Ready
or
Not

Jean Rover

Ready or Not
Copyright © 2023 by Jean Rover
Blue Agate Press
Salem, Oregon

ISBN: 978-0-9967130-3-0 (Blue Agate Press)
          978-0-9967130-4-7 (eBook)
Library of Congress Control Number: 2023907340

Cover design: designpointinc.com
Cover photograph: zengxiao lin on Unsplash

Manufactured in the United States of America

Also by Jean Rover

Touch the Sky

Beneath the Boughs Unseen

For Tara and Forester
*Until one has loved an animal, a part of one's soul remains
unawakened.*
Anatole France

BENSON BOY FOUND
By Richard Snow, Associated Press

FOREST LAKE Oregon—Nine-year-old Cody Benson who has been missing for six months was found alive yesterday in the Big Bat Wilderness area.

Klamath County Deputy Sheriff Ken Blake, who helped lead the intense search for the Forest Lake boy, said he is "well and healthy and was taken to a hospital in Klamath Falls, where he has been reunited with his family."

Cody disappeared while on an outing to find a Christmas tree with his grandfather. Hundreds of volunteers combed the wilderness area looking for him, and police investigated thousands of leads from the public. The boy was found wandering alone, not far from the place he first went missing.

Two weeks earlier, convicted sex offender, Len Roster, the subject of an intense manhunt after abducting four-year-old Jason Atwater of Klamath Falls, died by a self-inflicted gunshot wound to the head. Police recovered his body near the same location where Cody was found. Jason was unharmed.

"We're convinced Roster kidnapped Cody," Blake said, but offered no details about where the boy has been since he vanished on December 5 of last year or who brought him to the wilderness area after Roster killed himself.

Roster was also linked to the murder of a seven-year-old Grants Pass boy who disappeared last year after getting off his school bus.

Pete Benson, the child's father, said: "We don't have a lot of details yet, so we don't know what he's gone through. We're just happy to have our boy back."

According to the Klamath County Sheriff's Department, investigation of this case, which drew national attention, continues.

CHAPTER 1

Seventeen years later ...

Cody Benson folded the yellowed newspaper clipping and put his past back in his pocket.

After having lunch downtown with his department head, he swallowed two extra-strength Rolaids Softchews to fight off his upset stomach and heartburn. What would Chair Luci Maxwell think if she knew her bright, twenty-six-year-old, assistant professor of anthropology was on his way to see a shrink?

It wasn't the smoked ham and Gruyère cheese sandwich he'd had at *Le Rêve* that caused his indigestion. It was Luci's suggestion that the department needed him to do some preliminary field research with a unique tribe in a remote village in South America.

Alone.

The meeting with Luci replayed in his head as he walked. He had listened politely. A part of him wanted to leap at this chance of a lifetime. Instead, he sat there paralyzed. He set down his sandwich and took a deep breath.

Luci bit into her seared tuna salad and swallowed. "This is so good," she said, licking her lips. "And, I have it every time I come here. Anyway, I want you to think about this opportunity."

Cody started to sweat. "Oh, I will. I will."

"British and American oil companies are coming into the area. The enlightened ones are partnering with human rights groups trying to understand the culture of the indigenous tribes. That's where we come in."

His right leg bounced under the table. He sipped his Pinot Gris. *Stop.* He tried to persuade his brain.

"Some of these tribes have never been contacted. If not done properly, it could jeopardize their very existence," she said.

"I can see that. Progress ruins everything."

Luci's blue eyes widened. "I know. I know. But there's nothing we can do about that. With the demand for oil, they're *going* to drill. Look, it's a big step forward that they're even considering the native people and want our assistance. I immediately thought of you with your extensive background in the indigenous cultures of the Americas."

His throat tightened. "Most of my field work was in *North* America."

"Exemplar Oil is willing to contribute big research dollars to the university if we can help it finesse the culture."

"They're just going to destroy it anyway. Why don't they drill someplace else?"

"I know how you feel and I agree, but there are substantial benefits to this offer. The tribes are fascinating, and we'd at least get a chance to understand them. God willing, we can help preserve their cultures." At forty-five, with pageboy blond hair and bangs, Luci always drove a hard bargain when she made up her mind about something, but he couldn't say the words. How could he explain what he didn't understand himself?

"Anyway, you don't have to decide right now. Think about it over the summer—what it could do for Willamette University, your career, and eventually tenure for that matter. Think about the papers you'll write. Maybe even a book." She smiled and handed Cody a file folder. "Here, you can read the details for yourself."

He quickly set it down, so she wouldn't see his hand shake.

"It could put our department on the map. And the company is willing to bankroll all your expenses," Luci said.

Cody clutched the folder and headed up High Street. *Quit thinking about it.* It had rained earlier, but now the April sky was flawless blue with huge, puffy white clouds. The air smelled clean, and under other circumstances, hopeful. He took a deep breath. He knew something about Colombia. It was the fourth largest country in South America and the world's largest producer of cocaine. A beautiful region scarred by armed conflict, drug cartels . . . and *kidnappings*. He couldn't tell Luci about his past. Jesus. That was when he popped the Rolaids.

God, he needed to walk. He wished he had time for a run before heading over to Salem Hospital to meet with Dr. Ragu Aanandi, his psychiatrist. Maybe afterward, he'd take a jog through Bush Park. Gaze at the tulips. Unwind. May was inching closer. Then it would be finals week and the end of spring semester. He was lucky, wasn't he? He had a good job with a prestigious university and a bright future. It was just those damn panic attacks, dreams, the *fear of getting lost*.

Chanting and shouts from the front of the courthouse punctured his thoughts. A small group of twenty or so people clustered near the entrance carrying picket signs. It was a protest of some sort. The placards said "Save Banjo." Curious, he tried to move behind the crowd. A middle-aged, heavy-set woman in gray sweats approached him. "If you're here to join the rally, you can pick up a sign over there." She pointed to several stacked on the ground. "You from the humane society?"

"No, just passing through."

"Well, you look pretty spiffy. I thought maybe you were an official or something."

Cody had worn his navy blue blazer and khaki slacks for his lunch with Luci at the posh restaurant, and he always dressed up for his appointment with Dr. Aanandi. Medical professionals seemed to take you more seriously when you looked competent.

He glanced up at her placard, which bore a huge picture of a friendly looking German Shepherd. *Oh God. Did his past have to follow him everywhere? The dog was almost a dead ringer for Wolf.* He belched up the wild cherry flavor of his Rolaids and considered swallowing another one when he noticed her—that stunning brunette who came into Starbucks on Friday mornings. He usually sat off in a corner reviewing e-mail and reading Google News on his iPad, but he couldn't help but notice her. She was tall, dark-haired gorgeous, and always in a hurry. He'd said, "Hello" once, as he stood behind her in line to pick up his coffee, but she smiled and rushed off as if he didn't exist.

She seemed confident and kind. He knew she was caring because she never failed to stop and chat with the elderly homeless guy who sat on the bench outside the coffee shop every morning, his wheelchair piled high with a sleeping bag and a plastic sack of personal belongings. "Any change. Any change," he pleaded as people rushed past him.

Cody wondered if he was truly homeless or a crafty panhandler. He never sat in his wheelchair, just used it like a grocery cart. She, however, greeted the old guy and sometimes bought him a cup of coffee or a napkin-wrapped pastry. "God bless. God bless," he'd say.

Cody moved closer until he stood beside her. Maybe this was his lucky day. She waved her sign and spun in his direction shouting, "Save Banjo! Now." Her loud voice blasted into his right ear.

"What's this all about?" he asked, his ear still ringing.

"It's not fair. It's not right. The dog is innocent." She had beautiful, expressive brown eyes.

"What? Is he on trial?"

She gave him a swift, questioning look. "Don't you read the papers? They want to put him down, but it wasn't his fault." She pumped her sign up and down; then looped it around in the air. "We've got to save him," she yelled to the crowd.

"Hey, be careful," he said, ducking to avoid the swinging sign. "You almost took my eye out with that thing." He grinned. She grimaced, tossed her long hair, and turned away. *What a lame thing to say. Idiot.*

He lingered for a while. He liked dogs and felt sorry for Banjo. A photographer, probably from the *Statesman Journal*, was taking pictures. He vaguely remembered reading about this dog. It had bitten someone. That was it, but there were some extenuating circumstances, which he couldn't recall. He glanced at his watch. Yikes, he needed to get to his appointment. He stepped back.

"Ow!" someone said. "Watch it, you stepped on my foot."

He turned around. It was the brunette again. "Sorry," he managed. His nostrils whiffed her flowery scent.

She glared at him.

"Uh, gee," he asked, "does this dog have a chance?"

"He's got a lawyer. We sure hope so."

"A dog with a lawyer, well that . . ." He tried to think of something witty to say, but stopped when a tall man standing on the courthouse steps with a megaphone began speaking.

"Can I have your attention, please? Your attention, please." The crowd swayed with their signs and chanted, "Justice for Banjo. Justice for Banjo." A police officer came out of a door. He thrust out his jaw and stood, his feet hip distance apart, his arms crossed in front of his chest.

"What an enthusiastic group you are," the tall man said. "Thank you all for coming. We hope the county commissioners get our message. Now to honor Banjo, Joey Marks from North Salem High School is going to play a song, and you guessed it—on his banjo. It's called 'When the Angels Carry Me Home.' Take it away, Joey." A skinny boy with pimples hurried up the steps, smiled shyly, and strummed filling the air with twangy sound.

Cody turned toward the attractive brunette. He hoped to continue his conversation, but instead, saw her wave and call to another woman. "Hey, Dulcy, over here."

Cody's ears perked up to see if the approaching woman would say the gal's name so he could learn what it was, but it was difficult to hear over Joey's snappy banjo music and the hum of the milling crowd.

"Let's move off to the side," he heard her say when Dulcy approached. "So we can talk."

Cody watched them walk away. There was something about her. Why didn't he mention Starbucks and say that he'd seen her there? That would have been a better opener. Sadly, he'd struck out, but then that's the way it was. He could talk for hours on end about the details of Native American regalia or the bone structure of Kennewick Man's thighs, but when it came to women, his tongue always took a wrong turn.

CHAPTER 2

Cody fidgeted sitting in a comfortable, dark brown leather chair in the interview room of Dr. Ragu Aanandi's office. Located in the Center for Outpatient Medicine on the Salem Hospital Campus, it resembled a small living room with lamps, plants, and tasteful artwork all done in calm earth tones. The one splash of color was the rug, an eclectic collection of varying rectangles. He studied the brown, green, blue, red, and yellow geometric shapes, wondering if the rug had any psychological purpose. The area was a tranquil cocoon, the kind of space he wished he could stay in forever. He pulled a tissue from the box on an end table to dab at his nose. Spring air always aggravated his sinuses. He could hear the doctor walking up to the door, pausing, speaking to someone before turning the knob.

"Hello, Professor," Dr. A said. He carried a file.

Cody rose and shook his hand. An Asian Indian who had come to this country as a young boy, Dr. A grew up in the Chicago area. He had a slight frame, a pleasant face, and a full head of graying dark hair. "Looks like it's going to be a nice day out there," he said, gazing toward two tall windows.

"Yeah, I enjoyed my walk over here, but the pollen is making my nose run."

Dr. A handed him the Kleenex box. "Here, have another. I was over at the Hallie Ford Museum over the lunch hour. I see you have an exhibit there."

"Yeah, it's a small display of Native American portraits."

"They're beautifully rendered. I can't draw a straight line." He laughed.

"Thanks. I've been working on those over several years. Luci Maxwell, my department head, thought I had enough good ones for a show." Cody liked the doctor's calming manner and found it easy to talk with him. He first met Dr. A at the YMCA playing racquetball. After getting acquainted, Cody worked up the nerve to mention his struggle with anxiety, and Dr. A agreed to help him.

Dr. A sat on the sofa. He flipped through Cody's chart. "So how are things?"

"I think it's getting worse. The anxiety I mean. It seems to be turning into full-fledged panic attacks. And I'm having strange dreams."

"Okay. First things first. What seems to bring on the panic attacks?"

"I just came from lunch with Luci. She offered me an opportunity to do field work in South America with a remote tribe. I . . . I started sweating. My knees shook. It felt like I was having a heart attack. Like I was heading down a dark hole."

"Did you try the breathing exercises we talked about in the past?"

"I tried, but . . ." He had to chuckle. "I got caught up in the conversation. And when she said, I'd be going there *alone*, I forgot all about breathing. Period."

Dr. A smiled. "It takes practice. So going alone is what worried you?"

"I . . . I suddenly had the fear of getting lost . . . of something terrible about to happen. Last week I was driving in Portland . . . meeting my mother for lunch. I got lost. I've never had much of a sense of direction, but this was different. I started to sweat. My hands shook on the wheel. I felt like I was suffocating. I had to call my mother twice."

"Mazeophobia. It's the fear of getting lost. It's pretty common, especially in cases like yours. You got lost when you were a little boy. You were alone and frightened. Someone abducted you. Suddenly, your world turned upside down. It's no wonder you have a fear of strange places."

"But over the years . . . when I was growing up, things seemed to go okay. I mean it took a while, but it turned out all right. Now, everything seems out of control. Why now? I'm supposed to be an anthropologist, but I can't even get from point A to B without falling apart."

"You were eight years old when you were kidnapped. That was what? Twenty years ago?"

"Actually, it's been seventeen. But I just don't get it. Why all the angst now? When I've accomplished what I want. Have a job I love."

"It can happen. I've seen this quite often where a person's past reoccurs in waves. There's probably some deep underlying anxiety, something unresolved that triggers these attacks. Do you have any idea of what that might be?"

"No."

"Earlier, you mentioned dreams. What are those about?"

"I'm in a cave. It's dark. I see those eyes of his. They're wild. I'm scared. He reaches for me. He's trying to say something, but I can't make it out. I wake up and my heart is pounding." His lower lip quivered.

"This is the man that kidnapped you?"

"No, he didn't kidnap me. He saved me. And I lied about it . . . to save him. I've got to find him."

"Wait. You lied?"

"Yes." He wished he had some water for his dry throat.

"Cody," Dr. A. said, looking at the file. "We've been over some of this before. The police said a pedophile abducted you. A man named Len Roster. And you identified him as the man who took you."

Cody swallowed. "No, I never met that man."

Dr. A seemed puzzled. "I've read your file and the reports from the psychiatrists who examined you as a child. You were nine years old when found. Correct?"

"Yeah. It's just that I couldn't . . . I can't talk about this to anybody—my friends, my mother, my colleagues." He thought of Luci Maxwell and shuddered.

"It says here there was evidence to connect you to the pedophile. You had buttons or something of his in your pocket."

"I don't know how they got there."

"You struggled with the man perhaps?"

"I never encountered him, I swear. Look, I've done some research." Cody pulled copies of news clips from the pocket of his jacket. "This is the man I was with."

Dr. A read the main article. "Hmmm," he said several times as he read. "This Jim Fallingwater was a fugitive who committed a murder and escaped to the wilderness area. Folks believed he died there . . . froze to death."

"Yeah."

"But of course this happened, let's see, about twenty years before you were abducted. Correct?"

"That's right."

"This is a story that was known around your town, correct? It was a tragic murder in a small community. People talked about it for a long time."

"I guess."

"You could have heard this story and it fed into your fantasy. Then your mind used it to protect you."

"I don't know. I don't know."

"We call that phenomenon dissociation. The mind creates something to ease fear or pain."

"No, he was real. I know because . . ."

"This article says he froze to death."

"No, he was very much alive." Cody moved to the edge of his chair. He clenched his fists.

Dr. A's eyes focused on Cody's hands. "It's okay. This kind of thing is common with traumatized kids. Especially kids like you . . . according to your file, you had quite an imagination as a child."

"I'm not a child anymore . . . I know he was real."

"Listen, I totally understand. I grew up in a small town outside of Chicago. We had a story like that, too. Where this fellow shot his wife and then jumped off a bridge. People said his ghost stalked the woods. On Halloween, we boys even swore we saw him walking out there. The story just kept getting better over the years." He paused and looked sympathetically at Cody whose head hung over his chest. "What you need to do now is let it go."

"But I can't. See, here." He held out his right hand and showed Dr. A the scar on his index finger. "We . . . he made that cut there, and we became blood brothers. That's how I know I'm not making this up."

"Blood brothers?"

"He was Indian. American Indian." Cody's leg jiggled.

"Take a deep breath. Perhaps you were acting out. In other words, it's quite likely you did that on your own . . . to make your protective world real to you. That's also common. I once had a patient who was afraid of a big dog in his neighborhood. There was no evidence the dog ever bothered him. One day he came in with a bite on his forearm. Turned out he'd bitten himself."

"Look, I'm not some nutcase. I remember the cave we lived in. How he used to whittle and carve things . . . and he had this dog, Wolf."

Dr. A took a deep breath. "A man with a dog, living in a cave, a warm scene. You are describing Rousseau's noble savage. But of course, all of that is so impossible when you consider the freezing environment. No one could survive in circumstances like that for all those years. And now, after even more years, you think he's still out there?"

"Possibly. He gave me a carved dog . . . said it was my totem. I still have—"

Dr. A redirected their discussion. "What else do you dream about?"

What the heck is the use? Already, he thinks I'm crazy. "Sometimes it's my grandfather. He's lost. I'm trying to help him, but I'm lost, too. I'm shouting. It's snowing. Then he turns into Jim Fallingwater. I wake up shaking."

"Guilt."

"What?"

"Guilt. That's one of your triggers. You still blame yourself for your grandfather's suicide. He was supposed to look after you, and you wandered away on his watch. Devastated and overcome with grief, he committed suicide. The stress surrounding your abduction destroyed your parents' marriage. Two shocking things for a child to cope with. You blamed yourself for what happened to your family. That's normal. Children frequently do. Then you stored all of that away and went on with your life. Now, for some reason, it's bubbling back and beating you up."

"I have a hard time remembering him."

"Who?"

"My grandfather."

Dr. A didn't respond. Cody watched his hand as he wrote in his file. *Probably writing total fruitcake.*

Dr. A glanced up and smiled. "I can give you some medication for the panic attacks. That will help calm you. Wear a rubber band on your wrist. When you feel the panic about to start, snap it hard and tell yourself to stop. Continue with the breathing exercises. Learn meditation. A mindfulness group meets here at the hospital. Check that out. I'd also like for you to keep a journal. Record what you are thinking when the panic or anxiety begins. Then write down what you did to try to stop it. Try to be very detailed. You feel guilty about your grandfather's death, for example, and your parents' divorce. I think that's some of it. We'll continue to talk. It takes time, but eventually we will get at the core causes about what's going on deep inside. What about your personal life? You teach, you draw, you grade papers, you go home at night. Are you in a relationship?"

"No." He remembered his earlier encounter. Already he'd struck out. "I . . . uh . . . haven't had time." When he was a kid, his mother kept a short leash on him afraid he'd go missing again. He coped by studying art and burying himself in schoolwork, becoming an honor student, and keeping his nose in the books throughout college and graduate school. The resulting social awkwardness was embarrassing and not something he wanted to talk about.

"You need to get out there—socialize, go to the gym, join in. Do things that will take your mind off yourself."

"But this Fallingwater guy," he said, moving the conversation off his social life, "I feel that in my dream he's trying to tell me something."

"Perhaps the man that abducted you had an accomplice? Someone who looked after you?"

"No. No. There was no one else. I've got to find out what he's trying to say. Talk with him. If nothing else, thank him for saving me."

Dr. A set down his file and leaned back. "Okay, Professor. Go ahead. Look under the bed."

"What?"

"Look under the bed." His smile was calm. "My little daughter was afraid to go to sleep at night because she believed there was a monster hiding beneath her mattress. So, every night, we checked. Under the bed. In the closet. When we didn't find one, her fear eventually dissipated. So go ahead and look for your ghost. Whatever you discover can bring closure. Just make sure you write about it in your journal. In detail. I'll see you next month to find out how you're doing. Be sure and bring the journal."

Cody's face grew hot. "I know he exists. I was there."

"Like I said. Go take a look. Then let it go. Get on with your life."

Cody's hand stroked his brow. Dr. A was giving him permission. He wasn't expecting that. "I don't know where to begin." Suddenly, he felt tired.

"Sure you do, Professor. You know how to do field work. You're an anthropologist. You completed university, graduate school, and have a doctorate. You've got a terrific career going for you. You're an extremely talented artist and one hell of a racquetball player. Be grateful every day that you survived that bad situation in your childhood. Embrace your life in the here and now. I know you can do it. What is it they say? Ah yes, 'You can't turn back the clock, but you can wind it up again.'"

CHAPTER 3

Cody climbed the steps of the wide porch of the Queen Anne style house located in the historic district on Chemeketa Street. In the foyer, he picked up his mail from the credenza and headed up the tan-carpeted stairway to his apartment.

He heard the familiar thud coming from his bedroom. That, he knew, was Crackers jumping off the bed after waking up from a long afternoon nap. Crackers belonged to Anne Ferguson, his landlady, but the slate gray cat had developed a strong affinity for Cody. He often climbed up the backyard trellis, bounced onto the porch roof, and came in through the bedroom window Cody left partially open for him. Sometimes he arrived early enough to perch on the bathroom counter and watch Cody shave. Eventually, he'd knead himself a comfortable spot in the middle of Cody's bed. The cat with his unique senses loved classical music, especially opera, so Cody always tuned the stereo to the classical station before he left for the day. A few bars of something like Verdi's Triumphal March from *Aida* made Crackers' eyes turn to slits. He'd nod off until he got hungry; then he'd stretch his legs and make his way out and down to find Anne.

Cody tossed his mail and the folder Luci had given him about Colombia on the table. Crackers arched his back and yawned. "Just some bills and my *Smithsonian* magazine," he said to the cat. "Let's see what I have for you." Crackers rubbed against Cody's pant leg, purring and begging for the tasty tidbits he knew would be forthcoming. Cody reached into the cupboard and found his bag of treats. He laid three on the table and tossed the empty bag in the garbage. Crackers

jumped up and gobbled them. "That's all, now. I'm out." He showed
the cat his empty hands before pulling open the fridge door and
peering inside. "In fact, I'm out of just about everything." He poured
himself half a glass of milk and tossed away the empty carton.

After the meeting with Luci and Dr. A, he felt drained. The idea
of going for a run no longer appealed to him. He just wanted to crash
on the sofa, but knew he better make a trip to the grocery store while
he had the time. The rest of his week included student conferences,
grading term papers, developing final exam questions, and hosting the
pre-dinner for the semester's last campus lecture on "The Americas
before Columbus."

He changed into jeans, pulled on a sweatshirt, and hurried down
the stairs to his Subaru Forester, which he parked next to Anne's
black Nissan in front of the stand-alone garage. Cody hated grocery
shopping, but it was a boring necessity.

Once in the store, he reached for coffee, milk, bread, and cereal. Lots
of cereal. He never made a grocery list. Instead, he pushed his cart
down every aisle to jog his memory. Cheese, apples, bananas, some
frozen pizzas, a stack of frozen entrees, bags of Fritos, bread, chicken
nuggets, ground round, Hamburger Helper, hot dogs, Oreo cookies
for dessert, and a big jar of peanut butter. He knew it would make his
mother happy if he shopped the vegetable aisle, but he skipped it. He
could tolerate carrots, but unless you bought those baby ones, they
were too much work. You had to chop, scrape, or peel them, and
then somehow cook them. When you did, they didn't taste like much.
Instead, he opted for a case of V8 Vegetable Juice. He tossed in a
spiral notebook, so he could start the journal Dr. A recommended
and, oh yes, some sturdy rubber bands to wear on his wrist. Jeez, that
seemed so silly, but he dropped them into his cart anyway. He bought
three bags of cat treats to keep Crackers happy—one chicken flavored
and two tuna. Crackers liked tuna-flavored anything.

Once past the checkout, he wheeled his cart to the parking lot
and loaded his grocery bags into the back of his Subaru. His mind
kept replaying what Luci had said, but when he started to sweat, he
told himself to stop. He ripped open the package of rubber bands
and slid one around his wrist, just in case. He got in the car and
slammed the door shut. It bothered him that Dr. A didn't seem to
believe him. Usually, he wasn't judgmental. *Look under the bed.*

What kind of advice was that? Maybe his explanation wasn't all that clear. He shared his story with Dr. A, because medical records were confidential, but he knew he had to be careful. Oregon had the death penalty, and there was no statute of limitations for murder, so Jim Fallingwater, wherever he was, could still be arrested. Then what? A crunch and a loud blasting horn shattered his thoughts.

Damn it to hell, I backed into something. He jumped out to survey the damage. He stared at a crumpled dent in the side door of a blue Chevy Sonic. The other driver, a woman, walked rapidly toward him clutching her purse. She didn't have to say anything. He could tell she was mad. *Oh, God, no. It's her. The hottie from Starbucks. Did he have a target on his back?*

"You made a gigantic dent in my back door," she said, pointing. "Why don't you watch where you're going?"

"Gee, I'm sorry. I didn't see you back there."

"How could you not see me?" She demanded. "I even honked my horn, but you just kept coming."

"I . . . uh . . . had a lot on my mind."

"Don't we all. Welcome to life."

"Look, I said I was sorry."

"I'm running late. Have a lot on my plate, and now . . . now, I have a humongous dent in the damn car. Jesus. There's not a scratch on yours."

He bent over to inspect the damage. "It can be fixed. I mean it's not too bad."

"You just don't . . ." She stopped and peered at him. "Hey, wait a minute, you're that guy that stepped on my foot at the rally."

"I always seem to be apologizing to you for some reason."

"Exactly." She gripped her purse.

For a brief minute Cody thought she might hit him with it.

Instead, she said, "You're insured, aren't you?"

"Well, yeah, I'm insured." He fumbled in his pocket and pulled out his wallet.

"I guess this is my lucky day," she said sarcastically.

He showed her his insurance card. She grabbed it from his hand, pulled a cell phone from her purse, and snapped a picture. She didn't hand the card back. Her eyebrow shot up, like she couldn't believe what she was reading.

"I think, you're supposed to show me yours," Cody said lamely. "I mean, we need to exchange information."

Her eyes didn't blink. "Are you Cody Benson? Cody Andrew Benson?"

"Well yeah, that's what the card says."

"No, I mean the real Cody Benson."

He plucked at his shirtsleeve. "I guess I'm real."

"I mean from Forest Lake . . . in Southern Oregon?"

"I lived there for a while. Not very long, actually."

"Don't you know me?"

He gazed into her eyes. All he knew was that she was gorgeous. He didn't know what to say. He'd spent so much time studying and researching, he never learned to flirt. Whatever came out would be wrong. He stood there speechless.

"I'm Brittany. Brittany Bolin. We were in third grade together."

"Brittany! Oh my God. No, I didn't recognize you. You're all 'growed up' as they say." He tried not to stare at her breasts.

"We used to play together. Remember? Then you moved away. Right after they found you. I always wondered what happened to you." She dug in her purse, retrieved her insurance card and held it while Cody snapped a photo.

"My God, Brittany. It's been so long. Gee, I'm so sorry about your car."

"Yeah. But Cody Benson. I can't believe it."

"Listen, do you have some time?" he said. "I mean, I'd like to buy you a cup of coffee . . . or something . . . uh . . . to make up for the dent there."

"Well, I've got my groceries . . . and I'm going to make dinner for a friend." She laughed. "That's why I was so mad at you. But wait. Let me give you my phone number."

"Where do you live?"

"In some apartments over on D Street."

"Well gee, I mean we're practically neighbors. I'm over on Chemeketa."

She handed him a piece of paper with her number on it. "What are you doing here?"

"Well, the cupboard was bare. I was out of everything. And the cat needed . . ."

"No, I mean, what are you doing in Salem?"

"I teach at Willamette. I'm a professor of anthropology."

"Well, that fits."

"It does?"

"Well, you were always such a little know-it-all." She laughed. "I mean smart."

She had such a wonderful laugh. He loved her laugh. All he could remember about school in Forest Lake was that his teacher thought he was a pain in the ass. "What do you do? Here in Salem, I mean."

"I'm a third grade teacher at Northeast Elementary."

"Listen, I'll call you." He rubbed the back of his head. "Uh, maybe we could get together."

"Please do. I'd love to hear about your life."

"What's a good time for you?"

"Well, tomorrow after school. Say around 3:30."

"Do you want to just meet at Starbucks? Our usual place?"

"Sure. Gee, I'm so excited. Cody Benson, after all these years. Mother won't believe this."

"Uh, yeah, well, I'm excited too. I mean you're all grown up."

"You already said that." She laughed again. "Okay. I'll see you then."

He could listen to her laugh all day. "I'm sorry about your car. I mean, I'm really sorry."

"I know. I know. You've said that a hundred times, too. But look, I'll see you tomorrow."

He watched as she got into her car and pulled her shapely legs inside. *Hot damn.* Some days it *did* pay to get up. His hand shook as he twisted the key in the ignition. *She's Brittany.* He couldn't focus. *Brittany Bolin.* He reached for the rubber band on his wrist and snapped it three times.

CHAPTER 4

Cody stepped from the shower and toweled off. A coffee date should be casual, right? He pulled on his jeans and slipped a red sweatshirt over his head. Maybe he was too casual. Minutes later, he changed into a maroon short-sleeved shirt.

Crackers sat on the bathroom counter and watched Cody brush his teeth. "What do you think of this number?" he asked through a mouth full of white foam.

The cat swished his tail. "Meow." His grape-green eyes gave Cody his I'm-not-amused-and-don't-care-about-your-shirt look. He raised a paw and tried to swat a small ant crawling up the wall, but it disappeared into a crack.

"You gotta be quick, fella. Gee, I hope there aren't more of those. I better tell Anne."

The cat continued his hopeful watch.

"Brittany Bolin, can you believe that, Crackers? Brittany was my best friend in third grade. Hot damn. Who knew? Should I put on a different shirt?" He reached for the mouthwash and made loud gargling sounds, causing Crackers to arch his back and leap from the counter.

Cody spit green liquid, smacked his lips, and gazed at the mirror, his brown eyes wide. "This isn't right. I better do the blue one." He went into the bedroom and changed.

Back in the bathroom, he carefully parted and combed his medium length dark hair, cut longer in the back. Crackers jumped on the counter and busied himself batting a yellowish rectangle. His munching sounds drew Cody's attention. "What have you got there? Not my

Fritos!" His reach wasn't fast enough. Crackers grabbed it with his mouth and darted away.

Cody followed him to the kitchen. "Ah crap, I left the bag on the table. How many of these did you mouth? Huh?" He closed the package and tossed it in the cupboard. "You little thief. Salt and fat are not your friends."

Crackers, carefully guarding his prey, twisted his ears and turned away, not partial to lectures.

Ready to leave, Cody glanced at himself one more time in the small, round mirror by the door. "Well, fella, this is as good as you're going to get." He stood up straight, shoulders back and down as if preparing for a job interview, then dashed down the stairs to begin his walk to Starbucks.

* * *

At the coffee shop, he grabbed a table by the window overlooking the street, listening to the hum of small talk and the hissing sound of steaming milk. *Oh, God, here she comes.* As soon as she entered, he jumped up to greet her. "Hi," he said. She looked lovely in her royal blue sweater and jeans.

Her full lips smiled. "Sorry, I'm late. I had to park way down the block." Her cheeks were rosy. She tossed her dark brown hair away from her face.

Cody fumbled for words. "We must have vibed each other."

"What?"

"I mean we're both wearing blue."

"Oh," her facial expression perplexed.

"What can I get for you?"

"The usual . . . I always have a vanilla soy latte."

He led her to the small corner table. "I'll be right back." After ordering and waiting impatiently, he returned with her drink, a tall black coffee for himself, and two napkins. A heart design happily floated on top of her latte. *Ah, the fates are on my side.* Savoring the rich vanilla scent, he carefully set his caffeinated valentine in front of her.

"Thank you," she said. "Is that all you're having? Black coffee?"

"Yeah, I like mine black and plain. All that other stuff is pimp coffee."

"Huh?"

"No offense. I mean uh . . . that's how I learned to drink it, black, uh . . . nothing added. Not all gussied up like a street . . . I mean . . ." *Christ, I must sound like an idiot.*

Brittany's right eyebrow arched. "Whatever." She took a long sip. The heart design disappeared into her mouth. *So much for the fates.*

"Where did you go after you left Forest Lake?" she asked.

"Mom moved us to Portland."

"That must have been quite a change. I mean from little staid Forest Lake to the big city, especially after all you'd gone through."

"I worked with a counselor for a few months. Over the summer, actually. Started school in the fall."

"And then?"

"I pursued my interest in art and native peoples . . . did undergraduate work at the U of O. Went for my master's there and ended up with a doctorate in Native American Studies from Berkeley. Got a job teaching at Willamette. The rest, as they say, is history." He sipped his coffee.

"Dr. Benson. How impressive."

He shrugged. "Yeah . . . I guess. Actually, I'm just an assistant professor. And you?"

"My dad died when I was six."

"I remember hearing that."

"Mother still lives in Forest Lake . . . out in the country. She got a clerking job at the Mercantile in town. She couldn't afford to pay for my college, but she helped, and I worked part time. I went to Klamath Community College and then on to Southern Oregon University and majored in elementary education. I teach third grade."

"I certainly hope you're a better teacher than ol' what's her name." He grinned, slightly embarrassed. "I can still see her shaking her finger at me, and those awful brown boots she always wore."

"Miss Brackston. Eula Brackston. Yeah, she was a piece of work." She laughed. "I remember you gave her fits."

"Whatever happened to her?"

"She had a drinking problem . . . had to give up her job. Left town and supposedly sought treatment. No one ever heard from her. What about your family?"

"Well, when I, uh, went missing, they . . . my parents . . . their marriage crumbled."

"Oh, sorry."

"After the divorce, Mom finished her degree. Taught school for a while. Then went to law school in the evenings, at Lewis and Clark. She's now a lawyer with Watson & Creighton in Portland."

"Good for her."

"Dad remarried. Still works for the Fish and Wildlife department. I have a half-sister, Lacy. They . . . uh . . . live in Medford. I always felt responsible for that. The divorce, I mean. And then my grandfather. He . . . uh . . . committed suicide." His voice wavered. He wanted to snap the rubber band around his wrist. *God, not in front of her.*

"Don't. Don't go there." She reached over and patted Cody's hand.

The repeated touch of her warm, soft hand sent a blast of desire through him. His face flushed. To disguise his embarrassment, he gulped more coffee. Unfortunately, the hot liquid hit the back of his throat, causing a coughing spasm. "Sorry," he croaked through the napkin covering his mouth. When the coughing stopped, he used the napkin to nurse his dripping nose, and then blew into it like a honking goose.

A heavy-set woman seated at the next table reading a book while nibbling a chocolate muffin gave him a pitiful stare.

"You okay?" Brittany asked.

"Yeah." He wiped his lips with his soiled napkin. "It still gets kinda raw at times. I mean, when I think of my family and—"

"Here, use mine." She handed him her napkin. "It's pretty common for children to feel that way. The guilt I mean."

"The counselors worked with me, but . . . uh . . . I'm not a kid anymore."

"I should say not. You're quite a handsome hunk." She winked.

His face got warmer. "And you're quite a babe yourself." He made a clicking noise with his mouth. "Why are you laughing?"

"Because you still have those big brown eyes—those winsome, puppy dog eyes."

Self-conscious, he looked down. "Oh."

"So, have you ever been back to Forest Lake?"

"No. Never. Well, I've been to Southern Oregon many times, but never to Forest Lake."

"So you see him. Your dad, I mean?"

"I go down in the summer, and we go camping." His dad. It was hard to talk about him, because they never were that close. "He's okay. A good guy, actually. We're just on different wavelengths. He's black-and-white, up-and-down serious." Cody threw up his hands. "What can I say, he's an America-is-the-only-real-country-on-earth kinda guy." He waited. *Don't talk about religion or politics. Isn't that what Mom always said.*

Brittany burst out laughing.

God, he loved that laugh. To Cody, it sounded like Mendelssohn's "Songs without Words." "I guess you know we university types tend to lean to the left."

"My mother's a bit on the conservative side herself. So is most of Forest Lake." She rolled her eyes.

"And my dad, he doesn't think much of my penchant for art. Never did, now that I think about it." He remembered sketching a squirrel on one of their outings. His father pulled his tablet away, replacing it with a fishing pole.

"Art? You sort of mentioned that earlier."

"Yeah, I had a double major in school. I love drawing."

"Wait a minute." She leaned back, enabling Cody to sneak a peek at her breasts.

"As I recall, you used to draw in class instead of following instructions. That's what gave ol' lady Brackston fits." She giggled and slapped the table.

Cody laughed too. He sat up straight. He needed to impress her. "In fact, I've got a show over at the Hallie Ford gallery."

"You do? An entire show?"

"Well, actually, it's a small corner, but Luci, my department head, encouraged me to display the work. Do you want to walk over and see it? After we finish our coffee, I mean."

"Sure. When we're done here."

He checked his watch. "The museum stays open until five."

"Perfect."

There was an uncomfortable silence. Cody leaned forward. "I just have to ask. What was all that fuss over there at that rally for the dog?"

"Banjo, you mean. He's a German Shepherd." Her face turned serious. "He bit a three-year-old girl on the arm, a girl from his neighborhood."

"That's not good."

"You have to understand that his owners always let him lick the dirty dishes they set in the dishwasher. The kid was visiting, and I guess she smacked him on the nose and tried to pull him away. That's when he nipped her."

"Still, not good news."

"Yes, but don't you see? The owners allowed it. Licking the dishes. All the time. So, to Banjo, it was his food dish. You don't get between a dog and his bone. Someone should have supervised that child. Don't you know anything about dogs?" Her voice rose. She seemed irritated. The fat lady was staring again.

"*Yeah.* I grew up with a dog. Jack. He was a golden. And . . . uh . . . a friend's dog, Wolf." He winced. "I love dogs, actually. I just can't have one where I'm living now."

"Me neither. But someday."

"Was the child badly injured?"

"I'm sure the incident was traumatic for her. But no, not seriously. Her parents, though, had a raging fit. They want the dog put down. Banjo's owner, Lupe Garcia, and her daughter, Monica, love that dog. Lupe's a single mom. Doesn't have much money to fight back."

"Yeah, but once they bite. How do you know for sure . . . that he won't bite again?"

"Vets and dog trainers have examined him. They say he's well trained, isn't aggressive, and follows commands. But there's more."

"More?"

"The authorities say Banjo has a record." She made quote signs in the air when she said record. "Supposedly, he menaced, as *they* say, some kids in the neighborhood. But they were teasing him. Lupe didn't have a secure fence, and those kids got into the yard. They teased Banjo and threw pine cones at him. With a dog, that's a territory issue, especially for a German Shepherd. Lupe has filed a lawsuit. Well, with our encouragement and help. There are a couple hundred of us supporting her."

"Sounds like a flaming fudge bag." The fat lady, scraping muffin crumbs into her napkin, gave him a sharp look.

"We maintain Banjo is innocent because they provoked him. The parents of the girl who got bit and the cranky neighbors said Banjo did all those things without provocation. They brought in witnesses. So, Banjo got a death sentence. Can you believe that?"

"But with witnesses . . ."

"It's a marginal neighborhood. I think the girl's parents are after money. The people there have it in for the dog. And they don't like Lupe. She's trying to turn her life around, and I'm helping her. I think they're a bunch of liars."

"So it's complicated."

"Actually, it comes down to whether the dog was provoked or not. The law says a dog is dangerous if it does bad things for no reason. Our position is that Banjo was provoked." She raised her hand as if to strike someone. "Provoked. Provoked. Provoked."

The fat lady, chin in hand, studied them, a frown on her ample forehead.

Cody lowered his voice. "Take it easy. I believe you, but if they have witnesses, adult witnesses—"

Brittany exploded, pointing her finger at him. "Listen, we have a lineup of professionals . . . vets, dog trainers, that say otherwise."

"Excuse me," the fat lady said. "Could you two keep it down? I'm trying to read." She lifted her book.

"Sorry," Cody said.

The lady nodded. "Thank you."

"Where is Banjo now?" he whispered.

Brittany's fingers drummed the table. "He was at the Marion County Dog Shelter for several months. His health was failing. He lost a lot of weight. We've convinced them to move him to a pet hotel. That way, he can get more exercise and attention. He, of course, has to wear a muzzle." Her shoulders slumped.

"Not good. Gee, I feel for the dog."

Her eyes got teary; her voice shaky. "He deserves a second chance. Marge, the kennel manager at the pet hotel, says Banjo has never given her any trouble." Her expression perked. "That's another witness for our side."

Cody got brave. He reached for her hand and squeezed. "Listen, I support you."

"Thank you. He's a wonderful little being. I'm going to fight for him until hell freezes over." She put her other hand on top of his.

Cody didn't move. He wanted to stay there with his hand sandwiched between hers. *Forever.*

CHAPTER 5

Cody ushered Brittany through the glass doors of the white marble structure that housed the Hallie Ford Art Museum on State Street.

"Good afternoon, professor," said Mrs. Rodgers, stationed behind the curvy, wood paneled front desk. It matched the curvilinear design used throughout the museum. A long-time docent with blue-gray hair, she sized up his attractive companion through glasses sporting a beaded chain. "Nice to see you again," she said.

"Likewise, Mrs. Rodgers. This is my friend, Brittany Bolin. We're going to take a quick look at my show."

"Enjoy. Friends of faculty get in free," she said to Brittany.

As they passed, Cody glanced back to catch the coquettish smile that crossed Mrs. Rodger's face. She put thumb and forefinger together, giving Cody the "okay" sign. He smiled awkwardly, blushed, and quickly directed Brittany across the brown-tiled floor and up the marble stairs to the second floor.

"I have a small corner adjacent to the museum's permanent collection of American Indian Art," Cody explained. "We can check that out afterward, if you want."

The title of his show was simply *Indigenous People of Oregon.* Brittany paused to read Cody's bio under a small photo of him sitting at his drawing table.

"Already, I'm impressed."

"Boring stuff," he said, feigning modesty. He gently placed his hand on her back, guiding her toward his twelve drawings tastefully displayed on a cream-colored wall.

She leaned forward to examine a portrait of a young Indian woman tending a fire in front of her hut and another of a weary woman carrying a sleeping baby on her back. "Oh Cody, these are wonderful, so real and yet very unique in style. I love that little guy's expression. So peaceful, compared to the mom."

Cody beamed. "I did them all in graphite pencil and charcoal."

"The lighting and detail are exquisite." She stepped back and then moved closer again.

He continued. "I made the drawings from museum and library photo collections. Then I changed the perspectives and had my subjects looking in different directions. I included what I thought would be their emotions, or I put them in natural environments. I actually pulled the Klamath woman from a group photograph, but enlarged her to make a single portrait study. I added the fire."

"Her face is so serene compared to this guy." She studied the next portrait titled, *Captain Jack, Modoc Chief.* "That is one miserable looking dude."

Cody drew the chief with a tear on his cheek. In the background was his idyllic world before the white man invaded it and a ghostly face of a young girl floating in the sky. "You know the story of Captain Jack?" He hoped she didn't, so he could expound.

"Well, kinda. The Modoc were a Southern Oregon tribe."

"Southern Oregon and parts of California . . . around Lost River."

"He was a renegade, I remember. Did some way bad things." Her mouth tightened.

"He and a small band of followers refused to stay on the Klamath Indian Reservation. The attempt to bring them back resulted in the Modoc War in the late 1800s. Jack and his band shot two peace commissioners, one of which was a U.S. Army general." He paused and rubbed his forehead. Brittany seemed intrigued. "They eventually caught up with Captain Jack and his accomplices. They were hanged at Fort Klamath for the murders in 1873."

"I guess justice was served, then."

"There were atrocities on both sides, but the Modoc died defending their homeland, although their story isn't told that way." Cody's right hand jabbed at the air to bring emphasis to that point. He took a long breath and shook his head. "All Captain Jack wanted was a piece of land for his tribe, but the government wouldn't even consider that. The cost of the war was twenty-five times more expensive than the land

Jack wanted to feed his people. After the war, the Army rounded up the men, women, and children and sent them to a reservation in Oklahoma where they were poorly treated. Captain Jack's daughter, Rosie, died there."

"Rosie," she said softly, studying the drawing, her brown eyes wide with concern. "Rosie. That must be her ghost in the sky."

"Yes, Captain Jack loved his daughter."

She bit her lip. "Native American history is sad . . . and tragic."

"They made the families watch the hangings."

"Oh my God. How cruel." She took a deep breath. "I don't ever remember hearing Captain Jack was a father."

"The settlers came west for gold and cheap land. They never considered that the land was already occupied . . . by families."

"I include a unit on American Indians for my third graders. I try to teach a different story from what they learn from TV and the movies. I cover their culture mostly and their love for the land."

"There was a lot of duplicity and broken agreements. Be sure to include that."

She seemed taken aback by his tone. He worried he sounded too pedantic.

Looking directly at him, she said, "I can tell you feel *strongly* about the way they were treated."

"Well yeah." He folded his arms. "The bottom line is we took their land and gave them smallpox and alcohol. We annihilated ninety-five percent of their population. Talk about a holocaust."

"Obviously, the settlers didn't understand Native American culture," she said, "and, as I consider today's world, I see us making that same mistake. Just look at our foreign policy over the years. The Middle East."

"Don't start me on that."

"Hey, maybe next fall you can come and talk to my kids. Have you ever thought about doing that?"

"No. But I'd like to. I'd have to simplify my diatribe." He laughed. "I don't usually present to children."

"They're a lot smarter than you think." Brittany shifted her eyes to another drawing. "I love this picture of the wolf."

"Actually, it's a dog."

"Really?" She looked closer at the drawing of the animal standing majestically in the snowy wilderness. "But it says *Wolf* under the drawing."

"That was his name."

"Oh, but why . . ." She didn't finish her thought. Instead, she focused on another portrait. Underneath, the title said, *Lost.* She grasped her hands behind her back and leaned forward. "This one is especially intriguing. There's just something about this fellow's eyes. They seem wild, wounded maybe, but sad in a way."

Next to the portrait were some studies of the "lost" Indian sitting near a campfire making a woodcarving of a deer and a second one of him playing a flute for a small child.

"Why are these called *Lost?*"

"Does he look familiar?"

"You know. Now that you mention it. Kinda." She tilted her head. "But I don't know why. He's obviously modern. I mean, he's wearing jeans and what appears to be a ski jacket."

"Actually, it's Jim Fallingwater." He closed his eyes and waited for her reaction.

"Should that mean something?"

He opened his eyes to study her face. "From Forest Lake."

She looked down, pressing her two index fingers against her temple as if thinking. "Hey, wait a minute. That name . . . that was a long time ago. Didn't he kill someone?"

"Yes." He waited for more.

"Why did you draw him?"

"I'm . . . uh . . . doing some research. Anthropology stuff. I want to study the effect of modern life . . . uh . . . society on native peoples." He hoped he sounded convincing.

"The detail in his face, that scar on his forehead. How did you know what he looked like? I don't imagine there are pictures of him in museums."

"I drew from memor—I pulled old newspaper clippings and, uh, studied them. His situation seemed like a good one to zero in on." *God, I almost blew it.*

"But the historical aspect all happened before we were born. It's not like *today.*"

"Exactly, but he's an excellent case study. I mean, he was isolated from his tribe. What was going through his head? What drove him to kill? Did he fit into our society? Probably not. Many modern Native Americans don't feel like they belong anywhere. I think we could learn a lot from his case and apply it to contemporary times." His lie was sounding better all the time.

She glanced at the ceiling. "I'm trying to remember. I think he was in love with her . . . I can't recall her name."

"Christie Jenkins," Cody said.

She snapped her fingers. "That clicks. Her dad used to run the Shell gas station. I think her mom went off the deep end over the loss of her daughter. I remember Mother talking about that. People in Forest Lake talked about it, too. For a long time, until . . ." She hesitated.

"Until what?"

"Until you were kidnapped, and then found, walking alone in the wilderness. 'A miracle,' people said. 'He got away.' After that, they forgot about what's-her-name and talked about *you*. Every Christmas, someone would bring up your story. Some still do."

"They do?"

"Oh yes, you're some kind of folk hero." She paused and moistened her lips before continuing. "At least around Forest Lake."

If she had reached out and slapped him, he couldn't have been more surprised. He didn't think anyone in that dinky, dusty town would even remember him. All he could think to say was, "Jeez."

"Hey, the drawing of that Jim guy playing a flute by the fire with a small boy . . . he looks like you . . . when you were little."

Recovered, Cody smiled. "You're very shrewd. That *is* me."

She stroked her hair. "So why are you in that scene, clever boy that you are?"

"Well, I'm the artist. So, I put myself in the drawing. Pretty ingenious, don't you think?"

"Yeah, except who would know that? Only people who knew you back then."

"Exactly. It's sort of my little secret. The great masters were always painting in their secrets. So, this is mine." He waved his arm like Vanna White presenting a new refrigerator. "Ta da."

"It must have been a love story. Right?"

"Love story? Me?"

"No, not *you*. I mean this Jim and Christie."

"I don't really know."

"I can't remember exactly. What happened to him?"

"He . . . uh . . . was arrested. Escaped. Ran away to the Big Bat Wilderness area, got caught in a blizzard, and froze to death. I, uh, am told." He didn't even blink when he said that.

"She died. He died. Why did he kill her? I hope it was a love story."

Cody snuffled a laugh. He had her going. Maybe "looking under the bed" as Doctor A had recommended wouldn't be that hard. "That's what I want to find out. I guess I'll have to go down there and do research." *God, If I don't get lost.*

"Mother has a Native American friend that does some work for her. Maybe you could talk to him."

"What tribe?"

"I don't think Bobby has one. Bobby Blaze. He's lived in the area many years. Real pleasant fellow. He might've heard of this Fallingwater guy. You'd like him. He's an artist, too."

"What does he draw?"

"He's a sculptor. Makes metal art out of trash mostly."

"Really."

"Yeah. Listen, my birthday is coming up. Why don't you come home with me? Lance is out of town."

"Lance?"

"My boyfriend."

Cody's muscles stiffened. "What?" He stifled a gasp. "Oh . . . uh . . . you have a boyfriend?" He forced a smile.

"Well, yeah." Her voice rose, her face brightened. "And you? Do you have someone who would object if I took you home with me?" She tweaked his cheek, grinning mischievously.

The smile dropped off his face. "Uh . . . well no . . . uh, I've been pretty busy." His neck and cheeks flushed. It felt like a freaking 500-pound gorilla was jumping on his chest, crushing his lungs. "With uh . . . my career."

"I've got you blushing." Brittany laughed her wonderful, melodious laugh. This time, Cody didn't hear Mendelssohn's piano.

"I know Mother would love to see you again." She turned away and stared at the Jim Fallingwater portrait. "There's something in those eyes . . . a yearning maybe." Her eyelids fluttered. "I think it was a love story," she said, her voice dreamlike.

"Wouldn't your mother object?" Cody sputtered. "I mean, you bringing home another guy. I mean, if this Lance, is your—"

"Oh no," she said, still engrossed with the portrait. "I think of you as my *brother*. I always did."

Brother? She thinks of me as her brother? He didn't care. He turned away, reached down and snapped the rubber band hard against his wrist. *Ouch!*

CHAPTER 6

Artie Bradshaw and Gilbert "Toad" Holloway were the first regulars to arrive at Dottie's Café. They took counter seats next to the kitchen, so they could include Roy, the easygoing cook, in their conversation.

In Forest Lake, Dottie's Café was still the town's gathering place, although Dottie Johnson, now in her 80s, sold the restaurant several years ago to Roy and Pasty Kirkland, and retired to a small bungalow not far from the city park.

"After the divorce, Berny got the house," said Artie, his oversized rear-end wiggling the red counter stool. "All she does is sit home on her fat ass."

Patsy, a tall attractive woman, ten years Roy's junior, automatically set two mugs in front of the men and filled them with coffee.

Artie took a hefty swig. His voice jumped up three octaves to mimic Berny's whine. "'The dishwasher's broke. We gotta doctor bill. What am I supposed to do?' In the next breath, she's talkin' about going to Disneyland. What the hell, Disneyland."

"Dig into your biscuits and gravy," said Roy. "That'll make a young feller like you think life's worth living."

"At least for a while," Patsy added in her loud, raspy voice. She set one plate of two halved-biscuits, smothered with white gravy and chunks of sausage by Artie, along with a second one loaded with scrambled eggs, bacon, and hash browns.

Toad sized up Artie's pile of food. "You eat all of that you're gonna need your own area code." Toad drowned his stack of pancakes in syrup, careful not to get a drop on his ham. He earned his nickname because of the three cysts above his left eyebrow, a dark mole next to his right nostril and a pink one on the end of his chin that moved up and down when he talked.

"I pay her a humongous alimony check every month, and she's talkin' Mickey Mouse." Twenty-seven-year-old Artie got Bernice pregnant his senior year, dropped out of high school, found a job at the Shell station, and still worked there as a grease monkey. "Hell, I can't even afford toilet paper."

Roy, a man of medium height, with wavy gray hair and a seriously full mustache, grinned, "They're having a big sale on that over at Tillden's Grocery. A pack of six mega rolls equals twelve-four regular ones. I'm just sayin'."

"Yeah, but those mega rolls are so fat, they don't fit on the roller," said Patsy. "If you use the john, you'll notice I set the roll on the tank until it thins down some." She smoothed her frosted dark hair, which was cropped short like a boy's and combed straight back over the ears.

"Ha," Toad chuckled. "Lookin' at the size of Artie's breakfast, he could use a big roll."

Artie tugged on his camouflage hunting hat which he wore skewed to the right and never removed, even indoors. "Ver-r-r-y funny. I'm pouring my heart out here, and all you guys care about is ass wipe." He stuffed his mouth with biscuit and tipped his coffee cup. "Now she wants me to go over there and cut the grass."

"Yep, Yep," said Toad. "I learnt a long time ago, wimen's trouble. That's for sure, by golly." A retired ranch hand and an old dyed-in-the wool bachelor, he had lived alone in a single-wide trailer on the Lyle Janes' ranch for years. After Lyle passed, and the family sold the place, he moved to town. "Course those two youngin's of yours is fine boys."

"Yeah, but their ol' lady is ruining them. 'Daddy, I want this. Daddy, buy me that.' Do I look like I'm made out of a sack of dough?"

"Nah, you look like you should be on Weight Watchers." Toad poked fun at Artie's ample belly, which he tried to hide under a pair of overalls and a red-and-black plaid shirt.

"Aw, you've gotta face that only a mother could love," Artie shot back. "Now that the government's messing with healthcare, maybe you can have your mug reset. But don't start me on the government. I got enough problems with Berny."

"You two need to can it," Patsy said, refilling their cups. "You sound like two little brats in the back of a car on a long trip." The direct opposite of mild-mannered Roy, Patsy had the tact of a bulldozer.

"Speaking of cars, Berny let the oil run down and burned out the engine driving to the beach. Now she wants a different one. I can't believe it. She's crabbin' about not having money, then she drives to the coast. You think she'd a brought it in to me. Of all the goddam stupid things." He mimicked her again. "'What if I get stranded? I'm a woman alone.' Why the hell don't she just stay home."

"Can't you fix her car?" Roy asked.

"Nah, I'd have to replace the whole engine. It's best to junk it." He shoved a fork full of biscuit into his mouth, a dribble of gravy escaping down his chin.

"I heard Alma Selby over on Fourth Street has her car up for sale," Toad said. "Givin' up driving. Actually, I think it was the daughter's idea." He cut his ham into small pieces. "Well, Alma's livin' in town and can pretty much walk places as long as her legs don't give out. I don't know how much she wants for it."

"What kinda car is it?"

"It's a green Ford sedan. Don't know the model."

"It's a Taurus," Roy said.

Toad speared his ham with his fork. "Can't have a lot a miles on it. I betcha Alma's got more miles on her than that car of hers."

"Aw, I think I know the one you mean. Nothin' to write home about," Artie said. "Her grandson drove it around and banged it up good a couple of times. Say, how can you afford that new Silverado you're driving? Janes must have paid you a bundle."

Toad's fork, with a piece of ham on the end, stopped in mid-air. "Hell, I didn't get it hanging over a bar at Benders, spending money on those floozies."

That little dig went right over Artie's head. "Aw, loosin' up. A guy's gotta have some fun."

"You should take a look at Alma's car," Roy said.

The bell over the door jingled. Bobby Blaze sauntered in. A big man, with a full face, glasses, and graying black hair pulled back into a single braid, he seated himself at the counter next to Toad.

"But you know what?" Artie continued. "What I really need is a new huntin' rifle."

"It ain't huntin' season." Toad said. He dabbed at his lips with his napkin. "You got a bunch a months before you need to worry about that."

"Criminy," Bobby said, "When has that ever mattered to Artie? Most of the meat in his freezer is illegal."

"Hi ya, Bobby," Pasty greeted him. "Want the regular?"

"Yeah. Go heavy on the fried baloney. I'm really hungry this mornin'."

Patsy turned and hollered in Roy's direction. "Double on the baloney, hash browns, three over easy, white toast, and a large Pepsi."

"I already know that," Roy yelled back. "It's always the same."

"I said *double* the baloney. Didja get that?" Pasty barked.

"Yeah. Yeah," Roy muttered. "I got it."

The Kirklands kept bologna in the fridge for Bobby. And, they willingly did substitutes for other regulars, which is why townsfolk considered Dottie's Café their second home.

"Your gut must be lined with galvanized steel," Artie said. "Your ancestors never ate that stuff. No, they'd be out there huntin' buffalo. How can anybody drink pop at this hour?"

"How many buffalo you seen in the woods lately?" Toad asked.

Bobby ignored Artie's remarks. "Where's Dottie this morning? I brought her a hunk of Sue Bolin's carrot cake." Bobby helped Mrs. Bolin keep up her five acres out in the country. In return, she let him use her barn for his welding business. Bobby repaired farm equipment and dabbled in welding art.

"Her arthritis is acting up again," said Patsy. "I'm taking over some soup for lunch. I'll take the cake to her then. That'll make her day. I know she loves Sue's carrot cake." She brought Bobby a tall glass of Pepsi with a straw.

"Ah, thanks, Patsy." He took a long, noisy pull.

Artie continued to taunt Bobby. "Hey, instead of that rot gut stuff, get him a beer. They say the fastest thing on an Indian reservation is a beer truck. The next fastest thing is the Indians running after it."

Bobby set his glass down. "You know, Artie, I could make a monkey out of you, but why should I take all the credit?"

No match for Bobby, Artie changed the subject and went back to whining. "I was supposed to take over for Dad after he passed, but Ma had to go sell our drugstore to Walgreens."

"I miss the old soda fountain, but I can't picture you runnin' a drugstore," Patsy said. "You'd have to be nice *all* day."

"I know how to be nice. Jeez."

"Well, you couldn't tell it from the talk going on here. I don't know why men think insulting each other is conversation."

"It's just a guy thing." Artie rattled his empty coffee mug on the counter like a two-year old in a high chair.

"Well, it's stupid." She folded her arms across her chest, like a school principal about to lecture an unruly child. "And quit banging your cup. Didn't your mother teach you any manners?"

"Excu-u-u-se me. Jeez. Anyway, I'd just like to have a cool two million. A nice little stash that Berny couldn't get her hands on. You know, so I could buy anything I wanted without worrying." Artie pushed aside his empty biscuit plate and began working on his eggs and hash browns.

"Garsh." Toad's mouth dropped. "Two million? What're you smoking? That's a lotta money. You better start buyin' lottery tickets . . . and prayin'."

"As long as you got a roof over your head and enough to eat, you should be happy," Roy said. "When all is said and done, rich people aren't any happier than the rest of us."

"He's certainly got enough to eat." Bobby winked at Patsy. "Sorry, just couldn't help it."

"Well, things gone and changed around here," Toad said. "The population's bucked up to around 2,000, and we got more tourists than ever comin' in now that they built that ski lodge on Big Bat Mountain and added those cabins over there at the lake. You must see more business at the station."

"Yeah, but what the hell, I get paid the same. I don't know how much longer I can last there at the garage." Artie gave the ketchup bottle a hard thwack over his hash browns. "My back keeps actin' up and my right knee is givin' out. I was thinkin' I could go out on workers' comp. I even filed a claim. Damn people turned it down. Said I came that way or some darn thing, like I was born with a sore back. The claim and all, that made Ed real upset."

"That figures. Your boss is the one that pays for the comp insurance, you know," Roy said from the kitchen. "Every year it goes up."

"When I'm not working on cars, Ed expects me to get out there and pump gas. All day, I'm up, down, up, down."

"What you need to do is take off your paunch," Patsy said. "Get off your butt more."

"I'm off it all day. What do you think happens at the garage? And that Ed, he keeps me runnin'."

"Maybe you need to duct tape your mouth. I figure one of your ends is the problem."

"Whooowheee," Artie chortled. "Patsy, you got enough tongue for twenty rows of teeth."

"And if you don't watch your mouth, you aren't gonna have any," she shot back.

"Aw, give me a little sympathy. I work hard, and Berny just spends it all. I work my butt off at the station."

"Well, your mile-high breakfasts sure ain't gonna shrink your ass," Toad said.

"I gotta keep up my strength. Every day it's something. There's always some clown with a problem. I don't know why in the hell the people drivin' here for recreation don't get their cars checked out before they take off."

"Those *clowns* are your customers," Bobby said. "Hey, Toad. What you fixin' to do today after you and Cliff come back here to do your checkers game?"

Toad waggled his eyebrows. "Goin' over to the hardware store and talk to Stan. Then go home and watch the TV. Take my nap, until it's time to eat again. I wished Cliff could get here earlier, but his wife won't let him outa the house."

"I need someone to help me haul an old water heater out of Sue's basement. I want to move it over to the barn. She said I could have it for my welding art."

"What are you going to make out of an old water heater?" Pasty asked.

"I'm gonna cut it up, add on a few things and make a dog statue for Brittany."

"Sue's girl?"

"Yeah, she's got a birthday comin' up. She's a teacher up in Salem."

"They grow up fast," Patsy said.

Toad wadded his napkin and tossed it on his empty plate. "Well, sure, I could help with that. You want me to meet you out there?"

Rrrrmmmmm. Rrrrmmmmm. The sound of a chainsaw came from Artie's shirt pocket.

Toad snickered. "It's just the ringer on his cell phone. Used to be a flushin' toilet."

Bobby shook his head. "Jeez, I thought he was passing gas."

"Yeah, Ma." Artie said into his cell phone. "Yeah. Look, I can't get over there today. Yeah, I know the windows need fixin', but it's just gonna have to wait. Yeah. Yeah. Yeah. Look, I'll talk to you later. I'm trying to eat here. I know you cook, and I could stop over there, but I'm here. Okay?" He tucked the phone back in his pocket. "I just wish everybody would get the hell off my goddam back."

* * *

Artie strolled into Benders out on the highway and took a seat at the far end of the bar. "Hey Al," he said to the bartender. He ordered a beer. The big screen TV on the wall over the counter thankfully scrolled text because it was impossible to hear over the noise and the Johnny Cash song playing in the background. Artie fumbled in his pocket, pulled out a cigarette, nervously lit up, took a long drag, and blew a cloud of tension into the already smoky air. He sipped his beer, waiting and watching the rear booth in a shadowy corner near the back. He looked at his watch. *9:00 p.m. Remey should be here.*

Tootie, a redhead in tight jeans, approached carrying her pool cue. "Hey Artie, want to play a few rounds?"

"Nah, not right now. After I finish my beer."

She climbed on the stool next to him. He could tell by her rheumy eyes that she was already a little tight. His arm reached across her back until his fingers found the side of her breast. "Want a beer?" He squeezed. Tootie giggled.

"Later cookie," she said. "I'm on a roll." She slid off the stool and headed back to the pool table where she joined a big-stomached guy in a cowboy hat and boots who was chalking his cue.

Between swallows of beer, Artie shot glances to the back of the bar. *At last.* Remey was sitting there in a blue hoodie, which didn't hide his cascading rolls of fat. Artie signaled the bartender and ordered a beer for Remey. He waited until Mandy, the server, delivered it. Remey lit up. That was the signal.

Artie took his beer, sauntered over and slid into the booth. Remey busied himself reading e-mail on his cell phone. At first glance, Remey was all neck. Stubble covered his chubby cheeks which merged into his massive quadruple chin, making him look like an overweight pelican.

"Here's the stuff." He handed Artie a small package under the table.

Artie glanced over his shoulder, pulled a rolled-up wad of money from his pocket.

"Count it out," Remey said. He flicked ashes into the ashtray.

Artie checked his surroundings again. "Here? You want me to count it in public?"

"Yeah, just turn your back and be quiet about it."

Artie shifted in the booth, undid the rubber band, and laid out the money as he counted softly.

"That ain't enough," Remey said. "You're short." He tapped his fingers on the table. "Again."

"Aw, just by a little. I have to wait until payday. I told you about the divorce . . . Berny, she . . ."

"We can't just keep supplying you."

"Aw, I just need some stuff for my back, you know, for the pain."

Remey leaned forward, his lips curled downward into a sinister smirk. "You gotta pay up."

Artie squirmed. The click of the pool balls seemed louder. "I will. I will. Payday is comin' up. Just give me a little time."

Remey scooped up the bills Artie left on the table and stuffed them in his pocket. "You could make big bucks being a slanger. Taking it to the next step, if you get my drift."

Artie held up his hands in self-defense. "Nah, Nah. I don't want to do hard junk."

"We got good quality mud from Mexico."

"I get depressed. I'm just tryin' to kill my pain." Artie's armpits were wet.

"They all are, friend. But street deals, they could take care of your little debt problem." Remey took a drag from his cigarette and blew the smoke in Artie's face. "Like over at that trailer court."

"Ray's?"

"Lot of potential there."

"Yeah?"

"Lots of it . . . a chance for some real dough, fella. And there's the school."

"Aw, not the school."

"Small town America. It's a growing market."

"Aw, I got kids. I'm a local boy."

Artie's folks used to run the Rexall drugstore which meant they knew just about everybody—people that depended on them to fix everything from sniffles to hemorrhoids. The plan was for him to learn the business once he graduated high school, but he hated being all cooped up, working with ledgers. His joy was cars. Fixin' them up. Driving fast. Loving the grease under his nails. Hanging at Dave's Bowling Alley. Rasslin' with Berny in the back seat.

Things changed fast. The folks sold out to a chain pharmacy. He married Berny when she was two months pregnant and found that job at the garage. After that, life was same ol', same ol'.

"I'm tellin' ya. It's everywhere. And, if it's not you, then some other lucky dude'll be cashin' in."

"Uh-huh."

"Why not you?"

"It's just . . . my back hurts . . . and Berny—"

"You push enough, and you kiss that friggin' job goodbye."

"Yeah?"

"I'm tellin' you. Think on it." Remey tipped his glass, finishing his beer. "Because you gotta pay up. Otherwise, the boss, he's gonna be mad."

"Yeah?"

"Real mad."

"Oh, I will." Artie gripped his glass. He wiped his sweaty brow with his sleeve. Loud strains of a Reba McEntire's "I Want a Cowboy," filled the room. A few people laughed and swayed to the music, bumping into each other. The smell of fresh popcorn hung in the air.

"Hey Artie." It was Tootie again, calling from the bar. She swiveled her buttocks on the bar stool.

Artie turned toward her. His face flushed. "Yeah?"

"Wanna dance, baby cakes?" She was eating popcorn from a large yellow bowl on the bar. She threw a handful in his direction, giggling as it scattered on the floor.

Artie gave Remey a pleading look.

Tootie crossed her legs. "I'm ready for that beer now." She leaned back on the stool and impatiently jiggled her right foot.

"I better go." Artie welcomed the chance to get away from Remey. "It's scorin' time. Heh, heh."

Remey sized up Tootie, his eyes stopping at her low-cut tank top, a sleazy, knowing expression on his face. "Yeah, and while you're getting' it on there with Miss Big Jugs, think what I told ya. Okay?

Their eyes locked. Artie nodded.

Remey stood up. "I'm outta here." He slithered out the back door.

CHAPTER 7

Lance. Lance. Lance. If he heard any more about Lance Helms his head would split. Cody left the freeway near Eugene and rolled out onto Highway 58 through the lush Umpqua National Forest filled with tall, green conifers, waterfalls, and wild rivers. *Thank God we're about halfway there.* Once they broke clear of the valley, the sky beamed a brilliant blue.

Brittany leaned back. She nursed the vanilla latte she ordered at a Starbucks "drive-thru" where they'd stopped earlier. "I told him all about you, when we were kids. . . how you were kidnapped. I'd like you two to meet."

I can hardly wait. "What does this Lance do for a living?" Cody reached for his black coffee in the cup holder.

"He's a lawyer," she bubbled. She held her latte between her knees and worked at tearing open a bag of pretzels. The sweet vanilla smell of her coffee drink floated in the air. "I don't know why these dang packages are so hard to open. Anyway, Lance works for Janes Timber, a lumber exporting company in Portland. You've heard of William Janes?"

"Actually, no."

"Well, it's his company. They export logs around the world. He's also a state representative. Representative Bill Janes. Does that ring a bell?"

"Kinda. Now that you mentioned the legislature. I still can't picture him."

Brittany was off Janes and back to *Lance. Lance. Lance.* "That's how I met him. Lance is his legislative aide. I took my kids for a tour of the Capitol Building. Lance spotted us and took over . . . led us to some behind-the-scene places we'd never see on the regular tour. Then we got to meet Representative Janes."

Cody gave her a sideways look. *Britt was so naïve. Lance didn't spot them. He spotted her and moved in. Probably didn't give a damn about the kids. He liked that about her, though. She wasn't stuck on herself.*

"He drives a Camaro ZL1 convertible, white with a black top. It's a $60,000 car, you know."

"Uh-huh." *What exactly was it about women and cars? Something he never understood. Madison Avenue advertising stuff.* "And now you're riding in a Subaru. You must feel like Cinderella at midnight."

She laughed that wonderful laugh. "Oh no. It's just that I'd never ridden in a Camaro. Well, until I met Lance."

"A man isn't his car, Britt," Cody said.

"I know that. Jeez. Lance is a really nice guy." She laughed again, still struggling with the bag of pretzels. "You're the only one that calls me that."

"What?"

"Britt. You used to call me that when we were kids." She laughed again. She reached over and gently stroked his knee. He wished she wouldn't do that, now that he knew she thought of him as her *brother.*

Pop! Brittany yanked the pretzels bag open with such force, half the contents flew through the air. "Oh God, now I've messed up your car."

"Not to worry," said Cody, picking a pretzel out of his hair. "I'll let Crackers in, and he'll vacuum it in a jiffy."

"Crackers?"

"My landlady's cat. He was a stray who used to sneak up and steal the Ritz crackers she set on her patio table. She adopted him. Now, he thinks my apartment's his man cave. I caught him stealing my Fritos." He looked over at Brittany and chuckled. He knew any story about animals would melt her heart.

"Ahhh. How sweet. A junk food kitty. I'd like to meet him."

"Just stop by with a bag of potato chips, and he's your man."

"Want some?" She pushed the pretzel bag toward him.

"No thanks. I can't chew, sip, and drive at the same time."

"Lance says Bill Janes is planning to run for the U.S. Senate. He's in his late fifties, so it's now or never. Lance is all excited—he's expecting to go with him."

Cody, delighted to hear Lance might be leaving, almost let out a whoop.

"Well, he thinks Washington will be more exciting than timber. I'm not sure how I'd adjust, though."

His desire to hoot gave way to a stab in his chest. Of course, if Lance eventually went to Washington, he'd want Britt to go with him. "So why isn't Lance here celebrating your birthday?"

"I always celebrate with Mother. I mean, she's all alone. When Lance gets back, we'll probably go to dinner or something. Lance isn't all that comfortable in Forest Lake. It's awkward for him. You know what I mean?"

"No, what do you mean?"

"Forest Lake is a bit of a . . . backwater. Lance just doesn't know what to do with himself. He's not very outdoorsy. And . . . uh . . . he's uncomfortable around Mother. After the first six words, he dries up, goes out on the back porch, and buries himself in his cell phone. After we eat, he's ready to go. I can't really visit when he's around."

"Hmmm." Cody couldn't resist. "Sounds like a snob."

"Oh no, he's . . . just so busy . . . you know. The small town pace is different."

"So what is he, Janes' puppet? He can't stay off his cell phone for a few minutes."

"Janes is a real neat guy. He has a pure white Akita dog." She smiled. "He takes Blanche everywhere. When the legislature is in town, he takes her to work."

That sounded like Britt, Cody thought, judging a person by his dog.

They passed Klamath Lake, drove through Klamath Falls and finally cut to the highway that would lead to Forest Lake.

"The sky is so blue over here. That's what I miss about home," Brittany said.

"Yeah. I wish we had more time so we could get off the highway and explore a few things. Well, so does this Lance have a dog? A cat? A parakeet?"

"No. He's always on the go."

"I see." He didn't really.

* * *

Ahead, he saw the plain green sign: *Welcome to Forest Lake. Population 2025.* The town did seem bigger than he remembered, but other than that, it was just a collection of flat buildings bisected by the highway. They passed the Shell station, the Dairy Queen, and Tillden's Grocery.

"I'm hungry," Brittany announced, "for *real* food. It's almost one thirty. Let's stop in at Dottie's. You remember the café?"

"Just barely." The actual place was a blur. He and his grandfather had lunch there just before they headed out to find a Christmas tree, and their lives went to hell.

"We can use the restroom and get a bite to eat before we head out to Mother's." She leaned forward and pointed. "There it is up there . . . to the left, across from the motel."

Cody slowed the car and turned into the parking lot. Dottie's Café was a gray-shake building with a gabled roof, an entry porch and two large front windows shaded by green awnings. On one side were steps, on the other, a ramp for the handicapped. A wooden staircase wound up one side to what appeared to be an upstairs apartment. The building was adjacent to a large parking lot just off the highway, giving easy access to truckers.

Cody got out and paused. He looked up at the window—Dottie's apartment, his grieving grandfather hung himself there. He swallowed hard. *Stop! Don't panic.* He meekly followed Brittany up the concrete stairs. A bell jingled when she opened the door.

"Well, look who's here," Patsy called from behind the counter. "Brittany Bolin." The lunch crowd had thinned, a few regulars sat at the counter.

"Guess who I have with me?" Brittany said. Three men at the counter turned to see.

"Well, I don't know, but he's damn handsome," Patsy said in her loud voice. "If I was a little younger, I'd blow in his ear."

Cody blushed.

"Cody Benson," Brittany blurted. "*The* Cody Benson."

"Oh my gosh," said Patsy. You're kidding." She hurried from behind the counter to shake his hand. "I've never met you, but I'd recognize you by those eyes. You have the most wonderful eyes." She turned toward the kitchen. "Roy," she called, "Come on out here."

Brittany continued with the introductions. "You remember Artie Bradshaw." Artie sat there with his baseball cap skewed sideways and stared. "He was in school with us."

"Sure." Cody extended his hand. Artie returned a weak shake. "The last time I saw you, I think you tossed my hat out the bus window." He tried not to stare at Artie's thick gut. The guy had morphed into a blimp.

Artie smirked. "Aw, that was years ago."

"And this is . . ." Brittany paused. "I'm sorry, I can't remember your name.

"Gilbert Holloway. Folks call me Toad." He nodded. "Garsh, I'm pleased to meet ya." He extended his hand.

"And of course, Ken Blake. You remember Deputy Blake?"

Cody stiffened. *The cop. That was the cop who questioned him. Older, full head of gray hair, a little thicker at the waist, but that was him. No doubt about it.*

Blake smiled broadly. He got off the stool, gave Cody a warm hug, and patted his back. "Hey, fella," he said, "I spent a lot of hours worrying over you." He stood back, holding Cody at arm's length. "You look great."

"Thanks. I see you're still wearing a badge."

"Don't let that fool ya," Patsy said. "He's a snowbird. He and Lydia spend winters in Arizona."

"Actually, I'm sorta retired, but I still work as a reserve deputy. Merrill Korman is the Chief Deputy in these parts now."

"And Dottie," Cody asked. "Is she still around?"

"Dottie sold the cafe to Patsy and Ray years ago," Brittany said.

Patsy laughed. "She comes in here for breakfast, now and then. Still tells us how to run the place."

Blake continued to stare at Cody. "You know, I occasionally bump into your father when Lydia and I go to Ashland to see a play." He rubbed his jaw. "He's darn proud of you."

"He has to be. He's my dad." *Proud. Really? Since when?*

"Aw, what brings you down here?" Artie asked.

Brittany jumped in, "He's doing some research, looking into the Jim Fallingwater case. Remember that one?"

Artie looked away, bored. Toad sat up straight, seemingly interested.

Cody bristled. *Oh God, why doesn't she quit talking. I shouldn't have said anything.*

"Jim Fallingwater?" Blake pursed his lips. "Why?"

"I'm an anthropologist. Uh . . . with Willamette University. In Salem. I'm studying the effects of modern society on Native Americans."

"But Fallingwater . . ." Ken started to say. His eyes watched Cody. "That's a really *old* case."

"Yeah, but his case is open and shut. I mean there's a beginning and an ending. A tragic ending. It's a good case to study for that reason. It's complete . . . I mean from an anthropological point of view." *Get a grip. I sound like a mumble bumble bullshitter. And, I am.* He wished Blake would quit gawking at him.

Artie's moony eyes scanned Brittany's body, like he was undressing her. "You're looking swell, Brittany. Bring your car by anytime; I'll take a look at it. Before you drive back."

Way to go Artie. Change the subject. Phew.

"Thank you Artie, but Cody drove me down here."

Artie shot a glance at Cody. His lips tightened. He looked away and picked at his chin with his thumbnail.

Roy came out of the kitchen, wiping his hand on his apron. "So you're Cody Benson. Gosh, it's nice to see you. We still have your picture up there on our wall." He pointed.

Brittany pulled Cody's arm. "Yeah, look over here."

Tacked up in the middle of other photos of men with fishes and people celebrating birthdays was a large framed newspaper clipping. "Boy Found," said the yellowing article in tall, black type over his third-grade picture, and a photo of the Big Bat Wilderness area. *There it is. My source of stress. My* . . . He fingered the rubber band on his wrist.

Pasty returned with a camera. "We need an update." Brittany started to move out of the way. "Oh no. Stay put. I want to get both of you for my wall." She peered through the viewfinder and waved with her hand. "Move in closer."

Cody put his arm around Brittany. He could smell her fragrant hair. He wanted to linger there forever. *Not a feeling "a brother" should have.*

"Say cheese," Patsy called and snapped away. "Wait, one more. People will love this. We talk about you down here all the time. You were our last big story."

Artie, not amused, said, "I've gotta get back," He grinned at Brittany. "Be sure to stop in."

"Oh. I will if we have time."

"Good to see you," said Cody.

Artie tugged at his hat. "Yeah," he said. "Later." He stalked out the door.

Toad shook Cody's hand, giving him another once over. "Nice to meet ya. You too, Miss Brittany. Sorry, I gotta run, the Orioles is gonna be at Tampa Bay."

Blake stood eyeing Cody. "Lydia will be so happy to hear about you," he finally said. "So, you're a professor?"

"Yeah," said Cody, embarrassed. "Actually, I'm an assistant professor. I . . .uh . . . my specialty is indigenous peoples."

Blake's eyes widened. "Very impressive."

"Tell Lydia, hello," Brittany said as Blake made his way to the door. She turned to Cody. "She was my sixth grade teacher." The bell over the door jingled and the deputy was gone.

"Well, what'll it be," Patsy said, bringing out her order pad.

Roy beamed. "Whatever it is, it's on the house."

CHAPTER 8

Cody stepped out of the car, stretched his legs, and drank in the smell of freshly cut grass. He'd never been to Brittany's house even as a kid. Now, he could see why hotshot Lance never wanted to spend time there.

A large, lumpy yard surrounded the small, white two-story farmhouse, which badly needed a coat of paint. The concrete porch, with no steps, was set close to the ground. Above it, four columns supported the overhang. A wooden porch swing that had seen better days hung on the right side. Above the swing, a horde of gnat-like insects flew in a circle enjoying the spring sunshine.

Two long double-hung windows faced the porch on either side and one upstairs window peeked out above it. There was no garage. Brittany's mom, he saw, parked her car in the open shed by the barn next to a riding lawn mower.

"Our house is modest." Brittany explained as if sensing his reaction. "I hope that's okay with you. I should've mentioned it before. If that's a problem, you can always stay at the motel in town."

Cody assured her, "Mom always said it didn't matter what type of house people lived in as long as the floor was clean and the roof didn't leak."

"After my father died, Mother did the best she could . . . took a job clerking at the Mercantile. Still works there, but it doesn't pay a whole lot. The place belonged to my dad's folks. It was free and clear, so we stayed here on the five acres, rather than move into town. It was a great place to grow up."

Brittany's mother, he knew, never remarried, and her father had been a Forest Lake mail carrier. "Charlie was so dependable, you could set your clock by him," Cody remembered his mother saying. "He was one of a kind. Everyone liked him."

Inside, the living room was neat but simple—sofa, easy chair, TV, a scratched oak coffee table, electric wall heater. Not much else. The pea green carpet was clean but worn. Brittany had lived a humble life. Cody didn't realize this when he was young, but he could see it now. He remembered, she always brought her lunch in a brown bag. The house had a cozy feel, and some wonderful tomato-basil smell wafted from the kitchen.

Sue Bolin came into the room, carrying a dishtowel, hugged her daughter before greeting Cody. "My, I'm so happy to see you." She set the towel on the sofa arm, extended her hand, and hung on to his with both of hers. They felt rough, like they were used to work. Sue was an older, tired version of her daughter, the same face but with shorter, chin-length gray hair. She wore a simple, blue paisley blouse over black poplin pants and black Keds-style canvas shoes.

"Brittany told me all about running into you."

Cody grinned. "I guess I'm the one that ran into her."

His attempt at humor apparently went right past Sue. "Bobby's coming for dinner, too," she said.

"Bobby Blaze," Brittany said. "He's a long-time friend. He helps Mother manage out here by herself. You'll like him. I think I told you, he's Native American."

"You mentioned that. I'm eager to talk with him."

"Cody's doing some research on Native Americans," she explained to Sue.

Sue nodded. "I'm sure Bobby can help you with that."

Cody sniffed the air, "Something sure smells good."

Sue beamed. "I'm cooking up my own tomato sauce. We're having lasagna."

"One of my favorites. Nice spread you have here," Cody said, trying to keep the conversation going.

"We used to have a cow and some chickens for our own use. Charlie always put in a big garden. Now I do the garden and rent the field to a neighbor who runs a few cattle. Bobby uses the barn for his art and his welding business. He helps me out a lot. If there's a hole in a fence or a slat out of the barn, I call Bobby. I'm glad he's around."

"And, I don't worry about her being out here alone," Brittany added.

"I made some tea. Thought maybe you'd like a snack before you bring your things in. It's a long drive down here."

"Just a bit, Mother. We had lunch in town."

They sat around the large round table with a dark brown wood-grain Formica top that stood in the middle of the kitchen. There was no dining room. The stove and refrigerator were avocado green. The floor was bamboo-colored linoleum. In spite of its modesty, the kitchen, with its light green walls and cluttered counters, seemed homey.

Sue took the teakettle from the top of the woodstove and poured black tea into three cups. "I made a fire this morning. I know it's spring, but it's still chilly outside." She set out a small plate of soft oatmeal cookies with raisins and chocolate chips.

"These are delicious," Cody said. "You know, I remember these. I used to pilfer them from Britt's lunch when we were kids."

"He was always after my cookies." Brittany laughed.

Oh, baby. "She always had two cookies, but instead of giving me one, she'd break off pieces and parcel them out."

"I've been making these for years," a pleased Sue said. "They're always a big hit at church potlucks. Got the recipe from the book that came with my very first electric range years ago. I added the chocolate chips for Brittany." A big, black fly buzzed over the plate.

"Now how did he get in here?" Sue asked. She waved it off.

"Leave it alone, Mother." The fly escaped to a window and eventually sunned itself on the sill. "Then I found out he had his own stash of cookies—peanut butter," Brittany continued.

"Yeah, but I shared them with you, too."

"Only after I threatened to cut you off."

"She was a tough negotiator."

"I'll send some home with you," Sue assured Cody, obviously enjoying their banter. "It's so good to have both of you here."

"Want a bite?" Bobby teased Brittany at dinner. He held a forkful of meat-laden lasagna toward her.

"Absolutely not. Usually, he's trying to pawn off bologna sandwiches."

"I'll bet you could make a mean lasagna out of bologna. Ever tried it, Sue?"

Sue made a face. "No, and I don't plan to." She glanced at Brittany "I don't know. I worry you don't get enough protein." She passed the French bread.

Cody looked puzzled.

"I'm a vegetarian."

"I made a meatless portion for her," Sue said.

Cody helped himself to the bread. That explained the salad she'd had at Dottie's. She'd said nothing while he gobbled down a hamburger and fries.

Sue winked at Bobby. "It's too bad Lance couldn't be here for Brittany's birthday. You remember Lance?"

Bobby buttered his bread. "Yeah."

"Lance is very busy, Mother. He's working on a special project for Bill Janes. Janes Timber exports logs internationally. Lance may have to go to Japan or maybe China. I'm not sure which."

Sue's face brightened. "Lance is so right for her," she said to Bobby. "Smart, handsome, and he makes good money." She turned to Cody. "Salad?"

"Thank you." He piled the greens onto his plate. *Lance. Lance. Lance.* Probably can't keep his pants zipped. Cody felt like a large serving of chopped liver.

Sue smiled at Brittany. "You'll have to invite Lance over again when he's free."

Bobby cleared his throat. "So, you're an anthropologist," he said. "A professor?"

"Yes, with Willamette University." He was glad they were off Lance.

"Ah, Willamette. They always sponsor a great pow-wow. Drove all the way over there in March."

"Were you part of the entertainment?" Cody asked.

"No, I sell my metal sculpture. I made three thousand dollars."

"Wow," Brittany said.

"Sold the big deer I made to some guy from Lake Oswego. Not bad for something I made out of worn car fenders."

"Cody's here to do research on Native Americans," Brittany said. "He's looking into the old Jim Fallingwater case."

"Fallingwater?" Bobby seemed surprised. "Why for God's sakes?"

"I'm researching the effects of modern society on Native American culture," Cody quickly added. "I'm . . . uh . . . especially interested in assimilation in smaller communities. I mean what turned this guy into a killer, and could he have gotten a fair trial?"

Bobby frowned. "I wouldn't waste my time on some dead guy."

"I've read a lot about the case in old newspaper articles. Just want to fill in the blanks."

Bobby licked his lips. "If you want to explore Indian ways, why not go out to the res? The Klamath Reservation down here. There are plenty of young bucks who'd be willing to talk with you. They're folks that's done lotta good. We'd rather be remembered for that than . . . murder."

"You should contact Dottie Johnson," Sue said. "She knew this Jim and, of course, you knew Jim and Deputy Blake were boyhood friends."

Cody reached for his water. "Actually, I didn't."

"Oh yes. They both grew up here. That's the story anyway. Some folks think—"

"Go talk to Indian people in the here and now," Bobby said. It sounded like an order.

"I plan to. But I'd like to use the Fallingwater situation as a launching story. Fallingwater's case ended tragically—"

Bobby wouldn't let go. "You should've just gone over to that pow-wow in Salem. Lots of opportunity there."

"Once I discussed Fallingwater, I could bring my treatise up to modern times. You know, interview the current tribal folks, and maybe some entrepreneurs, such as yourself. I mean I'm really in the planning stages about how I want to structure this. What's your tribal heritage?"

Bobby slowly sipped water from his glass and then set it down. "My father was Modoc. My mother was a bunch of things, including a little Dutch."

"Fallingwater was a full-blooded Modoc," Cody said.

"Fallingwater was a long time ago. People here would like to forget about it. That was an ugly time in this town." He paused and gave Cody a level look. "My advice." He tapped the table hard with his hand. "Don't. Go. There."

His reaction caught Cody off guard.

Brittany shot a glance at him, which said let it drop. "Um, we held a rally in front of the courthouse for Banjo. I think I told you about him?"

"He's that dog you're trying to help," Sue said. "And?"

"He's still incarcerated. A hearing's coming up."

Bobby helped himself to more lasagna.

Sue refilled her water glass and handed the pitcher to Bobby. "I don't know, rallies and all. Be careful. Someone might get hurt. People can get pretty emotional over dogs. Does he have an owner?"

"Yeah, and she supports us. She's a single mom. No way can she afford to fight for the dog."

"Once a dog bites, it's pretty hard to save 'em," Sue said. "You know down here, they shoot the dog—"

"Mother," Brittany said, her shoulders slumping. "He didn't just bite someone. He was provoked. *Provoked.* That's a big difference. Trust me. We're going to *save* him."

"Honey, you always had a soft spot for the animals, but some—"

"We're going to *save* him."

"I don't know. They're gonna do what they're gonna do," Sue said.

"Over my dead—"

Cody lifted his water glass. "Here's to the birthday girl," he said, defusing the discussion. He grinned at Brittany.

Sue pushed back her chair. "I say bring on the cake." She flipped the switch on the coffee maker and brought a tall chocolate cake with swirls of dark icing to the table. She lit the three candles on the top. "Now, you can make a wish."

"Wait, wait, wait." Cody led the birthday song while the coffee maker gurgled in the background. Brittany closed her eyes and blew out the candles. Afterward, she cut four generous servings while Sue poured coffee.

"You make a helluva cake," Bobby said, taking a big bite. "The frosting's enough to put a man in heaven." He licked his fingers.

"Chocolate everything is Brittany's favorite," Sue said.

Cody let the delicious frosting linger on his tongue and sipped coffee, which tasted like it came out of a can. "You should enter this in the state fair."

Just then, the big fly landed on the table. Sue waved her napkin. "That darn fly." The startled fly buzzed off.

When they finished the cake, Bobby jumped up and returned with a large, awkwardly wrapped package that he placed on the floor. "Presents," he announced, "Time for presents." Brittany clapped her hands and pulled off the paper.

"Oh Bobby, this is wonderful." She hugged the metal dog sculpture. "Just absolutely wonderful." The seated, three-foot high dog had an open mouth and a lapping tongue.

Bobby beamed. "I made it out of hubcaps."

Cody touched the shiny sculpture. He whistled. "That's a lot of hubcaps."

"I find 'em along the road, or I get a bunch from the garage in town. Polish 'em up. I made his tongue and his ears outta Sue's old water heater. You can set it outside."

"No, no, someone might steal it." Brittany gave Bobby a big hug. "I'll find a place for it inside my apartment."

Sue handed Brittany a card in a blue envelope. "Open it."

Brittany carefully tugged open the flap and read the card. "How sweet. You always find the best cards. Oh, and a gift card to Krystal's Boutique. How'd you ever get this down here?"

"Had cousin Dulcy pick it up."

Dulcy. That name. Cody had heard it before. The other woman at the rally. They were cousins.

"But this is too much money."

"You can add to it. Get yourself something nice. You'll need it now that *Lance* is taking you places." She smiled at Cody.

Lance again. Cody pulled a small package from his pocket. "It's kinda tiny, but inside is someone special to you."

"Lance?" she giggled. "He's too big to fit in there."

Cody felt tightness in his stomach. "Just open it." *Lance, Lance, Lance. Jesus. Was there no escaping him?*

"Banjo!" Brittany blurted. She dangled the bracelet with the small German Shepherd charm. "Thank you. How perfect." She leaned toward Cody and planted a loud kiss on his cheek.

Cody's entire face and neck lit up. He glanced at the cake crumbs on his plate and then up into Sue's not amused face.

* * *

The next morning after a leisurely breakfast of scrambled eggs and toast, Cody planned to drive out to Big Bat Mountain, near the place where he'd gotten lost. He'd never been back there, but felt comfortable going as long as Brittany was with him. He also wanted to contact Dottie Johnson to find out when she'd be available to talk. Instead, he frittered away valuable time fixing a malfunctioning toilet. The house only had one bathroom. After the last flush, the water kept running.

Sue worried about having to call the plumber. "They charge so much. And, I just replaced the water heater."

As it turned out, it wasn't a big problem, the overflow pipe had slipped off the fill tube. Cody had lived in enough apartments to know the fix. "It looks like you should replace the flapper, too." He showed Sue. "That's this black thing down here that keeps the water from flowing into the bowl. I'm sure Bobby can do that for you. Just have him pick one up at the hardware store. It only costs a few dollars."

"I'm so glad you were here," Sue said.

Cody's few minutes of fame wilted when he carried their luggage to his Subaru. The back tires had been slashed. Cody dropped the suitcases and rushed to inspect the punctured tires. "What the hell."

Sue's hands cradled her face. "That's never happened out here. And, on a Sunday!"

"I suppose everything is closed," Cody muttered. *Damn it to hell.*

"It's creepy that's what," Sue said. "Is anything missing from your car? Do you think I should call the sheriff?" She hurried off to check her own car and to walk around the house.

"Artie," Brittany said. "I'll call Artie. He'll help. I know he will." She headed toward the house.

"My car's okay," Sue said, coming back from the shed. "Doesn't look like anything else was touched. We've never had vandalism out here before," she insisted.

Brittany returned carrying her cell phone. "Artie is still in bed. He has to go to the garage to get tires." She handed the phone to Cody. "You better talk to him. He needs details about the tire size."

* * *

When Artie finally arrived, he spent the first few minutes flirting with Brittany, who acted as if he was a hero. "Oh Artie, it's so wonderful of you to come out here . . . especially on a Sunday."

Artie touched the bill of his skewed hat. "Aw, no problem. So good to see ya, again. You, too, Mrs. Bolin." He ignored Cody. "I brought two tires," he said to Brittany.

Cody rolled his eyes. "Earth to Artie. It's *my* car we're talking about here."

Artie grinned. Cody showed him the spare, hoping to save some bucks.

"I'd have to inflate that one a bit. You know they lose their air over time," he said.

Unlike some people, Cody thought.

He gave Cody a hotshot smile. "Spares are flimsy. It's best with an all-wheel drive to replace both tires. When ya get home, take it to the shop there and have 'em take a look at all four. Tires need the same amount of tread to maintain even stability on the road."

Ka-ching. Cody massaged the back of his neck, visualizing dollars flying from his wallet.

Artie took his time jacking up the car, removing the wheels, and replacing the tires while Brittany watched and Cody paced. Afterward, Artie lingered and made small talk with Sue and Brittany. Sue invited him in for a cup of coffee and served him cookies. "I guess none of us will make it to church this morning," she lamented. She plopped down on a kitchen chair and asked about his ex-wife, his mother, his kids and a half-dozen other people in town.

The big fly was back. It landed on the table, rubbing its forelegs together. Bored, half-listening and extremely irritated, Cody picked up the morning newspaper, which was still in its plastic sleeve, and slammed it against the table. Bam! Sue jumped. Dishes rattled. The fly buzzed away.

"Don't do that," Brittany said horrified.

Sue wrinkled her nose. "You missed it."

Artie smirked.

Stunned, Cody said. "What?"

Brittany's eyes flared. "The fly wants to live as much as you do!"

"It's just a fly, what the hell—"

"You take a glass, capture it, and put it outside," she said in her teacher's voice.

Artie's lips curled up into a big-ass grin.

Sue's eyebrows rose, but she looked straight ahead.

Cody's face flushed. Exasperated, he checked his watch and turned to Artie. "How much do I owe you?"

"Aw, just a minute. I have to get my clipboard from the truck." He opened the door as the fly sailed out over his head.

Brittany clapped her hands. "The God of second chances," she said.

From the window, Cody could see Artie sitting in the cab taking his sweet time figuring and chatting on his cell phone. *The guy moves like molasses.*

Artie eventually sauntered in. "Well, it's not too bad." He gazed at Brittany with a moonstruck smile on his face. "I'm not chargin' you for mileage."

Cody inhaled sharply. Brittany smiled. "How sweet of you, Artie."

"Aw, it's nothin'. Glad I could—"

"Who the hell would do this?" Cody blurted. He hastily wrote out a check on the kitchen table.

"Aw, kids. Just kids," Artie said with a glint in his eye. He folded the check and stuffed it in his wallet.

By the time Artie left, it was almost 2 p.m. Sue was making noises about lunch, but Cody insisted that they head back. "We'll catch a bite on the way." There wouldn't be time to go out to the Big Bat and look around the way he wanted. He wasn't in the mood to track down Dottie, and back in Salem, he still had papers to grade for Monday.

It took forever for Sue to wrap some of her cookies and find just the right-sized sack to put them in. Then she had a sweater that she'd bought but didn't like once she'd gotten home and thought Brittany might want it. Of course, Brittany had to try it on.

Shit. He was glad when they were in the car headed north. They drove away in silence. If he was going to make any progress with his search for Jim, he'd probably have to come back on his own. *Alone.* That thought upped his anxiety level. His throat felt furry.

"Sorry about the fly," he finally said.

"Yeah, well, no harm done." She paused. "I . . . uh . . . I'm a Buddhist."

That explained a lot, but he couldn't help but wonder what ol' Lance thought about that. He didn't sound like a guy who'd sit cross-legged in his three piece suit.

"I believe in a reverence for all life. We share this planet with *all* other beings and everything in the environment."

"Uh-huh. As a cultural anthropologist, I've studied all kinds of spiritual paths. I don't care what people believe as long as they don't dump a helping of it on my plate or beat me over the head trying to make me swallow it." That drew a smile. "So, are you a follower of a particular school or branch—Theravāda, Mahāyāna, Zen, Tibetan?"

"I'm a bubblegum Buddhist."

His jaw dropped. "What?"

"It means a more secular approach. I see it as a philosophy, coupled with meditative practice and mindfulness. It gives meaning and peace to my life."

"Uh-huh."

"Have you read any books by Stephen Bachelor?"

"Actually, no."

"He's British. A wonderful author, former monk, and noted scholar. He's a proponent of secular Buddhism. He wrote books like *Buddhism without Beliefs* and *Confessions of a Buddhist Atheist.*"

"And does your mother know that? I mean that you're Buddhist, sort of'?"

Brittany sat up straight, folded her arms, and looked directly at him. "I *am* a Buddhist. Just an evolving one. And, in case you haven't noticed, I'm also an adult." She paused. "I'm serious about what I believe."

Cody gripped the wheel. Oh, he noticed all right. He stared straight ahead. "Sorry. I guess I keep stepping in it."

She sighed. "It's okay. You couldn't have known. Actually, I'm the one that's sorry . . . about the tires I mean. That's just so unusual. Weird."

"I don't know what it is about that guy. I get the distinct impression he doesn't like me."

"Artie's okay. You weren't exactly chums in grade school."

"Man, you'd think he'd get over that. We were just little kids. But it wouldn't surprise me one damn bit if he wasn't the one that did the slashing."

"Oh no, I don't think he'd do that."

"He was slobbering all over you, like he created the opportunity."

"Artie was just being Artie. You know, the kids blamed him when you disappeared. Said his bullying made you run away."

"I didn't run away."

"Yeah, but the kids knew Artie picked on you. They blamed him for a long time, until he just sort of melted into the background and stayed there . . . if you know what I mean."

Cody said nothing. He saw how Artie looked at Brittany, and he knew that look. The idiot. She was way out of his league, and he was too stupid to know it.

"I used to feel sorry for him," she said. "He was always overweight, wasn't good at sports, never had a date for the dances. Got hooked up with Bernice Langston. First thing you know, she was pregnant and they got married. They both dropped out of school. Two kids later, there was a divorce."

Cody leaned back in the seat and relaxed his tight grip on the wheel. Britt had a heart of gold, but there was something about Artie that stuck in his craw.

<h1 style="text-align:center">CHAPTER 9</h1>

Honey paced on the top level of the Pringle Parkade in Salem, waiting for the payoff from some guy he only knew as Shades. He lit a cigarette and tossed the match on the concrete.

Honey, short for Honeyman, was tall, muscular and built like a tank with a shaved head and a long scar on the side of his face. He wore jeans and a jacket. He fingered the button on the switchblade in his pocket. Nobody messed with Curt Honeyman.

"He'd be the guy wearing dark shades," said Shooster. "That's all I was told. I'd a took the job myself, but I don't got the connections down there if you catch my drift." Honey had hooked up with Shooster in prison. Shooster served eight years for armed robbery. Honey was in for the big GTA—Grand Theft Auto. He got released after five years. Now that they were both out, they worked in a body shop out on 25th.

He didn't know who Shades was exactly. Neither did Shooster. A pal of a pal and some guy named Remey contacted Shooster who fingered Honey. All Shooster had said was that Shades needed a job done, and that there was "lotsa bills" in it.

Honey needed money. Then maybe he could get out of the shitty room he rented in Felony Flats. What the guy wanted was a lot easier than pushing joints and chalk dust in back alleys. In fact, it almost seemed like a cakewalk.

Honey checked his watch. Almost 2:00 a.m. Everything was closed—the Italian restaurant, the barbershop, and the wig place. The empty parkade seemed like a giant concrete tomb. What if some cop drove through? Just checking. Honey'd hightail it to the stairwell. Shooster had warned him to avoid the elevator. You could stumble into someone, even at 2:00 a.m. Some friggin' tramp, some homeless guy. Even when zonked, they had eyes. Come on foot. Take the stairs. That's the way Shades wanted it.

He took a drag from his cigarette.

Wait. He heard footsteps on the stairs. Slow, echoing. Tap. Tap. Tap. Now he could see him—a tall, shadowy figure walking slowly in his direction. Honey felt for his switchblade, just in case. The man wore sunglasses like Shooster said. God, they were dark, big and wrapped around his head. He had on a long black coat and a black brimmed hat pulled down over his forehead. Honey looked down, focusing on Shades' expensive tasseled loafers.

"You Honey?" He had a solid, confident voice.

"Yeah." He could see a red feather stuck in the side of Shades' black hat. Honey dropped his cigarette and mashed it with the tip of his steel-toed boot.

Shades reached inside his coat, pulled out a wallet and flipped it open.

Honey eyed the wad of money in there

"Here's a grand for you and a grand for your friend. He did good on such short notice."

"Yeah," said Honey. He reached for the cash. It was a lot for a small job.

"I don't want anyone to get hurt. We just need to scare him off."

"Right," said Honey. "Scare him." He stared at the man's thin lips. There was nothing else in the face to focus on. Honey stuffed the money in the pocket of his jacket.

"Keep an eye on him," Shades said. "I'll let you know."

"What if I need to contact you?"

"Nobody contacts me. *I* contact *you.*"

"But . . ."

"Got it?"

"Right," said Honey.

"Good," Shades said. "I don't want anybody getting hurt."

"Sure."

"You watch for the signal. A piece of red paper on your windshield. Then you meet me here . . . same time . . . same circumstances. Say nothing to no one."

"Got it."

"I mean it."

"Yeah."

"Okay, then."

Shades turned and walked away, as slowly as he'd come. Honey stood in the cold spring air, waiting for him to go down the stairs. Once the footsteps stopped, he sauntered over to the east side of the parkade, carefully looked over his shoulder, and peeked over the ledge. He saw the dark figure cut through the park in front of the insurance company, walk toward the pond, and disappear into the darkness.

CHAPTER 10

Brittany ran her hand through her hair and paced. "It's a black-tie charity dinner in Portland. Leukemia or something. God and everybody will be there."

Getting ready for her big date with Lance was too important to do alone, so she called on her cousin, Dulcy, for help. Big-boned with dishwater blond hair, Dulcy was older, almost thirty.

"Wow," Dulcy said, after Brittany slipped into the dark blue satin sheath with a V-cut portrait neckline. "You look just like Keira Knightley. The color is great on you, and it fits so well. You have great taste."

"Lance gave me the name of some woman at Krystal's Boutique. Stella something. She helped me pick out the dress, like she knew exactly what he'd like."

"You got the dress at Krystal's?" Dulcy's lips made a low breathy whistle. "This must've set you back a bundle."

"I used my birthday gift card, but when I still hesitated, Stella said it was on sale."

Dulcy's eyebrow rose. "I bet that's something Lance told her to say."

"Oh, I don't know."

"Whatever." Dulcy fingered the soft fabric. "I love this little side flourish here."

"Stella called it a stitched cascade or a faux wrapped skirt something or other."

"Well, whatever it is, it's sexy . . . and expensive."

Brittany took a deep breath. "I'm a bundle of nerves. A lot of big shots will be at the dinner—Lance's boss, Representative Bill Janes, people with money. I want this to go so right . . . but I'm still a small-town girl at heart.

"There's nothing small about you. You're tall, beautiful . . . and Lance is so perfect for you."

"Thanks Dulcy, but my stomach feels like jelly."

"You're gonna be fine."

"What about my hair? Up or down?"

"Let's pull the front up." Dulcy pointed to a dinette chair. "Sit here." She brushed the top half of Brittany's dark hair up and pinned it in back. "There, that adds a little sophisticated lift at the crown, but the length is still down around your shoulders. Go, take a look."

Brittany dashed to the bathroom and studied herself in the mirror. "You could've been a stylist," she said coming back to the dining area. "Did you ever think about that growing up in Roseburg?"

"Nope. Not my calling. I love social work, helping people in need. Not the hoity-toity crowd." She reached for the hairspray and lightly sprayed the top of Brittany's hair.

"Do you think these shoes are okay?" Brittany pointed to her black patent heels.

"They're fine. Oh, one last thing." Dulcy went to her purse and pulled out a blue sapphire pendant necklace. "Dave gave me this on our anniversary. It will be perfect with your neckline. You need something there."

"Oh gosh, Dulcy. That's so special."

"It'll calm you down. If you get nervous, just think that Dave and I are right there with you."

"Oh, that's sweet. I'll take good care of it."

"Relax. You will not turn into a pumpkin at midnight." She gave Brittany a big hug. "I gotta get home and tend to the kids before they drive Dave up the wall. You'll do fine. Just be yourself an' knock 'em dead with that smile of yours. Tomorrow, you can tell me all about it."

Brittany watched Dulcy go. She was so lucky. Dave was devoted to her and their two young children. Totally.

Growing up with a single mom had been fine. She loved her mother, and she knew she did the best she could. God, the woman worked her fingers to the bone so her "little girl" could go to college and "have a better life" as she always said. But as a kid she always felt like the odd one out. Her classmates had siblings . . . and a father. Maybe that's why she and Cody bonded in grade school. They both were only children. She knew it was a cliché, but she just wanted a house with a white picket fence, some kids . . . maybe four . . . and of course a dog . . . maybe two. Then Lance walked into her life . . . hopefully for good.

* * *

Brittany heard the supercharged engine of Lance's white Camaro pull up in front. She watched through the window as he stepped out and stretched his six-foot-four frame. He smoothed his dark auburn hair, which grew naturally in a thick, wavy pompadour, and walked confidently toward her first floor apartment.

She didn't wait for him to ring the bell. She flung open the door and twirled around in her satin dress. "Ta-da," she said, "How do I look?"

"Gorgeous. Just gorgeous," he said in his confident radio announcer voice that seemed to fit his athletic build. "C'mere beautiful," He pulled her close; she rested her head on his broad shoulders. He lifted her chin and kissed her on the lips. "Oh, and you smell so good. That Stella did a damn good job." He held her at arm's length, his golden brown eyes smiling. "She always takes care of my girls."

"Your girls?"

"Secretaries, campaign workers, clients, volunteers, yada . . . yada. Those kind of girls."

"I see." She laughed.

"I have something to go with the dress," he said.

"You do?" She hoped it wasn't another necklace. She needed to wear Dulcy's.

He reached into his pocket and pulled out a small box. "Open it."

Brittany eagerly flipped up the top. "Oh Lance, it's beautiful." Her face flushed. She buried her face in his shoulder, drinking in his faint, woodsy smell.

"Happy belated birthday. It's a one-carat diamond solitaire. Well, gee don't cry, we still have to drive to Portland and do the dinner."

She grabbed a tissue and carefully wiped away tears, not wanting to smudge the mascara she'd worked hours applying. "Help me put it on."

75

He took the ring from the box and gently slid it on her finger. "See, it's a perfect fit."

"Perfect," she repeated. Everything Lance did was *perfect.*

"Actually, I wanted to give it to you over a special birthday dinner, but things got in the way. You know, my schedule can get a little dizzy, so I thought it would jazz up your dress."

Her face moved toward his; she kissed him again softly, enjoying a tender moment in his strong arms. When they pulled apart, she said, "Not just my dress . . . my life . . . our lives."

"Exactly." He flashed a broad smile, showing his full set of perfect white teeth. "Can't wait to show you off to the crowd."

Brittany loved that smile, so certain, so calming.

A b-z-z-z-z-z sound came from his pocket. "My cell phone's on vibrate. I have to take that." He went off to the side and paced in his polished, expensive shoes while he talked. "I told them to contact you. Yeah . . .Yeah. We got our lawyers working on that, so just keep your head down and keep going at it. Perfect. We can discuss that before I head off to Asia. Look, I gotta go. I'm in the middle of something . . ."

Brittany held her hand out and stared at the glittering ring. She felt like Cinderella. She wanted to shout the news to her mother, Dulcy, the world. But why during this special moment, was her prince talking into his cell phone?

* * *

Inside the elegant Crystal Ballroom of the Benson Hotel, women in their best finery and men in sophisticated suits, holding glasses, nibbling hors d'oeuvres, milled under the soft light of Austrian chandeliers. Beautiful bouquets of purple and white flowers stood on tall brass stands along the walls and smaller, matching arrangements topped the tables. Heads turned as Brittany walked in with Lance. He stepped away, shook a few hands, and quickly returned with flutes of sparkling champagne.

"Oh Bill," Lance called when he saw Representative Janes approach. "I have someone you need to meet—my fiancée, Brittany Bolin."

"Your fiancée. How wonderful." He took a sip of his champagne. Janes was tall, trim, with close-cropped white hair, clear blue eyes, and a reassuring smile. "I'm so glad to finally meet you. I've heard so much about you. Congratulations."

"Thank you," Brittany said. Janes continued to smile, but he seemed to be staring. It made her uncomfortable, so she said, "I understand you're a dog lover."

"Yes. I take Blanche, my Akita, everywhere. Well, not here tonight," he joked. "Formal dinners make her nervous." He paused. The silence was awkward. "And you?" he finally said.

"And me?" Her hand touched Dulcy's necklace.

"You have a dog?"

"I live in an apartment. But you may have heard about Banjo. He's the dog incarcerated by Marion County. Actually, he's on death row."

"Yes. I believe that was in the papers. Well, down in Salem . . . where they seem to search for news."

"I'm trying to save him."

"I didn't realize you were involved."

"I . . . we could use your help."

Lance winced. "Looks like we got a good crowd here tonight," he hurriedly said. "I see the Bakers made it."

"The dog is innocent." She looked directly into Janes' eyes. "He deserves a second chance."

Not amused, Lance stiffened. "Actually, Brittany's a third-grade teacher, part-time activist. Heh, heh."

Brittany didn't let go. "Your support would certainly help."

"We don't need to get into that now," Lance interrupted.

Janes smiled. "That's a local, county issue, you know. Not really my area." He sipped his champagne. "As I recall, the dog attacked a child."

"Nipped. And, only because he was provoked . . . teased."

"I don't know." Janes shook his head. "I mean, he bit a—"

"We need some leaders behind our push. Respected leaders." She felt Lance squeeze the back of her arm.

"I have a big heart for dogs."

"I know. That's why I'm asking."

"Supporting a vicious dog, "Lance said, "not exactly a good campaign move."

"He's not vicious," Brittany insisted. "We've got evidence of that."

Janes drained his champagne glass and handed it off to a passing hotel staffer. "I'd need to know more of the details. I'd certainly be willing to write a letter in support . . . if it's prudent. Maybe a letter to the editor."

"And to the county?"

Lance squeezed her arm harder. She ignored him.

"I'd be willing to consider that. Like I say, if it's prudent."

"Oh, thank you."

Janes winked at Brittany. "Have her send the details of the case to Mitch," he said to Lance.

"Sure. Perfect. Listen, I have some people you need to meet." He spirited Janes away.

Brittany found herself standing alone, sipping champagne. She chatted briefly with a banker and his wife and a lawyer couple. She looked across the ballroom and noticed Lance had left Janes' side and was laughing and talking with some other young women. A short, blond woman appeared to be pawing him with too much familiarity. She felt a pang of jealousy, but then it was his job. He was a lobbyist, lawyer, point man. He needed to mingle.

She looked at her beautiful ring. It all seemed so hurried. She had anticipated a more romantic setting, candles, music, but now wasn't the time to dwell on it. People were moving toward the tables. Suddenly, Lance was at her side. "Sorry for the distractions," he said. "I needed to touch base with a few people." She saw someone escort Representative Janes to the head table.

Lance directed her to a round table of eight. Individual salads and baskets of bread had been set out. An older man and his plump wife with short, spiked orange hair and dour face took seats next to Brittany. They introduced themselves as Stan and Nancy Whiles. The pert blond woman she'd seen earlier sat on Lance's other side. She said her name was Shelley and that she was a lobbyist with some forest industries association. Someone named Neil sat next to her. Across the table were two older women, one with short, thinning brown hair and an oversized nose; the other in a red dress had frizzy gray hair that needed conditioner. They quit talking long enough to give their names, but with the din in the room, Brittany couldn't hear them.

A server with a white towel over his arm opened the bottles of red and white wine on the table and offered to pour. Brittany accepted a glass of Merlot, even though she'd downed a glass of champagne earlier. Usually, she was good for one drink, but considering the occasion, she felt like celebrating. The alcohol made her head feel foggy. Lance was asking Neil something about the Asian timber market.

"Give it a rest," Shelley said. "You guys are always talking shop." She had a space between her front teeth. She turned toward Lance. "You really should stop by next Saturday," Brittany heard her say. "It's going to be a splendid party." Someone passed the bread, followed by the dressing, and they began working on their salads.

The Whiles were in a serious discussion about the sweetness and dryness of certain wines. "Chardonnays are aged in oak. That's what makes them toasty and buttery," Stan said.

"I was hoping for something with more of a bite, like a good Pinot Grigio," Nancy said. "I know they have some back there." With the hair, she reminded Brittany of a fuzz ball.

Suddenly Stan turned to Brittany. "Have you seen the sommelier? "

"Uh, no."

"I think he passed by here a minute ago." He craned his neck and looked over her and then to the other side.

"You mean the wine guy?"

"Well, yes." He pursed his lips. "The *sommelier.* I see you're drinking red."

"It's Merlot."

"A bit too soft for me. My wife would prefer something else." Nancy grinned. Stan swirled the white wine in his glass and smelled it. "Chardonnays are so down market, don't you think?"

I so don't care, Brittany thought.

"There will be a lot of good contacts there, you really should," Shelley said to Lance. Brittany strained to hear the rest but couldn't make it out because Stan kept chatting in her ear. She sipped her Merlot and smiled.

"You should always sniff your wine before you taste it, don't you think?" Stan sounded condescending.

"What?"

"Your wine. You should always sniff it."

Brittany gave an obligatory sniff.

"What kind of wine do you usually prefer?" He asked.

"Other people's. Mostly, I drink other people's." She lifted her glass. "Cheers," she said.

"I thought all of Lance's girlfriends were wine connoisseurs."

"I'm not one of his girlfriends. I'm his *fiancée.*" She shot a glance at Shelley, who continued to fawn over Lance. Brittany tried to hear what she was saying. It sounded like, "Carrie will be there." *Who was Carrie?*

Stan kept talking. "After a while, one's palate matures, don't you think?"

Her jaw tense, Brittany held up her glass as if looking through it. "You know, I think we should take all these grapes so full of antioxidants and give them to the world's starving children. Once they're *all* fed, then we can titillate our palates and ponder about silly things like dryness and sweetness . . . whatever. I mean, we should think about what we're doing. We take our fine grapes and excellent grain and turn it into alcohol. It takes a lot of land to raise these things . . . and not for food . . . but for drink, which isn't all that necessary when you consider other needs." She paused and added. "Don't you think?"

Stan's eyebrows shot up. He looked like someone just dropped a turd into his worldview.

"Goodness," Nancy said.

"Sorry, I can't help myself," Brittany said. "I'm a third-grade teacher in a low income district. There is so much need out there."

Lance, overhearing the last bit of the conversation, hurriedly changed the subject to sports. "Boy, did you see the playoff game, Stan? Miami really cleaned up."

Stan mumbled something in reply.

Brittany picked at her salad.

After the sports talk, Stan turned away from Brittany. The Whiles never said another word to her. The servers arrived with the main course, a choice of roasted pepper stuffed chicken breast or butternut squash ravioli in sage-brown butter sauce.

The women across the table were talking about some couple. The one with the enormous nose said, "Well, they have to travel or they would kill each other. I mean Lyle is two quarts low. I don't know why she married him."

The one with the frizzy hair replied, "Well, they've been to forty-two countries. That's something."

"Yeah, and they come back just as dull as they left," the other said.

Lance went back to talking with Neil about timber. Shelley stared at her. Brittany picked up her water glass with her left hand, so Shelley could get a good shot of the ring. She was glad when the dessert and coffee arrived. God, she needed the coffee. She clasped Dulcy's necklace again.

After dinner, Bill Janes gave a brief speech about the great work of the foundation and handed out plaques to volunteers. "I'm so proud to chair this year's leukemia drive. And just tonight we've added another hundred thousand to the pot. Thank you so much. You're wonderful people, each and every one of you." There was a hearty round of applause.

"Oh, and one other thing before I sit down. I'd like to make a toast to two special people. My able assistant Lance Helms and his special friend, Brittany . . . uh . . . Bolland. Tonight, he proposed and she accepted." A low murmur of laughter rippled through the crowd and they applauded. Stan and Nancy gave a chilly smile. Shelley fingered her glass and looked away.

"Where are they?" Janes scanned the audience. "Please stand."

Lance put his arm around Brittany and pulled her close. "Sorry he muffed your name," he whispered and flashed his perfect smile.

"Ah, there they are." Janes lifted his glass prompting the crowd. Shelley's glass stayed glued to the table. "Here's to your future," Janes said. "Your very special future."

* * *

After the dinner, Lance helped Brittany into the white Camaro. He turned on the seat warmers to head off the chilly evening. They headed back to his condo in the West Hills, where they would spend the night. They drove in silence, listening to the hum of traffic on a busy Saturday night, staring into the headlights of oncoming cars. A light rain dropped beads on the windshield.

Lance flipped on wipers. "Look, you offended Stan and Nancy Whiles. They're two of our biggest donors . . . not only to the leukemia fund, but to Bill's campaign for U.S. Senator."

"I was only speaking my mind. I mean, there was so much excess at the dinner when people . . . children . . . are out there in the world starving."

"That's crazy talk. Wine is a big industry in Oregon. And it's a clean industry. Stan is on the wine board. Don't forget that."

"He's also full of himself. And, it's not crazy. It's a fact."

Lance sighed. "And you shouldn't have asked Bill to help with your dog case right off, like that."

"He seemed eager to help".

"You have to pace those things. Not pounce on people."

"Well, *excuse* me."

"Look, you have to get used to my world. In my job, there's a lot of networking with all kinds of people. Some of them are hard to swallow, but you never know when you might need them . . . for a favor . . . or for whatever."

"Uh-huh." More silence.

"Oh, honey," Lance said. "Tonight we got engaged. It's our big moment. Let's change the subject."

Her face drooped. Her head ached from the alcohol. *Big moment. Really?*

"Look, cheer up. I've got some wine. We still need to have our own celebration."

That's all I need—more wine.

"Come on, honey. Don't let it get you down. You looked absolutely stunning tonight. He reached and squeezed her knee.

"I just have to be me, I guess."

"Well, I love that *me* in you, tiger." He laughed and looked over at her. "Salem's such a backwater. It's no wonder it narrows your focus."

"Really? Some of those so called 'with it' people were annoying."

"You just have to learn how to blow smoke up their asses. There's a whole big world out there, girl. And it's gonna be ours. All ours. Okay?"

"Oh, all right," she patted his thigh.

"Perfect then. Just perfect," he said.

CHAPTER 11

During his next appointment, Cody told Dr. Aanandi about his frustrating trip to Forest Lake, the faulty toilet, the slashed tires, and the girl from his past. He couldn't help it. He talked a lot about Britt. In fact, almost every word that spilled from his mouth was about her.

"We're, uh, just friends. I mean she has a steady boyfriend, but, uh, you know, it was nice to see her again. Her mother. There wasn't time to drive by my old house, or make other contacts."

"But you at least went back to the place. The town. That's a good start. How was your anxiety?"

Cody smiled to himself. "We used to share cookies when we were kids."

Dr. A exhaled. "Cookies?" His eyes widened.

"Yeah, Britt and I, we . . ." He caught himself.

Dr. A flashed a sympathetic smile. "And your anxiety? Let's get back to that."

"Sorry. I was frustrated about the interruptions, but it wasn't like panic. Not with Britt being there. When she's with me, I feel whole. I mean calm . . . or something."

"Hmmm. Perhaps this girl you speak of can help you in your quest to resolve your past . . . as a *friend*."

"I can't count on that." Cody's self-esteem wilted. "All she talks about is this other guy. He's some big-shot lawyer with political connections and money. Drives a flashy Camaro."

Dr. A looked him directly in the eye. "First you tell me the story of the noble savage, and now you're telling me the one about unrequited love." He quit making notes. "Oldest story in human history."

"Oh no. *Love?* No, we're not in love." His hands fanned the air to emphasize that point. "She's already involved. I . . . uh . . . dented her car. Well accidentally." He knew he was rambling, but he couldn't help it, the words spilling out, gushing like a fire hydrant.

Settling back in his chair, Dr. A said, "In this world, Professor, you have to face your tigers or they will eat you."

"My tigers?

"Your challenges, your demons." He paused again and smiled. "Your competition. You've read *The Life of Pi?*"

"Uh-huh. And saw the movie. But what—"

"It is only when Yann faces the tiger in his boat and deals with him that he finds salvation."

"But this Lance guy . . ."

"And then we discover the tiger is an allegorical symbol of himself. Well, in my opinion."

"Uh-huh." *What the hell? Tigers? Boats?* "See, I'm not in his league. I don't care about material things. I'm a teacher."

"But of course, you like her? You trust her?"

"Well, yeah. When I was a boy, she was my only friend . . . but she's smitten with this guy."

Dr. Aanandi steepled his hands, making a little rooftop. "Face your tigers, Professor." He paused. His dark eyes sparkled like an East India cupid. "My advice? Ask her to help you."

* * *

The size of Brittany's engagement ring blinded Cody when she waved her hand in front of his nose. They were meeting for coffee at Starbucks, supposedly to chat about their trip to Forest Lake. He was so gobsmacked, he spilled his coffee. He reached for his rubber band, but it wasn't there. *Shit. I left it in the bathroom.*

"So, when's the big day?" he asked while sopping up the spilled coffee with several napkins.

"Well, there isn't one . . . yet. Lance is on his way to Asia on timber industry business."

"That huge diamond must give your finger a big workout."

She looked down at her hand. "It's gorgeous, isn't it, but the wedding is going to have to wait until Lance gets back. He'll be gone most of

the summer on business for Janes Timber. It's a really important deal."
She cut her cinnamon roll with a fork and sipped her vanilla latte.
"Bill Janes is counting on him to . . .What's the matter, you seem . . .
uh, I don't know, anxious."

"Anxious?"

"Well, your leg is bouncing. You're practically shaking the table."

"Oh."

"Unless we're having an earthquake somewhere." She smiled at
him and pushed her roll toward him. "Want a bite?"

"Oh no. Thanks." He paused. *Face your tigers, isn't that what
Dr. A said? It's worth a try. I do trust her.* "Listen, can I talk to you?"

"Isn't that what we're doing? Talking?"

"I mean . . . about my kidnapping."

Her eyes got serious. She set down her latte. "Okay. Sure."

"I need to talk to someone I can trust."

"Shoot."

He looked around and lowered his voice. "It was a lie."

"What?" She placed her elbow on the table, her chin resting on
her fist.

Words tumbled from his mouth. "Len Roster did not kidnap
me. Jim Fallingwater saved me. I can't talk to anyone about this because
Fallingwater killed that woman, and there's no statute of limitations
for murder. I never had a chance to thank him, and I—"

"Wait. Hold on." She held up her hand like she was being sworn
into a high office. "Take a deep breath. What are you saying? You
were saved by some guy that's dead?"

"That's just it. He wasn't dead."

"Seriously, everyone in Forest Lake knows—"

"Yeah, but I was there. I don't care what they say."

She threw up both hands. "Well then . . . why did you lie? Why
didn't you tell the truth? You were safe. He couldn't have hurt you."
She licked frosting from her fingers.

"I bonded with him. He was my friend. I liked him. He made
me feel important. I wanted to protect him, save him . . . just like he
saved me. We were blood brothers."

"Blood brothers? Are you kidding me?" Her jaw dropped. "I'm
just trying to grasp all this. All these years, I . . . everyone thought—

"I know. And Ken Blake interviewed me when I was a kid and
asked me about Jim. Told me he was a bad man who killed a woman.

Stared at me like he suspected something. I looked him straight in the eye and lied. I knew this Roster character offed himself." His voice rose. "I *had* to protect Jim . . . only back then I didn't really know who Jim was, but I do now." His hand slapped the table.

A bald man, sitting nearby, in slacks and a white shirt, with a soft stomach that challenged the shirt's buttons, looked up from his wireless tablet.

Brittany lowered her voice. "Whoa. Slow down. And this story now, about wanting to research Indian cultures."

"It's my way of finding out where Jim is without getting him in trouble."

"So, you think he's still alive? Out there some place?"

"Yeah, out there. Or someplace else."

"He sounds scary."

"I was never afraid of him. I just felt, sensed, that he wouldn't hurt me. He had these wild looking eyes, but he didn't have the heart of a killer. I don't know why he murdered that woman, but there's got to be a reason. Not that it justifies anything. There are so many questions I need answered. But I have to know. If he was a cold-hearted killer, why did he save me? What did he want from me? Why did he risk discovery by returning me? I was a kid for crying out loud. How could he be certain I wouldn't talk?"

Brittany held her head. "Whew. I'm still trying to grasp all of this."

"He changed my life. I was only with him for six months, but I felt closer to him than to my own dad. I still do."

Her eyes widened. "Really? Was your dad abusive?"

"No. No. He just didn't get me."

"Oh."

"Still doesn't. There's more to this story. My shrink said maybe none of this happened." He cringed, trying to tell if she thought he was crazy.

"You were gone for six months, so we know *it* happened."

"He meant the Fallingwater part of it. Dr. A called it dissociation. He said I could have heard this story about Fallingwater, and then used it to survive those months of captivity. You know . . . imagined it, to get through an ordeal."

"Maybe your shrink is right. Maybe you should listen to him."

"I never met Roster. He never had me."

"Well, if this Jim guy *is* still out there, he may not want you to find him."

At least she wasn't laughing. "I've got to find out what happened to him. If he stayed on the mountain, I suspect he's dead. If I find him . . . his bones, his remains, I want to give him a decent burial. At least. Something. Something to fill this hole in me." He placed his hand on his chest.

She leaned in, her eyes serious. "Maybe Jim will feel threatened. He may not recognize you. He may kill you. He may be crazed."

"Look, this is something I've got to do. It's been gnawing at me. I have dreams. Anxiety. I just have to . . . to resolve it."

"Well then, I guess you have to."

"But there's a problem."

"Good god, another one?" Her voice rose. The man at the next table was staring again.

"I suffer from Mazeophobia."

"Mazeo *what?*"

"It's the fear of getting lost. A fear of strange places. It's an anxiety disorder. More like panic."

"That's understandable. I mean getting lost got you kidnapped   or whatever. Or, maybe you're just jousting at windmills."

"Look, I've never told anyone else about this. Not my mom . . . not my dad, God, he'd freak out . . . no one . . . well, just my shrink. Will you help me? I mean go with me? Help me resolve this?"

She hesitated.

Maybe I shouldn't have said anything. "Listen, I know I sound like a frigging nut case."

"You're right, you do. I don't know. I mean, I have to think about Lance." She looked toward the windows.

"I really do want to research the cultural implications of the Fallingwater case. What drove him to kill? Why did he run?"

"Well, for starters, Oregon has the death penalty . . . and he wasn't white. Duh."

"It's a deeper question. I mean, what was it in our culture that made him the way he was. Clearly, he didn't fit in Forest Lake . . . but then neither did I."

"Now you're going professor on me."

"Well?"

"Well, what?"

"Are you in? Will you help me?" He looked like a puppy dog begging for a treat

She twisted her napkin.

He eyed the big diamond on her left finger.

The bald man closed his tablet and stuffed it into his shoulder bag. Leaving, he stopped at their table. "I don't have any idea what the problem is here, but for God's sake help the poor sap. I can't take it anymore." He strutted off.

Embarrassed, Brittany took another bite of her roll and washed it down with her latte. She set her cup back on the table. She looked at the ceiling thinking, and then directly at him. "I'm in."

CHAPTER 12

Before heading south, they shopped for groceries at the Center Street Safeway. Brittany insisted they avoid Tillden's Grocery in Forest Lake because it was a hotbed for gossip.

They planned to stay at the old Humphries place in Whiteside, a spot in the road about five miles from Forest Lake. "I've known the Humphries since I was a little girl," Brittany had explained. "They're gone for the summer visiting grandchildren. I told them I would check on their house from time-to-time. We can stay there. That way, Mother won't be in the way, and people won't bother us."

"I never heard of Whiteside."

"There's nothing there except a gas station, convenience store, and a small church. It's an older house set back from the road—three bedrooms, one bath. Yada,yada, yada."

After watching Cody pick several boxes of frozen dinners from the freezer case, Brittany pulled out her own list and labeled Cody's grocery shopping skills as "nonexistent." She took over the cart and collected several pounds of apples, oranges, grapes, and bananas. Then she headed for the clumps of spinach, carrots, broccoli, and bags of salad greens.

When he thought she wasn't looking, Cody slipped in a jar of peanut butter.

"I saw that." A grin crept onto her lips. "Actually, it's a good fat."

Once they filled the cart, they sailed through checkout. In the parking lot, they loaded their bagged groceries into the back of the Subaru. Brittany climbed in the passenger seat while Cody returned the cart to the receptacle, leaving the rear gate of the Forester open. When he turned to head back, he saw a kid grab a sack of groceries and dash away.

Cody sprinted to the car, slammed the rear door shut, and jumped in. "Hang on!"

"What happened?"

"A kid just swiped one of our bags."

He threw the car into reverse and took after the kid catching up with him just as he reached the street. The car screeched to a halt. Cody jumped out. "What the hell do you think you're doing?"

"Nothing." The skinny boy clutched the paper bag close to his chest.

"Yeah, right. And that sack you're holding just fell outa the sky."

"For my family." His dark eyes widened, his mouth opened revealing a row of square teeth; he looked like a scared monkey. "We don't have nothing . . . to eat."

"Where do you live?"

"Over there." He pointed southeast.

"How old are you?"

"Thirteen."

"What's your name?"

"Omar."

"Omar what?

"Omar Ramirez."

"Get in."

"No. No." He offered the bag back to Cody.

"I said get in." Cody grabbed the boy's arm and motioned toward the back door.

"Where we going?"

"I'm taking you home. You better not be lying."

"I don't want—"

Cody ushered Omar and the bag of groceries into the back seat. "I said get in. Now, which way?"

Omar directed them to a rundown duplex located off 14th on an alley-like street. There was a chain link fence around a tiny overgrown front yard. Cody carried the sack of groceries, and he and Brittany followed the boy to the door. Omar stopped, his eyes anxious as if he was on the way to the principal's office. "Go on," Cody ordered. "Open it."

The door creaked open.

"Omar?" A thin woman with long, dark hair turned from the sink in the kitchenette situated along one wall, startled to see the boy with two strange adults. A small girl clung to the pant leg of her jeans. A younger one played on an old couch in the attached living area. A table stood off to the side and an unmade mattress bed on the floor buffered the wall near a radiator. The dingy room smelled musty.

"*¿Quiénes son estas personas?*" she asked Omar.

The boy hung his head. The little girl quit playing and skipped toward them. "Appo," she said, pointing to the plastic bag of red apples peeking from the top of the paper grocery sack. Her smudged face needed washing.

Brittany and Cody exchanged glances. "Mrs. Ramirez?" Cody asked.

"Yes." She glanced at Omar. "*¿Ha sucedido algo?*"

"*Nada,*" he mumbled. His shoulders tightened.

Mrs. Ramirez turned to Cody, "Something happen?"

"Uh, your son won some groceries at the store. We . . . uh . . . just wanted to help him home with them. They're kinda heavy." He handed her the bag.

Omar's shoulders loosened. His lips formed a nervous smile.

"Oh, Omar. *Justo a tiempo.*" She moved toward Cody. "We're out of everything. My husband, he got hurt while working."

The little girl bounced impatiently on her feet. "Appo," she insisted. Her small finger jabbed the air. "I want appo!" she pleaded to Brittany.

Brittany reached in, opened the plastic bag and handed her an apple. "We better wash it first." She led the little girl to the sink.

"You from the store?" Mrs. Ramirez asked.

"Let's just say we're helping him get these things home. And . . . uh . . . there's some more back in the car." He motioned for Omar to follow him.

"Oh my," Mrs. Ramirez's hands circled her face. She picked up the younger child and held her close.

"Look Omar," Cody said once outside. "Don't steal. It just makes things worse. Okay? Otherwise, you're gonna break your momma's heart."

Omar stared at the ground like a scolded puppy.

"Okay?" Cody asked again.

"Okay."

"Just a minute." He reached in his pocket and pulled out a card. "I'm a teacher at Willamette University. You know that place?"

"Yeah."

"Well, I'm writing my cell phone number on the back here." He handed it to the boy. Omar stood quietly, staring at the card.

"If you ever need something, you call me, okay."

"Uh-huh."

"Look, you don't want to spend the rest of your life stuffing olives with pimentos, do you?"

"No."

"Then listen to me." Cody reached for the two other bags. "Here, you take one, and I'll carry the other."

Inside, the little girl sat on the mattress eating her apple. Drool ran down her chin. Her tiny sister sat next to her with a slice of whole wheat bread, tearing off small pieces, putting them into her mouth.

"Thank you. Thank you so much," Mrs. Ramirez said after they set the two bags on the table.

"You're very welcome," Brittany said. "I guess we're done here, Cody."

"You folks have a nice day," Cody said. "Good job, Omar. Enjoy the groceries." He winked.

They were almost to the car when Omar came running. "Wait," he called. He threw his arms around Brittany and buried his face in her chest. "I am sorry."

She patted his back. "Honey, things are going to get better. I know they will."

They left Omar standing on the sidewalk as they drove away.

Brittany dabbed her eyes. "What you did back there was wonderful. I talked with the mom when you went to the car. The dad does yard work and injured his leg. They really need help."

"It sure looked that way."

"I opened the fridge to help put some of the things away, and there was hardly anything inside."

"Jeez."

"I'm going to call my cousin, Dulcy, and tell her about Omar and his family. She's a case worker. She'll know how to get them the help they need."

Cody grinned. He felt like a different person when he was with Britt. Stronger. Self-assured. Something. He chuckled. *Tigers.*

"What's so funny?"

"Well, I just hope Mrs. Ramirez knows what to do with all that tofu you bought."

CHAPTER 13

The warm, yellow June sun inched its way to the center of the cloudless sky. Seconds later, the noon whistle from the sawmill, just outside Forest Lake, pierced the air with its high-pitched shrill.

At Dottie's Café, Patsy laughed. "That's a dying trend." She stuck tickets on the kitchen order wheel for the customers seated in a booth by the window. Ken and Artie sat at the counter drinking coffee, waiting for their food.

"What is?" asked Ken.

"The noontime whistle. Lotsa mills shutting down these days."

"Aw, I'd miss it if it weren't here," said Artie. His chubby fingers tapped the counter. "It's gone off at this time ever since I was a kid."

Patsy brought him his double cheeseburger, a pile of extra fries, and a raspberry milkshake. "Just last week, I was servin' some folks from the Midwest who were on their way to the lake. They thought it was a tornado signal. Roy couldn't leave it alone. He came outa the kitchen and told 'em that it only blows when a big one is expected." She hooted and licked her lips. "Well, their eyes got real big. They set down their forks and asked for the bill. I had to explain he was just kiddin.' God, they looked nervous."

"Yeah," said Roy coming to the counter with Ken's burger and fries. His mouth formed a big smile under his mustache. "Isn't that amazing? They were gonna pay up before they ran for their lives. So we told them their lunch was on the house. I still can't get over that."

Ken reached for the ketchup. "I wish we could solve all problems with free meals."

"Why?" Roy asked. "What's up?"

Ken carefully cut his hamburger in half. "Oh, we're having some problems with drugs at the grade school of all places. Now the pushers are down to the twelve-year-olds."

Roy gave a long-drawn whistle of astonishment. "Woo-wee."

"There's no damn place that's safe no more," said Patsy. "When I was a kid, you could wander anywhere. If you got in trouble, you knocked on somebody's door, and they'd see you got home, or whatever."

"What are you findin'?" Roy asked.

"Marijuana, OxyContin, and meth. Especially meth. Meth doesn't take months to grow."

"Jesus," Roy said. He blew out a gust of air and headed back to the kitchen.

Artie's face darkened. "Hey, send the ketchup down this way."

Patsy slid the bottle down the counter. "You're welcome," she said sarcastically.

Artie struck the bottle bottom, making a thumping sound. A river of red pooled on the side of his plate. "Aw, you know, that's a goddam shame. I got kids." He passed the bottle to Ken.

"Be grateful yours aren't in school yet," Patsy said. "Where does that stuff come from, anyway?"

"We don't know any local source at this point," Ken said. "Cops always watch for those trophy houses . . . those big fancy places that suddenly crop up in some out-of-the-way place."

Artie dunked his fries in ketchup and shoved a handful in his mouth. "Ya need to look for a double-wide with a Mercedes in the driveway."

"Don't talk with your mouth full," Patsy said.

Artie's bloodshot eyes narrowed. "Criminy, if I needed my ol' lady around at lunch, I'da brung her." He wiped ketchup from his chin.

"Speaking of double-wides," Roy said from the kitchen. "There's always been drugs out there at the trailer park." He set an order on the counter for Patsy.

"Yeah, we know," Ken said, "and those folks are pretty tight-lipped. But goddam, the grade school."

"What about the high school?" Roy asked.

"Yep, stuff there, too. But that's not new. More meth there, though, and a couple weeks back, Ronnie Anderson got into his grandma's pain pills. Some of the older kids lie their way into Benders."

"Maybe folks comin' up from California bring it in," Patsy said.

Ken held a fry in his hand and used it like a pointer. "We know drugs travel along the I-5 corridor and end up in Medford, Grants Pass, and Klamath Falls. Much of it comes in from Mexico." He nibbled the fry and reached for another.

Patsy picked up the coffee carafe. "Makes ya yearn for the old days. The worst things we did was smoke cigarettes and snitch a beer." She stepped away to refill the cups of the other customers.

"I thought being a reserve deputy, helping Merrill out, would be a way easier job," Ken said to Artie, "but it's beginning to balloon." Patsy returned and filled their mugs.

"I've been helping with a drug education program. Went over to the grade school and gave a talk to the kids. Little Toby Meeks came up to me afterwards and turned in his aspirin."

Patsy laughed. "I didn't think kids were supposed to have aspirin. Doesn't it give them a rash or something?"

Ken's dark eyes twinkled. "Toby confessed to emptying the aspirin tablets down the toilet, so he could have the bottle. Filled it with Red Hots. He wouldn't admit it, but I think he was playin' drug dealer. Something he saw on TV."

Artie lifted his double cheeseburger, holding it tight to keep it from falling apart. "Aw, good god," he said before taking a healthy bite.

"Yeah, I took his bottle away. Told him next time I was gonna arrest him. He was wide-eyed, but what really scared him was when I said I was gonna tell his momma."

Patsy gave a long sigh. "Jeez. He must be hangin' around older kids."

"Could be. We know some of those sixth graders have tried meth. It makes me want to puke."

Patsy rang up bills at the register for customers ready to leave. "Be grateful school's gonna be out in a few days."

"Yeah, but there's always those kids that hang around the playground in summer. And those pushers know how to get to 'em."

Roy placed three finished orders on the counter. "You know, when people are outta work, they get desperate. I think that has somethin' to do with all this drug stuff."

"You'd have to be pretty desperate to push to kids," Ken said.

Roy nodded. "Yeah, and the mills here don't get the timber they need to make two-by-fours. They keep sellin' those raw logs to the Chinese. On top of that, you got the environmentalists. Some counties are so hard hit with layoffs, they can't hire police. They're talkin' about having the state send in the National Guard."

Ken shook his head. "When people aren't workin' they steal or deal. And, there's no income to tax."

"Aw, the chinks are takin' over everything. Buying up the timber and pork plants. How come they got so much money?"

Ken gave Artie a sharp look. "It's called the global economy. And, a *chink* is a small crack—not a people."

"Aw, you know—"

The bell on the door jingled.

In walked Toad, talking to himself. "Get those empty boxes from Tillden's, buy duct tape . . ."

"Hey Toad, how come you're so late?" Artie asked.

"Well garsh, I'm plannin' on movin' And I don't know what I'm gonna do with all my stuff."

Artie snickered. "Aww, Toad. You got stuff?"

"Where you movin' to, Toad?" Patsy asked.

"Over onto Fourth Street. Got me a bigger place. Got a garage, an upstairs, and a garden."

Patsy set a mug in front of him and filled it with coffee. "What's wrong with the little house you had? That seemed like just the right size for an ol' bachelor like you."

"There's no garage for my pickup and my tools. Bought the Beck place."

"The Beck place." Ken's eyebrows raised. "What you gonna do with three bedrooms?"

"Right now, I'm worried about packin,' and I'm gonna plant me some tomatas."

"Ain't that place gotta basement?" Artie asked.

"Yep. And one of those outside sheds."

"I'll be damned. You gonna be swimmin' over there in all that space. You're gonna have to get yourself a wife," Ken teased. "Maybe rent a couple of kids."

"No siree. Not gonna tangle with no woman. Made that mistake years ago, and I promised myself if I ever did it again, I'd hire someone to shoot me in the head." Toad played with a mole on his chin. "Bobby's gonna help me. But he said I got to get the stuff packed."

Artie slapped his knee. "Christ almighty, that should be easy. All ya need is two boxes."

Ken laughed, too. "I'll bet you haven't got a blasted thing in your kitchen, except a cup and a pot. You ever use the stove?"

"Toad's got the cleanest stove in all of Klamath County," Patsy said. "The oven's so clean, doctors from the clinic sterilize their instruments in it."

"I got to pack my canned goods, all my beer, and my spices."

Roy's ears perked. He couldn't resist. "Ha. Toad. You got spices? What the hell for?"

"Garsh, the nice ladies from the church give me a spice rack back when I moved to town."

Artie, laughing, throttled the counter with his hands. "Aw, that was ten years ago. You ever used them?"

"Salt and the pepper most of the time. I got cinnamon and some red stuff."

"Toad," said Patsy, "throw the damn things out."

"My ol' man always said don't be quick to throw stuff in the burn barrel. Someday it's gonna look good ta ya."

"Throw. Them. Out." Patsy said. "Before you poison yourself, or God forbid, someone else."

A lull in orders, Roy poured himself a cup of coffee. He stood by the flat screen TV watching Senator Ted Cruz giving an interview on climate change. "Bobby helping you move is like two Republicans searching for truth. What the hell does Bobby know about packing?"

"He said between his pickup and mine, we can do it in one shot."

Not listening and still watching Cruz on the TV screen, Roy said. "That damn fool. Not long ago, he was frying bacon on the barrel of a machine gun."

"Jesus." Ken shook his head. "No wonder nothing gets done in Washington."

"They say the trouble with fryin' bacon that way is that you can only do one slice at a time," Patsy said seriously. "And then it's half raw." She turned to Toad. "You want your regular?"

"Yep," he said.

Artie looked glum. He finished his milkshake with a gigantic slurping sound. He set it down and wiped his mouth with his sleeve. "You know this milkshake didn't quite cut it," he said.

"What's wrong with it?" Patsy asked.

"Didn't taste like the berries."

"Well, how about I fix you another one. Vanilla?"

"Nah, I gotta go." The sound of a buzz saw came from Artie's pocket. "Now what?" he muttered. "Yeah, yeah." he said into his cell phone. "Look Berny, I'm just headin' back to work, and I'm already late. Aw, if the washer's broke, call somebody. Yeah, yeah, I'll pay for it."

He left a tip on the counter and followed Patsy to the register. His shoulders slumped. "You know the world's on the road to hell when the chinks buy up everything, and the rest of us struggle to pay a repairman." He squeezed his eyes shut like he was feeling pain.

"I worry about Artie," Patsy said after he left. "He sure seems down in the mouth."

"He's always down 'bout something. I think it's his divorce that soured him," said Toad. "His wife got the house, but it's headin' into foreclosure."

"Well, his mom was in here the other day complaining about the all the time he spends over at the casino outside of Klamath Falls."

Toad perked up. "Did he win somethin'?"

Ken winced. "I thought his favorite hangout was Benders."

Patsy wiped down the counter. "If he's down to a bar and a casino, it's not good. Not good. That poor guy needs to get a life."

"At least he's got a job," Ken said. "At least he's got a job."

CHAPTER 14

If age brings the face you deserve, then Dottie Johnson earned a happy one, Cody decided as he and Brittany sat in the living room of her small home on Fifth Street, patiently waiting for her to return from the kitchen with refreshments. His memory of her was fuzzy. He'd only met her briefly when he was eight years old. His grandfather had taken him to lunch at her café just before they'd left to get Christmas trees in the snowy wilderness, where he ended up lost in a swirl of white.

Dressed in a short-sleeved blue blouse and elastic waist jeans, Dottie had greeted them warmly. In her early 80s, her thinning hair was completely white, cut in a short straight bob. She'd combed it neatly and had applied a touch of lipstick to her mouth. Her fingers were crooked with arthritis, and she had little dimples in the crooks of her elbows. Despite some deep laugh lines on her face and her slightly bent shoulders, she had aged gracefully.

The room, which smelled of freshly brewed coffee, seemed crowded with her life. On the wall, she'd tacked up a set of orange owl plaques with huge glass eyes and wire wings, a plain wooden cross, and pictures from her café days in groupings that would affront a savvy interior decorator. On an end table, a cluster of huge amber acrylic grapes rested on a white crocheted doily surrounded by several pill bottles, a jar of Vicks, and a glass of water. There was a TV in the corner and an afghan hung over the arm of her flowered sofa.

Over coffee and peanut butter cookies, Dottie caught up on their lives, impressed that both of them were teachers. She was especially eager to hear about Brittany's engagement.

Blah, blah, blah. Cody munched cookies and jiggled his leg while Dottie oohed and aahed. *Gag me.* He was glad when they finished,

After a few more pleasantries and the amusing story of how Cody and Brittany literally "ran" into each other, Dottie was ready to be interviewed.

"I think I explained over the phone that I'm doing research on the effects modern society continues to have on Native American culture, and that I'm planning to use the old Jim Fallingwater case as a springboard."

"Yes, you did. I even heard about that in town."

"Seriously? They're talking about my—"

"I heard it at the café. You know, you young folks have all those gadgets—cell phones an' what not, but down here, you just have to set foot in town to find out what's what." She beamed like she just landed a punch in favor of older adults against encroaching technology.

Cody smiled back. "I . . . uh . . . plan to present a paper on my findings to the American Anthropological Association's annual meeting. Brittany is assisting me for the summer."

Dottie grinned at Brittany. She easily believed Cody's story. "How nice. Let me get us more coffee."

After refilling their cups, she settled back and began talking about Jim Fallingwater. "I always liked him. As an Indian kid, he never did quite fit in around here. His ol' man was an abusive drunkard. His mother wasn't much either. I tried to get her a job an' all . . . after the father died, but she couldn't hold it together. The folks never had a pot to pee in or a window to throw it out of, as they say. That takes its toll on kids."

"Did he have any relatives . . . friends that you might know of?" Cody asked, his pen poised over a notebook.

"He and Ken Blake were real tight."

"Right."

"You should talk to Ken. He knew him better than most folks."

"Anybody *else*?"

"Not that I can think of right off. He did come into the café for breakfast every mornin' with a bunch of fellers from the sawmill. I don't recall their names. Some of them old codgers might still be around. You could check out at the mill."

Cody wrote down D&R Lumber.

Dottie bit into a cookie and chewed. "Jim had problems controlling his anger. Like a bull seeing a red flag. Ken always said that was the result of Jim's abusive father. The old drunk. And, I have to say, there was lots of prejudice around here then. Still some pockets of it."

Cody nodded. "That's understandable. Small rural communities are isolated from other lifestyles and cultures. As a result, they're underexposed to differences. It's pretty common. Of course, there are prejudices in larger cities, too. It all comes down to fear."

"A sister," Dottie said. Her face brightened as if she just offered the right answer on a quiz show. "Jim had a sister. Can't remember her name. She was older, but as soon as she came of age, she ran off with some fella. Never heard from her again. Jim never talked about her. He was pretty much on his own."

Brittany leaned forward. "Tell us about Christie Jenkins. Was it a love story?"

Cody rolled his eyes. *Here she goes again. Getting all moony.*

Dottie folded her arms, her eyes serious. "Christie was a beautiful girl. Red hair. Blue eyes. Nice figure. She was a talented artist." Her shaky finger pointed to the wall. "That painting of the lake and Big Bat Mountain is hers. That one over there is one she did of the café. She was waitressing for me to get money for art school."

Cody got up and took a closer look. "Nice. Great detail for watercolors." He reached out and lightly touched the frame around the one of the Big Bat. It was a painting of the mountain in springtime with its snow peak reflecting in blue lake waters. Memories of Jim and his time in the cave flooded his mind. He could almost smell its musty dampness. His throat tightened.

"Cody's an artist, too," Brittany said. "He does wonderful portraits."

He was grateful that Brittany had jumped in. It gave him time to compose himself.

"Oh my, you grew up to be a talented young man."

"He's got a show at the Hallie Ford gallery in Salem."

"Your mother must be very proud," Dottie said. "After all you went through. How is your mother?"

Cody grinned sheepishly. I didn't go through anything, he wanted to shout. I wasn't molested. Instead, he said, "Mom's a lawyer in Portland. She did okay for herself."

"Back to Christie," Brittany insisted. "Were they lovers?"

"I don't know about a love story," Dottie said after Cody seated himself again. "I mean, I know Jim was smitten with her, an' she flirted with him whenever he came to the café. Lord, she flirted with most of the men to get big tips. Those lonely ol' fools. Her parents would never have permitted the relationship. He being Indian an' all, and a sawmill worker. She was just seventeen. Full of big ideas. She had her heart set on the bright lights somewhere else. She was destined for some big art school back east. At least that's what she said. To be honest, I was surprised to hear that they were out there together . . . at the lake, I mean." She gestured toward the painting.

"I've studied old news clippings about the murder, but I'm curious about the local reaction at the time," Cody said, hoping he could glean a local contact from her response.

"Wowee." Dottie's eyebrows shot up. "They were mighty mad. The Jenkins were churchgoers, and they did a lot for the town. She was so young, an' Jim musta been in his mid-twenties. I have no idea what happened. The only thing I can figure is that something set him off. But I have to say I think it's better an' all that he died out there in the wilderness. I don't think this town coulda stood a trial and neither could Mo or his wife.

"Mo?" Cody asked. *Bingo.*

"Mo Whitefeather. He wasn't any relation, but they came from the same tribe. He kinda took over after Jim's father died. Took him places, I mean. Showed him things. Camping, hunting, those kinda things. He always thought of Jim as his son. Mo was a real good guy. I always liked him. Loved the wilderness. Knew it like the palm of his hand. He died on the mountain, you know, searching for you."

Cody's eyes widened. He hastily scribbled in his notebook. "I didn't know that."

"He was up in years. Going out there got to be too much for him. Too much."

"Where could I find out more information about this Mo?"

"You could ask Ken. Other than that, I don't know. Wife died long before Mo did. He pretty much kept to himself. No children. Bobby Blaze lives in the house Mo lived in. He might know something."

When she mentioned Bobby, Brittany and Cody exchanged glances. Cody cleared his throat. He looked at his notebook. "Did Christie have siblings? Close friends?"

"She was an only child. The folks are passed. I don't know who she chummed with, and she went to the church. I suppose she had friends from school, but they never came into the café." Dottie took a swig of coffee. "I hope these cookies are all right. I got them from

Tillden's. I don't bake much anymore. I know Cody liked peanut butter when he was a little boy." She smiled.

"He still does, and they're fine," Brittany assured her. She winked at Cody.

Dottie frowned. "Taste a little dry to me. Not like what we used to serve in the café."

"They're good, honestly," Cody said. "I better quit eating them." He paused, pen poised over his notebook, and gave Dottie an earnest look.

Dottie took his nonverbal cue. "Let's see, where was I? Oh, Jim was a good football player in high school. Lettered an' everything. That probably was the best time in his life. Graduated. Got a job pulling green chain out at the D&R. Had a small apartment. Boughta ol' pickup. Then his life all went up in smoke. He seemed to be a real nice guy. Used to come in an' help me carry things that were too heavy. Helped me get the wood in, an' lift those big sacks of flour. Big, tall, a nice lookin' boy. Always willin' to help. He was a talented woodcarver." She set down her cup, got up, and shuffled to the fireplace mantel in her pink scuffs. She returned with a carved bird sitting on a branch. "He gave me this once. I think it was for my birthday or something." Her hand touched her forehead. "My mind fails me at times. Look at the detail on that thing."

Cody fingered the bird. Of course, he remembered, Jim had many carvings of animals in the cave. He'd given him a carving of Wolf, his dog, which he still had. For a brief moment, he saw himself giggling, dropping wood shavings into the fire and Jim's wild, amused eyes staring at him.

He passed the bird to Brittany who held it up to the light in her palm. "Nice," she said. "Very nice. It's a song sparrow."

"I remember thinkin' it was a darn shame." Dottie said. "He could've been so much. Both of those kids could've been somethin'."

"So, Jim died on the mountain?" Cody probed, his face innocent like a choirboy on a Christmas card.

"He was arrested but escaped. Ken was the one that was bringin' him back to the county. Somehow, he got away." She hesitated and let out a long breath that ruffled her bangs. "Wowee. There was a big hullabaloo about that."

"He got away from Blake? Is that what you're saying?" *Sweet Jesus.* Cody almost dropped his notebook.

"Folks here thought maybe Ken let him go on purpose."

Cody gripped his pen like a reporter. "Did he?"

"I never bought that story. Ken is honest as the day is long. That Jim was clever. I think he reeled ol' Ken in."

"So, Blake—"

"Someone saw Jim running off toward the Big Bat Wilderness. Wasn't too long after that a terrific blizzard hit. Then, over the summer, they found evidence. I don't know what all, but it got reported that he most likely froze and the animals got to him. Ken almost lost his job over the escape. I remember that. Well, at the time he was workin' in Klamath Falls. Then, he got reassigned back here. Been here ever since."

"So, they never actually recovered a body?" Cody asked fishing.

"Like I said, you should talk to Ken Blake. They were buddies since grade school. He'd know a lot about what they found and what made Jim tick . . . or quit ticking. My mind is old. Makes things get foggy. That was such a long time ago."

Dottie seemed to be getting sleepy. She yawned a couple of times and apologized. "I musta stayed up too late last night watching the TV." She laughed. "You know when you get to be my age, you doze during one program, wake up in another, and can't figure things out."

Brittany giggled. "Sometimes I do that myself. I come home tired from teaching school, plop down, and try to catch up on the news. What-do-you-know, I wake up in the middle of *Jeopardy*."

Cody sensed it was time to go. He rose to his feet and thanked Dottie for her time. Brittany carried their cups and the plate of uneaten cookies to the kitchen.

Dottie slowly walked them to the door. "Your grandfather, Sam, was a real nice fella. Just a darn shame what happened there. You know, he just couldn't forgive himself. He felt responsible for losing you, but I want you to know he loved you." There was a little catch in her voice when she said that.

"Thank you for that," Cody said. "I appreciate it. I never had the chance to really know him."

She kneaded the skin of her turkey neck. "You know, I often think. If he just could've waited. Toughed it out a bit. He would've been walkin' on air when they found you."

Cody could see Dottie was getting emotional. "Who knows why things happen." He reached out and hugged her. "You've been very, very helpful."

"I'm sure glad you two dropped by." She shook Cody's hand. "I always wondered what became of you. Good luck with your research. An' give my love to your mother. She and I had a lot of long talks back then."

She took both of Brittany's hands in hers and glanced at her ring. "I sure hope he's right for you, honey."

CHAPTER 15

Back at the Humphries farmhouse, Cody and Brittany settled down in the small living room for a quick pizza dinner and debriefing.

"It seems stuffy in here," Cody said, thinking the musty smell came from mold in the crawlspace or from the faded brown carpeting.

"It's old house smell," Brittany assured him, coming from the kitchen with two bottles of cold Heineken.

He jerked up the sash of one of the aging double-hung windows to let in fresh air. Despite the rustic odor, the Humphries' living room had a comfortable feel with its well-worn couch, easy chair, and brick fireplace. A wicker basket of kindling sat off to the side. A large mirror hung over the fireplace and an old-style TV stood in one corner. There were no pictures on the walls.

Cody slipped off his shoes and fired up his mobile hot spot to access the Internet. Relaxing on the couch with his notes and iPad, he feasted on the pizza, but only picked at the salad Brittany had made.

She curled up with her small Apple MacBook in the cozy brown armchair with crocheted armrest covers.

Being in the house with Britt made him feel like they were a couple, but his stomach quivered because he realized it was temporary.

"Well, so where are we?" Brittany asked.

Cody flipped through his notebook. "We got something, I think. There's this Mo. He must have been Jim's lifeline."

"How do you figure?" She hoisted her pizza in the air and tilted her head back to swallow the strings of hanging cheese like a baby bird accepting a worm from its mother's beak.

Cody glanced at her and smiled. He loved the way she did that. "Well, Jim had things in the cave . . . frying pans, tools, popcorn, coffee."

"Popcorn. Really?"

"Yeah, really. He couldn't have stolen all that stuff. Sometimes, he'd go out on a trek and come back with canned goods. Mo must've known he was out there and helped him. It makes sense. Mo. Hmmm."

She wiped her hands on a paper napkin. "Maybe he's the one who hid him in the first place."

"Could be. Dottie said he was a father figure, and really familiar with the area."

She reached for another piece of pizza, took a bite, and set it down. "Why don't we ask Bobby?"

Cody's hand cupped his chin. "That night, during dinner at your mom's, he seemed angry about the whole thing."

"I think the idea of you wanting to feature a murderer in your research offended him." Brittany typed on her keyboard. "Hey, I just did a search on the Internet for Jim Fallingwater."

Cody hooted. "And? You got the cave address, right?"

"All I got under Falling Water was a house that Frank Lloyd Wright built in Pennsylvania." Her faced turned serious. "So, are you going to talk with Blake?"

He clenched his teeth. "I know I'll have to eventually, but I need to think long and hard about the best way to approach him." He took a long swig of beer. "Probably, our next step is to go out there . . . into the wilderness, I mean . . . to try to find the cave, but first I need to get a feel for the place." He paused and stared into space.

She gave him an understanding look. "That's got to be emotional for you. Especially with your Mazie thing."

"Maze-o-phobia." Cody said it slowly. "But you'll be with me." He looked at his naked wrist. When he was with her, he didn't bother with the rubber band. "That'll make all the difference, but I must see what we're up against. You know, kind of like putting your toe in the water before you jump in."

She smiled, rearranged her legs, and tossed her mane of dark hair. "I'm glad you find me comforting."

Oh, baby, if you only knew. "I'm going to try and punch out a plan."

"How do we find the cave? We don't even know where to look."

He closed his iPad. "I have some archeologist friends that I've worked with before. We'll need maps and a GPR system."

"A what?"

"Ground Penetrating Radar. Archeologists use it to explore the earth's subsurface. It uses radio waves to discover differences in the soil. Various soil textures or rocks reflect unique radio waves, which show up on the machine's screen. You make note of those and then use a computer software program to interpret the findings. You can also use metal detectors, which, in our case, would really be helpful because Jim had a lot of tools, most likely provided by that Mo character."

"Fascinating," she said, "I had no idea," but Cody could see she was half listening and continuing to surf the Internet.

"There are new techniques, too. Like GIS, Geographic Information Systems, which archeologists use to create environmental models," he continued.

"Uh-huh."

"I know Jim's cave was near a natural spring, because when the weather got better, I went with him to fetch water. During winter, we melted snow. Hopefully, we can identify sources of water, which could give us a clue about where the cave might be. Old maps or other historical documents could also help, if we can find them. They've built a ski lodge up on the mountain. I wonder if the contractors have any research they might share."

"Hey, I got an e-mail from Dulcy. She says Representative Bill Janes wrote a letter to the editor about Banjo. Oh wait. She included the link to the newspaper. I'll bring it up."

"And?"

"He's so sweet. Listen to this part:

. . . I encourage everyone to consider the circumstances that caused Banjo to bite a young girl. All evidence suggests that this dog was provoked. As a legislator and lover of dogs, I not only support human rights for people, but humane rights for animals as well. As Albert Einstein once said, 'Our task must be to free ourselves . . . by widening our circle of compassion to embrace all living creatures and the whole of nature and its beauty . . ."

Brittany hesitated and swallowed. She read the last sentence aloud again. "That's beautiful." She wiped her eyes with her napkin. "This makes me so happy. That Bill Janes is . . . did I tell you I actually met him?"

"Yeah, you did." *A thousand times with Lance, Lance, Lance.* "I hope that letter does some good. That poor dog must be stir crazy."

"We should contribute something to Janes' campaign." She continued reading e-mail. "Dulcy says she made contact with your landlady. She's forwarding your snail mail. Dulcy's forwarding mine. Says we've got bills. Oh, I see there's a hearing coming up about Banjo. I'll have to go back to Salem for that."

"We both will at some point," Cody said. "I'll need to touch base with my archaeologist friend and see if he'll let me use his equipment."

Finished with dinner, they took their dishes to the kitchen. Cody set his empty beer bottle on the turquoise Formica counter. He rinsed pizza grease from his hands in the pedestal bathroom-style sink by the door.

Brittany put the bottle back in the cardboard container which was sitting on the linoleum floor. "Good thing we brought the beer with us," she said. "Otherwise, we'd be drinking good ol' Bud Lite from Tillden's."

"I don't suppose they have a brew pub here?"

She wrinkled her nose. "Are you kidding me? The only bar is Benders way out on the highway and it's a dive. Open the door and the air will knock you over."

"Another reason to head north."

"You didn't finish your salad." Brittany held the bowl of now wilting greens toward him. "Didn't you like it?"

He waved it away. "I ate most of it. Vegetables are too rubbery . . . squeaky. Salads never stay on the fork for me, and they taste like shi . . . grass."

Brittany tilted her head back and filled the room with her warm, contagious laugh. "You sound like a little kid. Stick with me, Professor, and by the end of summer, you're going to be a changed man."

He watched her scrape the sad mixture of lettuce and kale into the garbage container under the sink. *I hope so. God, I hope so.*

"There's no dishwasher, so I'll wash these," Brittany said. "Then I'm going to hit the sack. I'm tired." She ran water into the kitchen sink and pulled a bottle of Dawn detergent from the cupboard underneath.

Cody yawned. "It's been a long day." He reached for a dishtowel. "Here, I can dry those."

"Just leave them in this rack to dry." She grabbed her suitcase, which she'd parked by the round oak table and headed toward the stairs.

"No," he said, still holding the dishtowel, "take the downstairs bedroom."

"You sure?"

"Yeah, that way you'll be closer to the bathroom. Women have smaller bladders than men," he teased. "Across all cultures."

"Okay Professor, but keep the stair light on, so you don't break your neck when you have to get up in the middle of the night. You can use the bathroom after me."

Cody grinned. "Don't spend all night in there." He sat on the couch surfing for articles on soil textures, listening to the pipes in the old house making knocking sounds when Brittany ran water in the bathroom. He heard the door open.

"It's all yours," she called.

He didn't look up. "Okay, in a minute."

"See you in the morning," she said and waited.

"Yeah. Goodnight."

The house got quiet. He closed the living room window, drew the blinds, pulled the shade in the kitchen, and checked the doors before heading into the bathroom to clean up. Afterward, he pulled on a T-shirt and pajama bottoms and carried his things up the creaking stairs to a small bedroom with sloped ceilings and flowery wallpaper. Outside it was pitch black. He lay awake in the dark listening to old house noises. *Jim, where are you? Alive? Dead?* He could almost feel the damp cave, see the flickering fire, and hear Jim's knife scraping wood as he carved late into the night. His mind switched gears. Brittany was sleeping downstairs. Just a few feet away. *In the same house.*

* * *

Light streamed through the window. Cody lay half-asleep in the small, hard bed. He thought he smelled coffee. He bolted up when he heard pounding on the bedroom door.

"Cody, are you awake?" Brittany called.

"What?" His eyes blinked. "What's the matter?"

"Are you decent?"

"Yeah. I guess." He sat on the edge of the bed, hurriedly trying to smooth his rumpled hair.

Brittany dashed in, already dressed in jeans and sweater with her hair neatly combed. "I went outside to catch a breath of fresh air," she said, her eyes wide. "I found this attached to the front door." She thrust a piece of paper in his face.

"Wah?" He rubbed sleepy eyes. "Let me see that."

In large black letters, it said simply, *Leave. NOW!*

* * *

Cody checked the rearview mirror as he and Brittany drove toward the Big Bat wilderness area, mid-morning sun and blue sky promising a pleasant day. No one was following them.

"That note on the door creeps me out," Brittany said.

"Yeah, but we can't let it stop us." Sure, the note was unsettling, but his mind was busy steeling itself for his return to the spot where he'd gone missing.

"Maybe some narrow-minded people don't think we should be there together. I mean unmarried. Under the same roof." She fiddled with the zipper on her jacket. They sped past stands of trees, farmhouses, barns, and green pastures dotted with grazing, white-faced cattle.

"We can get married if it bothers you." Cody grinned at her and winked. She didn't seem amused. He cleared his throat. "Uh, besides, when they see that big rock on your finger, they probably think we're engaged."

Brittany glanced at her left hand. "You know what I mean—shacking up." She hunched forward.

Considering her mood, he weighed his words carefully. "It's not unusual for guys and gals to share housing these days. It's pretty common."

She took a deep breath and smoothed her hair. "I *know* that, but people down here are strait-laced. Isolated."

He passed a slow-moving farm vehicle struggling with the steepening grade of the highway. "What people? No one knows much about us. We're staying outside town, at a spot in the road."

"You'd be surprised how news flies in Forest Lake."

"Maybe that's the ethnography I should be studying. Does gossip bother you?"

"No, I just think tacking a note like that is weird. Mean spirited. Threatening."

"Agree. Maybe it wasn't meant for us. Maybe it was for the property owners."

"I can't see how. Reba and Eldon Humphries are two of the nicest people you'd ever want to meet. They raised five children."

"That looks like the turnout we want up there," Cody pulled over and switched off the ignition. They sat for a moment staring out at rocky ground, trunks of towering pines and the green splendor of mixed conifers. His fingers tapped the steering wheel. His leg started bouncing.

"I can tell you're anxious. Meditation can help with that. I'll show you."

"Here? In the car?" He gave her a wary look, like she was about to perform some dark magic.

"Anywhere. Sit up straight."

"Should I turn on some classical music?" He reached toward the CD player.

"No. Put your feet flat on the floor and place your hands in your lap like this." She positioned her left hand palm up in her right hand. "Close your eyes. Breathe. Count your breaths. Inhale on the in-breath, exhale on the out-breath."

With each breath, he could hear her counting in her calm, comforting voice. "Focus on your breathing," she was saying somewhere off in the distance. "If your mind wanders, come back to the count." He wanted to stay there, listen to her. Breathing deeply . . . holding it . . . exhaling. Again and again. Such a feeling of well-being. Where were they?

"Ten," she said. "Now open your eyes."

He hesitated, clinging like an unborn child comfortable in the moist warmth of its mother's womb, not wishing to be pushed out. His eyes blinked open.

She smiled at him. "Better?"

"Yeah."

"We'll try some longer sits back at the house."

"Dr. A mentioned meditation. I . . . I just never—"

She winked and gave him a thumbs up. "It gets easier the more you do it. Okay then, we're ready."

Outside, it was windy. They grabbed their backpacks, pulled on hats, and headed into the peaceful, almost timeless, wilderness.

Brittany breathed in the fresh, resinous scent of the forest. "It's beautiful out here, but I have to say it all looks the same. I can see how a kid or anybody, actually, could get lost." She brushed stirring insects away from her face.

They continued walking, listening to squirrels moving in the brush and birds fluttering overhead as they followed narrow animal trails. When they came to a clearing, Cody pointed to another trail leading uphill. "Let's head up this way."

"Does any of this look familiar?"

"No, when I was a kid all I remember was snow, being with my grandfather and . . . Wait. See that big rock over there?" He pointed to a good-sized brownish boulder with a flat top. "Hmmm. I think this is where Jim left me that day." He slowly turned around, taking in the landscape.

"He abandoned you?"

"He told me to wait there and then walk to the highway. Apparently, a maintenance crew passed through around noon. I think he wanted them to find me. Of course, I don't really know." They sat on the boulder's flat surface. "It's not like he could just saunter into town and say 'Hey, I found this kid.'"

"Maybe Jim didn't just find you. Maybe he took you."

"He nursed me back to health. He never hurt me."

"Maybe he was lonely."

"He set me free."

Brittany pulled off her backpack. "I'm hungry. I think this is the perfect place to have lunch." She unpacked food while Cody supplied bottles of water. Brittany passed him a cheese sandwich and baggies holding grapes, carrots, and broccoli.

Cody wished he had some chips and a Snickers bar. Britt was a health nut.

She lowered her voice and nudged him. "Look over there! Quick!"

"Where? What?"

"I just saw a deer. You missed him. I should've had my cell phone ready."

"There will be plenty of opportunities for photos. When we come back, we'll need to bring camping gear and our equipment." He finished his sandwich and savored the tart taste of the purple grapes. "We'll need to spend a few days out here and mark where we've been, so we can find it again. I hope you don't mind camping." He ate one small carrot but didn't touch the broccoli.

"Did some of that as a kid," she said, as she chewed. "Roughing it sounds like fun." She started packing away the leftover vegetables. "So, how are you doing emotionally?"

He took a long swallow of water. "Not bad. It helps to come back here."

"What's the matter?"

"The sun. See it right above the tops of those fir trees?"

She shielded her eyes with her hands. "Yeah, it's bright."

"Jim told me to wait until the sun rose above trees like that and then walk down to the highway."

"Right about noon, so you'd meet that maintenance crew."

"Yeah. I'm pretty sure this is the place." He turned and scanned the forest. "So, I think we need to walk that way." They pulled on their backpacks and headed in the direction he suggested.

Cody pointed to the ground. "These are deer tracks. Jim always followed the animal trails. I bet they'll lead us to water." He led the way, pushing aside brambles and vines. He took Brittany's hand and helped her over a fallen tree trunk.

He stopped near a small grouping of cedar trees and plucked a frond of pointy green leaves. "It's incense cedar. Native American tribes used the branches in steam baths and for medicinal purposes. They believed it brought good energy and drove out the bad kind. Jim used cedar to carve animals, wood spirits, and magical flutes. Sometimes he tossed cedar branches in the fire for the fragrance." He handed the frond to her, his eyes meeting hers and holding. "It's special to me."

Brittany took the frond with both hands and sniffed its spicy scent. "Special," she repeated. She tented her palms and faced the trees. "I bow to you in gratitude," she said softly. She squatted, placed both hands on the ground, "and I touch the earth." She closed her eyes for one brief meditative moment. When she opened them, she stood and gave him a wide smile.

"Uh . . . thank you," Cody said.

"When you see the connection between all things . . . when you really see that, there's no turning back. I sense that your friend, Jim, felt that way."

"I guess . . . yeah." *What is she talking about?*

She reached toward him and gave his shoulder a tender pat. Then she carefully tucked the cedar frond in her pocket and began walking ahead.

Cody hurriedly joined her; they pushed on in silence until the deer trail narrowed and forked like a Y. The right fork seemed to wind through dense forest; the other rock-strewn and steep.

Brittany lowered her voice to mimic Robert Frost. "Two roads diverged in the wood, and I—I took the one less traveled by."

"And that made all the difference." Cody finished the stanza and laughed.

"Well, scout, now what?" Brittany asked. "Which one do we take?"

He checked his watch. "I think we'd better turn around and head back. We've been walking over an hour. I'm really at a loss as to where to go next. God knows, I don't want us to get lost."

"Jim Fallingwater," Brittany called out to the stillness. "Where are you?"

"What the . . .?"

"Well, if he's out here, maybe he'll hear us."

Cody laughed and nudged her shoulder. "You crack me up. Let's head back. We need to regroup."

"It's certainly been wonderful exercise," Brittany said. "Now, do we drop breadcrumbs to remember where we've been?"

"This wouldn't be that hard to find. We're not in that far. On our next trip, we'll use metal stakes or pin flags like surveyors use. We'll pull them up once we're done. The folks that manage the forest don't like people to leave permanent markers."

When they reached the turnout, Cody pressed the remote on his key fob. Nothing. He pressed it again. Still nothing.

"What the heck? The key fob isn't working."

"Do you have a spare?"

"No." He went to the driver's side, inserted the key and manually unlocked the door; then reached over and unlocked the passenger side so Brittany could get in.

Cody got behind the wheel, inserted they key into the ignition. *Nothing.* He pumped the brake and tried it again. No luck.

"Christ, now what?" He slapped the steering wheel.

"We're not out of gas," Brittany said, checking the gauge.

Cody reached for the lever to pop the hood and jumped out. Brittany quickly joined him. He released the safety catch and peered in. "Look there. One of the battery cables is cut."

"But the car was locked," she said.

"Someone must have jimmied the lock. We better check to see if they took anything." He opened the glove compartment and shuffled through papers, the car registration, a disposable camera, some loose change, and a tiny box of stale raisins.

"As far as I can tell," Brittany called from the back seat, "nothing's missing. But we didn't really leave anything of value. Just blankets, a change of shoes, and the cooler. I had my cell phone and wallet in my backpack."

"Yeah, me too. Nothing much in the glove compartment." He slammed it shut.

"Were they going to steal the car?"

"They wouldn't have cut the cable if that was the plan."

She whipped out her cell phone. "No use. I'm not getting a signal. Now what?"

"I can tell you everything the Kennewick man wore and ate, but when it comes to car engines, I'm clueless. There's nothing to do but walk until our phones pick up a signal."

"We better take our backpacks with us," Brittany said.

"Damn it!" Cody muttered. "We're already tired from hiking and now we have to hoof it." They headed down the highway. "There isn't any traffic, and no one knows we're here. Wait, here comes a car."

Brittany looked wary. "I'm *not* hitchhiking."

Cody waved his arms. *Oh, God no.*

CHAPTER 16

A police cruiser pulled up alongside, and the officer rolled down the window. "What are you two doing out *here*?" Ken Blake squinted at them.

"Car trouble," Cody muttered. He instinctively put his arm around Brittany as they stood there.

"You run outa gas?" Ken asked.

"Nah, someone tampered with it. Cut a battery cable."

Ken raised an eyebrow. "You leave valuables in the car? You see anyone around?"

"We had our backpacks with us. Didn't look like they took anything. Just messed with the engine. The hood locks from the inside, so they must've sprung the lock to cut the battery cables."

Ken seemed to be staring. "That's odd."

"No kidding," Brittany said.

Cody reached into his back pocket for his wallet. "I have Triple A. If we could get a lift to where I could call . . ."

"I'll radio for assistance," Ken said. "Get in. I'll drive you back to your car. You got your card?"

Brittany climbed in the front. Cody fished out his AAA card, handed it to Ken, and reluctantly hopped into the back seat. Brittany turned and smiled at him through the steel mesh cage barrier.

He shrugged his shoulders as if to say *now what?*

She mouthed the word *breathe.*

He drew in air and slowly released it, but he still felt like a snared rabbit. The seat was made of smooth, washable vinyl, but it smelled sour. He'd seen some awful scenes on YouTube of cops trying to manage drunks and other druggies who threw up, spit, and worse. He listened while Ken contacted the garage in Forest Lake, gave the make of the car, and explained the problem. Sitting in the back sucked. He was grateful they hadn't walked very far and glad when they arrived back at the turnout.

Ken jumped out, opened the back door for Cody, and returned his card. "Let's take a look under the hood."

After Cody flipped the hood latch, he and Brittany joined Ken up front. "Hmmm. Cut clean through. I guess now we wait for the tow truck. Doesn't make much sense, but I'll file a report." His eyes narrowed. "So, how's your research going?" He looked from Cody to Brittany. His eyes settled on her engagement ring.

"I . . . uh . . . I'm just barely getting started," Cody said. "I've interviewed Dottie."

Brittany quickly added, "I'm helping him, uh, for the summer."

"When I've completed my research, I'm going to present my findings to the national anthropology convention. Comparing and contrasting then and now. How would Fallingwater fare today?" The words came easy. His story was getting better every time he told it.

Ken folded his arms. "Why'd you come up here?"

"I wanted to see the place where I got lost."

Brittany smiled calmly. "He's never been back here. It's therapeutic."

"Uh-huh," Ken said. "Interesting." He cocked his head to one side.

Brittany glanced at Cody and then back at Ken. Her eyebrows arched; her chin jutted. She got that same look whenever she defended Banjo. "I . . . uh . . . understand you and Jim Fallingwater were friends," she said.

Pow. Cody stiffened. Leave it to Britt to cut to the chase.

"Yeah. Jim had a rough life. Abusive father, not much of a mother. Terrific football player, though."

Cody followed Brittany's lead. "I guess Jim's lack of a good family life explains things. I mean, what happened. The murder?"

Ken rubbed his chin. "It took its toll. One time in a drunken binge, his father shot his dog."

"Shot his dog?" Brittany winced. Her hands clasped her face. "How cruel."

"He knocked Jim around, too. Sad. That dog was the only thing in the house that loved him. Jim had anger. Maybe rage is a better word. Can't blame him for that. He never had a support system like the rest of us."

"Except for Mo Whitefeather?" Cody asked.

"So, you heard about Mo? From Dottie?"

"Yeah."

"Mo was good to Jim. Taught him a lot of things. Took us on treks into the woods. Just a real nice guy." He shook his head. "The murder almost killed him. He just withdrew into himself."

"Did you talk with Jim . . . after the murder?" Cody asked.

"Uh-huh." He hesitated and gave Cody a long, suspicious look, like maybe the conversation was over.

"What happened that night with Christie?" Brittany blurted. "Was it a love story?"

Cody flinched. *Here we go again.*

Ken smiled. "Well, I don't know about that. He told me he wanted to marry her, and she laughed at the idea. Then he just lost it. That's no excuse for what happened."

"So, he was in love with her then?" Brittany prodded.

"She was a beautiful girl. Just a damn shame on both counts. I wanted to help him, but that damn guy. You probably heard he escaped from my custody. Damn near killed me doing it."

"No, actually, I hadn't heard that," Cody lied. His eyes blinked. He rubbed the back of his neck.

Ken's lips pursed. "Let my guard down. Responded as a friend, a pal. I was young. Stupid. Then he ran to the mountain."

"And died up there." Cody quickly finished the story.

Ken narrowed his eyes at Cody. "That's what they say. A horrific blizzard hit." He paused, his eyes boring into Cody. "I always wondered how you got back out of there. I mean with your kidnapper being dead for a couple weeks before you were found." He folded his arms. Waited.

Brittany shot Cody a reassuring gaze. He took a deep, calming breath. "You know," he said with a poker face, "I have no memory of that. It's a big puzzle in my mind as well." He forced himself to look directly at Ken. "My therapists told me that kids block those things. To cope. Sometimes pieces come back. Sometimes they don't."

"Still, it seems strange—" Ken began.

"Here comes the tow truck," Brittany said almost too gleefully.

They turned in unison to look. The conversation stopped. *Thank God.*

"Oh no," Cody moaned. "Christ, it's Artie Bradshaw."

A smiling Artie stepped out of the truck in his plaid shirt and bill cap on sideways.

Cody couldn't help himself. "Why is it every time something happens to my car, you show up?"

"Aw, that's easy. I'm the only mechanic in Forest Lake. We got the three-A contract. Help out lots of tourists. Need to see your three-A card." He smirked.

After recording the information, he checked under the hood. "Seems like a cable is cut."

"Jeez, Artie. Tell me something I don't know," Cody said.

Artie flashed a big Cheshire cat grin that made Cody want to puke. "You been playin' with the car?"

"Hell no." Cody doubled his fists. He imagined dropkicking Artie over Cooper's Hawk Canyon.

Artie went back to his truck and returned with tools and parts. After some time, he poked his head around the hood. "Go ahead and start it."

Cody got in the car and turned the ignition key; the engine hummed.

Artie slammed the hood down. "I was able to rebuild the top part of the cable and reconnect it. You'll want to take it into the dealer when you get back home and have it checked again. Everything else looks good."

"Thank you, Artie," Brittany said. "You're so handy."

Artie beamed. "Hey, no problem." He gazed into Brittany's eyes, while Cody handed him his credit card.

Artie winked at Brittany. "Stop by the shop sometime. I'll buy you a cup a coffee over at Dottie's."

"Oh well, sure sometime. That's if I get time."

Cody watched Artie waddle back to his truck. *Why did she have to play up to the jerk?*

"You have any other calls for vandalism lately?" Ken asked Artie when he returned with Cody's receipt.

"Nah, just regular tourist stuff." Artie smirked. He eyed Cody as if he were the problem. He tugged at his hat. "See ya at Dottie's tomorrow," he said to Ken and headed back to his truck.

Ken said, "I'll follow you guys until we get close to the Lake Store, then you'll have cell phone coverage, so you can call if you have any more trouble."

"Thanks, Ken," Cody said. He extended his hand. Ken had a firm grip.

Cody and Brittany climbed into the Forester and drove away with Cody watching the cruiser in the rearview mirror.

"Well, that was a godsend in a lot of ways," Brittany said. "We got to talk with Ken without all the formality, and we learned something, too. About Jim, I mean."

"Ken seems like a nice guy, actually. Although he acted very suspicious."

Brittany nodded. "You think? I thought his stare was going to bore a hole in your shirt."

"Yeah, and he seemed to gape at your ring."

"His wife was my sixth-grade teacher. She started the little library in town for the kids years ago. Nice lady."

When they reached the Lake Store, Ken flicked his cruiser lights as he shot past and Cody waved his appreciation.

"So," Brittany said, "Now we know why Jim killed Christie. Sounds like unrequited love, and he couldn't handle it."

"Hmmm. You could be right," Cody said, deep in thought.

"About their relationship? Of course, I'm—"

"No, I mean about us. Someone slashed my tires when we visited your mother, which, by the way, Artie didn't mention. Then you find a threatening note. Now this."

"So, it's like someone is stalking us?"

"Yeah, and that someone doesn't want us here, or at least not *me*."

CHAPTER 17

Half-awake and stiff from sleeping on the couch, Cody awakened to pounding on the door. He blinked into light filtering through the blinds. The clock on the wall said 8:00 a.m.

He bolted up wearing a white T-shirt and red plaid boxers. Not thinking, he flung the door open and found himself staring into Sue Bolin's angry face. He rubbed his eyes. "Oh, hi," he said, and looked again.

She glared at his boxers. "Well, I never," she gasped. Her jaw tightened. "You! What do you think you are doing here with my daughter?"

"Nothing . . ." he said, his voice gravelly, his mind still foggy. "We were just sleeping." He tried to smooth his unruly bed head.

"Sleeping together!" Her face flushed; she pushed past him. "Brittany!" She called. She moved toward the kitchen. "Brittany, where are you?"

Brittany sauntered into the living room, sleepy-eyed, hair disheveled, wearing only a long, knee-length, navy blue T-shirt with a yellow canary cartoon character on the front. "Mother, what on earth is the matter?" She placed her hand in front of her mouth and yawned. "What are you doing here?"

"You're engaged. You shouldn't be here . . . alone . . . sleeping with . . . with him." She pointed an accusing finger at Cody.

"What?" Her eyes widened.

"How would Lance feel about that?"

"Lance? He's in Asia."

"So, he can't trust you?"

"I'm just helping Cody."

Sue shot a glance at Cody's boxers and then back to Brittany's long T-shirt and her bare legs. "It looks to me like it's more than helping. People in town are talking. They're saying terrible things."

"Let them talk. We're not doing anything wrong. And I'm disappointed that my own mother would stand there accusing me. Want some coffee? I'm about to make coffee."

"Hmmph. Why don't you go home," she said to Cody.

Cody crossed his arms and scratched at his ribs through his T-shirt with both hands. "Look, Mrs. Bolin . . . Sue . . . nothing is happening here. We're just doing research."

"I'll bet you're doing *research*. The least you could do is get dressed."

Cody looked down at his underwear; then bounded for the stairs.

"Look Mother, this is all innocent. I was uncomfortable sleeping down here on my own after someone left a nasty note on our door . . . and more. Cody agreed to sleep on the couch. We. Are. Not. Doing. It."

Sue's hands cupped her exasperated face, pulling down her cheeks, exposing the red rims of her lower lids. "Honey, think about Lance!" she gasped. "He can offer you a wonderful life. Give you all the things I couldn't. You'll be set forever. He'll take you places you've never dreamed of. Don't throw it all away."

Brittany's voice softened. "I know you want the best for me, Mother, and I love you for that, but Cody and I are just friends. I'm helping him for the summer. Nothing more. I expect you to believe me. I . . .uh . . . I told Lance I'm assisting a Willamette University professor with research. He's okay with that. Once we're done here— we're done."

Cody emerged in his jeans and sweatshirt, his hair hastily combed. He smarted at Brittany's last words.

"Right?" she said to Cody.

"Sure . . . I mean right." He looked at Sue. "Done."

She shook her finger at Brittany. "Why didn't you tell me, then? I knew you planned to look after the Humphries' house. But I didn't expect you'd be living here with . . ." She waved her hand in Cody's direction. "With him!"

"Mother, stop. We needed a place to . . . a base to operate from. Cody will be bringing equipment. We're gathering documents. This just made sense. It's free and it's private."

"All that trouble over a dead Indian. What am I supposed to tell people?"

"Tell them what I just said. Now, would you like to sit down for a while and have coffee?"

"Look. I've got to get to work. Think about what I told you . . . about losing Lance." She glared at Cody. "Think real hard." She spun around, headed out the door, and slammed it behind her.

Brittany let out a long sigh. "Jeez, I'm sorry about that."

"Look, if me being here is causing trouble . . . I don't want to hurt you, or cause a big rift with your mom, or . . ." He swallowed. "Lance."

Brittany's upper lip stiffened. "Look, our being here together is just a working arrangement. If those narrow-minded ol' biddies can't deal with that, it's their problem." She folded her arms. "Now, I know why I left Forest Lake. Do you want coffee? I could use some coffee."

Cody followed her into the kitchen, admiring her long, bare legs. "I like your T-shirt," he said.

* * *

Tootie came out of the shadows of Benders Bar & Grill, smelling of smoke and soured beer. She pulled off Artie's hat. "Hi big fellow. I've been waiting for you." She tugged at the blue plaid shirt he wore and planted a kiss on his lips.

"Aw come on, give me back my hat."

The Juke box played Jimmy Buffett's "Too Drunk to Karaoke," while people danced and bumped into each other on the tiny dance floor. Someone shouted "Yeee Haw!" and clapped. The noise went directly to Artie's head where a headache was forming.

"I could use a drink," Tootie said, as she pushed the hat back down on his head, the bill pointing sideways.

"Aww. Yeah?" He put his arm around her and led her to the bar. He wasn't in the mood for Tootie, but it was hard to shake her once she glommed on.

"Yeah, cookie."

"I thought you'd be out there dancin'."

"I was babycakes, but I'm tired now." Dressed in tight jeans and a revealing snug coral tank top, she perched on a barstool and reached for a handful of popcorn from the big yellow bowl on the counter. "It's Jimmy Buffett night," she said and munched. "All night."

"Aww, I'll buy ya a beer, but I'll bet it's not your first one."

"Not tonight. Margaritas are half-price. Don't you want one? It'll make you pucker."

"Nah, I can't handle the salt on the rim." Artie ordered Tootie a Margarita and a beer for himself. "I don't know why they have to gum the glass up with salt."

"Whatsa matter, honey? You look so-o-o sad." She tweaked his plump cheek.

"Aw, cut it out, Tootie."

Tootie dropped some popcorn down her tank top. "Ya want a treat, honey?" She wiggled her boobs.

Al, the poker-faced bartender, set down their two drinks.

"Can't ya be serious for just a second?"

"Boy, you're grumpy." She sipped her Margarita. She winked at the glum bartender and pointed at Artie. "He's almost as grumpy as you."

Al didn't respond. He swept stray popcorn off the bar, pulled out a white cloth, and wiped the surface.

Artie looked toward the back of the room. It was 9:00 p.m. Remey should be there, but the booth in the corner was empty.

"I think my babycakes is in a foul mood."

"Nah, I'm just tired. Lot of work at the garage today. Spent the afternoon fixin' a muffler and exhaust system. My back's kicking in."

Strains of "Margaritaville" drifted through the room. "Wanna step outside and get some air?" She giggled. "If you know what I mean."

A big, rangy man with a sweaty, leather face ambled over. Artie recognized him as Dale, a Benders regular. He smelled like Chinese food gone bad.

Dale pulled out a cigarette and tapped it on the bar. "Hey, ya got a light?" he said to Artie in a gravelly smoker's voice.

Artie whipped out his lighter. Dale sucked in smoke and plopped onto the bar stool next to Tootie.

Artie stretched his arms and glanced at his watch again. *What if Remey doesn't show?*

Tootie and Dale were in a conversation about a row of ants Tootie spotted in the women's restroom. "Makes you wonder where else they are," she said.

Dale gave a ringing laugh and belched.

"Hey," Tootie wailed. "I mean ants travel, man."

Finally, Artie spied Remey's tubby body plopping down in a booth in the dark back corner. Artie slid off his stool. "Take care of her, wouldya?" he said to Dale, who barely nodded. Artie turned to the surly bartender. "Send a beer to the guy in the corner. I gotta see a man about a horse."

Artie hesitated until Mandy, the server, delivered the beer. Remey lit up and blew a cloud of smoke. That was the signal.

Artie headed for the john. Benders' crapper was a dim, smelly closet with dingy cream-colored walls, an overflowing wastebasket, and mystery puddles on the floor. Artie's head was swimming. He stared into the chipped mirror. His eyes were puffy and he needed a shave. How had it come to this? *I'm not a bad person. I just got reeled in like a trout.* He combed his mind for answers, but he didn't have to rake far. He'd wracked up his back working at the garage and ended up in traction. Then, Berny, his wife, walked out, taking the two boys—his whole world. It had all rained down at once. He knew a little weed would help with both kinds of pain, plus help him keep his job. *That guy that used to hang at Benders, what was his name . . . Baines? Raines? He pointed me to Remey.* Remey offered a cure which picked him right up. Only it didn't last.

During his meeting with Remey, he'd need to hold his own. Artie reached into his pocket, pulled out a plastic baggie, and shook two white tablets into his palm. He ran the faucet in the sink with a brown stain, cupped his hand under the running water, and gulped, waiting for the rush. He took a piss and flushed the toilet. In a few minutes, he'd be jumping around like a crackbrain.

Out in the hallway, he fumbled in his pocket for a cigarette, nervously lit up, took a long suck, and blew a cloud of tension into the already smoky air. He ambled over to the bar, grabbed his mug of beer, and edged his way to the back booth as the jukebox blared, "Come Monday."

Remey sipped beer, read messages on his cell phone, and puffed away on his cigarette like he always did. He nodded as Artie slid into the seat across from him but continued to stare at the phone.

Remey's silence made Artie uneasy, but then the drugs began to kick in. He felt emboldened. "I'm tired pushing joints and crap to the kids. They're out there watching me. I could get sent to the big house."

Remey slowly looked up. His fat chin wobbled. "Who's watching you?"

"The cops. I can feel 'em."

"You feel 'em?" His eyes bored into Artie. "Like they're ghosts or somethin', huh?"

"This is a small town, I—"

"A deal is a deal." He gave Artie a level look. "We own your ass, man."

"Look, my house is in foreclosure. My wife and kids are gonna be on the street. She needs a car."

"Your ex-wife you mean."

"She's the mother of my kids. The house needs repairs."

Remey snickered. "You owe us eighteen grand."

"One of the kids is sick. I don't have insurance. I'm having to pay rent and a mortgage. I need help now. It can't wait, and I can't push enough stuff. I'm a mechanic. I have a job to do. I can't be runnin' off all the time."

"A deal is a deal," Remey said again.

"And, I'm tired of playing your stupid games, spooking Benson. It don't make a lot of sense." His mouth was dry. He took a long drink from his mug, but it didn't help. He took another one. His tongue seemed numb.

"Relax."

"I need some dough quick."

"Ha. We paid you dough. And what did you do? You blew it all gamblin' away at the casino, man. Then you used stuff and didn't pay for it."

"Look . . . I need . . ."

"I don't give a fuck what you need. Get off your fat ass and earn it. Lot of action in Curry County. The county's fucked for funds. Cops can't police it."

"Curry County? Way over there. Hell, what are you thinking?"

"Look, man. You're in debt." He slammed his hand on the table. "To *us*."

The loud slam crashed like thunder in Artie's ears. He looked over his shoulder, but the loud music muffled Remey's outburst. He turned back to the table. "I get caught, and I'm gonna go public with it."

"I wouldn't make the boss mad."

"You tell Mr. Big, I know who he is."

"What are you sayin'?" Remey's massive quadruple chin quivered a bit. It gave Artie courage.

"Yeah. I have my ways of knowing," Artie bluffed. "You get a few people drunk around here." He could tell he had Remey's attention. He wanted to hammer him, but his eyes burned and his speech slurred. Across the room, the thump of pool balls striking each other pounded in his drug-addled brain. "And I'm gonna spill it, unlesh you come through wish shum big bucks." Maybe he should've only swallowed one of them tablets. "Now."

"Man, you been sniffin' somethin' before you wobbled over here? Your pupils are as big as hub caps, and your words are bumping into each other."

"Come on. Werse talkin' hardball."

"You, hardball? Hah!" Remey snorted. "We got another job for you."

"I don't wants it."

"You don't gotta choice, fella. We need you to plant some coke on our . . . friend."

"Aww, what for?"

"So, we can get his ass arrested. Idiot."

"Aw, he's getting wise to me."

"You better make sure he doesn't. Think, man. It's a chance for you to work off your debt."

"I don't wanna . . . I don't wanna do that no more." The bar seemed to be spinning. He took a deep breath.

Remey jammed his cigarette in the ashtray and put his cell phone back in his pocket. He pulled out a small packet and slid it across the table. "Here's the stuff you plant." He eased himself out of the booth and pointed his finger in Artie's face. "We. Own. You. Don't never forget it."

"Hey, where you going? We're not done here. I need shum . . ."

Remey bent down and put his face right into Artie's. "You better think about those kids of yours. Don't want nothin' to happen to them. Understand?"

Those words clobbered Artie like a steel hammer to the head. He opened his mouth, but no words came out. For a brief moment, he saw freckle-faced Denny with his first baseball mitt and his small son, Randy, soft, brown curls, little hands, reaching for him. "Read to me, Daddy."

Remey glowered. "You're smashed. Let me know when you got that job done, okay? And Keep. Your. Fat. Mouth. Shut. Got it?"

Remey turned and disappeared out the back door, leaving Artie alone with his beer. The alcohol-drug combo made his stomach churn and his hands numb. He had to get outside to puke. He stood up, but felt shaky. If he could get to his pickup, he'd lay down in the front seat. *Maybe I took the wrong pills. Can't ever tell how pure stuff is.* He stumbled toward the back door. Where was Tootie? God, he needed her now. He looked over his shoulder toward the bar. She wasn't there. Then, through the smoky haze, he spotted couples dancing to the plunky strains of Buffett's "We Are The People Our Parents Warned Us About." He buried his face in his palms.

CHAPTER 18

Back in his Salem apartment, Cody dressed for his appointment with Dr. Aanandi while listening to violinist Joshua Bell playing *Chopin's Nocturne in C Sharp Minor.* He gazed out the open bedroom window into the green tops of fully-leafed trees. A perfect June day—breezy, sunny and in the mid-70's. He could hear the rush of Mill Creek below. He sucked in the air's fresh, earthy smell. His landlady, Anne Ferguson, had potted red geraniums that sat on the stone wall overlooking the creek. It felt good to be back.

He wrote out his rent check on the kitchen counter. Thump. Crackers jumped up, brushing against his arm. "You know, I actually missed you, you crazy feline, kneading my chest at night, sneaking around, hogging the couch." He stroked the cat's head. Crackers purred like a miniature motor boat. Cody reached into the cupboard and gave him a treat, which he eagerly gulped. He rubbed against Cody again, purring louder, dead set on another. "Okay, okay. Just who do you bug when I'm not around? Huh?"

Cody grabbed the check he'd written. "Let's go see Anne. She's waiting for us." He hurried down the stairs with Crackers close behind. He found her out on the patio overlooking the creek, sitting at her small table shaded with a bright rose umbrella. She was a petite woman with curly white hair and determined blue eyes.

"Thank you," she said when Cody handed her the check. "Have a seat. I made coffee." She reached for her thermal pot, filled a mug, and handed it to Cody. "It's been a long time since we just sat and talked." She grinned. "And, I've missed all that violin music wafting from upstairs."

131

"Gee, do I have it on too loud?"

"I actually enjoy it."

"I turned it up a bit this morning. It's such a beautiful day."

"A bit breezy, but that's fine with me." She placed the check in her pocket. "How long you figure you'll be gone?"

"Probably most of the summer. Depends on what we find."

"Now, what is it again you're doing?"

"I'm . . . uh . . . researching an incident involving a Native American that happened a long time ago. He lived in a small, all-white community and got in trouble. I'm trying to extract out how isolation, prejudice, socio-economic conditions, plus a dysfunctional family played into his outcome. Then I'm going to transition into modern times. Things haven't changed much for some people . . . in some communities. Native Americans still face a lot of prejudice."

"What's all that equipment you've been lugging in have to do with that?"

"Well, he . . . my subject . . . uh camped out in the wilderness for a while. Then apparently froze to death. I'm working with some archeologist friends to find the exact location of his camp. His personal story will add color to the rest of my research." Each time he explained his quest, the details got better.

"Sounds complicated and a bit icky, especially if you find his bones."

Cody laughed. "Not really, and I love playing with archeology equipment. You know, I minored in archeology."

"Interesting. Here, have a cookie. Fresh baked this morning and your favorite—peanut butter chocolate chip."

Cody eagerly reached for a cookie. "Did I ever tell you you're my favorite landlady?"

Anne's face brightened. "Yes, many times, as a matter of fact, especially when I have cookies." She handed him a paper napkin. "You know, if I had to live my life all over, maybe I would've studied archeology." Her finger jabbed the air, like it always did when Anne wanted to make a point. "Ancient studies fascinate me. On my last trip to Greece, we went through some fabulous old ruins." The breeze rippled her stack of paper napkins. Anne anchored them under the plate of cookies and adjusted her sweater. "Of course, when I was a girl, our choices were pretty limited—nurse, secretary, or teacher."

"But you loved teaching junior high, didn't you?"

"Oh yes, but I look at you, and I think I could've studied anthropology or archeology or something just as grand and taught it, too. But I guess I can't complain. I've been meaning to thank you for the boy . . . Omar. He's working out fine. He's been pulling weeds, helping me put in the garden." She pointed to two raised beds filled with tomato starts and other tender green plants. "Yesterday, we got out the rest of the patio furniture. Next time he comes, we're going to wash the downstairs windows." She bit into her cookie and took a sip of coffee. "Sometimes, when he's finished working, we have lunch. He's a bright kid, actually. I gave him some books to read. If we have time, we talk about them. Right now, we're working our way through *Huckleberry Finn.* There's a lot more in that story than adventure." Her pointing finger punctuated her opinion.

"Oh, Anne, that's wonderful."

"I guess the family is getting food stamps, but I always send a little something home with him . . . especially for his little sisters. You know, cookies, muffins."

Cody reached for a second cookie. He could see that worrying about Omar and his family had energized Anne. "How's his father doing?"

"Well, Omar said he's going to be able to look for work next month, so I assume he's on the mend. He's getting some assistance for his medical bills, too. I took the kids shopping at garage sales for clothing and some little stuff. We even managed to get Omar a used bike. Now, he does errands for me."

Hooking Omar up with Anne was probably going to change the boy's life forever. "That'll make Britt really happy," Cody said. He blushed and looked down.

"Why don't you bring your girlfriend around? I'd like to meet her."

"Actually, well . . . she's not my girlfriend . . . she's more of a colleague, helping me for the summer on my research."

Anne's face took on that teacher expression as if she were listening to a student explain how he lost his homework. "I see."

"We're just friends. We knew each other in grade school."

"Uh-huh. Well, I'd still like to meet your *friend.*" She tilted her head and narrowed her eyes. "Bring her by sometime."

"She's over attending a hearing on Banjo, the dog they've condemned. "You've probably heard about that?"

"Oh yes. There's been quite a fuss over that dog. I've read several stories about the whole thing in the paper." Her finger sliced the air again. "I had half a mind to go down there and straighten those folks out. I hope it works out well . . . for the dog, I mean."

"Britt is very involved with the group that's trying to free him." Cody beamed when he mentioned her name and smiled to himself.

Suddenly Crackers jumped up on the table. His grape green eyes focused on something in the yard and blinked softly. He swished his tail back and forth and hoisted it in the air, the tip twitching.

"I suppose now he's into stealing cookies."

"No, look over there." Anne pointed toward her azaleas.

Cody spotted a small, calico cat crouching under the shrubs. "Ah, another cat in the king's territory."

"Actually, it's his girlfriend. Not to worry, though, they're both fixed."

"Crackers, you sly dog. No offense." He held up both hands as if to defend himself. "No wonder you're all puffed up."

Anne's blue eyes focused on Cody. She gave him a knowing smile. "Love will do that to you."

<h1 style="text-align:center">CHAPTER 19</h1>

"Hello professor," Dr. A. extended his hand. "And how are you on this splendid Friday afternoon?"

"Pretty good, actually." Cody forced a smile; his right leg bounced. Dr. A. had a calming persona, but just being there in that office threw him off-center. Part of it was the psychiatric stigma. He could visualize those future job or insurance applications and *that* question. *Have you ever had psychiatric or psychological therapy?* He had read somewhere, that socially speaking, it was better to be an ex-convict than an ex-mental patient, but then—

"Let's see," Dr. A. said, interrupting his thoughts. He'd seated himself and flipped through his file. "The last time we talked, you were planning to go off and do some research. So, how's it going?"

"I've barely scratched the surface. Oh, I've learned some things about Jim's personal life and the murder."

"And?"

"Apparently, it was a crime of passion."

"Hmmm."

"He was in love with this woman, and she treated his intentions as a joke. I guess she laughed at him."

Dr. A's eyebrow shot up. He said nothing, so Cody chattered away.

"He had anger management problems, most likely caused by an abusive family situation and prejudice. My next big step is finding the actual cave. You know the one he . . . and I . . . lived in for some clues on where he might be."

Dr. A. gave him a skeptical look. He cleared his throat. "So, how are the panic attacks?"

"Much better. Especially, when I'm with her . . . uh, Britt."

Dr. A smiled. "Your friend?"

"Britt. Yeah. She's my assistant." He smiled self-consciously.

"Ah yes. I remember now."

Cody held out his wrist. "Look, no rubber band."

Dr. A grinned. "Ah, professor, I think you're in love. Perhaps it is your cure."

Cody dropped his hand and sat up straight. "Oh, no, no," he protested. "She's a colleague. We're staying in . . . I mean, we set up our operation in a farmhouse."

Dr. A. put down his pen. "Hmmmm," he said, a smile in his eyes. "So, she's moved in with you?"

"We're just sharing housing. Her fiancé is over in Asia." He knew he was rambling. "He's some big shot timber executive."

"She's engaged to someone else . . . and she's living with you?"

"Well, yeah. But we're just friends. This is temporary. We're not . . ."

Dr. A looked bewildered. "I see, but it's very comfortable for you."

"Sort of. Well, it was. I mean they . . . someone left a note on the door ordering us to leave."

"Whoa! You were ordered to leave?"

"It was a note left on the door. Not signed. It just said, 'Leave now.'"

"Very strange."

"Yeah. And then someone cut the battery cable on my car and before that slashed my tires. I—*we*, think it's all related."

Dr. A sat silent, like a computer processing information. "But of course, you reported all this to the police?"

"Well, no actually. I mean a cop did stop and help us when we were stranded. But, because of the situation with Jim, he's still a wanted man, and all. I can't involve the police."

Dr. A wrote something on his chart. He looked up. "You're sure these things are happening?"

"Absolutely. We had to get a mechanic out to fix the car."

"What about your girlfriend . . . perhaps she knows something about all this?"

"Britt? No. It's making her uneasy. Actually. I can't figure out why they . . . anyone . . . would care about what we're doing. I mean, an anthropologist doing research is so uninteresting. It doesn't make a lot of sense."

"Hmmm." Dr. A. frowned. "Maybe this Jim character, if he exists, doesn't want you to find him." He studied Cody's face.

"How would he even know I was looking for him?"

"Perhaps this ghost has someone who is helping him."

Cody bristled at the suggestion that Jim was fantasy. "Ah, come on." He gripped his palms. "I told you I know he's real. I was there. I'm not some nut case."

Dr. A focused on Cody's hands until he quit wringing them. "Okay. Okay professor. Relax. I have another thought."

"Yeah?"

"Maybe your colleague . . ." Dr. A made quotes in the air with his fingers when he said that last word. He paused and started again. "Perhaps your colleague's fiancé isn't as far away as you think."

* * *

Back at his apartment, Cody changed into jeans and a sweatshirt. He was hungry, so he checked the fridge. There wasn't much in there except some cans of cola, a jar of peanut butter, and an apple that had seen better times. He retrieved the pop and tossed the apple in the garbage. Maybe Britt would want to do dinner.

His visit with Dr. A left him feeling like he was trapped in a revolving door. The good doctor still seemed to feel that his story about Jim and a cave resulted from his dissociative disorder. Stay on your anti-anxiety medication and see me next month, Dr. A advised. He also suggested the possibility of using hypnosis to help get at repressed memories. Something to think about, but he was getting better, wasn't he? He felt calmer and wasn't having the dreams. Maybe he didn't need a shrink anymore. No, talking with Dr. A helped, and he genuinely liked him. Besides, he was going to prove to the doctor that he was right about Jim.

The beginning strains of Camille Saint-Saëns' *The Swan,* the ringtone for his cell phone, stopped his thoughts. "Britt, hi, I was just about to call you. So, how'd the hearing go?"

"Not well." She sighed. "They didn't reach a decision."

"But I thought they were on the verge . . ."

"The parents of the injured child are making a big stink." Her voice was impatient, irritated. "Some of the neighbors came and testified. They want Banjo destroyed."

"Oh Britt, I'm sorry."

"Yeah. The pits. I got to visit Banjo. He isn't thriving. He's sad. He's thin. He has to wear that muzzle whenever they take him for walks." She paused and sniffed. "Representative Janes also showed up . . . as a dog lover. He doesn't have any authority, but we were happy to have his support." Her voice choked. "I don't know if Banjo's going to make it if they don't resolve this soon."

He heard a sound like static coming from a radio and knew Britt was blowing her nose. "I wish you were here so I could give you a supportive hug." Silence on the other end. "Maybe that's their strategy. Let the dog languish, and then they won't have to make a decision."

"I don't know. I can't seem to focus right now. Damn politicians."

"That's for sure. Is there anything I can do?"

"Uh, no. Why don't you go back to Whiteside on Sunday. I'll drive down on my own and catch up with you again Monday evening."

Cody felt a stab in his gut. He was hesitant to go without her. "Are you sure? I can wait."

"No. You go ahead. I'm going to pick up a few things and then, when I get there, I plan to spend some time with Mother to smooth things over. You know?"

"Okay. Well, how about dinner tonight? Something casual. We could order a pizza. It might help to just talk."

"Thanks, but I need some time. Alone. To think. To grieve. I don't know what."

He heard the radio static again and knew she was crying. He didn't want her to hang up. "I guess Omar is doing well with Anne."

"Yeah, that's what Dulcy said. Look, I gotta go, there's someone at the door."

Then she was gone. He looked down at his wrist. *Oh God, I need my rubber band!*

* * *

Cody reached the farmhouse in Whiteside late Sunday afternoon. He carried in his belongings and the archeology equipment. *Now what?* The house seemed strange and empty without Britt. He tried calling her cell phone, but when it went to voice mail, his heart picked up a pace.

Sweat beaded on his forehead, and his throat felt sore. The telltale signs of a panic attack, just when he thought he was making progress.

Shit. Cognitive distortion.

Isn't that what Dr. A called it? This was so silly. She'd be here tomorrow. He opened his duffel bag and found the medication Dr. A prescribed and swallowed a tablet. He missed Crackers and his apartment. Most of all, he missed her, especially the yoga sessions they did in the darkened Humphries' living room, followed by mindful meditation—Britt sitting cross-legged with a tiny Buddha statue in front of her; the lighted candle, the glowing stick of incense, the sagey-healing smell wafting through the air. The sound of the small singing bowl she tapped three times to begin a session and twice to end it played in his mind. Sure, he fidgeted and snuck peeks at her, but the overall result was one of calm, and it helped. God, it helped.

Famished from the long drive, he heated a frozen pizza and smeared a handful of Doritos with gobs of peanut butter. The food stuck in his throat. He craved beer, but didn't think it wise to mix alcohol with his anxiety meds, so he drank iced tea. *What to do? What to do?* He whipped out his sketchpad and did several quick drawings of Britt from memory. *I just need to breathe deeply. She'll be coming in tomorrow.*

Finally, he headed upstairs to bed, turned on his iPad, signed into Cloud Player and listened to soothing ocean flute music while he scanned e-mail and Google News. *Nothing new.* He propped up the pillows, leaned back, and thumbed his way through the latest edition of *American Indian Quarterly,* hoping sleep would claim him. When his eyelids drooped, he switched off the lamp.

Something jarred him awake. It sounded like a slamming car door. He jumped up and scampered to the window. With no outside lighting, it was pitch black. So dark, he could barely see his car. His ears perked. Nothing. *Just jitters?* He jerked the comforter off his bed, grabbed a pillow, and headed down to sleep on the couch. After placing his cell phone on the end table, he scanned the living room for a suitable weapon, settling on the fireplace poker, which he laid on the floor within easy reach. Staring into the dark, listening to the old house creak, he drifted off again.

Jim pointed at something.

"I've been looking all over for you," Cody said

Jim frowned. "Don't go there."

"Where?" Cody asked.

The wild eyes bore into him. "Be careful." His big hands reached out. "Don't tell. Never ever tell."

Cody could feel Jim pulling him, squeezing him. His mouth moved, but Cody couldn't make out the words. Suddenly Jim turned into a huge Crackers sitting on his chest.

Cody gasped, sat straight up, his heart pounding in his ears. Another damn dream. *What was that?* Tapping noises near the front door, like someone was messing with the lock. His cell phone said 2:03 a.m. He bounded up, gripping the poker. What would he do if someone actually broke in? And, why would they do that? He hurried through the house turning on every light, so whoever it was would know someone was there and awake. Maybe it didn't matter. Maybe they knew he was alone. A thud sounded somewhere. Could his mind be playing tricks? He retrieved a straight-back chair from the kitchen, jammed it under the doorknob, and returned to the sofa where he sat hugging a pillow. He needed Brittany. God, he really did.

* * *

Cody awoke with his head buried in the pillow and a foul taste in his mouth. All the lights were still on. His eyes were puffy and his head ached. After dressing, he made coffee, waiting briefly for the caffeine to clear his foggy head. Poker in hand, he headed out to have a look around. As soon as he opened the door, he saw it.

Another threatening note was neatly tacked to the door. *Jesus!* He ripped it free and slid it into his pocket.

That would explain the tapping noises he'd heard. He locked the door and did a complete circle around the house, checking every window. Nothing seemed amiss. *The car!* He sprinted toward it. Everything looked okay, but he hopped in and fired up the engine just to make sure. So, it was just the note. *Weird.*

Back in the house, he secured the door lock, poured another cup of coffee, and bolted down toast and cold cereal. Periodically, he peeked through the drapes to see if anyone was around. He spent most of the day listening to music, making lists, and mapping the trek they would make into the wilderness to find the cave. Around 4:10 p.m., a car pulled in.

Britt!

He dashed out to give her a welcoming hug and to help her carry in her things. "You look bushed," he said when they were both inside.

"It was a long drive. And, I haven't been sleeping well. I brought some groceries."

"Yeah, I brought some stuff, too." Cody was eager to talk. "I couldn't sleep either. In fact, this morning I found . . ." Brittany turned away. She seemed detached, like she couldn't focus. *This isn't the time. This isn't the time.*

Once they tucked the groceries away, Cody hastily toasted cheese sandwiches while she tossed a salad. He pulled two beers from the refrigerator. "How'd it go with your mom?"

"Mother has calmed down a bit. Lance called while I was there and that made her feel a lot better."

"So how is Lance?" He remembered what Dr. A said. "Still in Asia?"

"Well, yeah. I guess things are going okay over there. He misses me. I miss him. Once I put Mother on, she started pressing him for a date for our wedding."

"So, when is it?" Cody asked, waiting to be slapped.

"Oh, it's still up in the air. Lance has got to work on Representative Janes' run for Congress. But he insisted we shop for *the* dress."

Cody set down his fork and took a gulp of beer. His throat still burned.

"Mother had this idea that she was going to make the dress, and that we'd be getting married in Forest Lake. Lance nipped that in the bud. I mean, there's no way Lance would get married out in the middle of nowhere."

"That's okay with your mom?"

"Oh yes. Lance told her it would probably be at some big, fancy country club." Brittany smiled. "And he's paying for everything. Cool. Don't you think?" She folded her arms.

"Oh well, yeah. I guess." He wanted to puke.

"Poor Banjo," she suddenly blurted. "The commissioners keep postponing a decision. I think they're being pressured. Apparently, the little girl who was bitten is the niece of some prominent developer."

"Really."

"Yeah, really, and I wonder why, if he's so concerned, so high and mighty, why he stands by and lets her live in that crummy neighborhood." She pushed pieces of lettuce around on her plate and barely touched her sandwich. "I mean being his niece and all. I think the jerk's attracted to the publicity. Likes the limelight." She massaged her lower back. "Do you have any Advil? I've been on the road for over four hours. Now my back is feeling it."

"Just Tylenol. We can pick up Advil in town tomorrow. Can you wait that long?"

"Get the Tylenol. I need to lie down." She carried her dish to the sink and headed toward the couch with a glass of water.

Cody retrieved the pain reliever from his bag upstairs. Brittany swallowed two tablets. Just as she did, her cell phone rang.

"Hi Dulcy. What? Yeah, there's a set here." She signaled to Cody. "Turn the news on. Hurry!"

He rushed to the set and fiddled with the remote. It was an older, clunky set, but soon a picture emerged.

"Dulcy says it's all over the news."

"What is?"

"Banjo! Quick. Channel 8. She said someone broke into the pet hotel and kidnapped him."

"What? You're kidding."

Brittany paced, running her hand through her hair as she talked to Dulcy. "If someone hurts that dog, I'll . . . Okay. Okay, Dulcy. Talk to you later." She rotated her shoulder blades making popping and clicking sounds.

They plopped down on the couch, eyes glued to the TV. The news anchor just finished talking about a local strawberry festival.

"Back in May," he said, "we brought you the story of Banjo, a two-year-old German Shepherd, who's on trial for biting a child. Steve Mason, down in Salem, has the latest."

The reporter stood in front of the pet hotel. "For a year now, the dog has been housed in this pet hotel outside Salem awaiting his fate . . . until Sunday night. That's when police believe someone scaled the fence at the facility, broke a window, and snatched Banjo from his kennel."

"Oh my God," Brittany wailed.

"Sh-h-h," Cody said and leaned forward.

The camera cut to the distraught manager of the facility pointing to a broken window. "This is the first time something like this has *ever* happened," he said, his eyes wide as if he'd just seen a flying saucer.

The camera flashed back to Steve Mason. "Banjo had been sentenced to die for biting a three-year-old child on the arm. The girl wasn't seriously injured, but her parents insist that the dog be destroyed. They also say the dog had previously menaced children in the neighborhood. In Marion County, a dog can be destroyed if it is determined that the animal caused injury without being provoked."

"He was provoked!" Brittany yelled at the TV.

"Banjo's supporters, however, argue that the dog was provoked."

"You bet he was," Brittany yelled again. "We've got vets and trainers on our side. Why don't you mention that?"

Cody reached over, put his arm around her, and squeezed her shoulder. "Calm down," he whispered.

Mason continued. "Witnesses allege the child got between the dog and his food and hit the dog in the face. They also claim that other neighborhood kids teased the dog. State Representative Bill Janes testified at the Friday hearing on behalf of Banjo and urged his release."

The camera zoomed to Janes. "Hopefully, this dognapping will bring closure for Banjo's owners. I just hope the dog is off to a new and happy life."

"He's so-o-o nice," Brittany gushed.

"Shhhh," Cody said. "There's more."

"We contacted the dog's owner, Lupe Garcia, but she had no comment. Police are treating the case as a burglary and have alerted Portland area authorities to watch for suspicious persons trying to drive, fly, or sail away with a German shepherd. Roy, back to you."

"Thanks, Steve. Gee, I can't imagine anybody trying to board a plane with a dog in a suitcase," he joked. The female anchor laughed. The station cut to a Cialis commercial of two people in separate bathtubs holding hands on a sandy beach.

Cody glanced at Brittany who punched a number into her cell phone. "What are you doing?"

"I'm calling Lupe. Dang, she's not available. I can't believe this." She rubbed her head and paced. "I just can't believe this."

"Maybe Lupe's heading across state lines with Banjo in the trunk."

"She has a child and a job. I doubt that."

"It seems like whoever stole him had good intentions. That's good news."

"I hope so. God, I hope so." She jumped when her cell phone rang. "Lupe! I'm so glad you called. Do they have any idea where Banjo is or who did this?"

"That's better than some stranger." She looked over at Cody with a relieved smile on her face. "She says they think it was an inside job."

CHAPTER 20

Cody reached into his pocket and nervously fingered the small wooden dog. Jim Fallingwater had carved for him. Standing at the trailhead, he took a deep breath, glanced at the endless woods and inviting sky. *Where are you, Jim?* The big day had finally come—an opportunity to fix the broken pieces of his past. That's why he was here preparing to trek into the Big Bat Wilderness, Mazeophobia and all, with someone else's girlfriend.

Before heading out, he and Brittany had spent hours at the REI store in Medford, buying gear and getting advice. Luckily, they found a very helpful store employee who had actually hiked the Big Bat to the summit. They peppered him with questions about the terrain, water purifiers, Dromedary bags, portable battery packs to recharge cell phones, food, and everything else they'd need for what Cody figured would be a two-or-three-day trek.

After collecting outdoor gear and doing research, he and Brittany had taken some quick trial hikes to test their stamina under the weight of their backpacks. Their preparation had consumed three weeks. Then, they decided to wait until after the Fourth of July to avoid the outdoor enthusiasts who would drift in for holiday recreation.

"There never used to be much of a trail here," he explained as they headed in. "Now, you can follow the main trail all the way to the summit."

"But we're not going to the summit, right?"

"Correct." He glanced at the topographical and environmental maps he'd gotten from the U.S. Forest Service and from Tracy Bly, his Willamette University colleague and an accomplished geology professor. Tracy was an avid hiker and had done some work in the Big Bat Wilderness with his students. He loved talking about the massive gouges left by ice age glaciers, blocky basalt formations, and the mountain's history as a young volcano.

"Hey man, I'd be happy to trek in with you." Tracy had said, his face eager.

Cody forced himself to look directly into Tracy's eyes. "Uh . . . no need. Me and a cousin are going in to find a spot we explored as kids. There was a cave, a spring, and a creek, as I recall. We, uh, promised ourselves we'd go back there one day."

"Understand," Tracy said to Cody's relief. "So, it's personal." Tracy marked out all the possible water resources and areas that could contain caves. "Give me a call if you have questions."

Cody tagged their departure point from the main trail with one of the orange reflective trail markers he carried. He also had an ample supply of reflective tape. "This is the stuff hunters use when they're moving through unfamiliar territory. It even glows at night."

Brittany pulled her hat close around her ears. "Ha, we're a modern day version of Hansel and Gretel, dropping reflective bread crumbs."

"When we're done with our expedition, we'll need to remove them." He shifted his backpack to get comfortable. "I notified the Forest Service so they wouldn't freak out."

They tramped along the boulder-strewn trail, through a forest of Shasta red fir, mountain hemlock, lodgepole, and ponderosa pines. Manzanita and other evergreen shrubs lined their trail. There were still patches of snow on the ground. Occasionally, a bird flitted through the air while startled chipmunks darted deep into the underbrush.

"We need to turn off this trail at about a little over a mile-and-a half. Jim always followed the ones animals made. Animals go where there's water. I know there's a spring and a creek near the cave because when the weather turned, he took me with him to get water."

"I brought bear spray in case we run into one," Brittany said.

Cody laughed. "They'd be more scared of us."

Brittany slapped her neck. "Jeez, these mosquitos. They're just laughing at my repellant."

"Keep covered up," Cody said.

After walking a good part of the morning, they stopped. His shoulders ached and Brittany looked tired. Warm and sweaty, they collapsed on a log, took long swigs of water, and swallowed a lunch of trail mix and cheese rounds.

Brittany kneaded her calves. "I work out at the gym, but my legs are killing me. Even our trial hikes didn't prepare me for this."

"Walking steep rocky terrain is a lot more challenging than a treadmill." Cody set down his water bottle, perused the map, and checked his compass. "As near as I can tell, we need to turn east and then head straight, which will take us to a higher elevation."

They trudged up the trail Cody selected. The underbrush from both sides started closing in on them, but they pushed through, sometimes stopping for Cody to snip a branch with the small clippers he carried. After hiking one-hour-and-a-half, he halted again. "I think we're going in the wrong direction. According to Tracy's map, we should have had a view of Cragger's Rock which he intended for a marker."

"What's *that*?"

"A marker is—"

"No, I mean that? Like something tramping in the brush?" She grabbed his arm, her eyes wide. "A bear maybe?"

"Let's go," Cody said. He ushered her in front of him as they hurried back the way they came. After trucking on for another two hours, Cody suggested they stop and camp. "I need to study the maps some more. We don't want to be out here walking around once it gets dark."

"Good idea. I'm exhausted." She helped him set up their two-person dome tent in a clearing next to a fallen tree.

Cody sprayed the tent with mosquito repellent and suggested Brittany rest inside while he finished setting up camp. He carried a small butane camping stove with him, but because it was chilly, decided to pull dead wood off standing trees and make a fire. He piled the dry wood in front of a boulder to block the wind and arranged stones in a ring for a makeshift fire pit. Once he got the fire going, he boiled water for dried soup mix and instant coffee.

Refreshed, Brittany pulled out crackers, peanut butter, and bananas. She sipped the warm coffee. "Sure makes you appreciate Starbucks, doesn't it?"

"Yeah, but at least it's wet and warm." As they ate, Cody checked the map.

"How much farther?" she asked.

"Well, it depends. Hopefully, we're going in the right direction."

"Hopefully? We don't want to end up getting lost out here." Brittany slipped out of her hiking boots and massaged her feet.

"That's why I put down the trail markers and reflective tape. If we get turned around, we can just follow the stakes back down." Cody fumbled in his pack until he found his journal, the one Dr. A told him to keep. He felt good inside. He had braved his way into the wilderness and hadn't once felt a panic attack or paralyzing fear of getting lost. That he attributed to a good map, compass, trail markers, and being with Britt. Especially Britt. *She's salve for my anxiety plagued soul*, he wrote. *What will my life be like after Britt?*

The sun cast a shadow over the mountain and filled the sky with yellow orange and pinkish streaks. Brittany loosened her ponytail and brushed her hair. "That's just an amazing sunset."

Cody closed his journal and tucked it in his pack. He and Britt used the fallen tree for a backrest and stared at the sky for a long time. Once the sky darkened, it filled with sparkling stars.

"Such a beautiful starry night—something you don't see much in the valley." Brittany moved closer to him. "I'm not getting fresh. I'm just cold." She pulled on her wool hat. Cody smiled, and reached for her.

"It's such a big world," she said, looking up at the stars. "I keep thinking about Banjo. Wondering how he is . . . Lance is happy Representative Janes stood up for Banjo. He thinks it'll help with the election. He says people like that. It humanizes politicians."

The last thing Cody wanted to talk about was Lance. "I just hope Banjo is okay."

"Me too. All life matters. Banjo wants to live as much as we do."

"And he ought to."

Cody reached into his pack, fished out his iPad, and began reading.

"What are you doing?"

"Catching up. This is a book about the Paleo-Indian migration to the Americas from Siberia."

"Egads," Brittany said, irritated.

"It's on my Kindle app."

"So, I guess I'll just sit here and talk to the squirrels while you read."

"It's based on genetic evidence."

"Uh-huh. That's great, Professor. Just great." She waved her arm toward the sky. "Such a lovely night, and you're back in ancient times."

"Actually, about 15,000 B.C."

"Who knew?" She rolled her eyes.

A few clicks on his iPad and violin music floated through the air. "How's that? Chopin's Nocturne in C sharp minor."

Haunting but smooth strains made by a 300-year-old Stradivarius violin drifted through the rough and craggy wilderness.

"It's beautiful," she whispered.

"I downloaded it onto my iPad. The quality is kinda tinny."

"Shhh," Brittany said, her expression totally relaxed, like someone getting a scalp massage.

"It's Joshua Bell," he said after the last note played. "His music always calms me."

"Who is he?"

"One of the most celebrated violinists of our time. He's coming to Salem next year to play with the Oregon Symphony. I'm addicted to his music."

"I've never been to the symphony. It's not something Lance is into."

"You can come with me."

"Next year seems so far away." She looked up at the starry sky again. "And, who knows where I'll be." She held out her hand. "Mrs. Lance Helms." The engagement ring on her left hand glittered in the glow of the fire.

Cody stiffened. He tapped his iPad to bring up another piece— Bell playing Ave Maria.

Brittany leaned her head on Cody's shoulder. Her eyes got moist. She reached for Cody's knee and gave it a little squeeze.

"What's the matter?" He pulled her closer. "Are you okay? Are you too cold? Maybe I should put more wood on the fire."

"It's such a beautiful night. Who'd a thought after such a long time we'd reconnect."

"Yeah." He looked into her eyes and she looked back.

"This is a special moment for me." Her moist lips parted, her eyes shimmering.

"Yeah."

Her face moved close to his, her hair brushing his cheeks, soft and fragrant. He turned toward her, his mouth about to touch hers.

She jerked away. "What the?" A beam from a spotlight splashed directly on them.

Cody leaped to his feet. "Who's there?"

The spotlight jiggled over them, hit the tent, moved to the side and faded away.

"What is it?" Brittany jumped up.

"Who's there?" Cody shouted again. His hands tightened around the hatchet he'd used earlier to chop wood.

"I hear someone running." Brittany yelled. "Over there!"

Cody dashed off in the direction she pointed, but he only went a little way into the brush and returned, not wanting to leave her alone and vulnerable.

"What do you make of that? Who'd be out here?" she asked, her hand rubbing her forehead.

"I don't know. That was a spotlight. It could be a deer poacher."

"Way up here? We're way off the main trail."

"Yeah. I don't know. I'm not a hunter." Cody piled more wood on the fire. "Just making the fire big, so they won't think we're deer, or bear, or whatever the hell they're after. I wish we had a gun."

"A gun? Oh my God."

"Just a thought. So many crazy things have happened. None of which makes any sense."

"Why would anybody care what we're doing?" Her voice trembled.

"Look, I didn't want to upset you. But while you were gone, I found another note at the house. Tacked on the door. It said, *Leave. While you still can.*"

"What?" Her eyebrows rose. "My God. Why didn't you say something?"

"You were so distraught over Banjo."

"Yeah, but that's—"

"And then weeks went by and nothing happened. I didn't tear this one up. I saved it for the handwriting."

Brittany threw up her hands. "Oh great. And what are we supposed to do? Walk around Forest Lake and ask for writing samples? Like, we're looking for a needle in a haystack."

"We just need to keep our eyes peeled. Eventually, this stuff has to add up."

Brittany's arms hugged her shoulders. "Oh, God . . . There's no cell phone coverage, and no one knows we're out here."

Cody didn't immediately answer. He put his arm around her and pulled her close, but it felt different now. It wasn't about romance, but fear. They sat by the fire for a long while. "We don't have a lot of options out here," Cody finally said. "We can't stay up forever. We'll just have to be vigilant."

"I'm dead tired from all the hiking. My body feels like I've been run over by a herd of something." She reached in her pocket, retrieved two Tylenol, and swallowed them with a swig of water.

Cody fed the fire and brought the hatchet and a four-foot craggy tree limb inside the tent for weapons. They unrolled their sleeping bags, laid them on the ground cover, and inflated their blow-up pillows. After removing their jackets and hats, they decided to sleep in their clothing in case whoever was out there returned.

Brittany, still leery, moved her sleeping bag close to Cody's. Cody opened his Swiss Army Knife and set it beside him. He rested his shoulders on his pack, so he could be ready for whatever.

Now sound asleep, Brittany snuggled against him. *They had almost kissed. That close.* He listened to her deep breathing, drank in the sweetness of her scent, and then leaned over and kissed her gently on the forehead. He gripped the knife. *No one is going to harm her.*

CHAPTER 21

Cody awoke with a start, his hand still clutching his knife. He glanced at Britt quietly snoozing. Everything inside seemed okay. He unzipped the tent flap, grabbed his pack, and slipped out in the daylight careful not to disturb her. After a brief look around in the brushy landscape, he hurriedly changed into clean underwear and socks.

Despite the chill, he didn't make a fire, since they would leave after they ate and broke camp. Instead, he heated water on his butane stove. When Brittany emerged from the tent, he handed her a cup of hot water. She breathed in the fresh air and stretched, her hair freshly brushed and tied back in a ponytail.

"After I got up, I checked things out," he said. "I didn't see footprints or anything else. Just zip. So, I guess we're okay. We can head back down if you're not comfortable continuing."

She wiped sleep from her eyes and yawned. "Continue," she said and dropped instant coffee crystals into the cup. "We've come this far." She sat on the log and stirred her coffee with a plastic spoon. "Maybe it was him?"

"Who him?

"Jim Fallingwater. Maybe he's out there."

Cody sipped coffee. "Seriously?"

Brittany reached into her pack to pull out energy bars, dried apricots, and almonds she'd crammed into little plastic bags for their breakfast. "Maybe," she said between bites, "you should've yelled, 'Jim Fallingwater. It's me, Cody.' I mean, he probably wouldn't recognize you as an adult. Maybe he thinks we're cops."

"Cops?" Cody ripped the wrapper off his energy bar. "What an imagination."

"Or, maybe it was Big Foot."

"Yeah right. With a spotlight. C'mon. Let's get going." He covered the embers of their evening fire with dirt. They washed their faces with cleansing towelettes, used just enough water to brush their teeth, sprayed their clothes with insect repellent, and rubbed the cream version on their faces, necks, and arms.

"Why are you laughing?" Cody asked.

"I was just thinking about Lance, and how he'd die before he'd ever live this way." She applied lip balm.

"Loverboy's not a camper? Not even a Walmart parking lot?"

She rubbed her lips together. "Mr. Perfect only camps in hotels—expensive hotels."

Cody had never met Lance and didn't know what he looked like, but now he had a new name for him—candy-ass. "I camped there one time, at Walmart."

"What?"

"Yeah, it was my senior year. I did it for a research project. One of my first on-site adventures. Studying the culture at Walmart."

"Are you kidding me?"

"Seriously. I got the store's permission to camp in the parking lot. I rented a small camper, ate meals at the store café, and washed up in the restroom. I observed, took notes, recorded what I saw. Got to know the Walmart greeters." He looked at her out of the corner of his eye. She was listening attentively. "Ate a lot of hot dogs."

"Yuk. And your conclusion, Professor." She tucked her lip balm into her pocket.

"I went there with some preconceived notions. Left knowing a lot of good, average folks, just trying to make it. Some characters, too. There was one old guy they called Ozzie. He came there every day with Scooter, his dog. He'd go inside, get a hot dog, come out, sit on a bench in front of the store and feed half of it to Scooter." He mimicked the old man's voice. "'They got a good buy on turlit paper inside. Be sure and have the mac and cheese, sonny. Damn good." He was such a regular, some of the workers there set out a water dish for the dog. Sometimes, they'd bring Ozzie coffee. Before I left, I bought him a big bag of dog food." Cody paused, his voice emotional. "The guy hugged me. Had tears in his eyes." He glanced at Britt. So did she.

"Aw, that was sweet." She turned away as if embarrassed and began rearranging her back pack.

He hadn't meant to stir up emotions, just take a shot at ol' Lance. "You can learn a lot hanging out with average folks. I learned how lucky I was." He couldn't resist a last jab. "Maybe Lance needs to come down to earth and rub elbows with the masses."

She didn't answer. She pursed her lips, zipped up her pack, and announced. "There, I'm ready."

After breaking camp, they hit the trail and walked for two hours into the woodsy silence; then faced one of their many right-left-or-straight-ahead dilemmas. "Let's take a break," Cody said. "We can think better if we're rested." They slipped their packs from their sore shoulders, leaned against a rock, drank water, and ate Snickers bars. Cody whipped out the maps and checked his compass.

Brittany rubbed her arm muscles. "Well, Professor?"

"I think we should go straight." He got up, put down another orange marker. They tramped on, Cody thinking about Jim. "You really have to hand it to Fallingwater, making it out here all those years."

"Yeah, but he knew what he was doing."

"One time when I got scared, he said, 'When you're part of the wild, you don't need to fear it.'"

"Oh no." Brittany wailed.

"What?"

"We need to stop. It feels like I have a blister on my foot." Brittany plopped down on the ground and removed her hiking boot and sock.

Cody immediately pulled the first aid kit from his pack. On long treks, he knew, a foot wound, even a small one, could become serious and end their adventure. Fortunately, it was a small blister on her heel, which he treated with Polysporin. Her foot was dainty and soft, but red in places where it rubbed her boot. He placed a small Band-Aid over the blister, put a bigger one over that, and massaged her foot from the toes to the heel, enjoying the feel of her warm skin. "I hope that does it."

"That felt so good. Maybe I'll let you massage the other one."

He'd love to knead her entire body, but they had to make time. He checked his watch. "You better try walking on this one."

She pulled on her stocking, laced the boot, and walked around as if she were trying on new shoes in the mall. "I hate to start up again, but I guess we have to."

"Is the foot okay?"

"It's not the foot. It's my whole body."

"Yeah mine, too. I'm feeling muscles I didn't know I had. Let's keep going. See if we can get in six miles before lunch."

They moved on, walking until they approached a small, grassy meadow. Brittany pointed to a clump of yellow and blue wildflowers. "Aren't those pretty?"

"Yeah, really. Let's get some shots." Cody snapped several pictures of her standing and then sitting among the blooms, including close-ups as she leaned forward to see if the flowers had fragrance. The sun reflected off her dark hair. A gentle breeze blew wisps that strayed from her ponytail against her face. Her full lips curled into a sensuous smile. He zoomed in on her.

"You need to get in on this, too," she said, getting up. "Let's take a selfie." She grabbed her cell phone from her pack. They both stood together, he pulling her close, relishing the opportunity to hug her. He pressed his sweaty cheek against hers.

"Ready?" She asked.

"Shoot." They smiled into the distance.

"When we get back to civilization," she said, moving away, "I'll send you a copy." She stuffed the phone back into her pack.

They trudged on again, Cody still tingling from their spontaneous hug, taking one rocky and dusty step after another. They didn't talk, they just walked until he abruptly stopped. "Wait. Listen. Do you hear that?"

"Uh-huh. It sounds like running water. Could it be?"

They hurried along the narrow trail until it led them down to a small, clear creek that smelled fresh. A few chickadees sung overhead in the trees.

"Jesus. Water." He felt like Columbus spotting land. Cody plopped down and pulled out his map. The creek wasn't on it, but then it was so small. He looked up, frowning, "You know, I think we must be behind or west of the area where the cave could be."

"If you say so. I sure as heck don't have a clue where we are."

"I remember the spring-fed creek didn't run in front of the cave." He put down some more markers. They continued to follow the creek until they decided to break for lunch.

"We're close. We're damn close. I just feel it." He unloaded his butane stove and boiled water, which he poured into freeze-dried packets of black beans and rice. While waiting for the food to rehydrate, they splashed in the creek, washed their faces, hands and stocked up on water from the spring that bubbled nearby.

Cody checked their food packets and handed one to Brittany.

"This stuff isn't half bad," she said, taking a bite. "We're living high now." After lunch, they gathered their trash and Brittany tucked it into her pack.

"Jeez, I hate to leave this spot. It's so inviting," Cody said, and pointed, "but I think we need to trek in that direction." They packed up and headed out. "Look up there," he yelled after a few minutes with an eager glint in his eye.

Brittany shielded her eyes with her hands. "What? Where should I look?"

"That big boulder and the rocky ledge. That looks familiar. It could be the one Jim used as a marker when he was out tramping around in bad weather." He slipped off his backpack and pulled out the case carrying his portable metal detector. After assembling it, he made a wide sweep of the area. Nothing.

He moved in closer to the ledge. The detector started beeping. He bounced on his feet. "I'm getting a reading," he called excitedly. "That's good news."

"Well, it doesn't look like a cave."

He used his metal detector again. "I still get a reading. It's stronger here. Hear that?"

"So? Now what?"

"The entrance to the cave could be here . . . blocked by all these rocks." He set down the metal detector and started pulling the rocks away. Brittany took off her pack and helped. Cody reached for his hatchet and then the portable shovel. They worked for an hour clearing away rocks and debris. Sweat drenched Cody's shirt.

Brittany wiped drips from her brow. "I'm sure glad we had a good lunch."

"Eureka!" Cody shouted, staring down a dark, deep cavity. He pulled out his flashlight and poked his head in. "This is it!" His heart pounded.

"Let me look." Brittany crouched down and gaped into the black hole. "I can't see much. How can you be sure?"

"I'm going in." He disappeared down into the rocky entrance. He was only gone a few minutes, when he popped back up. "C'mon."

She hesitated. "I don't know. It's pretty dark in there . . . and steep. Are there spiders?"

He motioned for her to follow. "The big rocks inside work like steps. Just follow me."

"What about snakes?"

"There's none of that. Turn on your flashlight. Take it slow." To himself, he muttered, "That I can see."

Brittany eased her way in.

"Easy, easy," Cody said as they descended. At last, they were standing on a damp, cool cave floor. He zoomed his flashlight around. Brittany did likewise. "This is it! This is it! Look, here's the old frying pan." He held up a rusted iron pan. "And look at this. This is what's left of the fire pit."

"You actually recognize this stuff?"

"Oh yeah. Oh yeah." He gripped his flashlight, shining it around the cave. "He left a lot of his tools. There's his lantern."

Brittany's light focused on a dark clump of something she couldn't identify. "I just hate to touch this stuff. It's all grimy and moldy." She coughed. "The air is rank. It smells like a horse barn."

"Well, the cave's been closed . . . for years."

"Do . . . do . . . you see a skeleton . . . like is he dead down here?"

"It appears he left in a hurry. Didn't take much of what he had. And over there, looks like old, rusting canned goods that have seen better days."

"Where'd he get canned goods?"

"I don't know. Probably stole them . . . or maybe that Mo fellow helped him. Jim, or somebody, went to great lengths to cover the entrance to avoid detection."

She wrinkled her nose. "God, I can't get used to the smell."

"Yeah, but when you're living in the middle of it, you don't notice it so much." Cody laughed. "You have too much to do just to stay alive."

Brittany flashed her light up and around. "I hope there aren't any spiders in here. I'll just die if I see a spider."

"That's the least of our worries. Spiders, I mean. Here, hold this." He handed Brittany his flashlight.

"How could anyone survive here?"

"We always had a fire going . . . and the cave entrance was open and much bigger. That made a huge difference. Look, here's the side cave."

"Another cave?"

"Lava flows can make a bizarre network of caves. This was a rare place. I can see why he chose it. Flash light over here."

"Where does that go?"

Cody poked his head into the side cave. "It leads somewhere to the outside. I was never allowed in it, but I know Jim went out that way. He used it to access a latrine, he'd dug somewhere out there."

"Didn't you use it?"

"No, it was cold, snowy. I used a bucket and then he carried the stuff out."

"Gross."

Back in the main cave, Cody picked up some gray-weathered carvings and a walking stick with a carved Indian head. "My God, look here. These are some things Jim carved. And over here. This small bow. It's mine. Jim made it for me. I used it for target practice in the cave."

"Let me see that." She held up the small, stringless and now warped, stick-like bow and flashed her light on it. "So, you remember this? It doesn't look like much."

"Yes. Yes! Holy wow. This is *the* cave." He twirled around. Then he stopped and reached up and felt around a ledge.

"What are you doing?"

"He used to write in a notebook and then store it up here, so I couldn't get to it. Bingo. Feels like a metal box, but it's stuck. I'll have to get my ax. I also need my camera to document this site and the stuff in it. I'll be right back." He grinned. "Don't go away."

"Yeah right. Like where would I go? Don't break your neck on those rocks. I don't want to get stranded down here."

Cody quickly returned, tucked his camera in his pocket, and used his ax blade to loosen the box and pull it free. Trying to open it with his hands failed, because rust had welded it shut. He carefully picked at the lid with his pocketknife until it gave way.

"These are his journals!" he blurted, moving the flashlight on the contents. "Or, at least what's left of them." He cautiously opened the old, brown cover of a spiral-bound notebook. It was very fragile. "I need more light."

Brittany hovered next to him. "Give me your flashlight, too." She pointed both at the notebook. "How's that? Can you read anything?"

"No. The writing is faded. Moisture damage." He ran his finger down a crinkled page. "I better stop. I don't want to ruin these. I'll have to find an archeologist specializing in imaging science to see if there's any way to enhance the readability. These journals might be our best shot at finding out what happened to him."

He set the box down. "I was right, Britt. I wasn't crazy." He picked her up and swung her around. "This is where he lived. This is where I stayed. Proof at last. Proof."

When he set Brittany down again, she almost lost her footing. "Okay, Okay." She laughed, steadying herself by grabbing his arm; then letting go. "Let's come back down to earth."

He wanted to hug her. *Get a grip. She's not yours. She trusts you.*

"You found it. Now what, Professor?"

"We need to cart these things out and then seal the cave entrance before we take off."

She shook her head. "Eeew. We can't take all this stuff."

"Just a few things to evaluate. The journals for sure. We'll probably need to return at some point for more clues." He retrieved the small digital camera from his pocket and took several shots. Afterward, he rolled through the LCD screen to review the photos. "Some of these are dark, but they'll do. I can probably lighten them up and enhance the quality with Photoshop."

Along with the rusted metal box, Cody handpicked a few small animal carvings, which he planned to show to Dr. A, his little bow, and the carved walking stick with the Indian spirit head. He had Brittany go up first. When she reached the outside, he handed her the items.

Once out, he carefully wrapped the metal box in a soiled T-shirt and slipped it in his pack. He protected the small carvings with toilet paper and his dirty socks. It was the best he could do. He fingered the small bow, remembering how Jim patiently taught him to use it and fastened it to his pack. He would carry the walking stick.

Afterward, he and Britt worked at covering the cave entrance with the previously removed rocks and fallen limbs. Cody did not leave any markers close to the cave.

"How's the foot?" Cody asked as they made their way back.

"Not bad, actually, but after all the hiking and lifting those rocks, I'm exhausted."

He checked his watch. It was already late afternoon. "We better find an off-trail camping spot. Keep your eyes peeled for a good one." They followed the orange markers down and set up camp under a clump of pine trees. Cody fired up the butane stove and heated water.

Brittany passed him the hand sanitizer which they carried to conserve water. "Let's celebrate." She pulled out two freeze-dried packets of vegetable lasagna and handed them to Cody to rehydrate. Dessert was the last of the bananas and Snickers bars.

The blue sky quickly darkened. They took turns in the tent, sponging off the trail dust and changing into sleep pants and T-shirts. They hung their sweaty hiking clothes on branches to air out and dry.

Before finally zipping the tent flap, Cody pulled the hatchet from his pack and placed it in easy reach next to his knife, just in case. He also set Jim's walking stick close to his sleeping bag and blocked the tent opening with his pack. That thin piece of nylon covering the tent entrance was the only thing protecting them from whatever lurked in the dark woods.

"It sure feels good to change into different clothes," Brittany said as they relaxed on their sleeping bags, relying on the light of their battery-powered lantern. She rubbed lotion on her feet and arms.

Cody sketched out his own map, noting key areas of the terrain to identify where they'd been.

Brittany yawned. "I'm bushed. All the physical activity and that high carbohydrate meal wiped me out."

When she climbed into her sleeping bag, Cody dimmed the lantern. She quickly drifted off to sleep. He tucked his map away and wrote in his journal, trying to capture every feeling, every detail of his discovery. *Camping out here with some of Jim's things makes him feel so close.* He could picture Wolf, Jim's dog, sacked out by the fire and Jim's big hands whittling a piece of wood into a bear or a deer. He paused to watch Brittany sleep, the swell of her breasts rising and falling with each breath, her soft hair framing her face, so beautiful in her blue T-shirt with little half-moons across the front. None of this would have been possible without her. The thought of her eventually leaving and marrying that big shot candy-ass was painful. It hit hard like a fist to his gut. He retrieved his small sketchbook from his pack.

In the dim light, he quickly penciled Brittany lying peacefully in deep sleep. He stopped when she said, "Hurry. We have to get away."

"Away? I'm just sketch . . ." Then he realized she was talking in her sleep, most likely dreaming about the spotlight incident. Maybe he should wake her, but she shifted her body. Her left hand brushed the side of her face before she drifted off again. The sight of her engagement ring brought him back to reality. He slapped the sketchbook shut, switched off the lamp, and listened for snapping twigs, or the footsteps of predators—animal or human. Finally, his eyes closed.

The next morning, shortly after 5:00 a.m., they pulled on their still damp clothing, swallowed coffee and a breakfast of freeze-dried scrambled eggs. Once they broke camp, they hurried on, retracing their route, facing the challenges of a trail sometimes flat, other times steep, almost always rocky. Just before noon, they reached the pullout, arranging their backpacks and the stuff Cody retrieved from the cave in the back of the Subaru.

"I can't wait to jump into the shower," Brittany said. "We both smell of trail dust and cave. I guess we just stink."

Cody checked under the hood and inspected all four tires. "Looks like we're set to go." He fired up the engine and they pulled out. "I halfway expected the car to disintegrate and to see our ol' friend, Artie Bradshaw, show up again with his tow truck and that smirky grin on his fat face."

Brittany laughed. "Do you really think he had anything to do with our car troubles?"

"Yeah, I do. He always seemed to be so happy to see us stranded. I think he has a crush on you and resents me."

"Maybe. I think I told you that when you disappeared, the other kids blamed Artie because he was such a bully. But then he was just a kid, an unhappy kid. He was overweight. Not good at sports . . . or much of anything. Spoiled by his parents. I don't think he ever had a date in school. Sadly, his marriage failed. And, he never did get out of Forest Lake."

"That was then. This is now. When we get back, I'm going to try and get a sample of his handwriting."

"Really. I don't know. Those notes at the house seem to be directed at both of us."

"Right now, he's my prime suspect. Maybe I'll just get right in his face and flat-out confront him." Cody's thoughts shifted. "Do you want to stop at the Lake Store? We can use the restroom, get some decent coffee, and a sandwich or something."

"Sounds good. Then let's head straight home, so I can jump headfirst into the bathtub and just soak the dirt off my aching body."

They pulled into the gravel parking lot at the store. Once he set the emergency brake, Cody whipped out his iPhone and tapped the keyboard.

"Hey, what are you doing?" Brittany asked.

"I'm texting Dr. A, telling him I found the cave . . . the cave for crying-out-loud. Now, he won't think I'm two quarts low. I can't wait for his response."

Brittany laughed her wonderful laugh. "That's hysterical. I mean, you sending a message to a shrink to prove you're not loony. But think about it, Cody. Really. Oh, not the crazy stuff, but you—the Mazeophobia suffering, anxiety-ridden you—actually came through and found the cave." She placed her palms together and bowed to him. "I'm proud of you."

"Thank you," he said, his face beaming. "I could never have done it without your support. I should be bowing to you."

She looked up, gave his shoulder a playful punch and grinned.

He smiled back. It was hard not to get lost in those dark eyes.

CHAPTER 22

The next morning at Dottie's Café, the inviting aroma of coffee, eggs, and hash browns promised to restore their still-tired bodies. Above the counter, the television beamed an interview with Miley Cyrus on the art of twerking as dialogue scrolled on the marquee beneath. "Ah, civilization." Cody scowled at the screen and directed Brittany to a booth near the window.

Since there wasn't much left in their fridge, they'd decided to grab a bite before shopping for groceries. Most of the breakfast crowd had gone. Toad Holloway and Bobby Blaze sat at the counter. Artie was missing, much to Cody's relief. He had absolutely no desire to hear him flap his pudgy jaws slobbering over Britt.

"Hi kids. Be there in a sec," Patsy called. She tended the cash register for a couple of truckers—one tall, with an olive complexion, graying hair and a short beard; the other stocky with jeans sagging in the rear and a face like a basset hound. They both looked glum.

"You take care, Patsy," the tall one said. "That's all ya can do in times like these." As they walked toward the door, he turned to his friend. "Just shocks the bejesus outta me."

"Yep," said the other. "Yep, there's no safe place no more." He reached in his pants for his cell phone. "I gotta call the wife." The bell on the door jingled as they exited.

Patsy fumbled around the counter, spilling a jar of drinking straws.

Bobby swiveled on the counter stool and shot a glance at their booth. "Where have you two been?" His voice was curt.

"Hiking. Just hiking," Cody said.

"Where at?"

"Oh, out by the Big Bat. Why, were you looking for us?"

Bobby's eyes narrowed. "I thought you came here to do research."

Cody didn't appreciate his abrupt tone. *The guy must've skipped his morning bran flakes.* "Yeah well, you know what they say, all work and—"

"Your mother's been looking for you." Bobby gave Brittany a grim look. "She's mighty worried."

"Worried? What—"

"I can't believe Artie would be doing that," Patsy blurted. "Makes me feel bad for all the ribbin' I gave him."

"Lookit," said Toad, "You never can tell what a guy will do when he's pushed. He was about to lose his house. Not that things were spiffy between him and his ex, but, oh my garsh, his boys woulda been on the street."

Patsy came from behind the counter, stood in front of them, and plunked two cups down hard. "Do you wanna look at the menu?" she asked while pouring coffee.

"No," Brittany said. "I'm going to have the delicious veggie omelet."

"I'll have the same."

Brittany gave Cody a wide smile. "Really?"

"Really." He took a sip of coffee. "With everything." He winked at Brittany. "I'm going all the way."

"Two veggie omelets loaded," Patsy called to Roy.

"What gives?" Brittany asked Patsy. "It seems like a morgue in here."

"Haven't you heard?"

"Heard what?"

"Artie Bradshaw is dead."

"Dead?" She sat up straight and exchanged glances with Cody.

"What happened . . . was he in an accident?" Cody asked.

"Hardly." Patsy swallowed and rubbed the back of her neck with her hand, like she couldn't bring herself to say anymore.

"Apparently," Bobby said, "he was shot."

"Oh my God," Brittany's mouth hung open.

Cody set down his cup. "Whoa."

"Yeah," Bobby continued. "In the head. Up by the Big Bat. We've been waiting for Ken to stop in here to get more info. They said on the news, it coulda been drug related."

Brittany winced. "Drugs? Artie? Our Artie?"

Ray came out from the kitchen. "Oh, his boys, his boys." He threw up his hands. "But you know, there's been someone pushin' drugs to the kids at school. Maybe that was Artie. And that just makes me so goddam mad."

"Artie had some real bitterness in him," Bobby said. "Always lookin' for the next good deal. Gonna get himself outta the garage."

Patsy fiddled with her order book and then tucked it in her pocket. "I know he seemed sorta down the last few times he was in. Like, somethin' was squeezin' him. But I just can't get my head around this."

"And his mother?" Brittany asked. "Is she okay?"

"She's just beside herself," Patsy said, "as you can imagine. Ladies from the church have been over there pretty regular. Course the police have been over there, too."

Bobby slid off the stool and plunked money down on the counter. "I don't need change," he said to Patsy. He turned to Brittany. "You be sure 'n call your mom." He glared at Cody.

CHAPTER 23

After leaving the restaurant, Cody and Brittany made their way to Tillden's Grocery, where Artie's demise was the talk of the day.

Two older men, who usually sat on the long bench in front of the Mercantile and smoked pipes, huddled in the cereal aisle. They each carried red plastic shopping baskets. The one in bibbed overalls reached for a box of All-Bran. "I heard Bradshaw hung out at Benders a lot. Fooling around with some floozy. It's no wonder it come to no good. You need some cereal, Curt?"

"No. No. The wife just wants me to pick up sugar." He checked his list. "And baking powder. Clem over at the garage said Artie was missin' work. You know somethin's wrong when a guy can't show to work."

While Cody felt little affinity for Artie, he never ever expected such a tragic end. For a moment, he pictured Artie alone out in the wilderness surrounded by thugs, scared, confused, pleading for his life maybe. The sadness drained him. His shoulders sagged, stunned that the dark underbelly of a bigger, meaner world had touched quiet, innocent Forest Lake.

He regained his composure and pushed their full grocery cart to the checkout stand where a solidly built woman with rolls of fat under her sweater and a small square pin that said *Mable* worked the cash register. She had blond marcelled hair, penciled eyebrows, and red lips. "The whole town is buzzin'," she said as she scanned Freda Longworth's groceries. "Berny and the two boys was just in here the other day. Feel sorry for them kids to lose their father that way."

Freda, an older woman, no makeup, straight short gray hair, held in place with a bobby pin, handed Mable her coupons. "I don't know what young folks these days see in drugs."

"Yep. Makes you wonder what needs fixin'."

Freda opened her purse and hunted for her checkbook. "They need more of God in their lives. That's what."

Mable rang her bill. "Fifty nine, ninety-nine," she said. Her pudgy finger had short red nails.

Freda slowly wrote her check; then pushed her cart toward the doors.

"What's new with you?" Mabel said, watching Brittany unpack their groceries on the counter. She sized up Cody.

Brittany smiled. "Not much, just trying to replenish the cupboards."

"I hear you're getting' married soon." She glanced at Cody bagging the groceries.

"Uh-huh."

"Nice lookin' fella you got there." Cody politely grinned and hurriedly filled paper bags.

"I see somebody likes peanut butter," she said as a big jar of Adams slid down the counter. She paused when she scanned Brittany's tubs of tofu. "Never did know what people did with this stuff." She held one up. "Looks like rubber to me. You cook this?"

"Sometimes."

"That's eighty-nine dollars and thirty-nine cents." She printed out the bill and handed it to Brittany. "You kids have a nice day."

"I'm so glad to get away from the talking potato chip," Brittany said, as they loaded groceries into the back of the Forester.

"What?"

"Her hair. Mabel's hair looks like one of those ruffled potato chips."

Cody raised his voice to mimic Mabel. "Whad' ya gonna do with all that tofu, honey? Build an Ark?"

Brittany swatted his shoulder. Her wonderful laugh comforted him.

* * *

Once they reached the farmhouse, Cody stopped the car so Brittany could check the mailbox. "Nothing," she said, "Just advertising junk."

He was glad to be away from town, back to where it was peaceful. He drank in the fresh country air. Each carried in a bag of groceries.

Instantly, they knew.

Drawers were pulled out and their contents dumped, cupboards were open, Brittany's laptop was on, pillows were off the couch and scattered.

"Oh my God," Brittany wailed. She set the groceries on the kitchen counter. "Who did this?"

A chill ran up Cody's spine. He remembered the night he spent alone in the house and the noises he'd heard, like someone picking the lock.

Brittany followed Cody as they checked each room. Mattresses were moved off the beds, and the contents of their suitcases dumped on the floor.

"It doesn't appear they snatched anything that belongs to the Humphries," Brittany said when they returned to the living room. "The china and silverware are still here. Nobody touched his big jar of pennies."

She quickly checked the files on her computer. Satisfied her password wasn't breached, she shut it down. "A stranger touching our things. It makes me feel so violated." Brittany's face flushed.

"Dammit." Cody massaged his neck. "The things I brought back from the cave are missing. I set them right over there, next to the sofa."

She threw up her hands. "Why would they take just those things? They aren't worth anything."

Cody didn't answer. He turned and headed for the door to check outside. "I didn't find any threatening notes. No windows are broken," he said when he came back in. "I wonder how they got in."

"Maybe they picked the lock. Heck, the backdoor just uses a skeleton key."

"I checked that door. It's locked." He slapped his forehead. "Yikes, the journals! I put them in the closet in my room." He leaped up the stairs, taking two steps at a time, and came back down carrying the rusted metal box still wrapped in his soiled T-shirt. "They didn't get this. Thank God, I kept it covered."

"They probably thought it was dirty laundry. Shouldn't we report this to the police?"

"We can't. There will be questions about the stuff taken, where we got it, and why we had it."

"Maybe we could omit that part?"

Cody was adamant. "*No police.* What we need to do is head back to Salem so I can hand these journals over to Evan Carlisle, my archeology colleague. Evan's done work with archivists. He may know a paper conservator who could make out what they say. I think these journals are our best chance of finding out what happened to Jim."

They worked at putting the house back in order and shelved the groceries, only stopping briefly for a lunch of cheese, chips, green grapes, and beer. After lunch, they started packing their suitcases, stopping when they heard a knock on the door.

"Now what?" Cody peeked out the window. "Oh, Jesus God! It's Ken Blake."

Brittany opened the door. Cody stood behind her.

Blake took off his hat. "Sorry to bother you. You probably heard about Artie."

"Yes. We did," she said. "And needless to say, we are saddened, not to mention stunned."

"Do you mind if I come in?"

"No. Not at all." She gave him a weak smile.

"Looks like you're packing up?" Cody's suitcase was open on the couch.

"We need to get back to Salem for a while," Cody said. "University business. Then we're coming back."

"Uh-huh. I'm helping Merrill tie up some loose ends, so I need to ask you a few questions." He whipped out his notebook. "As you know, Artie Bradshaw was murdered. They found his body out in the Big Bat Wilderness area."

"Where exactly?" Cody asked.

"Can't say. It's an active crime scene. I understand you were hiking out there."

News travelled fast in Forest Lake. "We were," Cody said, "but we didn't have anything to do with Artie . . ."

"Uh-huh. I'm wondering if you saw anything?"

"No, we—"

"But we camped overnight," Brittany blurted. "And while we were sitting in front of our tent, someone flashed a spotlight on us."

Cody cringed. *Why'd she have to say that?*

Blake, writing in his notepad, stopped and looked up. "And?" He stared at Brittany's engagement ring.

"That's all."

"I said, 'who's there'?" Cody added. "No answer, we—"

"Yeah, we heard someone running away."

"The next morning, I checked around. Nothing." Cody held out his empty hands. "Figured it was some deer poacher."

"We didn't know about Artie until we stopped in at Dottie's for breakfast," Brittany added.

"Where abouts were you?"

"I'm not too sure," Cody lied. "Not . . . uh . . . too far off the main trail."

"Not sure?"

"We were just doing recreational hiking, enjoying the trek, and stopping to take pictures . . . that sort of thing."

"And?"

"We needed something to do," Cody said. "Forest Lake is pretty dead."

Blake looked from one to the other. "Uh-huh, so why didn't you just hike out? Why'd you camp overnight?"

"Well, we weren't in any hurry . . . and we were tired," Brittany said.

"When did you start this . . . hike of yours?"

"We left Monday morning," Cody said.

"And you got back when?"

"Wednesday."

"So, you actually spent two nights in the wilderness. Why two nights?"

Cody's eyes narrowed. "It's summer," he said, irritated. "We're both teachers on break. I used to camp a lot with my dad."

Blake didn't look up. "Uh-huh. Pete. So, how's Pete?"

"He's doing well, still working as a wildlife biologist. They live in Medford."

"Spent some long agonizing days with your dad back in the day."

"So I've heard."

"How is your research going? I mean into the Fallingwater situation."

"Actually, I'm kinda sinking in a dry well. We know his crime was one of passion, that he had a rough childhood, had to deal with discrimination in an all-white community. Yada yada yada."

"I see."

"So, is it true?" Brittany asked.

"Is what true?"

"That Artie was involved in drugs, maybe pushing to kids?"

"I can't say a lot about the details. We're in the middle of an investigation. But, yeah, drugs appear to be involved. He was shot in the head, execution style. That's been in the news."

Brittany folded her arms. She looked sick. "That's just so sad."

"Yeah. Especially when it's a hometown kid. You know? His mother is heartbroken." He paused and swallowed. "I knew Artie, when he was a little kid. I guess I knew all of you when you were kids."

Brittany teared up. She wiped her eyes with her hand. Cody moved closer to her, wrapping his arm around her shoulders.

Blake gave them the once over and then slapped his notebook shut. "If you remember anything else about the incident you described . . . the spotlight . . . or anything that seemed out of the ordinary, give me a call."

"We certainly will," said Cody.

They watched from the window until Blake drove off. "Well, what do you make of that?" Brittany asked.

"If I was out here to do serious research, I could write a helluva paper on how fast news travels in small towns. Other than that, well, we were in the Big Bat Wilderness, so I guess it makes sense that Blake would check us out."

He paused and glanced around the room, his eyes lingering on the spot near the sofa where he had set the items they recovered from the cave. "Something smells. Somebody knows Jim's alive and where he is. Somebody that's here . . ."

Brittany bit her lip. "You're scaring me again."

CHAPTER 24

Back in Salem, Cody awoke to the weight of Crackers snoring on his chest. The lighted dials on the clock showed 6:05 a.m. Cody gently slid Crackers onto the bed. "It's time to get up, partner." He padded into the bathroom before heading to the kitchen to make coffee. It was going to be a good day. Evan had Jim's journals, and he thought he could do something with them. Plus, he seemed happy to have a summer project.

While waiting on the gurgling coffee maker, Cody flipped open his iPad mini to check e-mail. There was a message from Dr. Aanandi. The header said, "Congratulations!" The message was a Joseph Campbell quote:

> *"A bit of advice*
> *Given to a young Native American*
> *At the time of his initiation:*
> *As you go the way of life,*
> *You will see a great chasm. Jump.*
> *It's not as wide as you think."*

"Keep jumping, professor. Looking forward to hearing the details. See you soon, Dr. A."

Cody poured himself a cup of coffee. Crackers leaped up on the counter. "No Fritos today, so you might as well get down from there. Go see Anne."

Crackers ignored his suggestion and started batting the holder strap on Cody's small Nikon digital camera. "Knock it off before you break something." Crackers' paw kept it up. Cody reached for the camera. Crackers grabbed the strap in his mouth and took off.

"Whoa. Come back here, you little shit." Crackers dashed into the bedroom, out the open window, onto the porch roof, and down the trellis.

"Damn it." Cody, still in pajama bottoms and T-shirt, rushed down the stairs and outside to the front yard, just in time to see Crackers sprint up the large oak tree in the front yard, his mouth gripping the camera strap. Besides dozens of pictures of their trek, the camera had shots of Britt, things inside the cave, and the cave entrance.

"Godammit, Crackers. Get down here. You drop that and you're toast." He tried to spot the cat in the tree. He thought of going back inside to get treats. Instead, he moved toward his Subaru, which he'd parked on the street, so Anne's bridge players could use her driveway. Maybe he could jump up on the car roof and coax Crackers down.

"No, no. Professor!"

Cody turned to see Omar leap off his bike and run toward him.

"Don't go there!" he screamed. He crashed into Cody with his small body, causing Cody to take several steps backward. They both fell to the ground behind the thick tree trunk.

Crackers, startled by Omar's yelling, meowed and hurried off. The camera sailed down hitting the car's hood. The car exploded in a ball of flames, making a blast so loud it shook nearby houses and could be heard several blocks away.

Cody could hardly speak. He coughed, trying to clear his throat. Dust and a strong pungent odor filled the air. "What happened?" He untangled himself from Omar. "Are you okay?"

Omar didn't answer. Cody sat him up. "Omar?"

The boy rubbed his ears. "I can hardly hear you," he said weakly. He reached for Cody and clung to him.

Anne came running out in her bathrobe. "Oh my God!" she shrieked. The explosion shattered the front windows and the garage door was askew.

Several patrol cars with flashing lights appeared out of nowhere. An ambulance pulled in behind them. Three EMTs ran toward Cody and Omar.

Cody rubbed his right temple. "We're all right . . . I think. I just bumped my head on something." His ears were ringing.

Anne knelt beside them. She grabbed Omar, pulling him close to her chest. "Does anything hurt? Are you sure?" she kept asking.

"Let's just check you over to be certain," an EMT said. Neighbors streamed into the street and huddled in groups pointing. Shrapnel studded the tree trunk. Some of the bark had blown off. Branches littered the ground.

A police officer approached the EMTs. "Anybody hurt?"

"I think we're okay, but we'll need to transport them to make sure." Another EMT rolled out a stretcher. A second ambulance arrived.

Anne held her head. "My dear God!"

"What exactly happened here?" the officer asked.

"I saw someone messing with the car," Omar blurted. He looked at Cody. "I am coming to tell you. This man is bad. I don't know his name, but he is on the street. Selling drugs. Swearing at me. I saw him put something in the car. Under the hood." His eyes were big. Tears streaked his face.

"And what are you doing out this early?" the officer asked.

"I am coming to pull weeds in Miss Anne's garden. Before it gets hot."

Anne put her arm around Omar. "He does that," she assured the officer. "Then we have breakfast and discuss his reading."

Cody held an ice pack on his temple. "Where's Crackers? He was in the tree . . ."

"Oh, lord." Anne's hands flew up. "I'll look in the back."

While the police officer continued to talk with Cody and Omar, a *Statesman Journal* reporter and photographer showed up. The photographer, using a wide-angle lens, shot pictures of the sorry car and the house. The reporter headed toward Cody, but another officer kept him away, so he talked with the bystanders.

Anne came out carrying Crackers, his green eyes wide and wild. "He's still shaking. I found him in your apartment, hiding under the bed. I'm just so glad he's not hurt." She set him down. He immediately scampered away. Anne looked at the officer. "Cats have nine lives," she said. "Now, he's down to eight."

* * *

Emergency room doctors at Salem Hospital examined the two and then released them. Omar was shaken but had no injuries and Cody, also dazed, had a hefty bruise above his right temple.

After Cody spoke with Brittany by phone and assured her he and Omar were okay, she contacted the boy's parents and drove a distraught Mrs. Ramirez to the hospital to be with her son. Once they were released, she took Omar and his mom home and then drove Cody to his mother's condo in Portland to spend the night.

Cody's head hurt; his mind was reeling.

Brittany gave him a long hug and kissed his cheek. "We'll talk later," she said, as she prepared to leave. "I'm so grateful you're not injured." She paused. Her hand reached up and touched his lips. "Be. Very. Careful."

Cody grabbed her hand and kissed her fingers. "Maybe you should stay here. Don't go back alone." He didn't want to release her, but Brittany insisted she needed to touch base with Lupe and Banjo's supporters to learn if they found the dog.

* * *

The next day, Dr. Aanandi telephoned Cody to offer assistance, as did the Willamette University President, Luci Maxwell, his department head, and numerous colleagues. Cody assured all of them he was physically okay, but still shaken.

Not wanting repair people at the scene until the investigation was complete, the police boarded up Anne's front windows

Yellow crime-scene tape cordoned off the neighborhood while an army of federal and local investigators combed the site, gathering bits of evidence strewn near the house.

"You're lucky you ended up behind that tree," said Walter Sloan, the detective interviewing Cody, several days later, outside on Anne's patio. "We've pulled a ton of shrapnel from it."

"Yeah, every time I go out there, I bow to it." He fingered the bruise on his forehead.

"Our bomb unit and federal agents have determined it was some kind of improvised explosive device with a motion sensor. Probably designed to hurt you, but not cause a lot of structural damage to the neighborhood. None of the other homes or nearby vehicles were damaged much, just some broken glass. We had no reports of additional injuries. Just some lady down the street whose favorite teapot got blown off a shelf or something." He grinned.

"You have to unlock the hood of the car from inside. My car was locked."

"You'd be surprised how easy it is to spring a car door. These guys know all the tricks."

"Could a camera hitting a car set off a bomb?"

"Yep. It could. And the cat dropped it from up in the tree, so it hit with some force. The bomb would have gone off the minute you opened the door."

"I don't suppose your team recovered the camera?"

Sloan's eyes turned flinty. "I imagine the camera is in a jillion pieces. Probably floated in the air and landed at the Capitol." He paused, then leaned forward, his eyes level. "Tell me Mr. Benson, you got any enemies?"

CHAPTER 25

Grabbing his morning joe at Starbucks with Britt made Cody's life feel normal again. He sat facing the windows. The street outside was wet from a brief but badly needed summer rain. He watched a mother crossing the street with her skipping toddler and an older man with a beautiful fluffy poodle out for their regular morning walk. Life. Little everyday things. Things he wouldn't be watching now if he'd reached his car.

His hands shook at the thought, causing him to spill some coffee on the table. Soon summer would be over, and he had so much yet to do, but he lacked energy. And, he was always looking over his shoulder, suspicious of anyone who followed too closely or seemed to be staring. Then there was that nagging feeling about the decision he'd have to make in a few weeks about Colombia. His throat tightened. He dabbed his spill with his napkin and forced another swallow of black coffee.

"You're still on the front page," Brittany said.

"What?"

"In the newspaper. Listen to this." She read aloud from the *Statesman Journal.*

> *. . . Salem Police Detective Walter Sloan said someone planted a bomb in the car but declined to discuss its design or how it was detonated. "We don't know yet if Mr. Benson was the intended target or if this was a case of mistaken identity or an act of terrorism. The Oregon State Police Explosives Unit, the*

177

*FBI and its Bureau of Alcohol, Tobacco, Firearms and Explosives
are still investigating. At this point, we have no suspects."*

*Cara Branson, who lives in the Chemeketa Historic District,
said everyone was on edge. "The police aren't saying much,
but every day we see that van parked out there. The one that has
'Crime Scene Investigation' in big letters on its side. We're all
flabbergasted. Things like that don't happen here."*

"They sure are being tightlipped about the whole thing." She sipped
her vanilla latte, folded the newspaper, and set it down. "How is Omar
doing? They don't mention him in the article."

"Omar is a minor. Police don't want it known that there was a
witness."

"Can he identify the guy?"

He lowered his voice. "His description is sketchy. Heavy set.
Hispanic. Unshaven. He believes it was the same man that's been pushing
drugs on the street. Emilio. He said he saw him look around, fiddle with
the door, put something under the hood of my car, and run off. That's
all I know. The police are concerned about Omar's safety."

"He was the hero in all this. Too bad he can't come forward and
take a bow."

Cody touched the yellowing bruise on his forehead. "That kid
saved my life." He rubbed his eye with his finger. "I bought him a
brand new road bike with yellow wheels and handlebars."

"I hope it came with a helmet."

"Oh yeah, and a great bike lock, but right now it's parked in his
living room because the police want him to stay off the streets for a
while. Anne picks him up and takes him home. When this is all over,
we can have a big celebration honoring him."

"Who do *you* think did this?"

"You sound just like Mom. She's been calling every day to check
in, even called Detective Sloan using her lawyerly skills."

"Well?"

"She didn't find out any more than I know. I can't believe the
bomb was really intended for me. Detective Sloan wanted to know if
I had any run-ins with former students."

"And?"

"No. I can't think of a single one. We had a great year."

"Well, I think it's linked to Jim."

He looked at her as if she just sprouted two heads. "Why would it? Salem is miles away from Forest Lake. Why would anybody *here* care about me finding an old Indian? Jim's got to be in his sixties. It just doesn't compute."

She narrowed her eyes. "Think about it. Jim's the only one that's got something to lose if he's found. Jail time. Death row, possibly."

Cody waved her away. "C'mon. That's not the Jim I remember."

She gave him a level look. "Emphasis on *remember.*"

"Sloan thinks it's a case of mistaken identity. Maybe some drug deal gone bad."

She slumped her shoulders and sighed. "Well, now what?"

"I guess we head back to Forest Lake. I've got a loaner car until the insurance payment comes through. It's another Subaru Forester, but a bigger car with a lot of fancy do-dads. I'm a minimalist. I don't need a sun roof and all that crap. And, I bought a new camera. I lost all the shots of our trek."

"I still have some on my cell phone."

"Yeah, but you don't have the detailed shots of the cave entrance and the stuff inside," he said, his voice raising. "All of that is lost."

She didn't respond. After an uncomfortable lull in the conversation, Cody broke the silence. "A work crew replaced Anne's damaged windows. The cops took a bunch of shrapnel out of the front of the house and the garage. A vet examined Crackers. He's fine, but he's gun shy, been sticking close to Anne, and is leery about venturing outside."

"Oh, that poor baby. He saved your life, too."

"I'm giving him extra treats, but that doesn't stop him from stealing my Fritos. That's a good sign."

"Yay." She shook a victorious fist in the air. "Oh, that's my phone." She fished it from her purse and checked the screen. Her face lit up. "It's Lance."

Cody took a nervous sip of coffee. One phone call and ol' Lance siphoned Britt away from him.

"Hi sweetie," Brittany cooed into the phone. "I miss you, too." She glanced at Cody; then turned away. "Well nothing. I'm just sitting here having coffee with a friend. Well, yeah. I'm still working with Professor Benson from Willamette. Yeah, the research in Forest Lake."

Professor Benson? Jeez. He felt like an abandoned child.

"What's the matter? Remember, I told you—You are? That's wonderful! I'll see you in a few days then. Lots to tell you. I love you, too."

Her eyes smiled at Cody. "Lance is in Chicago. He's coming home."

* * *

Brittany left to run errands, so Cody headed toward the Willamette University campus. Walking helped him clear his head. He crossed the small bridge over the millrace and stood for a moment watching the ducks swimming and quacking. Was Lance really in Chicago or in his neighborhood planting a bomb? He'd always hoped Lance would get stuck in Asia. Forever.

Since the college didn't offer a summer semester, the campus was quiet. He needed quiet. After crossing the quad, he headed to his office in Eaton Hall where there wasn't much to do, except check his mailbox. Luci had sent more information on Colombia. He tossed it aside and called Evan Carlisle, his archeology friend.

Minutes later, he entered Collins Science Center. Evan's door was open. As soon as he saw Cody, he sprang to his feet and offered his hand. "So good to see you, man." He was tall, in his late thirties, with dark hair, graying beard and frameless glasses. After a few pleasantries and a discussion on the latest news about the bomb, they talked about Jim's journals.

"This stuff is in pretty sorry shape. Needless to say, most of the pages are moisture damaged and probably ruined beyond repair, but I was able to decipher pieces of it." Evan handed Cody several sheets of paper. "Here's a copy of a preliminary transcript of what I've found out so far."

Evan scanned his own copy. "From what I can tell most of the stuff is about nature, chores, weather. It appears he had a dog or some kinda pet. Also, something in here about a kid . . . maybe he had a son?"

Cody looked down. Evan didn't know about his past.

"There's a part about some woman named Chris or Chrissy. No last name. Says something to the effect that she was going to marry someone. Can't make out the who. Then, it says 'if only she hadn't said that.' Can't make out what. You can read all that on your own in the transcript."

"I don't suppose it said anything about his future plans?"

"Nope. Just about day-to-day stuff in incomplete sentences. He cut wood. He killed a deer. What were you hoping to learn?"

"Oh, I guess who the diaries belonged to. Where he might be. Uh, so I can return them."

Evan stroked his beard. "So far, this Chrissy is the only name I uncovered. I guess that's not very helpful. I can send them down to Steve Biggs, an imaging scientist and paper conservator in California. He probably could use ultraviolet illumination or some chemical process to increase the contrast of the ink, but thought I'd check with you first to see if you want to go through the time and expense. He might be able to decipher more, but just offhand, I'd say this is some guy writing mundane stuff."

Cody perused the papers, thinking. After a moment, he said, "Yeah, let's do it. That whole process that Biggs would be using to make the text more visible could be documented and used as a teaching tool for my students."

"Okay, then."

"Have Biggs look for names, especially full names."

CHAPTER 26

At his mother's insistence, Cody had dinner with her in her classy condo in Portland's Pearl District. Cally Benson, a family matters lawyer, was a young looking fifty-three with shoulder-length brown hair styled in a blunt cut and a few crinkle lines around her eyes.

She greeted Cody with a warm hug. "I've been worried sick about you." She wore black slacks and a red-fitted over blouse, which showed off her trim figure that she kept fit with yoga and workouts at the neighborhood gym. "I'm so glad you're here."

Dinner was Cody's favorite—linguini, green salad and crusty bread with olive oil and balsamic vinegar. Cody poured the Merlot.

"You seem a little down," she said.

"Wouldn't you be if you nearly got blown to bits?" He didn't want to mention that the major source of his angst was the fact that Lance, Lance, Lance would soon be back in the picture.

"I called the Salem Police Department." She dished linguini onto a plate which she passed to Cody.

"Again?"

"A lawyer in our firm has a contact down there, but it didn't produce a heck of a lot. Still don't know any more than you do. Mistaken identity is all I get from them."

"Yeah, I can't believe the bomb was meant for me. It makes no sense."

She passed the salad. "Be careful and *aware.* If you see something that makes you uncomfortable, report it. How are you coming with the Mazeophobia? Still seeing Dr. A?"

"Yeah. He thinks I'm making progress. I was until this happened." He looked over her head at the painting of stone columns supporting a lovely floral arch.

She gave him a skeptical look. "You know, if you ever get lost, just shoot a picture with your cell phone and send it to me. You know I'll come running."

"Mom, I'm not a little boy anymore." He twirled strands of pasta around his fork.

"I know, but a mother can't stop worrying." She leaned forward, her eyes level. "I was surprised to see Brittany Bolin. I didn't realize you two reconnected until she dropped you off last week."

Why doesn't she back off? "This is a really swell dinner, Mom." He sipped wine. That didn't stop her.

"I mean, I'm flabbergasted you didn't mention that you two reconnected. Brittany Bolin from Forest Lake. She's blossomed into a beautiful woman . . . don't you think?" Her eyes searched his face.

Cody blushed. "Now Mom, don't be getting any ideas. Britt is engaged." He drank more wine.

"Oh." Her face dropped. "She seemed really concerned about you. Is she planning on getting married soon?"

"I don't think they've set a date." *Gad, why doesn't she quit probing? It's the lawyer in her, that's why. And how would she like it if I delved into her relationship with Wyatt what's his face, that medical malpractice lawyer she's dating?*

"Well, you know in relationships, things can change." She reached for a slice of bread and dipped it in olive oil.

"Mom, did you see the big rock Britt wears on her finger?" He swallowed more wine.

"Well no, actually I didn't notice." She bit into the bread and chewed. "I was so concerned about you. You know, Cody, a solid relationship could be just the thing to help you with your anxiety."

She sounded like the good doctor. "Britt's fiancé is big-time rich . . . a lawyer . . . has a high-level position with a timber export company in Portland." The wine was making him mellow. "She's not going to tie her can to some college professor interested in the barter economy of indigenous people."

Cally's eyebrow rose. "Speaking of which, have you talked anymore with your department head about the Colombia offer?"

It sounded like she was asking if he finished his homework. "They've given me the summer to think about it."

"Summer's almost over, honey."

"And, I'm just not all that comfortable with it yet."

"Oh, Cody. Don't let some inner fear make you avoid a challenging assignment. Have you discussed that with Dr. A? You need to get beyond that, conquer it, so you can advance in your career."

He wanted the conversation off him. "Mom, do you remember the story about Jim Fallingwater from Forest Lake?"

It did the trick.

Her eyes widened. "Just that he killed a young woman, and her mother never got over it. What was the mother's name?" She tapped the side of her face with her index finger. "Myra, that was it. Myra Jenkins. She went crazy and died in a rest home. I actually talked with Myra when you went missing. Scary woman. Why?"

"Fallingwater was Native American. I'm doing some research on the Modoc tribe. I'm trying to use the Fallingwater case as an introduction and then bridge over to American Indians today."

She reached for the wine bottle and refilled her glass. "Hmmm. I think it was a relationship gone bad. Happens all the time, not just to a minority group. Our firm has a case right now of a young man who shot his wife in the head because he thought she was having an affair."

It was his chance to lecture. "There are more than a million Indians in the United States, and they are still trying to adjust to modern civilization. Some are very successful, some barely making it. I want to present a paper to the anthropology society on how Native Americans can or do assimilate and still hang onto their unique cultural heritage."

She sighed and rubbed her temple. "I guess the casinos in Oregon are doing quite well."

"Jeez, Mom."

"What does Fallingwater have to do with your general thesis?"

"Sociocultural anthropology. Assimilation in small towns. The Fallingwater case is a colorful one. I mean love affair, murder, escape . . . what turned Fallingwater into a killer and could he have gotten a fair trial? It's an intriguing springboard."

"As I recall, all that happened was that he froze to death."

Cody leaned forward. "Don't you see? Fallingwater didn't fit in, his family was dysfunctional, and there wasn't a Native American community in Forest Lake. It led to disaster."

"I guess. I know the Jenkins didn't approve of their daughter having a relationship with an Indian and as far as they were concerned, rape was the motive."

The alcohol loosened his lips. "I've been making trips to Forest Lake, talking with folks. Britt has been helping me." As soon as he said it, he wished he hadn't.

She set down her wineglass. "What? You've been spending time in Forest Lake? You and Brittany?"

"Yeah. Doing research. Mom, if Fallingwater was recaptured, what do you think would have happened to him?" Now he was probing.

She placed her elbows on the table. "He definitely would have had to do prison time. There were a lot of ugly racial feelings back then about what he'd done. I think the parents and others thought it was premeditated. He may have gotten the death penalty."

"And what would happen if he were found alive today?"

"Well, he'd still have to face charges. There's no statute of limitations for murder. He could get twenty-five years, which considering how old he'd probably be, that would be a life sentence."

"What if he did something good, like saved a life?"

"He'd still have to be accountable for what he did."

"It wouldn't matter?"

"The law is what it is." She pushed a wisp of hair behind her ear. "Why don't you spend more time thinking about that offer the university made for the Colombia research? Sounds like a great opportunity and right up your alley."

"Mom . . ."

"Think about it. If you took that assignment and succeeded, and I have all the confidence that you would, it might help end the anxiety you feel about getting lost and abducted." She pursed her lips. "I wouldn't waste my time on anything that happened years ago in Forest Lake."

CHAPTER 27

Back in Salem, Cody lay in bed, wide-awake trying to read an article on culturally significant Native American artifacts. He thought about the conversation over dinner with his mother and what she'd said, especially about Jim and how he'd end up doing prison time.

He'd always been close to his mother, but he'd never been able to tell her what actually happened when he went missing. All the child psychiatrists who examined him had convinced her that he was suffering from dissociation. Busy finishing her own schooling so she could support them, she proceeded cautiously and never really asked. He rubbed his eyes. He could hear cars going by on the street and smell the sweet fragrance of Anne's moonflower vines.

Once his mother left Forest Lake, "that cultural cesspool," as she called it, she'd never returned, and she always claimed that if they'd lived anyplace else, his disappearance would never have happened.

How could he have told her that he lied to save a murderer . . . that he liked and admired this man . . . that he saved his life . . . that he did more to boost his esteem than his own father ever did. He really didn't lie, did he? He just couldn't believe Jim would ever do anything wrong . . . and he was a kid. Just a kid.

He heard scratching at his door and the familiar "meow." He got up to let Crackers in. Still leery about being outside, whining at the door was his new mode of gaining entrance into Cody's apartment. The gray cat arched his back and walked past him as if to say, "What kept you?"

"Come on, Crackers. I have something for you." Cody reached into the cupboard and produced three tiny tuna treats, which Crackers gobbled up. He rubbed against Cody's legs and followed him into his bedroom. He hopped on the sill next to the open window, but didn't go out. Instead, he jumped down and onto the bed, kneading a spot next to Cody, his claws pulling up threads from the comforter. Cody stroked his back. "You're lucky I got that at Save-Mart." Soon Crackers was purring a calming sound.

"If Lance comes back, Britt won't want to continue," he said to the cat who, dead to the world, merely swished his tail. "She'll be planning her wedding. I need to get back to the cave for more information . . . take more pictures. Maybe pick up a clue as to where Jim could be. I hope the stakes I put down are still there. Why wouldn't they be? What if someone removed them?" Crackers curled into a ball.

"Oh God, I feel the panic coming on. I can't do this without her. What was I thinking? She's engaged." Crackers, most likely dreaming about chasing squirrels, snored. "You have such an easy life. Wish I was a cat." He took a drink of water from the glass on his nightstand, but it didn't help, so he got up and meandered into the bathroom to look for the bottle of tiny white anxiety pills Dr. Aanandi prescribed.

After downing a lone tablet, he climbed back into bed to wait for it to kick in. The bedside clock said 10:08 p.m. He picked up his journal but couldn't concentrate. His cell phone played the classical strains of *The Swan.* He sighed through his nose. *Now what?* Britt's number flashed across his caller ID. He instantly perked up. "Hi. I was just thinking about you. What's the matter? You're out front? Why are you crying? Wait, I'll let you in." He rushed down the stairs and opened the door to find Brittany pacing on the porch.

Brittany wiped her wet face on her sleeve. She was dressed in jeans and a navy blue hoodie. Her hair hung loose around her shoulders. She looked scared. "It's Lance."

"Just a second, let's go to my apartment. I mean, I'm out here in my pajamas." He put his arm around her and hurriedly led her up the stairs. "Do you want some coffee? I can make coffee."

"No," she sniffed. "Lance found the dog. He's going to—"

"What dog?" Cody pulled tissues from the box on the counter and handed them to her.

"Banjo." More tears trickled down her cheeks.

"He found Banjo!" He knocked the box onto the floor. "Are you kidding me?"

"At Mother's house. He went there looking for me. He thought I was in Forest Lake." She sniffed.

"He found Banjo at your mother's house?"

"He said he's going to take care of him. So it doesn't come out."

He shook his head. "You're not making sense."

She stamped her foot. Her voice rose. "I stole Banjo. He's at mother's house."

"What! You, you kidnapped that dog?"

"Exactly. Mother didn't know."

"Well, how did Lance—"

"He knew about Banjo and the hearings. My involvement. Remember, he helped get Representative Janes to vouch for the dog. And I confessed. I thought Lance would be on my side."

"Okay, slow down. I think I'm following this." He rubbed his head. "Actually, I'm not."

"I stole Banjo. I had to. He was wasting away. He would've died. I took him to Mother's house and told her he belonged to a friend who was going through a messy divorce. I asked her to care for him for a while. Mother never reads the newspapers. I thought he'd be safe in Forest Lake. I mean, who goes to Forest Lake?" She ran her hand through her hair, her face contorted like she just stepped barefoot into a nest of spiders.

"Do you want some water? Something to help you calm down. One of my pills?"

"No." She stamped her foot again. "We need to *save* Banjo. Lance said he was going to have someone take care of the dog, so this never comes out. He said Janes would look like a fool because he went out on a limb and defended a dog that his top aide's fiancé stole and lied about."

"Oh God." He slapped his forehead.

"He's going to have Banjo destroyed."

"What?"

"He said polls show Janes could be in a tight race. They can't chance a ripple. He said dog stories could blow up to be a big thing, like when Mitt Romney traveled with his dog in a crate on top of his car."

"Mitt Romney. Shit. Does your mother know?"

"Idiot."

"Your mother?"

"No, Romney."

"I mean about the dog? Does your mother know it's Banjo?"

"No, she doesn't"

"And . . . that there's some guy coming down there?"

"Oh, I don't know. I threw it at him."

"Threw what?"

"My engagement ring. I threw it at Lance. I won't let him kill Banjo."

"So . . . you're no longer . . ." For a brief moment Cody heard a violin playing the romantic *Pur ti Miro* in his head. Then he looked at Britt's tormented face. It brought him back to reality.

"Lance said, 'It's *just* a dog. You'll get over it.'" She cried. "He thinks this will pass, but it won't. I love Banjo."

"Okay, okay."

"It won't. It won't." She was crying again. "Just a dog. Just an animal. Well, that's all we are, too. Animals. Only we're too stupid to know it."

"Let me think. How much time—"

"He's sending someone out there tomorrow . . . I think." She held her face in her hands. "Actually, I can't think."

"We need to get there. Fast. Let me get dressed and grab a few things. If we drive all night, we should make it. Don't worry." He pulled her close and hugged her. Her hair was soft against his chin. "We'll get Banjo . . . and we'll do something. Maybe you should call your mother."

"No!" She pulled away. "She'll just side with Lance."

"Then we'll figure something out." He ran to his bedroom, pulled on jeans and a sweatshirt, hurriedly stuffed his duffel bag, and dashed out the door with Brittany. "Wait!" He ran back in and let Crackers out of his apartment. "Sorry fellow."

Cody ran down the stairs and jumped into the car. "It could take about six hours to get there."

"Bobby," she blurted. "We'll call Bobby. He's always been good to me. He helped pay for my college education. He's the only one there I can trust."

Cody tightened his grip on the wheel. He was getting in deeper. Now he was an accomplice to stealing an already stolen dog. What if they both got caught? What would Detective Sloan think . . . or Luci Maxwell . . . or the president of Willamette University? But Britt, oh Britt, he'd do anything for Britt.

* * *

They arrived at Britt's darkened house outside Forest Lake around 4 a.m. Cody killed the headlights and stayed in the car. He held his breath as Brittany pulled the hoodie over her head, carefully unlocked the door, and slipped inside. Seconds later, she emerged pulling the big German shepherd by the collar.

"Here we go." She pushed Banjo into the back seat.

His musky smell filled the car. Cody could hear him breathing. He missed having a dog.

"Wait a minute. I'll be back." She dashed into the house again.

While Cody waited, he visualized the headlines. Professor targeted in car bomb plot caught with a stolen dog while driving a loaner car from a local dealership. With a sunroof.

Banjo barked. Cody jerked to attention. "Shhh," he said. "Calm down, boy." He reached into the back seat and patted his head. "Lay down or something."

Brittany came running, jumped into the front seat. "Okay, now we need to get to Bobby's. Fast!"

She directed Cody down a dark, winding country road. Banjo's head poked between the seats. He gave Brittany a sloppy wet kiss.

"Shouldn't he be wearing a disguise or something?" Cody asked. "He's on the lam."

Brittany laughed. "Don't worry fella. We're not going to let anyone hurt you."

Eventually, they came to a gravel driveway. "Turn right there," Brittany said. Soon, they parked in front of Bobby's house. Brittany pulled out her cell phone, punched in numbers, and waited.

Cody watched her face. *What if Bobby wasn't in there? What would they do with the dog?*

"Bobby, this is Brittany Bolin. We're out here parked in your driveway. I need your help."

In seconds, a light flashed on. The front door opened and there stood Bobby, bleary-eyed in his plaid, faded bathrobe, thick hairy legs sticking out beneath, feet in worn bed slippers. His long salt and pepper hair hung loose around the shoulders. "What's going on?"

Brittany spilled the whole sordid story. Cody tried to fill in the gaps.

Bobby seemed confused. "Wait, wait. You're both talkin' at once. You better come in."

Brittany let Banjo out. He lifted his leg and peed on a bush, and then the three of them followed Bobby inside.

"I had to save him. I just had to. It was the right thing to do." She patted Banjo whose tail made an earnest show of appreciation. "Just look at his sweet face."

Bobby's house was small. An easy chair served as his convenient closet with jeans and sweat shirts piled over one arm. Newspapers were scattered on the floor beside the couch. Several months' worth of metal sculpture magazines covered the coffee table, along with a few stray tools and empty coffee cups. A bulky television stood in the corner accompanied by a pair of well-worn work books.

It took Bobby a while to catch up. He scratched his head, staring at Banjo who was inspecting his cluttered living room. "I dunno . . . a stolen dog? And, the cops, they're lookin' for him?"

Brittany's dark eyes pleaded. "You've always helped me."

"Yeah," he said, "like you were my own daughter." He turned to Cody. "What've you got to say about this?"

Cody's body straightened. "Banjo deserves a chance. I'm in his corner."

"Good, so keep your mouth shut. I'll take the dog and hide him, but not here."

"Somewhere safe?" Cody asked, seeking assurance.

"I'm gonna try and get him to the Modoc reservation in Oklahoma."

Cody glanced at Brittany. "That far?"

"Look, he needs to get out of this state. He's . . . well . . . a hot dog." Bobby couldn't help but smile.

"A reservation?" Brittany's hand massaged her temple, an uncertain look on her face. "They won't hurt him?"

"Oh, God no. They'll love him to death. No one will ever look there. I have a contact that can help. No, leave the dog with me. Don't worry. Go back to your farmhouse. Claim you know nothing." He thought for a moment. "What about your mother? She's gonna wake up and find the dog gone."

"I opened a window and loosened the screen, so it would look like someone broke in."

Bobby groaned. "Christ. Now, we're into burglary."

Cody's eyes widened. "God, you're some tough broad."

"We've got to hurry." Bobby scribbled on a piece of paper and handed it to Brittany. "I don't have a cell phone, so I wrote down where I'll be and the number for Clint, my friend in Tule Lake. If you need to get ahold of me, say you're callin' about the sculpture I made or somethin' like that. I'll let you know when Banjo is safely on his way. I'll just give you a call and say 'mission accomplished.'"

Brittany stuffed the note in her pocket. She bent down, put her arms around Banjo, and kissed him on the cheek. "Sorry for all this, boy, but it's the best I could do. Be brave. Be brave for me." She gently stroked his head. "You're my boy. You'll always be my boy." Banjo whimpered like he understood and licked her fingers. "Everything is going to be all right," she whispered.

"Don't worry," Bobby said. "He's gonna be fine. I don't suppose you brought his food."

Brittany blinked tears. "No, I had to get out of there fast."

"I'll get some on the way," he assured her. "Now, you need to leave so I can hit the road."

Cody steered Brittany toward the door. She looked over her shoulder for one last look.

Bobby followed them. "Tell no one."

<h1 style="text-align:center">CHAPTER 28</h1>

The sun was coming up as they reached the farmhouse, shining its golden rays on the white, dry August grass. It was going to be another beautiful, but warm day. Brittany went into the bathroom, washed her face, combed her hair, and applied makeup. Afterward, she made coffee, while Cody toasted open-faced cheese sandwiches under the broiler for a quick breakfast. She filled two mugs, brought the food to the table, then leaned over and gave Cody a big kiss on the cheek. "Thank you. Thank you so much for helping me save Banjo."

His whole body tingled. His face flushed. She smelled like lilacs. "I'm glad I could help." He started to rise, intending to kiss her back, but it was too late. She bit into her sandwich and her mouth was full. He eased back into his chair.

She took a careful swallow of coffee. "I made it strong because we need to be on our toes. Mother will be waking soon."

Cody tipped his cup, taking two quick gulps. The bitter coffee hit the back of his throat, causing him to grimace and cough. "Jeez, it tastes like tobacco."

"Sorry," she said. "I thought it would help."

The landline in the house rang.

"Don't answer it," she cautioned. "I gave Bobby my cell number."

He dabbed his mouth with a paper napkin. "This is like waiting for the Governor to call with a reprieve."

Minutes later, her cell phone played a melodious ringtone. "Shoot. It's Mother." She winced.

"Calm down, Mother. What?" She paced while she talked. "Someone broke into the house." She winked at Cody. "They came in through a window? Are you kidding? Sure. Sure. What? The dog is missing? I'll be right there. See you in a bit." She clicked off the phone and looked at Cody. "Okay, I'm on."

* * *

Sue Bolin, her face distraught, was still in her pink rose-sprigged nightgown. Her gray hair needed a comb. "Someone came through the window. Look, it's wide open."

"Maybe you left it open and forgot. The evenings have been so warm," Brittany said.

"No, I didn't." She pointed with a shaky finger. "See, the screen is off. I didn't want to touch nothing. There might be fingerprints."

"Did you see anyone?" Brittany asked innocently.

"No. I came down to the kitchen to let the dog out, and he was gone. Just gone. I looked everywhere . . . even outside. I called and called. He didn't come. I didn't even hear anything." Her hands clutched her temple. "Oh dear, oh dear."

"Maybe my friend, Judy, the dog's owner, came back for him."

"Why wouldn't she come to the door like a normal human being? Why come in the middle of the night? And, through a window? That makes no sense."

Brittany's eyes shifted. "Uh, I'll give her a call. I mean . . . find out what's going on. Judy needs to know about the dog." She reached for her cell phone. "Um, the signal is better outside." She hurried out to the front porch and feigned a call.

When she returned, her mother was sitting slumped at the kitchen table. "I didn't hear a thing. Just slept through it. I don't know why the dog didn't bark. They could have killed me."

Brittany put her hand on Sue's shoulder. "I reached my friend. What a convoluted mess. Judy thinks the dognapper was her ex. That's probably why the dog didn't react. Uh, her ex did the same thing to her once before. They've been fighting over custody of the dog. That's why I brought him here."

"I'm going to call the police."

"Oh no, Mother." She crossed her arms and fidgeted. "We don't want to cause any more trouble for poor Judy. Think of it this way. At least the dog is back with someone who loves him. Judy's going to connect with her lawyer. Let's let them work it out."

194

Sue's lower lip quivered. "He broke into my house. God knows if he was alone. They could've attacked me."

Brittany's mind raced. "Judy said she can't afford the house payments . . . alone, so she's going to have to move to an apartment. The sad truth is she might not be able to keep the dog." Brittany gave a nervous laugh. "Wow, how things change." She reached out and patted her mother's arm.

"Where's your ring?"

"My ring?"

"You engagement ring? Did you leave it somewhere? You don't ever want to—"

"I broke up with Lance, Mother."

Sue's jaw dropped exposing several dark fillings in the back of her mouth. "You what?"

"We're no longer engaged. We had a fight . . . he, uh, is too controlling."

"Oh Brittany, no. Honey, go back. Don't walk away."

"I can't, Mother."

"Think about what you're doing. What you're giving up. All men are—"

"I can't live that way."

"Honey, look at this house." She waved her arm like a tour guide. "The kitchen sink is old, the faucet drips, the house needs paint. Think about our life here. All the things we didn't have."

"We had each other. That's huge."

"I know, honey, but consider what you'll be missing."

"It's a different world, Mother. I can support myself."

Sue stood, hugged her, and held her at arm's length. "Yes, but on a teacher's salary. *Think* for God's sake. Lance can offer you the big, shining world. You deserve that. Don't throw that away. Don't make the biggest mistake of your life. Promise me you'll reconsider," she pleaded.

Brittany took a deep breath. At least her mother was off the dog. "Oh, I will. I will."

* * *

"I think she bought it," Brittany said back at the farmhouse, filling Cody in. She plopped down on the couch and wound the ends of her hair around one finger. "Mother seemed more concerned about my future with Lance. She wants me to make up with him."

Cody winced. "So, are you?"

"I can't go there now. Frankly, I'm exhausted. Once Banjo is safe . . . I don't know."

"But what—"

"My head hurts. Do you have anything for a headache?"

"Yeah, in the bathroom." He returned with a glass of water and the Tylenol bottle. "Have you heard anything from Bobby?"

"No. I hope he and Banjo made it okay." She popped a tablet into her mouth and took a long drink of water.

Brittany's cell phone rang.

"Oh no." She put her finger to her mouth to shush Cody. "It's Mother." Her voice turned melodious. "Hi Mother."

"A man showed up asking about the dog."

"He did? What did you tell him?"

"Well, I never," Sue said, her voice angry. "I told him someone already took the dog. He got kinda rough with me. He tried to push his way into the house."

"Oh, Mother." She shot a pitiful glance at Cody.

"He was a big guy with a bald head and a scar on his face. Do you know him? Is he your friend's ex-husband?"

"No. I don't think so. I mean . . . uh . . . I only met him once."

"I told him he should know where his dog was. He said I wasn't making sense."

"Oh, gosh."

"He said I better be telling the truth. Well, I never."

"He didn't hurt you?"

"No, I grabbed the broom. I was ready to give him a swat. I said 'No wonder your wife left you.'"

"Oh, golly."

"He looked at me kinda funny. Then he stormed outta here."

"At least he's gone."

"Did you say anything about me, where I was?"

"No. I called Ken Blake."

Cody nudged Brittany, his eyes wide. "A cruiser just pulled up," he whispered. "It's Deputy Blake."

"I gotta go, Mother. Looks like Blake is already here. I need to give him all the details. Relax. Everything will be all right. As soon as we're finished here, I'll come right over."

"Now what?" Cody asked.

"Jesus, God," she wailed. "She called the police. Okay. Okay. Be quiet. Let me do the talking."

Blake knocked. Brittany smoothed her hair, a confident smile on her face.

"I suppose you know why I'm here," he said, when she opened the door.

"Yes, I just got off the phone with Mother. Come in."

Ken stepped in, looked around the room, and pulled out his notebook. "Okay, you want to start at the beginning?"

"I brought the dog . . . a German shepherd . . . to Mom's because one of my friends was going through a nasty divorce. Um, she and her spouse are fighting over the dog." She looked at Cody. "I brought it there for safekeeping."

"What's the name?"

"Cooper. The dog's name is Cooper."

He gave her a lame look. "I mean your friend's name."

"Well, it's Judy."

"Judy what?"

"Judy Phillips."

"Does Judy have a phone number?"

"You want her phone number?"

"Yeah."

"Ah, sure. Just a minute. I'll write it down." Cody, poker faced, handed her some paper. "Do you have a pen?" she asked. He handed her a pen. She scribbled Dulcy's number. "This is the best I can do. She's staying with a friend." As soon as Blake leaves, she'd be calling Dulcy.

"Breaking and entering is against the law," Blake said in his police officer's voice. He tapped his pen against his notebook. "It's burglary. It doesn't matter that it may have been the dog's owner. Is that clear?"

"Oh, yes, and poor Mother."

"Can you give me a description of the male dog owner?"

She tugged her ear. "Actually, I never met him. You might ask Mother. I mean, about what the guy looked like."

Ken's dark eyes narrowed. "I already did." He slammed shut his notebook. He looked from Brittany to Cody and then back to Brittany. "Are you in any kind of trouble?"

She shrugged her shoulders. "What? Me?"

"I mean, because if you are, let me help you."

"No, no, no." She rubbed her eyes. "I was just trying to help a friend." She threw up her hands, fingers splayed to indicate her frustration. "I had no idea how much animosity existed between the two."

"Okay."

"Um," she bounced on her feet. "Are . . . uh . . . you going to look for the dog?"

"Look, right now, we got a local guy shot dead over some drug deal gone bad. The town is on edge. So no, we're not putting out an all-points bulletin about a dog involved in some marital tug-of-war." He sounded disgusted.

"Sorry you had to come all the way out here."

"Look, you better call your mother. She's pretty upset."

"Oh, I will. I'm planning to go over there. *Soon.*"

She and Cody watched Ken walk away and climb into his cruiser. Cody blew out a stream of air. "Whew. Remind me to never cross swords with you."

"Do you think he believed me?"

"I guess."

Brittany smiled, but jumped when her cell phone went off. "Hello," she said into the phone. She turned toward Cody. "It's Bobby."

"Mission accomplished."

CHAPTER 29

"Poor Mother. I need to head over there to see if I can calm her down, reassure her. It makes me angry that the guy Lance sent there was so . . . rude."

Cody hesitated, thinking about that man. He worried about Britt's safety. "A thug, if you ask me. I'm going with you."

"Oh God, no." Brittany raised her hand as if she were stopping traffic. "That will just start her up again on Lance. I'm so relieved Bobby came through for us." She reached into her pocket and pulled out the note Bobby had given her. "Guess I won't need this. She set it on the counter.

Cody picked it up. "That's odd."

"What?"

"This handwriting." He went over to the couch, grabbed his backpack, and retrieved the note that he'd found stuck on their door. "Look at this."

"What about it?"

"The *I's* and the way he crosses his *t's* . . . they're pretty distinctive."

Brittany looked perplexed. "So what are you saying?"

"The handwriting on Bobby's note. It almost matches the handwriting on the threatening notes I found on our door. The paper is different."

Cody flattened the two pieces side-by-side on the kitchen counter.

Brittany shook her head. "I can't believe Bobby would do that."

"Here, look at them again. I wish I had a magnifying glass."

Brittany picked up the notes, held them up to the light and squinted. "They do look similar, but he only wrote a few lines. That's not much to go on." She closed one eye and looked closer. "We'd need a bigger handwriting sample to be sure."

"Why don't we just flat out ask him?"

"Then we'd be accusing him of something."

"Well yeah." Cody threw his hands up, his voice rose, "Threatening notes are illegal."

She got that look in her eye. The one she had when she was determined to save Banjo. "Bobby has never lied to me," her voice slow and even as if lecturing her class. "He helped out a lot when I was a kid. Saw to it that I got to go to the county fair. After Dad died, he gave me a puppy, so I'd have something to love. He even paid the vet bills. He's like family. I know he was angry about you wanting to explore the Fallingwater case. Took it like an insult. Maybe that's what it's all about, if it's even him."

"But threatening people?"

She folded her arms. "Like I said, it just doesn't seem like Bobby."

Cody leaned over the counter and perused the notes again. "Maybe we could stop in unannounced at his house in broad daylight. Take a look around. See if we find the things that were stolen."

"Look," she said, even more annoyed. "He just helped us big time with Banjo. We can't push our way in there."

"Okay. Then how about Dottie's? He usually hangs out there for breakfast. We could stop by and ask him about something . . . for directions somewhere . . . have him write it down. Then casually mention that his handwriting looks familiar, watch his face . . . show him the note I found tacked to our door."

"Just don't attack him. Let me do the talking."

"After watching you deflect Blake, the show is all yours, babe," he said, leaning against the counter with a smug smile on his face.

* * *

It was promising to be another muggy August day when Brittany and Cody arrived at Dottie's the next morning around 7:00 a.m. The smell of coffee and bacon hung heavy in the still air.

Cody steered Brittany toward a table by the windows. Toad sat at the counter with two other men Cody did not recognize.

"Hi kids, be there in a sec," Patsy called.

"No hurry," Cody said. He watched a couple put suitcases in their car at the Forest Lake Motel across the street. Once they slammed the trunk shut, they headed toward the café.

Brittany stared at *The Today Show* on the flat screen above the counter. Al Roker was in Scotland in search of the perfect kilt. She leaned toward Cody. "Remember when Bobby comes in, play it cool."

"Got it." He reached for a menu tucked behind the plastic napkin holder next to the wall.

Toad briefly glanced around, nodded at them, and then returned to his stack of pancakes. "Garsh, I guess they don't know no more about Artie," he said between bites, "and now there's all this talk about the sawmill maybe closing." He turned toward the man seated next to him. "Feels like our world is coming unglued."

"Yep, yep," the man said.

Patsy came to their table with glasses of ice water. "You guys are up early."

Cody looked up from the menu. "Thought we'd have breakfast where it's air conditioned."

"Whad'll it be?" she asked, her pen poised above her pad.

"Did he say the sawmill was closing?" Brittany asked.

"Might be. Some guy is buying up all the logs and sending them to China. Who was it you said, Clarence?" She looked at one of the older guys with a bleak, turtle-like face seated at the counter.

Roy came out of the kitchen. "Janes Timber Export is grabbing the logs off the Spencer place. Guess they're gonna ship 'em to China."

"There's not gonna be nothin' for us to mill," Clarence said. "I worked there twenty-five years makin' lumber." He set down his thermos and unscrewed the top, so Patsy could fill it with coffee. "If it shuts down, I don't know what'll happen. It's all I know how to do. Who's gonna hire an old guy like me?" He looked down at his baggy jeans and light brown work boots. "I gotta few years to go before Social Security."

"Janes Timber. That's Lance's outfit," Brittany whispered to Cody.

"Maybe that's what he's been doing over there in Asia. Greasing the skids," Cody said.

Roy folded his arms. "Aw, those guys can't log public lands as much as they want to, so they're out scrambling for private timber stands."

Toad played with the mole on his chin. "Garsh, that just ain't right. Social Security don't pay that much."

Patsy handed Roy their order.

"If the sawmill shuts down, that leaves us with ranchin' and tourism," he said, before heading back into the kitchen.

"I started workin' there when I was still in high school," said the other man at the counter. He was bald as a cue ball, had a prominent chin, and wore glasses. "They're treatin' us like we was jist a bunch of prawns."

"You mean pawns, Harold," Patsy corrected.

"Whatever. It all boils down to no job . . . the wife needs surgery."

"Here, let me fill your cup."

"Not gonna be any health insurance once the job is gone." Harold's lower lip trembled. "I heard they're hirin' up in Roseburg, but they're lookin' at guys with college degrees. Especially in electronics, now that they got computers telling machines what to do. Me and the wife don't even do e-mail."

Brittany sat up straight, her face determined. "I'm going to ask Lance about it," she said to Cody. "There's got to be some other way. Why couldn't they buy timber from some place where it wouldn't have such a devastating effect?"

"It's probably like Roy said. The federal government owns most of the forests. And, I don't think you can export logs off of public lands."

Patsy stood at their table with the coffee carafe and two cups.

"Have you seen Bobby?" Brittany asked.

"Nah, he hasn't been around for a couple of days. I figure he's out doing one of his art shows." She hurried off to wait on the couple from the motel.

Toad slipped off his counter stool, getting ready to leave. "Garsh, Bobby ain't here. Artie is gone. It's feeling mighty lonesome."

"Why don't you come and join us for a while, Toad?" Cody said. "Maybe we can cheer you up."

"Nah, I gotta get goin'. Gonna wash the pickup before it gets too hot. Could reach ninety today, they say." He plunked his money on the counter and hitched up his jeans. The bell on the door jingled as he exited.

Patsy brought scrambled eggs with toast for Cody and French toast for Brittany.

The two guys at the counter continued to talk about the sawmill. "The government spends more time protectin' woodpeckers and owls than they do us."

Cody bit into his toast. "There you have it, the effects of a changing workforce. Mills are retooling, turning to computerized machines. Then you throw in environmental issues and the global economy, and you've got a whole cultural shift."

Brittany reached for the maple syrup. "Sounds like fodder for another one of your studies."

"Yeah, who thought Forest Lake was such a mecca for sociocultural anthropology?" Cody watched a glum Clarence and Harold head out for their shift. "Think about it. The guys come in here every morning, eat breakfast, share their stories, fill their thermos bottles with coffee and leave all happy. A ritual really, something they've been doing for years. Then one day *POW*." He waved his hand for emphasis. "Everything's upside down."

"Impermanence," Brittany said. She cut her French toast. "Life is a constant state of flux. You have to detach. Live in the present moment."

"Can't see those two sitting cross-legged in a meditation hall."

"I know, and they're worried about their families."

Cody glanced at the wall clock. "Looks like we struck out thinking Bobby would be here."

She laughed. "We might have to have a lot of breakfasts before we run into him. I could get mighty spoiled."

Cody lowered his voice. "While we're in town, let's get some supplies and concentrate on another expedition to the cave. See if we can get more leads about Jim."

"Yeah, and then I better check in again with Mother to make sure she's all right."

Brittany got a box from Patsy for her leftover French toast, while Cody paid the bill.

"You guys stay cool," Patsy called as they went out, headed toward the parking lot. "We're in for a scorcher."

"I can already feel the heat coming up from the asphalt," Brittany complained. The shrill whistle from the sawmill sounded. She dropped her shoulders. "Sounds like the dying call of some endangered, sad bird."

"Oh, look, here." Cody bent down.

"What?"

"Someone dropped this." He scooped up a worn black leather wallet and opened it. "Good god, I've never seen this much money." He pulled out a handful of bills and whistled. "They're all 100's."

"Let me see." She moved close to him.

"Hmmm. It's Toad's wallet. Why would he be carrying all that cash in a musty old wallet?"

"We could leave it with Patsy. He's bound to miss it and come back. Is there an address in there?"

"Yeah, on his driver license. It says Juniper Street. Do you know where that is?"

"Yes. Don't worry. There aren't that many streets in Forest Lake."

"Look, there's a check in here, too."

"Maybe he doesn't trust banks or doesn't have an account. A lot of the old timers don't."

Cody fingered the check and whistled.

"What?"

"This check. It's for five thousand dollars."

Brittany's eyebrows shot up. "That much? How would he get that kind of money? I thought he worked as a hired hand. You don't think he's into drugs?"

"You mean like Artie?"

"Money like that doesn't just fall from the sky."

Cody held the check in the light. "It's from Janes Timber Export Company. Isn't that the company that they were just talking about—the one that's sending all the logs to China?"

"Lance's outfit."

"And the signature . . . it's signed by Bill Janes."

"Are you sure?" Brittany took the check in her hands and then gave it back to Cody. "We better track Toad down and make sure he gets this."

They jumped in the Subaru and headed out to Juniper Street, passing houses with parched, straw-colored lawns, until they came to the front of a nice, older ranch-style home. It was white with brickwork below the front picture window. A picket fence circled the front yard. Toad's blue Silverado, covered with beads of water that sparkled in the sunlight, sat in the driveway. A hose dripping water from the spray nozzle lay on the ground. Just as they stepped out, Toad came around the corner of the house carrying a green plastic bucket and a big yellow sponge.

"Hey Toad, nice place you have here," Cody called.

His left eyebrow raised in surprise. "Yeah," he said.

"You take care of this all by yourself?" Brittany asked. "Must be a lot of work for a dyed- in-the-wool bachelor like you."

His face lit with pride. "I got me a cleanin' lady. Comes in once a week." He glanced at his sorry lawn. "I mow the yard myself. Course it's all fried up now. Except for them damn dandy-lions. They're the only green thing out there."

"Wow, a cleaning lady. I could use one of those," Brittany said. "Must be nice."

"Well, I got me three bedrooms and two toilets." He grinned and paused, puzzled. "What brings you this way?"

Cody held out the wallet. "We got something for you."

Toad's face flushed. He raised his hands as if to push it away. "That's not mine."

"What? It has your name in it," Cody insisted. He opened the wallet. "Your driver license . . . cash . . . a check . . . made out to you."

Toad set the bucket down, grabbed the wallet, and tucked it in his pants pocket. "Lookit, you can't tell nobody about this." He nervously squirted detergent from a bottle into the bucket. "The money, I mean." The pink mole on the end of his chin trembled.

Cody exchanged glances with Brittany. "Oh, we wouldn't. We just wanted to return it."

"I mean, it's embarrassing, people givin' me money." He picked up the hose and gushed water in the bucket, making mounds of soapy foam.

"Someone gave you the money?" Cody folded his arms. "For no reason?"

Toad stooped to dunk the sponge in the bucket, stood up, and made a wide swath on the pickup's hood. "Lookit, I used to work for his uncle on his ranch."

"Whose uncle?"

"Bill's uncle."

"Bill who?"

Toad's eyes blinked. "Why, Bill Janes."

"The politician?" Brittany asked. "The one that runs that timber outfit?"

He stood and wiped his hands on his pants. "Bill worked down here in the summers a long way back."

Cody studied Toad's face. "Worked where?"

"On his uncle's ranch. Lyle Janes. Bill wanted to be a pharmacist. His ol' man had different ideas, so he sent Bill to Forest Lake in the summers." He dipped the sponge in the bucket again. "Thought it would make a man outta him, I guess. Bill was a sugar foot, you know. Sort've a sissy, so I took him under my wing."

"Apparently, it paid off," Cody said, grinning.

"I did some of the tough stuff he couldn't do or didn't have the stomach for . . . like fixin' bull calves. That way, he could drive the truck and run errands. Flirt with the wimmen." He chuckled. "Bill wanted to run off and live in the big city . . . you know, Frisco or LA."

Brittany pursed her lips. "I didn't know he had any connection to Forest Lake." She looked at Cody. "Lance said nothing about it."

Toad continued. "Janes wanted to get away from his hard drivin' ol' man, but in the end, he had no choice but to join the timber company. The ol' feller took sick, and Bill had to learn to run the business. And he's done all right. He's a big shot up north."

"Yeah," Brittany said, "And if things turn out, he'll be heading to Washington."

Toad seemed to relax. "Never did come back to Forest Lake that I knowed about, but each month he sends me a check. Guess he appreciated it an' all. I mean what I did fer 'im."

"From the looks of things, he must have been bend-over-backwards grateful," Cody said sarcastically.

Brittany nudged him.

"I was kind of a father figure, if you know what I mean." Toad's chest swelled. His lips curled into a proud grin. "I never had no family of my own. After ol' Lyle died, they sold the ranch. I never had nothin' 'cept that tin box trailer. So Bill, he comes through for me."

Brittany's eyes got dewy. She steepled her hands and brought them to her chest. "Well, that's sweet, Toad. I actually met Representative Janes. He helped me with a problem, too. He's a dog lover, you know."

"Oh yes, ma'am. Real nice guy."

"And he has a good heart."

"Yes siree." Toad's eyes narrowed. "You can't tell nobody about the money," he said in a low voice. "I'd be . . . I mean I'd never hear the end of it. Especially now, what with the sawmill maybe shuttin' down. People . . . would be mad. They kin turn really mean."

"Don't worry, Toad," said Cody. "It's not our business. All we wanted to do was get the wallet back to the right hands."

Toad took a deep breath. "Garsh, I really appreciate it . . . I really do."

Cody shook his hand. Toad dunked the sponge and went back to scrubbing the hood. They left him whistling, *When You and I Were Young, Maggie.*

He and Brittany climbed back into the Subaru. "I have to say that sounds odd." Cody turned the key in the ignition.

"Yeah. A flashy new pickup, a bigger house than he needs . . . a cleaning lady."

Cody grinned. "You left out the two toilets."

She stifled a giggle and gave him a little punch on the shoulder. "But that definitely was his wallet. I mean, his driver license was in there."

"Yeah, and that's what was really weird."

"How so?" She turned toward him as she fastened her seatbelt.

"Toad is the only guy I know whose driver license photo actually flatters him."

CHAPTER 30

So many bouquets of flowers arrived at the farmhouse that Cody was on the verge of hay fever. Like a fawning puppy, Lance, Lance, Lance was going all out to make up with Brittany.

"Y-e-hep, here's another one," said Carl, the slow-moving delivery guy from Sheila's House of Flowers. "We call this one, *Because You're Special.* Well, not you . . . her." He handed Cody a vase filled with enormous pink Gerbera daisies, orange roses, and assorted greenery.

"Thanks, Carl." He'd come so often, he and Cody were on first-name basis. "Britt is out visiting her mother. I'll see that she gets these."

Carl adjusted his navy blue billed cap. "Y-e-hep must be some special dame, or the fella sending them's a mighty love-sick moose."

"You have a good day, Carl." Cody couldn't resist. Once Carl left, he read the small, attached card. *Dearest Brittany. Please forgive me. I love you—Lance.* He pointed a finger toward his mouth to feign vomiting, then set the bouquet on the kitchen table. Soon it would join the six others on the coffee table in various stages of wilt, since the house sweltered in the summer heat.

He'd just gotten a glass of water and plunked in two ice cubes when he heard a powerful engine revving outside. "Now what?" He glanced out the window and spotted a fancy white Camaro convertible parked in the driveway. A tall man with an imposing muscular build stepped out, stretched, and slammed the door. The man's eyes searched the house.

A loud knock rattled the door and adjoining window.

Cody swung it open. "Yes?"

The man sized him up. "Is Brittany here?" His voice was deep and confident, like a radio announcer.

Tall, wavy auburn hair, blue polo shirt with an embroidered polo player on the left pocket, khaki pants, and expensive leather loafers— Cody knew who *he* was. He took a calculating sip of his ice water. "Who wants to know?" he asked innocently.

"I'm Lance Helms. Her fiancé."

"Sorry, she's not here." *Ol' Lance definitely was fetching with that sexy, three-ball announcer's voice.*

Lance smiled, revealing a mouth of perfect teeth. "Where is she?" He eyed Cody's flip flops, hairy bare legs, red running shorts and oversized white T-shirt with a coffee stain on the front.

Cody caught a whiff of Lance's musky, woody scent. *He smelled expensive.* "Don't know."

"Really?"

"She's a big girl."

Lance crossed his arms. "Let's see, you're that professor guy. What is it you do? Oh, that's right, study dead bones."

Cody focused on the Arnold Schwarzenegger arms. He managed a laugh. "That would be what archeologists do. Big difference."

Lance was not amused. "Look, professor. Brittany is *mine*. We had a spat. We're going to be married. So get the hell out of the picture. Got it?"

Cody took a sip of water. "Jeez, you'd think she'd have something to say about that?"

"I'm warning you." He moved toward him.

Cody held his ground, not budging from the doorjamb. "This is America, friend. She gets to decide."

Lance gritted his teeth. His eyes looked like hard, dark marbles. "I know people. You like your job at that dinky college in a backwater town, you better beat cleats or you're likely to get fired."

"Are you threatening me?"

"I'm a lawyer, professor." He rested his hand above his head on the doorframe, moving closer, a foot from Cody's face. "I'm *advising* you. So, listen carefully, a few phone calls to the right folks, and you're toast."

More water. Cody took another sip, swallowed, but didn't step back. He stared into Lance's eyes. "Guess what? You don't scare me."

"I could see to it that you never work again . . . at any university. Just like that." He snapped his fingers in front of Cody's nose.

Distract the intimidating bastard. "Speaking of jobs," Cody said. "We were, weren't we? If you want to make points with Britt, why don't you drop the decision to buy up all the logs from the Spencer place?"

"Britt? Oh, isn't that cute? And what does she call you? Baby cakes?" His muscular arms crossed his very fit chest.

Don't engage. He pictured Lance as an overgrown baby crying, "Mine, Mine."

"Do you have any idea what Janes Timber is doing to Forest Lake? A lot of good folks depend on that sawmill for a living."

Lance's eyes narrowed. "Progress, man," he sneered. "It's progress—capitalism." He practically snorted the words. "Something you would know if you had a *real* job."

"You're upsetting lives."

"It's a dinky mill, affecting what? One hundred people, maybe. Those folks have to learn to do other things. Move on. Get a life."

Way to go. He was no longer talking about Britt. "That's a big number for a small town. Most of those folks spent their whole lives at that mill . . . so their kids could have a better life."

"Aw gee, professor." He held up his thumb and rubbed his index finger over it, imitating a small violin. "It brings a tear to my one good eye . . . and it sounds like liberal drivel. Give Brittany this." He held out a sealed envelope.

It felt like an order. "Give it to her yourself."

"I could break you in two."

Cody's neck tightened. He would love to punch that smug face, but he was no match for Lance. No, this was a game of brain over brawn. Lance was full of himself, a stupid lizard brain. Cody took a slow, measured sip of water. "I can see the headlines now." He extended his hand in the air, moving it back and forth, like a clairvoyant reading the future. "Prominent aide to Representative Janes arrested for assaulting a college professor. Pre-election poll takes nose dive."

Lance's face reddened. He gnashed his teeth and put the envelope back in his pocket.

"How long do you think you'd be on Mr. Big's staff, huh?"

"You think you're clever, don't you, professor?"

Cody smiled, but he didn't answer. He could hear Lance's cell phone ping in his pocket indicating he had a text message.

Lance diverted his eyes.

In that moment of distraction, Cody stepped back. "Meeting adjourned," he said, then slammed the door, locked it, and waited. His neck prickled. He set his water glass on the table and whipped out his own cell phone in case he needed to call for help. He expected Lance to kick the door down and charge in like a mad bull. Instead, he heard the Camaro's engine roar. He peeked through the curtains just in time to see the car peel out of the driveway in a cloud of dust.

"Whew." He was shaking, breathing hard. Lance was a complete ass. A thug. Brittany was lucky to be done with him. She was, wasn't she? He jumped. His cell phone rang in his hand. He hoped it was Britt.

No, it was Evan Carlisle from Willamette. "Listen, we were able to decipher more from the notebooks."

"Great. What did you find out?" Cody glanced at his watch. After his tête-à-tête with Lance, he wasn't in the mood for Evan. He stared out the window, watching a squirrel decide where to hide one of the peanuts Britt left out for him.

"Not much. More routine stuff. But we did learn that your cave dweller was in love with this Chrissy woman."

"I believe the name is *Christie*."

"Could be . . . anyway, she was planning to marry someone else." He paused and then said, "Bill."

"Hmmmm." Cody rubbed the back of his head. The squirrel was hiding the peanut in one of Mrs. Humphries' flower pots. Not a good decision, Cody thought.

"You still there?"

"Yeah."

"You seem distracted."

"I just had a conversation with an overgrown asshole in heat." His neck ached.

"What?"

"Nothing . . . Just a lot going on in my life."

"Anyway, someone named Bill."

"Bill, huh?" The squirrel sat back on his haunches and seemed to be looking directly at him with beady, unblinking eyes. *Maybe he read my thoughts. Cute.*

"Bill Janes."

Cody turned away from the window, held the phone tight against his ear, and began to pace. "Did you say, Bill Janes?"

"Yep. As near as we can tell. I guess it could be James. But no, the "n" was pretty distinctive."

"Hmmmm."

"And then there's something about Tule Lake. We can't be sure if your cave dweller was going there or if someone else was."

"That's across the California border, right?"

"Yeah. I mean, the last time I looked."

"And?"

"That's about it."

"Okay."

"So, I guess we're done here," Evan said.

"Yeah." A low burst of breath came from his lips. "Can I get a copy of the transcript?"

"Yep. I'll send you the transcript of what we got . . . and the bill."

Cody rolled his eyes toward the ceiling. "Oh for sure, the bill."

"It's a doozy."

* * *

Brittany burst into the kitchen carrying a bouquet of red and cream-colored gladiolas which she said were from her mother's yard. "I don't know why you have such a problem with that Subaru. I love the car . . . especially the sunroof and the backup camera-thingy."

"It's a boat. People don't need to drive boats. So, how's your mother?"

"Mother is calming down. She had new locks put on all the downstairs windows and a deadbolt on both doors. I brought her a sweet night light. It looks like a little panda bear." She grinned and reached under the sink for a glass vase and began arranging the tall spikes.

"Jeez, with all the flowers already here," Cody said, "you probably don't need those glads." But he loved the way the tall, bright flowers framed her face as she fiddled with them, soft but striking against her dark hair and eyes.

"Mother insisted."

"You got another delivered bouquet. It's over there on the table. Criminy, this place looks like a funeral parlor."

"Oh." She walked over, opened the card and read it. "Hmmm."

Cody studied her face. *Was that a frown?* "And Lance stopped by."

"He did?" Her eyes rounded. She seemed happy.

He paused to make sure she was listening. "He threatened me."

"Threatened you?"

"Said I needed to beat cleats, or I'd never work again."

She rolled her eyes. "That Lance. He gets so emotional. He's been calling me every day."

"And?" He could feel his pulse in his throat.

"I let them go to voice mail. That's probably why he came out here. I don't think he would've hurt you. Mother says he's persistent because he really loves me."

"That's love?"

"She likes the fact that he's willing to fight for me." She gave him a coquettish look.

Cody threw up his arms. "Fight? What the—"

"Besides, I don't think anyone has ever told Lance *no* before." She set the small card down, returned to the counter, and continued to fuss with the gladiolas.

"He seems abusive . . . and totally insensitive to the sawmill plight. How can you—"

"You talked about the sawmill?" She looked at him as if he had two heads.

"When he threatened my job, I thought mentioning it would send his thoughts in a different direction."

"Hmmm. He's a little rough around the edges when it comes to emotional issues. What did he say about the sawmill?"

"In a nutshell . . . too bad, so sad. That's progress. And, there's more."

"About Lance?"

"No. Evan Carlisle called. He said Christie—the love of Jim's life—was actually planning to marry another man?"

Her eyebrows arched. "Really? So, it was a triangle?"

"The other man, he said, was Bill Janes."

"Our Bill Janes?"

"Seems to be. I guess we can't be sure."

"Are you kidding me?"

"Nope."

Brittany clutched the vase of gladiolas to her chest. "See, just what I thought. It was a love story . . . a complicated one."

"I never considered Janes."

"Wait a minute," Brittany's eyes widened. She set the vase down on the table next to the flowers Lance had sent. "Remember what Toad said? Janes worked for his uncle on a ranch outside Forest Lake. Maybe he knew Jim. Maybe he even talked with him or knew people he may have known. We probably need to visit with Janes."

"What's he gonna say? And after Lance threatened me, I'm not sure I want to."

"Representative Janes is a nice guy. He isn't responsible for Lance's behavior. It's worth a try. He was so kind to me at that hearing about Banjo. Very supportive. Took me to lunch. And I'd like to make an appeal for the sawmill myself. You know, try and save their jobs."

* * *

Another floral arrangement, yellow and white daisies in a white basket, arrived the next day. A small package wrapped in white paper and tied with a silver bow was attached. Cody watched Brittany open it.

"Oh my," she said. Her engagement ring was inside, along with a message from Lance, probably still begging for a second chance.

Cody was relieved that she didn't slip the ring on. Instead, she got out her blue stationery, seated herself at the kitchen table, and started writing.

"I want him to know I received the ring, and to thank him for all the flowers," she said. "A personal note is better than a phone call or a text at this point."

He tried to peek over her shoulder to see if she signed it *love, Brittany*, but she folded the note and slipped it into the envelope before he could glimpse the signature.

"I need a couple of weeks to think things over." She licked the flap. "I'll mail this tomorrow."

Afterward, she called Janes' office and requested a meeting. "He told me I should feel free to contact him if I ever needed assistance," she said to his appointments secretary.

The next day, Janes' secretary called back. He had to be in Salem on Tuesday for a speaking engagement, she told Brittany, and would meet her at *Le Rêve*, the fancy French restaurant.

They left early in the morning for the long drive to Salem. On the way, Brittany dropped her note to Lance in a mailbox.

CHAPTER 31

By the time they reached Salem, it was blazing hot and almost noon. Cody plunked change into the parking meter.

"I'm glad we're eating in a nice place. I'm hungry," Brittany said, as they walked toward *Le Rêve.*

"Me too, and tired. Not to mention warm. I wish it would rain." He pulled on his collar several times to vent his shirt.

Inside the restaurant, the server, wearing a black vest and white shirt, immediately seated them in the elegant main dining room per Janes' request. "I understand he's going to be a little late." He gave a knowing smile. "Not unusual." He distributed menus. "Would you like something to drink?"

Cody waved him off. "Oh, no, not me, thank you. Water will be fine."

"We'll wait," Brittany agreed.

"As you wish," he said, and turned away.

Cody drummed his fingers on the white tablecloth, drinking in the restaurant's basil, onion, and chicken smells that made his stomach growl. There weren't many other people inside, most likely due to the heat. He stared at an empty table by the windows. That's where he sat when he was having the discussion with Luci Maxwell about Colombia. That issue was still out there. A tingling sensation crawled up his spine. His throat parched, he was glad when the server brought water. He swallowed slowly and glanced at Britt. Her eyes were downcast, studying the menu, so peaceful and relaxed. "We should have brought a deck of cards."

"Quit bouncing your leg. Relax. He'll be here. Did I tell you Representative Janes has a white Akita named Blanche? He takes her everywhere."

"So, is she going to show up for lunch?"

"Don't be silly."

Cody glanced away and spotted a tall, trim man with close-cropped white hair rushing toward their table. He wore a tasteful oyster linen suit with light blue shirt and matching tie.

Brittany smiled. She offered her hand. "Representative Janes, how nice to see you."

"Miss Brittany. It's always a pleasure." He had clear blue eyes, set off with crinkle marks.

Cody stood up and extended his hand.

"And you would be?" Janes asked, puzzled

"Oh, this is my friend, Cody Benson." Brittany said.

Janes ignored Cody's offer to shake hands. His eyes turned icy. "Forgive me. I wasn't expecting two of you."

Brittany blushed. "Cody is a professor of anthropology at Willamette University. I'm helping him with a summer research project. I told your secretary, there'd be two of us."

"I see." He seated himself in the curved, ladder-back chair. "Well, let's start with some wine. Chardonnay okay with you folks? It seems to go well with everything, and they serve a good quality here."

"Sure," Cody said, and Brittany nodded.

The server reappeared. "Are you ready to order?"

"Ron, how are you?" Janes said.

"Fine, Mr. Janes. Your order?"

"Yes, uh, let's get to the food. We'd also like three glasses of Chardonnay." He looked at Brittany. "Might I recommend the *Le Coq au Vin Forestiere?* That's braised chicken with mushrooms."

She hesitated. "I need something vegetarian."

"We have a nice chickpea ratatouille," the server said.

"Oh, that sounds good." She sounded relieved.

The server turned to Cody.

Cody handed him his menu. "I always have the smoked ham and gruyere cheese sandwich, whenever I come here."

Janes looked like he just spotted a booger hanging from Cody's nose.

"And how is sweet Blanche?" Brittany asked while they waited for their food. "Is she—" She stopped when the server returned with three glasses of wine.

Janes lifted his glass. "Cheers," he said. "Now, you were saying?"

"I was wondering about Blanche, your dog."

"Oh, she's as feisty as ever. We had a nice long walk this morning. Got to do it early. Otherwise, it gets too hot. Have you heard any more about the dog . . . what was his name?"

"Banjo. Not a lot. Only that the newspaper reporter covering the story says he got tips from some people claiming they spotted Banjo on a ranch in Montana. Another said he was in Hawaii."

"Oh my, Hawaii. Probably wearing a flowered shirt and sunglasses." Janes laughed.

"The important thing is he's safe . . . and off of death row."

"Exactly." Janes raised his glass again.

 Cody fidgeted.

The server brought their orders.

"What can I help you with?" Janes asked. He speared a mushroom, chewed, and reached for his glass.

Two men in slacks and short-sleeved shirts entered the restaurant and were about to be seated. They carried their jackets. The tall one with thinning red hair and a pale complexion stopped and slapped Janes on the back. "Hey Bill, how's it going?" His companion was thickset and had a beard.

"Pretty well, Ralph" Janes said. "I just finished speaking to some key fundraisers. And you?"

"We're refugees from an interim committee on genetically engineered crops." He nudged his friend who chuckled.

Janes seemed amused. "Pretty heady stuff, huh?"

"Yeah." Ralph rolled his eyes. "Couldn't wait for lunch break." He stared at Brittany.

"This is Lance's fiancée, Brittany Bolin."

Brittany smiled.

Janes said nothing about Cody.

Ralph winked. "That Lance is one lucky guy." They exchanged a few other pleasantries before heading to their table.

"Enjoy your lunch." Janes turned back to Brittany. "Now, where were we? Oh, yes, what can I help you with?"

Brittany straightened her back. "I wanted to make an appeal for the D&R Sawmill workers in Forest Lake." She cleared her throat. "The timber you'd be buying from the Spencer place used to be sold to the sawmill. If you send it . . . the timber . . . directly to China, a lot of jobs will be lost. These folks are plenty scared."

Janes' eyes narrowed. "I thought this was about mending it with Lance." He sipped wine.

At the mention of Lance, Cody reached for his glass.

"Oh . . . no . . . the sawmill." Brittany clutched her napkin.

"Nothing stays the same, Brittany." He set down his drink. "Of course, logs have to be debarked before we ship them, so in the end, it creates jobs. But then that work wouldn't be done in Forest Lake. And, the export market does employ quite a few loggers, truckers, dock workers, not to mention foresters."

Brittany leaned forward. "But these workers and their families . . ."

"The government won't let us export timber logged from public lands, so we have to consider as many private stands as we can." He meticulously cut his chicken into small pieces and made an orderly arrangement on his plate. "My responsibility is to my own firm. My employees. Sure, I care about those sawmill workers. Sure, I worry about them, but if I don't buy the Spencer logs, someone else will."

She got that determined look on her face. The one that Cody knew so well. "But how much is enough? Surely there are other places to get logs . . . bigger stands . . . other states?"

Janes took in a quick breath. "Next to Alaska, Oregon has the most forested land." His lips tightened; he looked peeved.

Cody gently kicked Brittany under the table to clue her in that she was irritating Janes. It didn't matter, she kept going. "Uh, well I certainly hope you will reconsider, especially since you have connections to our special little town."

Cody perked up. *Way to go, Britt. Great transition.*

Janes pulled at the knot of his tie. "Who told you that?"

"Well, uh . . ." She gave Cody a help-me-out-here look.

"Actually, it came up in connection with Jim Fallingwater," Cody said. "I'm doing some research on the guy and . . . Did you know Jim Fallingwater?"

"Fallingwater?" Janes set down his fork.

"Jim Fallingwater from Forest Lake," Cody prompted. "He . . . uh . . . got into some trouble there some years back. Killed a woman, actually."

"Oh, that Indian fellow." He took a hefty swallow of wine. "Only ran into him a couple of times. He helped me fix my pickup once."

"She must have been beautiful," Brittany blurted. "The woman I mean. Were you both in love with her?"

"Whoa." Janes' face blanched. "Who told you about me and Christie?"

Why did Britt have to cut to the quick like that? Cody decided some fast answer was necessary. "No one. Uh . . . ."

"But then, how did you know? Seriously, who told you?"

Cody thought fast. He didn't think it wise to mention Toad's wallet, the notebooks, the cave, or that he believed Jim was still alive. "Uh, we picked up some information from an old police file. They interrogated Jim after he was arrested."

"There's something about me in a file?" He quit eating, reached for his wine, and again took a serious swallow.

"Not really." He knew that sounded stupid. Janes seemed very annoyed, like maybe the wine was getting to him. "Just that Fallingwater mentioned your name." He shot a glance at Brittany. She looked tenuous. "Yeah, so we're talking to everyone that was around at the time. Trying to get a picture of Fallingwater. What he was like. Why he might have done what he did. You know, sociocultural anthropology stuff for my research. They. . . uh . . . the people we talked to . . . mentioned that your uncle had a ranch there, and that you worked on it during summers."

Janes' eyebrows knitted. "Well, I did know Christie Jenkins. She was a waitress in the café there. What was it called?"

"Dottie's."

"Yes. Dottie's. It was the only place to eat in town, as I recall. Terrible food." He drank more wine and worked on his chicken pieces.

"And?" Brittany asked. She dipped a piece of French bread into her stewed vegetable dish.

Janes looked up, finished chewing, and swallowed. "Christie was quite a gal." He gestured in the air with his fork. "She wasn't what people thought. Not this sweet, little innocent thing. She was a real hottie." His face flushed. He smirked and glanced at his watch.

Cody felt embarrassed for him. Janes' comments were sexist and hardly appropriate for a respected member of the legislature, but he wasn't about to stop him.

"I don't know what happened that night. I was surprised that she was out with him . . . that Fallingwater character. I mean, she used to laugh at him behind his back."

"Why?" Cody's eye's hardened. He set down his sandwich, waiting for the inevitable answer.

"He was Indian." Janes appeared to catch himself. "Uh, not that that mattered . . ."

"Apparently, it mattered to her?" Cody asked.

"What I meant was he . . . uh . . . didn't have much of a future. Oh, Fallingwater seemed like a nice enough guy. It was awful what happened there, but that's all I can tell you. I was back at school . . . at Oregon State studying to become a pharmacist, but my father got sick and needed me to help with the business. Turned out to be the right thing for me."

Brittany's eyes got moony. *Here we go again,* Cody thought.

"Were you in love with her?" she asked.

Janes managed a tepid smile. "She was just a kid . . . and well, so was I. I was twenty something. But then . . ." His eyes got distant. "It was not to be. I didn't know about . . . she . . . Well, I just didn't know."

There was an uncomfortable pause. Cody and Brittany exchanged looks.

"Know what?" Cody asked.

"I meant we were naïve. Just a couple of naïve kids. We knew so little about life."

It was time to ditch the mushy stuff. "Did Jim have any other friends who I could contact?" Cody asked.

Janes didn't answer. It was as if Cody wasn't there. "Speaking of love affairs," he said to Brittany. "I know a young man who's pretty upset over losing his girl. Right now, in real time."

Brittany seemed surprised that Janes was so attuned to her personal life. "Uh, we're working on it."

"Good. Lance has a great future. He's a little intense at times, but . . . I hope you two work it out. Ellen and I never had children of our own. I think of Lance as my son. It would be really nice to have you as part of our extended family." He placed his hand over hers.

Brittany smiled.

Cody tensed. *Lance, Lance, Lance. Barf.*

Janes tossed his napkin on the table. "Well, look I've got to go." He signaled for the bill. "You don't have to rush off. Linger. Have dessert."

The server appeared. "Just put it on my tab," Janes said.

"Was everything okay?" the server asked, looking at Janes' half-eaten meal.

Janes pressed his index finger against his thumb signaling okay. "Perfect Ron, absolutely perfect."

Brittany stood up. "Thank you so much for lunch . . . and your time."

Cody made no effort to stand. "Yes, Thank—"

Janes cut him off. "Sorry to rush off." His voice was edgy. He hurriedly clasped Brittany's hand. "But, I have another appointment. Campaign stuff, you know." They watched him hurry away.

"Wham, bam, thank you ma'am," Cody muttered.

"What?"

"That's how it seemed. This was all a waste of time. We should have paced it better. I felt like we were all over him, and it made him uncomfortable. He is a respected member of the state legislature, after all."

"I agree. It never crossed my mind that he would think this was about Lance and me."

"Yeah, right." Cody watched the server clearing dishes from a nearby table.

"It sounded like he really cared for Christie," she said. "Once."

"Seriously? I got the impression he thought she was a slut."

"Well, eventually, maybe. Why was he so darn interested in who told us about him and Christie?"

"I don't know, but I couldn't tell him about the notebooks."

"He said he didn't know about her past."

Cody took a last bite of his sandwich. "I'm not sure that's what he said or meant."

"There was no discussion in any of the news clips we read implying Christie had round heels."

"Jeez, Britt, they wouldn't put that in the paper. Besides, she was seventeen—a minor."

"And why was she out with Jim, if as Evan Carlisle, your Willamette friend said, she was going to marry Janes?"

"Well, you're with me, and you *were* engaged." He studied her, hoping she would acknowledge her relationship with Lance was over.

"Yeah, but this is different. It's business."

Cody's heart sank. "I thought this meeting with Janes would lead to other contacts. We're running out of time." He set his napkin next to his plate. "It's August. School will be starting soon. And, we're nowhere. Now, I guess it's back to the cave, to see if we can find more clues."

CHAPTER 32

After the Janes meeting, Cody found being in the pristine wilderness, away from civilization, hiking into the quiet, still pines refreshing like savoring a cold drink on a scorching day. Some leaves on the woody shrubs started to change hue, tinging the air with the anticipation of fall. In town, Tillden's Grocery already had back-to-school supplies on its shelves—big boxes of crayons, Elmer's Glue, spiral notebooks, and Cody's favorite, soft Pink Pearl erasers. He wouldn't be buying any of those items, but seeing them conjured up feelings of fresh starts and hope.

The long trek back to the cave in the early morning hours proved easier and faster because of the markers he'd placed, the new map he'd drawn, and an overcast sky, which kept them reasonably cool.

Still, it was a bittersweet journey because it was the last outing he'd make with Britt. Soon, they'd both return to classroom duties, and she'd be leaving him, perhaps re-uniting with Lance. He remembered their hurried lunch with Janes, and how he'd urged Brittany to join their extended family, but treated Cody like he was a grease spot on a rug.

A few drops of rain hitting him in the face brought him back to the task at hand. In a matter of minutes, the wind kicked up and fat raindrops pummeled them. They rushed to take cover under a thick grove of trees.

Cody pulled a plastic drop cloth from his backpack so they could sit. "Hopefully, we can wait it out. If it turns into a vicious thunderstorm, we'll have to turn back."

"We might as well have a snack," Brittany said. She retrieved nuts, apples, and energy bars from her backpack.

By the time they finished, the rain had let up. "For a minute there, I thought maybe I'd have to pitch the tent," Cody said. He stuffed his water bottle into his backpack and took a deep breath drinking in the fresh earthy smell of the rain on dry ground. He stared wistfully at the landscape. Soon he'd have to face Luci and decide about Colombia.

Brittany gathered up their apple cores and energy bar wrappers to drop into a plastic baggy, but the wind snatched the paper and blew them out of her reach. "Darn. The last thing we need to be doing out here is littering."

"At least we try. Some people don't give a rip," Cody said. "You can leave the apple cores for the wildlife. They like stuff like that."

They headed out again into the damp, now muddy wilderness, trekking along until Brittany broke the silence. "And boots and pants and boots and pants and . . ."

"Is that some Buddhist chant?"

"No, clever boy. Haven't you seen that insurance company commercial? There's this sweet little pig that keeps the beat with those words. I'm pacing our hike."

"I don't watch much television."

"Gotcha then." She laughed her wonderful laugh. "I'll send you the YouTube link."

Cody gave her a quick grin. He was really going to miss her. He wondered if it was mutual.

They arrived at the cave and began removing the rocks covering the entrance. Once cleared, they turned on their headlamps. Cody carefully led the way down the rocky steps and Brittany followed. It was like climbing down into the eyehole of an enormous skull. Once inside, he turned on his new candlepower spotlight.

Brittany pulled out her own high-powered LED professional flashlight. "God bless REI," she said. "We can see so much more with these lights." They took off their backpacks, tucked away their headlamps, and placed their packs safely inside the side cave.

Cody flashed his light to the rocky ledge, checking to see if Jim had left additional journals. He felt around with his hand, but found nothing.

"Look, over here," Brittany said. "There are a few more wood carvings. Kinda moldy, but you might want to take them." She picked them up and set them aside. "They don't smell good, but I guess you could try to restore them. Let's check the side cave. He may have stored some stuff in there. Out of the way. Hidden."

Cody directed his beam in that direction as they moved toward it. "Not much in here. Just some old pieces of wood that he used to fuel the fire and what's left of an ax."

Brittany shined her flashlight on the rocky walls. "It's hard to imagine someone living in here long term."

P-S-S-S-T

What's that?" Brittany asked.

Cody turned. "It's coming from the cave entrance."

A splitting, crackling noise and then a loud roar followed by a furious shock wave knocked them to the ground and filled the air with smoke and dust.

Everything went dark.

Cody couldn't breathe. He felt a gash on his forehead and tasted dust in his mouth. He lay still for a moment, trying to get his bearings.

What had happened?

He jerked his body up. "Britt! Where are you?" There was no response. Then he realized she was partially beneath him. "Are you okay?"

No answer.

He scrambled to find his spotlight, his ears ringing, fumbling in the darkness, until he found it a few feet away, but still in the side cave. He fingered the button; the light flickered on. *Oh, thank God.* He flashed the beam in Brittany's direction. "Britt!" He saw her trying to sit up and rushed to her.

She groaned, bracing herself on her elbows. "My leg. I can't move it." She coughed and spit. "What happened? Was that an earthquake? It knocked me so hard."

Cody pointed the light toward the cave opening. His skin prickled. Through the dust, he could see it was jammed with shattered rock and debris. There was a faint acrid smell which could only mean one thing. "An explosion. Somebody—"

"What? I can hardly hear you."

He raised his voice. "I said it was an explosion. The entrance is blocked."

"Somebody did this? On purpose?" Brittany rubbed her ears. "Why?"

"I don't know. We moved into the side cave just in time, or we'd be confetti."

"How do we get out?"

Cody's heart rate doubled. He staggered toward the cave entrance and used his light to trace the area. He set it down and tried to remove debris, but there was so much of it. His throat tightened. He hurried back to Brittany.

She was sitting up and massaging her leg. "What happened to your forehead? You're bleeding."

"Something caught me in the head, or I hit it when I fell. I don't know." He wiped his wound on his sleeve. "It's not that deep, just messy."

"Are we going to die down here?" Her voice quavered.

"We're in the side cave. I know it leads to the outside . . . somewhere. It's our only hope."

"I can't, Cody. I can't. My leg feels worse. I can't get up."

He set his light down, so that it focused on her leg, and assessed her injury. He could feel swelling.

"No, don't touch!" she cried. "It hurts."

"Does anything else hurt? Like any internal injuries?"

"I don't think so, but my leg. You'll have to get help."

He froze.

Alone.

"I can't just leave you here." His muscles tensed.

"You have to. There's no other choice."

"Maybe there's some way to make a splint."

"No, I feel pain in my hip."

"Hang on. I'm going to pull you farther in where there's less dust in the air." *Maybe whoever did this is planning to blast the side cave shut, too.* He grabbed her under her armpits and carefully moved her.

"Stop," she groaned. "Please. It hurts."

"Sorry. This, at least, is better." Once he got her situated, he jumped up and searched in the rubble for her backpack. After he found it, he set it beside her and retrieved her water bottle. "Here, take a sip."

She took a drink, coughing in between sips, causing water to dribble down her chin. She managed another cautious swig. "That's better," she said. "I swallowed a lot of dust."

He pulled out her sleeping bag, unrolled it, and gently scooted her onto it as thoughts zoomed through his mind. *I shouldn't have*

*brought her here. What if I don't make it. Get lost? What if whoever
did this is still out there. What if—*

She put her arm around him. "Listen, Cody. I have to tell you
something."

"Oh Britt. I'm so sorry. I should never have involved you. I don't
understand who . . . why . . . this . . ."

"Listen —"

"I should have been more cautious. Just hang on." He struggled
to keep his voice steady. His throat was raw.

"Cody—" Her voice was thin and pleading.

"Please. Please, just hang on."

"Cody, dear Cody, listen to me." She raised her arm and pulled
him close. "I love you."

"What?"

"I love you." She kissed him lightly on the lips. They lingered together
for a brief moment.

"I knew it that day you gave Omar the groceries."

"The groceries . . ." He struggled to focus.

"Listen."

"Omar . . .Oh, that time at the store. You did?"

"Listen, I thought I wanted the world." Her fingers traced his
face. "But I just want you."

He rubbed away smudges on her cheeks and forehead. "I loved
you the instant I set eyes on you."

"But . . ." She coughed and cleared her throat. "You never said
anything . . . just talked about fossils, caves, bones . . . finding Jim."

"You were engaged . . . I . . .You never—"

"I wanted you to *choose* me . . . to want me for who I am . . . not
just some arm candy."

"Lance had everything. How could I compete with that?"

"Oh, lord. You're as thick as cement, but you have a good heart.
I'm not sure Lance even has one."

He reached for her, kissed her soft hair, her forehead, her lips.
His eyes started to water, wetting her face. *She loved him, and he'd
missed it. Missed it. Jesus.*

"Don't cry. Just hold me."

"Sure."

"Cody." Now she teared up. "We may only have this moment."
She wiped her face with the bottom of her shirt.

"Don't say that! I'll get help. Just hang on. Please hang on. Until . . . I come back for you." He stood up, stepped back, almost stumbling over something. His backpack. He pulled it free and jerked out his sleeping bag and first aid kit. He unrolled and unzipped the bag; then covered her with it. He opened the kit and found the Tylenol. "This will help with the pain. It's all I've got." He waited while she swallowed two tablets. He set his pack beside her. "There's more food and water in here. Can you reach it?"

"Yeah."

"Okay. And, I'll leave my lantern light with you."

"Cody, no matter what happens. I'll be with you . . . Here, take this." She slid off her bracelet with the Banjo dog charm that he'd given her for her birthday and pressed it into his hand.

Her words stabbed at him. She talked as if she were dying. He wanted to stay. He wanted to bawl. He fingered the bracelet. "Totem," he said.

"Totem," she repeated.

He dropped the bracelet into his pocket, then pulled his headlamp out of his backpack and fastened it over his sore forehead. "Okay," he managed to say. "I'm going." He started to leave, then came back, knelt down, and kissed her again. "Okay, now, I'm going."

CHAPTER 33

Cody scrambled through the bowels of the side cave, every nerve of his body quivering. The air reeked of bat guano. Within minutes, his headlamp flickered and gave out. *Shit.* He pulled it off, tossed it aside, and pushed on through the blackness like a tunneling mole, feeling the cave's rocky sides.

Over time, the cave must have narrowed. Pieces of rock, hardened dirt, or maybe bat shit struck him in the face. The blast could've loosened entire portions of the tunnel. If that were true, everything could collapse.

Bats. They carried rabies and lice. Their droppings caused "spelunker's lung" and God knows what else. He shuddered, but pressed on into the gloom, until the passageway tapered and blocked him. He didn't remember Jim complaining about getting through the side cave when he was a kid. Maybe there wasn't just one passage. Maybe in the darkness, he'd turned off into another lava tube and was winding toward oblivion. *Push. Harder.* His body was caught in a vice-like grip of stone walls. *What if I'm trapped here? What lies beyond?* His throat burned. His heart thumped in his chest, the chill of panic on his rigid body. He bit his lower lip, blood salting his saliva.

Stuck, he could neither turn around nor back out. Maybe he'd be trapped here forever, helpless. Maybe the cave would be their tomb, and years later, archeologists would discover their bones and try to surmise what had happened.

She loves me. Those words echoed in his soul. He pushed, sucking in his breath until his temples throbbed. Suddenly, he popped like a cork and landed in a larger chamber. He felt around with his hands, crawling on all fours in the dark until he was calm and realized he could stand. Then he inched on carefully for several more yards.

The passage couldn't go on forever, unless something about the terrain had changed, or if he were somewhere else. *Wait. I can see light! That is light, isn't it?* He rushed toward it, emerged into daylight and clawed his way through brambles blocking the exit.

"I'm out," he shouted to the stillness. "I'm actually out!"

He sat for a while to catch his breath, tears spilling down his cheeks. Tasting blood again, he realized his bitten lip was still bleeding. He wiped it and his face on his slimy sleeve.

He needed to find his way back to the front of the main cave so he could get Britt out. *Oh God. She loves me. Focus.*

He looked over his shoulder. No one there. He proceeded cautiously, climbing over the rocky mound, made slick by the recent rain, until he was on the other side and could see the actual cave entrance which was entirely collapsed. He tried to move the rubble with his bare hands, but there was too much of it.

"Britt! Can you hear me? Britt!" No answer came. *Hurry. Britt may not last. The oxygen inside has to be low.* He looked for the orange markers showing the way to the main trail. They were gone! Of course. Whoever was after them wanted to make sure they'd never be found. But who was that person? Bobby? He'd written those threatening notes, but could he be that cruel? Bury them alive. *Why?* Cody cringed. What to do?

He ran back to the cave entrance, where he spied a piece of a tree limb. He jerked off his sweatshirt and white T-shirt; then tied his tee tightly around the limb, making a white flag, which he punched into the debris covering the cave. If, for some reason, he was unable to return and others had to find the location, the flag would make it easier to spot.

He pulled his sweatshirt back on and headed out into muddy wilderness. What was it that Jim told him years ago? Something about following the sun, but there was no sun, just clouds. In his haste, he slipped and fell in the mud. Maybe he was going in circles. He thought of Britt in the cave. *How badly injured was she? How long would the lantern last? What about the food, water, oxygen levels? Injured. Hurt. Her life depends on me. Me alone. Do something, you idiot. Do something.* He trudged on. Stopping, slipping again, picking himself up.

When the sun gets over the big trees, walk down and out. Wasn't that what Jim had said? *Close your eyes. Think hard. Answers will come.* He sat down, squeezed his eyes shut, and saw Britt's face. "Breathe," she was saying. "Count your breaths." He circled his arms around his legs and laid his head on his knees. *Breathe. Just Breathe. The map. I drew a map. Remember it.* He tried to picture the map and the noted terrain features . . . the details . . . oddities. Those archeological digs. How did we . . .? Stop. Think. Observe. Plan.

Oh, merciful God, the sun was breaking through the clouds. Keep the sun aligned to the right shoulder and walk with the alignment. *And boots and pants and boots and pants.* Those words. Her happy laugh. *She loves me.* His thoughts shot back again to the student excavations he'd been on and survival tactics they'd learned. *How did we . . .? Ah, the make-shift compass.* He picked up a twig, held it over the hour hand on his watch and studied the shadow. North would be halfway from where the stick shadow is cast and twelve. It worked. There was just enough sun. *So if that's north, and we trekked east, then I need to go west in that direction.*

And boots and pants and boots and pants. Chanting those words to himself gave him a strange peacefulness. *Totem.* He reached into his pants pocket and fingered her bracelet. When he did, he felt his cellphone, which he thought he'd stuffed in his backpack. He slapped his forehead. *For Christ's sake. Plug in your brain.*

He pulled it out and kissed it. What was it his mother had told him at dinner that time when they talked about his Mazeophobia? Ah, yes. "If you ever get lost, just shoot a picture with your cell phone and send it to me. You know I'll come running." Hurriedly, he snapped photos of his surroundings and attached them to an e-mail message: *Mom, I'm lost out here in the wilderness. Britt is hurt. Help me.* He pressed *send.* Nothing. *How stupid. There's no connection. I'm going to have to finish this on my own.*

He trudged on, but stopped when he spied a scrap of litter. He stooped and picked up a wrapper and fingered it. *This is from Britt's energy bars. The ones that had blown away in the wind after our snack. It's like she's guiding me.* He stuffed the wrapper in his pocket next to her bracelet. *Totem.* He spotted the cluster of trees where they'd eaten. *I must be getting close to the main trail. When I get to the car . . . Dammit.* He didn't have his car keys. They were in the cave inside his backpack. His legs shook. *There's no cell coverage at the turnout either. My best bet is to flag down a car. Hurry! She loves me.*

Branches from the bushes swiped his face as he ran. *Be careful. This ground is rocky, wet, and slippery. If I fall and twist my ankle, Britt will die.* The highway couldn't be far. It's August. Tourist time. Someone would come by. He turned toward a rustle in the bushes. *What the?*

CHAPTER 34

A chunky, broad-shouldered man lunged and crashed into Cody. As they hit the ground, the big man on top of him, Cody glimpsed a deep scar on his attacker's face. The man flipped him over, grabbed his arms, and held him down. "Emilio," he shouted, "tie his hands."

Emilio. That name. He remembered. Omar had said the man in Salem who planted the pipe bomb was called Emilio. *The explosion in Salem. It was meant for me. But why?*

Once Emilio bound his hands behind his back, the scar-faced man approached and jerked him to his feet.

"What's this all about?" Cody demanded.

Scar Face, with his puffy eyes, baldhead and no facial hair, resembled a huge sausage. A stud sparkled on his left earlobe. "Just walk, professor. Another word and you're dead." He jammed a gun into Cody's ribs.

Emilio led the way down the trail, while Scar Face pushed him along toward the highway.

Cody's body hurt all over; his head ached from the blast, from the shove to the ground, from everything. None of this made any sense. "Listen," he pleaded, "My . . . There's a woman trapped in a cave back there. We've got to get help, or she'll die."

"You don't say," said Scar Face.

Emilio turned and sneered, exposing small yellow teeth. His plump face had an unkempt strap of hair on his chin and a thin mustache under his nose.

"Listen to me." Cody's voice rose. "You don't want to be responsible for her death . . . for involuntary manslaughter."

Emilio snorted. Scar Face gave Cody a shove. Once they'd reached the turnout, Cody spotted his Subaru and a faded, green Chevrolet sedan parked next to it. He glanced up and down the highway looking for help, but the men quickly heaved him into the Chevy's trunk.

Inside, it was dark and smelled like gasoline. The car doors slammed; the engine roared, and the car pulled out. Where were they taking him? Scrunched up against what felt like a spare tire and some cans, Cody struggled to get free. He had to save Brittany. How long had he been gone? She was trapped there alone with no serious medication. He remembered her warm kiss and her words: *I love you.* He kicked at the trunk lid with all his might. It was an older car; hopefully, he could spring it.

No luck. *What was that?*

He felt a familiar vibration coming from his pocket. His cell phone! Someone was calling him. They'd been driving for a while. They must be near a tower, which would mean they were heading toward the Lake Store. *Did my message to Mom go through?*

If he could just reach his phone, he could call 911. He squirmed trying to undo the bindings on his hands, bumping his head on the trunk lid. *I'm coming, Britt.* But alas, it was hopeless.

The car swayed as if the driver made an abrupt turn and then bumped along, shaking him inside the trunk. They must be off the highway on some rural road, somewhere deep in the forest, where they could easily kill him.

The car jerked to a stop. He heard the door slam, footsteps, and voices. "Let me do the talking," one of them said. Then silence. Were they just going to leave him in there? Footsteps again close to the car. The trunk flew open, the sudden light blinding him. Scar Face reached in, yanked him out, and drew his gun.

Once out, Cody spotted a baby blue Mercedes parked next to them.

"Move!" the man commanded through gritted teeth, forcing him up a narrow trail. They didn't blindfold him which meant they didn't care if he observed the surroundings, a sure sign that they were going to get rid of him.

Soon they arrived at what looked like an abandoned cabin made of gray, weathered logs that had seen better days. The one window facing them had broken panes, and a flimsy wooden door was propped open. Scar Face pushed Cody inside.

"About time, Honey," said a man, addressing Scar Face. The man, dressed in jeans and a red sweatshirt, was sitting on a wooden bench calmly eating cheese puffs from a bag. His thumb and forefinger were tinged yellow. A bucket-style, khaki fishing hat covered his head, and dark, wrap-around sunglasses obscured his eyes. A small red picnic cooler with a white top was beside him.

Cody quickly glanced around, trying to get his bearings. There was an old wood stove and metal framed bunk beds. Nothing else. The cabin smelled like an animal had rotted under the floorboards.

"You just couldn't let it go, could you, Benson," said the man, crunching a cheese puff.

"Excuse me?" That voice. He'd heard it before. He squinted at the man who was now draining his plastic water bottle. Cody studied every inch of him down to his red and black Air Jordan sneakers. It couldn't be, but it was. He was certain it was.

CHAPTER 35

Cally Benson, lips pursed, chin firmly set, drove as fast as she could to the Klamath County Sheriff's Office. She'd gone to Eugene to debrief a witness in a family matters case. While taking a break, she'd checked her iPhone and found a desperate e-mail message from Cody: *Mom, I'm lost out here in the wilderness. Britt is hurt. Help me.* She tried calling him, but when that failed, immediately notified the police, discontinued the interview, and sped south.

* * *

Matt Winslow, a solidly built Klamath County deputy with close-cropped blond hair, greeted her and escorted her to the windowless conference room where Sue Bolin sat, slumped behind a large, dark walnut table. Except for a round black-and-white clock, the walls were bare.

"This is Sue Bolin, Brittany's mother," Winslow said. "Do you know one another?"

"Yes, but it's been a long time," Cally said, extending her hand.

Sue gave her a tense, closed-mouth smile and a limp handshake. She uncrossed her legs, but didn't get up. Her eyes were red, as if she'd been crying. She wiped her nose with a Kleenex.

Although they were both in their early fifties, Cally thought Sue, with her white hair and deep lines around her mouth, had aged. She sat there in a rose-sprigged blouse that was buttoned wrong and black poplin pants.

Cally took the seat opposite her and adjusted her gray suit jacket and silk scarf. She brushed her hair back, staring into space.

"Would you like some coffee, Mrs. Benson?" Winslow asked. "You look drained."

"Please," Cally said, hardly thinking. "I've been on the road for three hours. I was in Eugene, on business, when I checked my phone." She waited while Winslow poured coffee from a carafe on a tray into a paper cup.

"Black is fine," she said, and he handed her the cup. The coffee tasted bitter. She took a sip and set it down. It didn't help the upheaval she felt in her stomach. "Do we know anything more?"

"Mrs. Benson, we've been studying the photos you forwarded, the ones Cody snapped with his cell phone. We believe that your son and Brittany are in the Big Bat Wilderness area. Because of the possibility of an injured girl, we immediately dispatched a search team. One lone hiker in the area reported that he heard something like a blast or maybe a gunshot."

"Oh, my God."

"At this point, we don't know if that's connected. We're trying to get more information. We are also trying to ping Cody's cell phone and Brittany's as well."

"Do we know how badly she's hurt?" Cally asked.

"Not yet." Winslow said. "Apparently, they didn't notify anyone of their destination. Is your son an experienced hiker?"

"I wouldn't call him a seasoned outdoorsman. He's a teacher, an anthropology professor at Willamette University in Salem." She paused. "None of this makes sense. I mean Cody suffers from Mazeophobia, the fear of getting lost."

"I don't know why he had to take her out there," Sue said pointedly. "Especially if he has no sense of direction."

The door opened. An older man in a police uniform rushed into the conference room. Winslow nodded.

"I'm so glad you're back," Sue said to the man. "Did you hear anything from Bobby?"

"No, he hasn't contacted me."

The officer offered his hand to Cally. He was older and heavier with a full head of gray hair. She instantly recognized him as Ken Blake, the deputy in charge of the search when Cody was a kid. His presence kicked up memories, the heavy snow, the flaming bonfire, Cody's empty room. A wave of anxiety coursed through her body.

"It's ironic that we come together again to find your missing son," said Blake.

"Yes," Cally replied, her voice tense. "I'm not sure I understand how, what has happened. Why are they out there?"

"What do we know?" Blake said to Winslow. "Any word from Bobby?"

Winslow looked at Cally. "Bobby Blaze, a family friend of the Bolin's, reviewed the photos and recognized some features of the terrain as being in the Big Bat Wilderness area. We've dispatched a National Guard helicopter from Kingsley Air Field. Blaze and Korman are flying over the area as we speak. Merrill Korman is the lead deputy from Forest Lake. He's also an experienced hiker. So we're in good hands."

"Bobby is very familiar with that area, too." Ken said. He took a seat next to Sue.

"Yeah," said Winslow. "He thinks he has an idea of where they might have gone. He said he followed the kids out there one time."

"Why?" Sue asked.

"I don't know. Blaze said they were interested in a cave. Maybe Brittany slipped and took a tumble on the trail or in the cave. Cody may have gone for help and got lost. Blaze said the cave is way off the main trail."

"I'm still confused," Sue said. "Brittany said nothing about a cave. She was planning to marry another man. Well, I mean, they were trying to get back together." Her face flushed; she tugged at the collar of her blouse. "Now this."

Cally said, "I know Cody was in Forest Lake doing research on that Indian, but a hike into the rugged wilderness doesn't make a lot of sense."

"What Indian?" Winslow asked. "Blaze?"

"No, that old case . . . uh . . . what was his name. Oh, Fallingwater. Something Fallingwater."

"Who?" asked Sue.

"Fallingwater?" Blake's eyebrows raised. "You know, he mentioned that a couple of times to me. I mean, his interest in that old case."

"I told her," Sue said. "Stick with Lance Helms. He's got a good head on his shoulders." She started to cry. "She's all I got." She dabbed her nose with her wadded tissue. "Lance is a lawyer. He knows people. Has anybody called Lance?"

No one answered. Blake patted her hand. "Don't worry, Sue. We'll find them."

Winslow's cell went off. "Excuse me, but I have to take that." He left the room. There was silence.

Cally said nothing. She got the distinct impression Sue was not pleased with Brittany's friendship with Cody.

Sue sniffed. "I just want to thank you for getting the ball rolling so fast," she said to Blake. She looked at Cally. "I called him as soon as I was notified that Brittany was missing."

Cally instantly understood. Usually, the police had to get their bearings, figure out if the report was valid, do preliminary work before dispatching a search team, but Blake's credibility with the force probably helped speed things along. "My thanks as well. I—"

Winslow burst into the room, carrying a piece of paper. He looked harried.

"What's up?" Ken asked.

Cally sat on the edge of her chair. "Have they found them?"

Winslow gave a long sigh. "We got a near fatality out in Forest Lake."

"Who?" asked Ken, surprised. He jumped up.

"An older fella." Winslow looked at the paper. "Gilbert Holloway. He's been shot."

"Toad, shot? Everybody likes Toad. What the hell happened?"

"Details right now are sketchy. Sounds like a home invasion. He's asking for you."

CHAPTER 36

Cody scanned the room again. Was he suffocating, still stuck in the cave and hallucinating? No. This was real, and the man crunching cheese puffs was Bill Janes!

"Britt," he pleaded, "She was with me in the cave. We need to get help. I'm begging you—"

"I don't know what it is with you, Benson," Janes said, while Honey jabbed Cody with his pistol.

"What the hell is going on?" Cody demanded. Were they planning to kill him, to clear the field for Lance? That couldn't be it. Britt was targeted, too, and no one cared. Janes was a responsible person, an elected official, a CEO. "I don't get any of this. What are *you*," he glanced at the other two men, "and those jerks trying to prove? Britt is injured, we—"

"You're like a cat, Benson. You seem to have nine lives." He took a sip of water from a fresh plastic bottle, popped another cheese puff in his mouth, and slowly chewed. "So, this time I had to be here to make sure the job got done right."

"This time?"

"That other fat ass failed so many times . . ." He removed his sunglasses and set them on the bench. "To discourage you."

"What fat ass?"

Janes' eyes looked weird, like he was on something. "Oh, come on Benson, wasn't he your dear friend?" He appeared to be taunting Cody and enjoying it. He looked at Emilio. "Artie . . . what the hell was his name?" He snapped his fingers.

Emilio shrugged, his upper lip curled into a sneer as if he were bored.

"Artie. You're talking about Artie Bradshaw," Cody said. "You killed him?" He'd been right, Artie was the one who tampered with his car.

"Ah, professor. Not me. I have people." He gestured toward the two men.

Honey's laugh revealed a set of crooked teeth. He stuck his pistol in his belt and seated himself on the lower bunk bed frame.

"Why? Why everything? How does any of this involve me?"

"Your friend," Janes said in a voice so cold, it could chill the August heat, "had a big mouth. Want some?" He thrust the bag of cheese puffs toward Cody, like a deranged person offering poisoned meat to a dog.

"Are you stupid? Do you think you'll get away with this?"

Janes took a long drink of water. "Yeah, I do. Haven't you heard, Benson? Money talks, bullshit walks." He folded the top of the bag and set it on the cooler. "You had to go poking your nose in other people's business. Fallingwater . . ."

Cody's eyes widened. "Fallingwater? This is about Fallingwater. Jesus Christ. What has researching an old, dead Indian have to do with anything?"

The tip of Janes' tongue licked the corners of his mouth. "Don't play cutesy with me, Benson."

It was beginning to make sense. Janes was a paranoid sociopath, stuffing his face with cheese puffs while talking casually about murder; a depraved politician, not letting anything stand in his way.

Cody remembered Janes' overreaction at lunch when Britt mentioned Christie Jenkins. It was almost like someone shoved a screwdriver up his ass. Yeah. That had to be it. "You were there that night, weren't you? And you killed her. You killed Christie Jenkins in a jealous fit." He was fishing, but it was the only explanation. "And scared shitless that it might finally come out and ruin your little election plans." He paused to test Janes' reaction.

"You're pretty smart, professor, too smart for your own good."

Bingo.

Janes lunged toward him. Every nerve in the left side of Cody's face throbbed after Janes slapped it hard, almost knocking him off balance. But Cody managed to stand firm and to return a glare. He could see the pupils of Janes' eyes were dilated. Along with the stinging slap, he'd caught a whiff of his attacker's expensive cologne. He smelled like Lance.

Janes was the first to break eye contact, looking over Cody's shoulder with a faraway expression on his face. "I followed them out there that night. I thought she loved me. I bought a ring." His voice seemed to trail off, but as his anger rose, it got louder. "And there she was with him, laughing, leading him on . . . making love in his dirty pickup." His face reddened. "She'd told me she was pregnant. And there she was screwing a bushnigger with my baby inside her." He tipped his water bottle, taking another sloppy swallow.

"For Christ's sake," Cody said. He could feel his left eye swelling shut. "She was just a kid. Only seventeen. Probably mixed up."

Janes spit a mouthful of water on the floor. "I was young too, with a *future.* I made a mistake, I mean with her. She . . . she lied to me. There was no baby." His voice turned raspy. He paused to clear his throat. "The windows were open. I could hear . . . everything. 'Billy boy,' she called me. Said my daddy was rich and I was her ticket out." Janes paused again and drank more water.

"She was laughing at Fallingwater. The fool had just proposed. She kept laughing. I heard a scream. The pickup door opened, and she fell to the ground. She had slashes on her clothing and some cuts on her arms. The stupid fucker tossed his knife and drove away. I'd hoped he'd killed her. But no. The bitch was screaming at me." His blue eyes got that icy stare again. He raised his voice to mimic hers. "'That goddam Indian raped me. He stabbed me. Help me.'"

"So you finished the job, didn't you?"

"I . . . My father wouldn't have . . ."

"Didn't you?" Cody taunted. Honey advanced.

Janes waved him back. "She would've ruined my life."

"So filled with rage, you couldn't stop. How many? How many times did you stab her?"

Janes smirked. "It all fit so well. Fallingwater was a savage who lost control. What did anyone expect? Poor bastard."

"All these years, you knew."

"He was a loser."

"He was ten times the man you are. No, I take that back, one hundred times."

"Shut up, professor."

"Squared."

"You just couldn't leave it alone, could you?"

"You dug this hole yourself. I had nothing to go on. You. Insecure. Bastard."

"Don't play games with me, Benson." He tossed his nearly empty water bottle on the floor. "You pumped Holloway. Got it out of him."

"Toad? What?"

"Let's just say," his mouth turned upward into a feckless smile, "there's nothing left to pump."

"You hurt Toad?" He felt a spasm of disgust. Everything about this man was malignant. "You're crazy, sick."

Honey jumped up. "You want me to take care of him?"

Janes waved him off. "In time. In time."

Time. That word seared his heart. "Brittany Bolin is trapped in that cave. She hasn't got much *time.*"

"So you sealed her death," Janes said.

"She doesn't know anything about this."

"We can't be sure, can we, professor?"

"What was all that shit about you wanting her to marry Lance Helms . . . to join your family."

"That was then. This is now. Things got too sticky."

"You just can't *feel,* can you, Janes?"

"Why you . . ." Janes lunged at him again. This time grabbing his neck.

Emilio pulled Janes back. "Take it easy," he said. He came up to Cody. He pulled a knife with a serrated edge and placed it against Cody's neck.

Emilio smelled sour.

"You watch your damn hole," he said, "or I'll hang you up like a pig and slit your throat."

Janes' thin lips smiled. "You're the *last* one standing in my way," he said to Cody. When you're gone, my secret dies with you . . . and the girl, well . . . nature will take its course. No one will know."

Cody's whole body tightened. Without him, there was no hope for Britt. His head hurt. His mind stalled, going round and round, like that little buffering hub on the Internet. He heard Dr. A speaking, *Face your tigers, Professor. Face your tigers.* Then Jim's voice from long ago: *You can still talk to me when I'm away. Close your eyes. Go to that special place inside.* What to do? His wrists were bound. He saw Britt, her arms outstretching. *Come . . . come back to me.* Beads of sweat formed on his brow. Another spark of memory: his encounter with Lance. *Brain over brawn.* His mental web page had loaded. A forced smile on his lips, he said with as much confidence as he could muster, "We left our backpacks by the cave entrance. When the blast went off, it splattered them, leaving pieces all over the area. My wallet. Her ID."

Janes' bloodshot eyes were round. "Is that true?" he asked Honey.

Honey shrugged his shoulders. "We lit the fuse. We had to get outta there fast."

"Bomb squads these days are highly sophisticated," Cody taunted. "They can analyze residue, piece things together. *Trace* them. Bow hunting season starts soon. The area will be crawling with archers. And, don't forget about my car."

Honey snickered. "Oh, don't worry, Benson, we'll take care of that."

Janes grinned.

"Be my guest," Cody said. "It's a rental funded by my insurance company. You can bet they're going to look into the matter." The three of them were stupid. Sick. Especially Janes. He looked smaller than Cody remembered. He knew the type, a pampered, spoiled rich brat, always getting his way, never growing up. This man was an elected official who supposedly ran an important company, but more than likely, he was a figurehead. As he said, he had people. People who came behind him with a shovel, scooping up the messes he made while he filled a chair. It had come to this all because Janes wanted to ensure that the truth about Christie Jenkins would never surface. Now, he was in it so deep. What did Dr. A call it when you messed with a person's mind until his own thoughts got the best of him? Ah, that was it, *mental masturbation.* It was his only hope. "The cave I found. That's where Jim lived," Cody said.

"Lived?"

"Yeah, Fallingwater didn't freeze to death like everybody thought. He escaped and hid out in that cave. I found it . . . along with some old journals he left . . . before he hightailed it out to God knows where. You probably remember, they never found his body.

"Oh, the journals are not in perfect condition, but he mentioned you and Christie in them. That's how I connected you two. Toad had nothing to do with that." He could see he had Janes' attention.

"Fallingwater didn't just drive off that night. No, he stayed and watched. I'm hoping he recorded what he saw. In great detail. The journals are now at Boston University being carefully examined by an old colleague of mine." He picked a university far away because he felt it sounded more believable. "So, you can kill me, but it won't matter. In a few weeks, he'll have the notebooks deciphered, and the police will piece it all together. Especially since Britt and I will be missing. The cave. The explosion. Evidence . . . especially evidence, will lead them directly to *you*."

"You're shitting me." Janes' eyes darted from Cody to Honey to Emilio and back again. He did that several times, like an animal not knowing which way to run.

"Am I? Just wait and see." Cody managed a sinister laugh. "And, when it all comes out, you're going to have a cozy little room on death row."

Something changed in Janes' expression. His face, seemingly etched with doubt, reddened. His eyes kept moving from Cody, to the men and back, as if his brain was fogged by whatever drug or drugs he'd swallowed for artificial courage.

Emilio, standing by the old wood stove, fiddled with the lid; then lit a joint, took a drag, and handed it to Honey. Cody needed to lasso Janes fast before those two potheads got so high, they were capable of anything. He could see them exchanging looks, and Emilio giving Honey some kind of a high sign. Janes was a dolt. He had no idea how much danger *he* was in.

"I'll make a deal with you," Cody said. "You pay me a cool two million, and the notebooks are yours. You get to play the hero. You can say you happened to run into me on the highway . . . saved me. Then we notify the authorities about Brittany. The press will eat that up. Think about it. State representative saves two lives. Yeah. People love stories like that. Then you and me, we go to Boston, I get the notebooks, hand them over to you. You give me the money, and I'm out of the picture."

Honey and Emilio exchanged looks. Emilio took another long drag on his joint, his eyes narrowed.

Janes' knuckles stroked his chin. "And Brittany?"

"Like I said, she doesn't know what's in the notebooks. She thinks our trips to the cave were outings. She bought my research bullshit. She's in love with Lance and is all gaga about a wedding. Already picked out a dress. So, there's no reason for me to stay around. Once you have the notebooks and I have the money, I disappear."

"Where?"

"Wait a fucking minute," Honey said.

Janes waved him off. "Let him finish."

"I'm scheduled to do some field work in South America. You can check on that. Just call the university. So I take the money, leave, and am never heard from again. After all, Colombia can be a dangerous place. With that much money, I'd never have to teach again. Besides, if anyone ever learned of our deal, I'd go to prison. So we'd both have something at stake."

"What about *our* deal?" Honey demanded.

"Your deal. Your deal." Janes was almost shouting. "You bungled it. That's why I'm here *now,* because you failed. Benson was supposed to be dead."

CHAPTER 37

Ken rushed to Toad's room at the Klamath Falls hospital and exchanged greetings with two detectives who were already there. "They beat him up pretty bad," one said to Ken in hushed tones. "Fractured his ribs and broke his arm. If that wasn't enough, they stabbed him, shot him in the gut, and left him for dead. A neighbor thought he heard something and went over to check on the old guy. Mr. Holloway asked to see you."

Ken approached the bed. "Toad, it's me, Ken," he said, softly.

Toad's swollen eyelids twitched. His face looked like hamburger. His left arm was heavily wrapped and in a black sling. A nasal cannula mustached his face, a bouffant blue surgery cap covered his head, and he had an IV attached to the back of his right hand. A strong antiseptic smell lingered over him.

"Ken?" he wheezed.

"Yeah, it's me." The sight of this kind, happy man in that condition turned his stomach.

"I never thought he woulda hurt me."

The two detectives moved to the foot of the bed. One flipped on a small tape recorder. "Who hurt you?" Ken asked, his voice angry. "Who did this to you?"

"I woulda never told, but I'm not gonna . . ." He gasped. "be quiet no more. No siree."

"Take it easy, Toad. You can say what you want. No one is going to hurt you anymore," Ken assured him. He reached over and grasped Toad's left hand. It was icy.

"That night." He stopped and took a breath. "Bill had blood all over him . . . h-he wanted me to help."

"Bill?"

"H-he said he'd been deer huntin'. . . I knowed it was a lie."

"What night do you mean?" Ken asked.

"I weren't to say nothin'. Or his uncle would be mad. T-takin' his gun and huntin' in the dark and all. R-real agitated like." Toad paused and swallowed. The heart monitoring equipment beeped.

"Easy, easy," Ken said.

"He cleaned himself up an' . . . an' slept in my trailer on the place. Next morning, he took off like a bat out of hell. D-didn't want coffee or nuthin'. I made up a pot, but he just beat it."

"Slow down, Toad. I'm not exactly following you." He squeezed Toad's hand.

"I knowed it was in the fall. He came in the night. T-the next day they found that young girl dead. I never saw him again. Didn't come back and work summers no more. Guess his Daddy got sick. I kinda wondered about it. But then I'd never seen Bill with a girl."

"Bill who? What girl?"

"The weather changed, an' we went into Halloween an' all. Always had a big party out at Benders. Lotsa beer and music." He gasped and began breathing hard. "I was younger then." Some spittle dripped down his chin.

"It's okay, Toad." Ken pulled a handful of tissues from the box on his bedstand and carefully wiped it away.

"There was lotsa talk about the red-haired girl and the injun feller who killed her."

Ken's eyes narrowed. He leaned closer. "Are you talking about Fallingwater and Christie Jenkins?"

"Bill was a real nice guy. And he done all right. He's a big shot up North. N-never did come back to Forest Lake that I knowed about, but each month he sends me a check. Guess he appreciated it an' all. Not telling . . . keeping him informed."

"What's Bill's last name. Can you remember?"

"Janes. Bill Janes."

Blake and the two detectives exchanged looks.

Toad took in a deep breath. His voice got high, like he might cry. "I-I'm worried about them two kids."

"Kids?"

His body started to shake. "I don't want them hurt because of me . . . of what I told."

"What kids, Toad?" Blake asked again.

"M-Miss Brittany and that young feller, Cody. H-he thinks they know."

* * *

The spinning blades of the National Guard helicopter cut through the air with Deputy Merrill Korman in the seat next to the pilot. Bobby Blaze seated behind them leaned over Korman's shoulder. They flew over the area that Bobby identified as the place where he believed Cody and Brittany could be. It was consistent with the general area where the witness said he thought he heard a loud noise.

"Look over there," Korman said.

"What is it?" Bobby asked.

"A white flag on a stick or something."

Bobby leaned forward. "Can we take it down closer?"

"Yeah," said Curt, the pilot. "Hang on." The helicopter juddered downward and hovered. "That's about as low as I can take it."

Bobby pressed close to the window, looking for familiar points. "That's it," Bobby said. "See that rocky ledge over there and that tree. I'm pretty sure that's where the cave is, but holy shit, it looks like the opening collapsed."

Winslow pulled out his binoculars to survey the area. "You don't think they were messing around and trying to blast something?"

"That doesn't make much sense," Bobby said. "Benson didn't strike me as the type that would play with explosives or guns."

"Cody must have gotten out somehow," Winslow said, "or maybe was on the outside when it collapsed. Then he went for help. Got lost. My guess is the girl is trapped inside. That's why the white flag is there."

"There's no place to land on that terrain," said Curt.

"I'll radio it in." Korman contacted dispatch, described the situation, and the white flag. With Curt's help, he gave the location. "Bobby Blaze, who's here with me and very familiar with the area, says there's a cave there," Korman told dispatch. "The girl could be inside. How close is the search team?" He waited for a response. "10-4. Get a crew up here fast. Notify the fire department. We're gonna continue to see if we can spot Benson . . . Yeah, 10-4. I'll wait."

Bobby cupped his ear to hear over the din of the rotors. "What's happening?"

250

Korman didn't have time to answer. "What's that?" he said to dispatch. "Okay, 10-4 Okay. That's odd. What would he be doing there?" He paused again to listen. "10-4. Just a minute." Korman turned to Bobby, his voice loud. "They've picked up a ping from Benson's cell phone. It's not in this area, but farther east. Over by Yoder's Creek. Could he have wandered off that far? That's miles from here."

Bobby looked puzzled. "Yoder's Creek? There's an old shack out that way. A cabin, well more like an old shack. Do you know which one I'm talkin' about?"

"Yeah, I've been there. Yoder's Hideaway? Used by duck and deer hunters as a kind of camp."

"Why would he be that far away?" Bobby asked.

"I don't know, unless someone else has his cell phone." Korman quizzed dispatch. "Did you say Yoder's Creek? That's miles from— what? When did that happen? Okay. Yeah. Right. 10-4." He turned to face Bobby. "There's more. There's been a homicide in Forest Lake."

Bobby sat up straight. "Who?"

"Toad Holloway."

"What! Who would hurt Toad?" Bobby's clenched fist pressed against his chin.

"A house invasion or something. Beat up bad. Shot. Died at the hospital."

"He's dead? Jesus. Toad. Have they made an arrest?"

"No. And get this. Before Toad died, he told Ken Blake something about a murder. Blake believes these kids could be in real danger."

Bobby shook his head; his eyes blinked rapidly. "I can't believe this." His voice quavered. "He was my friend. What's that got to do with the kids?"

"The killer thinks they *know* something."

CHAPTER 38

Honey's face blotched. "You're here, Janes, because you were supposed to bring the loot."

Emilio's eyes were almost slits. "You brought the dough, right?"

"Untie him," Janes ordered.

"What?" Emilio glanced warily at Honey, then back at Janes.

"I said untie him. Then we'll talk about money. A little something for everybody." Janes smiled as if he were about to hand out candy at a kid's birthday party.

Emilio approached Cody with his knife and cut the bindings from his wrists. Emilio smelled like rotten onions.

Cody shook his unfettered hands. He didn't know what Janes or his thugs were up to, and he didn't know what he would do if Janes discovered he was lying, but he didn't have a lot of choices.

Honey seemed edgy. "We need to *talk* about our payoff now."

Cody turned to Janes. A coolness washed over him. Lying was getting easier and easier. It was a long shot, but he took it. "For Christ's sake, Janes. *Think*. You just told them." He flicked his thumb toward Honey and Emilio. "What this is really all about. Covering up a murder. And, now, it appears, murders. Can you trust a couple of dopers to be quiet? Huh? I doubt it. They will always be on your tail for money . . . for the rest of your life. Blackmail."

"Goddam you, Benson." Honey pointed his gun and cocked the hammer. The tips of his ears reddened.

Cody raised his hands, palms outward as if signaling a truce. "Do you really think Janes is going to pay you and let you live? After what *you* know? Plug in your brain, fella."

Honey turned the gun on Janes. "We want the loot, *now.*"

"Okay. Okay." Janes' hands rose like a teacher quieting an unruly class. He sighed and paused. His eyes darted repeatedly from Honey's gun to Emilio. "Once I hand you the money, I better never hear from you again. Deal?"

"Yeah," said Honey. "Deal." His eyes slid toward Emilio who smirked.

"But first, put down that gun."

Honey hesitated.

Janes folded his arms. "Put it down now. We're all partners here."

Honey lowered his hand. Janes waited until Honey tucked it into his belt.

"That's better." Janes reached into the cooler, took out a large paper sack. "You'll want to count it," he said. He started to put the sack on the bench. As Honey lunged for it, Janes pulled a small pistol from behind the sack and calmly shot Honey twice in the gut.

"My God," Cody blurted, his ears ringing from the noise. *He's going to kill us all.*

Emilio jerked back, dropped his knife and raised both hands; then side-stepped his way toward the door, turned, and dashed out.

"Hurry," Cody shouted at Janes. " *We* can't let him get away. He knows!" He started for the door. "Let's go!"

Janes tore past Cody, chasing Emilio in hot pursuit. He fired a shot as he exited. Cody didn't wait around to find out if Janes shot connected, or if Honey was dead or alive. Once out, he took off in the opposite direction.

Out of breath, Cody crouched behind bushes, breathing hard. He had no idea where he was. He waited and listened. *Were those footsteps?* He crouched lower, pulled out his cell phone, and dialed 911. *Nothing.* He flinched when he heard more shots in the distance. *Did Janes land Emilio or was it the other way around?* He got up cautiously, checked both directions, and started running again before coming to a jarring halt.

He was looking down the barrel of a gun.

CHAPTER 39

"Freeze!" said the man dressed in black, a helmet on his head. "Put your hands up!"

Cody's arms flew toward the sky. He could see the words POLICE across the man's chest. "I'm Cody Benson. They kidnapped me."

"Turn around. Get down on your knees," the SWAT team member ordered.

Cody buckled his knees as fast as he could. "Brittany Bolin," he pleaded over his shoulder. "She's hurt. She needs help."

"Now, down on your stomach."

Cody hit the ground.

"Put your hands behind your back." The officer cuffed him, got up, and barked into his radio, all the time his gun pointed. "Yeah, okay," Cody heard him say, "I'll bring him in."

"On your feet." The officer marched Cody toward the cabin, still cuffed.

Why was a SWAT team here and why were they arresting him? "I'm the victim, goddammit." He gasped. "What's going on?"

"Keep walking," the officer commanded.

When he reached the cabin, he saw several other SWAT team members, all dressed in black, carrying guns. A medical team was on the scene. Two paramedics were transporting someone on a stretcher down the trail. Cody couldn't see who the person was.

Another officer, apparently the leader, came forward and greeted them. "It's okay, Steve," he said, "This *is* Cody Benson."

The police officer removed the handcuffs. "Sorry," he said." In situations like this, we can't take chances."

Cody rubbed his wrists. "Listen," he said, "My companion, Britt, she needs help . . ." He stopped. He saw Emilio, head bent down, in cuffs. Two officers escorted him down the trail. *Was Janes still out there, armed? Why can't I get through to these people?*

"There were three of them, right?" the leader asked Cody.

"Yeah, three," he answered, his voice weedy.

"Then, that's the last of them. I'm Sergeant Henderson." He extended his hand.

Cody felt dizzy, his handshake weak. He tried again. "Brittany Bolin, my companion, she's trapped in a cave," he pleaded, his mouth dry, his voice scraping. "I've got to save her." His eyes got moist. "S-She loves me," he said lamely.

Sergeant Henderson grinned. "I think you already have."

"What's that?"

"I take it you're the one that planted that white flag?"

"Yeah, but . . ."

"Just a second." He radioed dispatch. "Have we got an update on the girl? Yeah, Ms. Bolin. Okay. Right. Okay. I'll wait."

To Cody, those minutes seemed like hours.

"Un-huh," Henderson said into his radio. "10-4. All three are in custody. We're wrapping it up." He turned to Cody. "They've located her and are working to get her out. An ambulance is standing by at the trail head. Another one is coming this way for you."

"Is she okay?"

"We'll know more about her condition when they actually get her out. How about you? Your face looks pretty banged up."

His hand went to his face. Dried blood from his head wound caked on his forehead and temple. His eye was sore and tender caused by Janes' slap. His whole body ached. Acid crept up from his gut and burned his throat. The tension that had kept him going lifted from his body. He crumpled in a heap to the ground. His fingers clutched at the hard earth. He burst into tears thinking of Britt, alone in that dark, cold cave, waiting, just waiting

CHAPTER 40

The next morning ...

Several reporters lingered outside Sky Lakes Medical Center in Klamath Falls waiting for a spokesperson to give them an update on Brittany Bolin's condition. In the meantime, the website of the Salem *Statesman Journal* carried a story under **BREAKING NEWS**.

State Representative William Janes of Lake Oswego and a declared candidate for the U.S. Senate was arrested yesterday on several counts of murder, assault, and kidnapping. He is being held in the Klamath Falls County jail. Janes is the owner and CEO of Janes Timber, a log export business based in Portland.

Two other men, Robert Honeyman and Emilio Alberto of Salem were also taken into custody. Honeyman was transported to the Klamath Falls hospital where he later died from gunshot wounds. All three men—Janes, Honeyman, and Alberto—were captured after a shootout with a Klamath Falls SWAT team in the Big Bat Wilderness area near Forest Lake. According to police records, Alberto is a suspected drug dealer with ties to a Mexican cartel.

Janes is believed to be responsible for the murder of a Forest Lake woman, Christie Jenkins, some 40 years ago. The man, previously accused of her murder, Jim Fallingwater, escaped from custody and later perished in the wilderness.

"This all came down because a politician wanted to cover up a past crime." Chief Deputy Merrill Korman of Forest Lake said. Korman

also said police are looking into the possible connection of Janes and Alberto to the deaths of two other Forest Lake men.

Janes and Alberto were charged with the attempted murder and kidnapping of Cody Benson, a twenty-six-year-old Willamette University professor who was looking into the Fallingwater case, as well as the attempted murder of his companion, Brittany Bolin, also of Salem. Benson and Bolin were doing research in a cave in the Big Bat Wilderness Area when Honeyman and Alberto apparently detonated an explosive.

Firefighters and rescue workers removed Bolin from the cave. She sustained a leg fracture and other injuries in the blast and was taken to the hospital in Klamath Falls. Benson, who was treated and released, was not available for comment.

Janes' campaign headquarters had no comment, except to say they were stunned.

More details will be available when known.

* * *

Two days later ... Sky Lakes Medical Center

"The patient is sitting up and taking food," said Sue Bolin when Cody came into the hospital room juggling three paper cups of Starbucks Coffee. She pointed to the breakfast tray in front of Brittany.

Cody immediately went to Brittany's bedside and kissed the bruise on her forehead. "Just what the doctor ordered," he said, and set a vanilla soy latte on her tray. "And one for you, too." He handed Sue a tall regular caffé latte. The pleasant smell of coffee competed with the antiseptic hospital smell.

Brittany laughed. Her left leg was in a cast, sticking out from under the sheets and elevated on two pillows. She took a big sip. "Just what I needed."

"You're still a bit pale," Cody said to Brittany, "but you're looking better today."

"The nurse helped me wash my hair with my own shampoo. I feel like a new woman."

"She's had some respiratory therapy and is breathing a lot better, too," Sue said. She looked haggard after sleeping in a chair by Brittany's bedside since she was admitted, but happy her daughter was going to be okay. Deferring to Sue's need to be with her daughter, Cody and his mother had retreated to a Shilo Inn Suites Hotel.

Sue set down her latte. "I've never been able to get used to this dressed-up coffee. You have to get through all that foam stuff on top before you get to the drink, and then it's too sweet."

"Oh Mother, just enjoy it."

Sue took a tentative sip. "I don't know why they have to mess up a good cup of coffee."

"I had to search to find Starbucks," Cody said. "Finally found one inside Safeway."

"Well, okay then," Sue said. "Thank you. How are you doing?"

"Good. I had another long talk with Dr. A over the phone last night to clear my head. Mom's watching me like a hawk, and I'm an expert at dodging reporters."

Sue stood up. "Now that you're here. I'm going to go back to the motel to clean up and get some sleep. I'll be back this afternoon, honey." She gave Brittany a kiss on the cheek. "Is there anything you want?"

"Bring me something to read . . . some magazines . . . That would be good."

After Sue left, Cody leaned over and kissed Brittany on the mouth. Then he buried his face in her soft, fragrant hair. "I love you so much."

"I love you, too." When he released his embrace, she glanced at the bedside table. "Mother left her coffee. Next time bring her a can of Folgers." Brittany giggled and then got serious. "The police were here," she said.

"Yeah, I've been talking to them, too. Apparently, Toad told them a mouthful before he passed. They pinged my cell phone and found the cabin. The SWAT team was closing in just when Janes shot Honeyman."

"We owe a lot to Toad. When I get better, I want to visit his grave. Bring flowers. I guess I'll have to wait until I can walk."

"Don't worry, I'll carry you there." He hugged her again. "I never want to let you go." He kissed her passionately.

"It could take six to eight weeks before I heal. I'll probably have to use crutches and go through physiotherapy to regain muscle strength."

Cody planted a kiss on her head. "The important thing is that you made it."

"Lance called."

Cody sighed. *Why can't that guy just get the fuck out of my life?* The last thing he needed was to hear about Mr. Perfect. "I guess Janes is on suicide watch."

"Figures. Lance is pretty shaken up about the whole thing."

"Did it bother him at all that it nearly killed us?"

"He wanted to see me, but I said no. Then he wanted to talk to Mother and she said no."

"I can't believe that guy. Did he think he was just going to waltz in here and start where he left off? What a prick."

"Calm down. He said he knew nothing about Janes' past or his connection to those two thugs. He wanted me to know that."

"Do you believe him?"

"I don't know." She shrugged. "The acting CEO of Janes Timber let him go."

"Nice words for fired."

"He said Janes Timber is in shambles and will probably be sold."

"Aww. I can hear the whistle from the Forest Lake sawmill all the way from here."

Brittany lifted her latte as if making a toast. "Cheers to those good people. Anyway, Lance is moving out of state. Some place far away where they won't know about him or his connection to Janes."

"The farther the better."

"You know, I wish him the best. I hope he finds himself. He—" She stopped because of a knock on the door.

"Come in," Cody said.

Bobby Blaze scurried in, carrying a bouquet of fiery orange-toned roses and Asiatic lilies. He carefully closed the door and set the flowers on the bedside table. The radiant flowers lit up the nearly all-white room. Bobby's hair was neatly combed into a ponytail, and he wore a jacket over his jeans, like he might be going to church, if he belonged to one. He nodded to Cody.

"Thanks, Bobby," Brittany said. "They're beautiful."

"I ran into your mother. She says you're doing well."

"Have a seat," Cody said, offering him his chair.

"Nah, you sit there. Listen," Bobby said. "I need to talk to you guys."

Cody stiffened. He and Brittany exchanged glances. "Yeah, Bobby, you do. You left those threatening notes on our door, didn't you?"

"Yeah, listen . . ."

Cody stood up and folded his arms. "Why, for God's sakes?"

"Listen to me, will you?"

Cody took a step forward, inches from Bobby's face. "What the hell were you thinking?"

"Shut up and listen."

Brittany rubbed the center of her forehead. "Please. This isn't helping. And never, never forget, Bobby helped them find me."

Cody backed off. He hung his head and sat down. "Okay, but—"

"He wants to see you," Bobby said.

He looked up. "Who does?"

"Jim."

Cody's head jerked up. "Jim?"

"Jim Fallingwater."

"What! You know where he is." He was on his feet again.

"Yeah. I didn't know who *you* were."

"You're not making any sense."

"Jim is in Oklahoma. Eastern Oklahoma. He lives way out in the country with my cousin, Nola. Away from people."

"But the notes . . ."

"Look, there's a penalty for hindering prosecution of a fugitive. It could get you time in the slammer . . . five to ten years."

"But why—"

"I thought I could scare you off. I didn't know *why* you wanted to find out about him. My father, Frank Blaze, helped Jim get there years ago. If the cops find out, we'd all be in a sack of grunt."

"But he's innocent, Janes—"

Bobby took a deep breath. "Just listen. There are other issues. Okay? I've been in contact with Nola. Now, I know. You're the kid. He wants to see you. He's not well."

"He . . . he . . . wants me to come?" Cody glanced out the window and then back at Bobby. He didn't know what to say. All the years he spent wondering about Jim, struggling with haunting dreams, wondering if he was real or imagined. Scared. Afraid of getting lost. *Don't tell. Don't tell.* Briefly, he saw himself in the cave with Jim hovering over a glowing fire, Wolf by his side, the dog's big pink tongue lolling to one side. This man not only saved his life but changed it. After all he'd been through, he'd given up hope of ever finding Jim. Now Bobby was offering him up. Poof. Just like that. Just when he needed to stay close to Brittany. He felt a gnawing in his gut.

"Don't worry about me, Cody." Brittany said, pulling him back into the discussion. "You need to go. Mother will look after me."

His body tensed. "He's in Oklahoma. He remembers me?"

"You *can't* talk to the police about it. There's still the matter of assault . . . and my cousin and other folks hiding him. And that *other* incident . . . I mean there still are legal problems. Big ones. A whole lot of people could be in trouble. It's best that they continue to think he's dead."

"I never *ever* intended to involve the police. I—"

"Like I said. I didn't know who you were. I believed your cockin' bullshit story about doin' research."

"I just needed to find closure . . . to thank him. I—"

"Then you need to hurry."

CHAPTER 41

Cody and Cally boarded a Delta flight out of Portland for a four-hour trip to eastern Oklahoma. After a brief layover in Salt Lake City, they landed at Tulsa International Airport, rented a silver Nissan and drove the ninety miles to the small city of Miami, Oklahoma where they spent the night at a Hampton Inn. After a breakfast of pastries and coffee at the Inn, they made their way up U.S. Route 66 to a rural area outside the tiny town of Quapaw.

"All these years . . . you've carried that secret," said Cally, map in hand. "This is just mind-boggling. I always thought you were the victim of that . . . that pedophile, Len Roster."

Cody gripped the wheel. How many times did she have to say that? Heck with the past. He was thinking about Jim. What would he look like now? He'd be in his mid-sixties. He tried to picture an older Jim, but all that came up was the tall, muscular man with those dark wild eyes and big feet that he'd remembered. Bobby said he was ill, but how ill? Why did Jim want to see him? All the angst that charged his emotional circuits for almost two decades was heading for closure. "Remember, Mom. I've paid you." He finally said.

She smiled. "Well, you bought my plane ticket."

"Same thing. So, you're his lawyer . . . in case we need one." Would they need one? Bobby had said tell no one. There were other issues. What other issues? Tell no one. Tell no one. Well, except his mother.

"Yes, I get that. But he saved you. Damn. He saved my little boy."

"Jeez, Mom. Quit saying that. I'm *not* your *little* boy."

"I still have so many questions. Why didn't you ever tell me about him?"

"How could I?" he said, annoyed. His voice rose. "Like I said, he was wanted for murder. Even as a kid I understood what that meant." Questions. He should have grilled Bobby for more information, but once he learned where Jim was, all he wanted to do was get there.

"Did Jim tell you not to tell the authorities about him?"

"He told me nothing about his past. I didn't know anything about it until I got home. He just set me free . . . in his own way. He was my friend. I wanted to protect him. I asked him to come home with me. I thought he was coming. I mean, I was a nine-year-old kid."

"So, he was good to you? I mean he didn't—"

"He. Never. Harmed. Me. He made me feel like I mattered. Like I could do things, like I was a pint-sized version of himself . . . not like Dad."

He felt that familiar, confusing pang in his gut. He and his father were never close. He couldn't relate to Cody's love of art, classical music, his liberal worldview, or his passion for Native American studies. Not really.

"Anthropology?" his father had said, shaking his head when Cody had told him about his career choice. "Better think hard about that one. Teachers don't make much."

Still, his dad helped pay for his college education, attended all of his graduations, called him, and talked a long time when he learned of his recent near-death experience compliments of Bill Janes and his thugs.

Cally reached over and patted his knee. "I know your dad never had a lot of patience, but he meant well."

"He sees the world as black and white. No room for gray." He lowered his voice to mimic his father. "Cut taxes. Cut government. Repeal healthcare. Cut more taxes. Abolish welfare. Close the borders. Cut even more taxes. Global warming is a myth. Apple pie, wham bam, thank you ma'am."

Cally laughed. "He's a bit conservative, that's all."

"A bit? Sheesh. I feel sorry for Lacy. He's so controlling."

"Think about it, now. Your disappearance hit him hard. He's probably overprotective of his daughter. I can understand that. I know I overprotected you. We both carried a lot of guilt when you were missing and we thought molested, blaming ourselves and each other, even the police. Now, it turns out that never happened. The molestation part, I mean."

"I'm sorry, Mom."

"Oh, honey, it's not your fault. I understand."

Did she? Of course, he should have thought of that. Not just the guilt they initially felt, but all the years they believed he'd been molested, handled him with kid gloves, paid for therapy and counseling, and watched him like a hawk, only to find out now that it never happened. What a frigging twist. But it had been a head trip for him, too. Someday, they could all have a heart-to-heart talk.

He brought the conversation back to his half-sister. "Whenever I visit Dad, I try to spend time with Lacy. She's seventeen and confused. I'm hoping she'll enroll at Willamette when she graduates."

"What does your dad think of that?"

"He thinks it's too expensive."

"And Lacy?"

"I think she just wants to get away from home."

They drove on in silence, Cally studying the map.

Cody slowed the car. "We should be getting close, shouldn't we?"

"That could be it," said Cally. Her finger traced the map. "I think that's the road we should take."

They drove until they came to a solitary, lopsided mailbox with a dented top. Cally held out a piece of paper and scrutinized the fading numbers on the box. "One-thirty, that's the number Bobby wrote here." They made their way down a gravel driveway up to a modest one-story tan house with a dinky porch; a single window faced the scruffy yard. There was no garage. An older, dark green Chevrolet sedan was parked out front.

Cody knocked on the door. No answer. He waited and knocked again. He could hear footsteps inside. The door opened slowly. A large Indian woman with a pleasant face, graying hair, and a body like a flour sack cinched at the waist, peeked out at them.

"You must be Nola. I'm Cody Benson. This is my mother, Cally. I believe you were expecting us?"

"Come in," Nola said. Her smile revealed a set of strong, white teeth. Cody thought she smelled like cigarettes.

Cally extended her hand. "It's nice to meet you."

The living room seemed tired but lived in. There was a ratty-looking couch with bumpy cushions up against a wall, a cluttered coffee table, an easy chair, and a television in one corner. A folded blanket was slung over the back of the couch and a bed pillow leaned against an arm. It looked as though Nola slept there.

A large-framed print of a snowy mountain with a wolf and an icy lake in the foreground hung on the wall over the couch. It was not an Oregon wilderness scene, but the kind of thing Jim probably liked. Cody recognized Jim's work in the woodcarving of an eagle and several other birds, which sat in the middle of built-in shelves. Seeing them aroused a longing tinged with sense of an ending.

Nola stood looking at them, the white plastic fan in the corner blowing her hair. Cody's body tightened. His eyes fixed on a crack in the plaster.

"He's in there." Nola pointed toward a closed door. "I don't know if Bobby told you? He has emphysema and a congested heart." Her brow puckered. "He liked his cigarettes, and all those years living like a mole didn't help." She headed towards the door. "You can't stay long. It's hard for him to talk, and he tires quick. We're expecting the hospice nurse."

Hospice. The word jolted Cody. *End of life care.* They'd left in a hurry. Bobby didn't go into detail. "We understand," he said.

She motioned for them to follow. Walking behind her, Cody and Cally exchanged glances.

Nola pulled open the door. "Jim," she said sweetly, "They're here. Your visitors."

Cody's eyes locked on the big man propped up on pillows in a hospital bed. That explained why Nola slept on the couch.

Jim aimed the remote at a small TV in the corner, causing the screen to go dark. There was an air conditioner in the window.

He was thinner now, but still formidable. He had a full head of gray hair, parted on the side and hacked off at his chin. Oxygen tubes descended from his nostrils and looped over his ears. The tubes were hooked to a big white concentrator that made a soft hum. An acrid smell hung in the air.

Jim wore a clean gray T-shirt. A sheet covered his lower body. His big feet poked out the bottom. Wrinkles lined his face. When he grinned, Cody saw that some of his teeth were missing.

Those eyes. Cody had never forgotten them, and they still had a tinge of wild, except now he wore dark-framed Johnny Depp glasses.

He instinctively went to Jim and reached for his hand. It felt cold. "I'm so glad to see you," Cody said. "Finally."

Jim's eyes were moist. He gripped Cody's hand. "Kid," he said.

Cally stepped around to the other side of the bed. "I'm Cody's mother. I had to come to thank you for saving my son." She took Jim's other hand. "I'm also a lawyer."

"I don't know if they told you all that transpired back in Forest Lake." Cody said in a trembling voice. "You're innocent. I wanted you to know that."

Jim nodded. "Yeah." He managed a grin.

"Bobby called us," Nola said peering around Cody. "He sent me the newspaper story. I read it to Jim." She paused. "You can't stay too long. He's not used to visitors."

Jim hung onto Cody's hand; the two just looked at each other. "You're all grown up."

"Yeah." Cody tried to swallow the lump in his throat.

"Thanks for what you did," Jim said.

"Did?"

"Clearing things up about me. What you went through."

"I was trying to find you."

"You almost got yerself killed."

Cody's shoulders relaxed. "It was worth it."

Jim's grin spread to his ears. He tightened his grip on Cody's hand.

Cody wished he could tell him all about Brittany, how they met, how they found the cave, his job as an assistant professor, his art show at Willamette, every detail of his life, but he knew it would take too much time, and Jim might not understand. He jumped when he heard a loud knock at the front door.

"Oh, that must be the nurse," Nola said. The oxygen concentrator started to beep. "She'll just have to wait." Nola bent down to adjust the dials on the equipment. The knocking continued. "Hold your horses," she shouted. "Why the heck doesn't she just come in? She's been here a dozen times. There, I think I got that thing to stop making that noise." She headed toward the living room.

If the nurse was coming, Cody knew he'd have to hurry. "I-I always wanted to thank you for saving me. You have no idea how much the time spent with you changed my life." His voice choked. "I—"

He heard Nola's loud voice. "You can't go in there. Wait! Stop!"

Cody turned and saw the look of surprise on his mother's face, just as Ken Blake brushed past Nola.

His eyes widened like he'd seen a ghost. "You followed us?"

Nola threw her hands up. "I couldn't stop him."

Jim eyed the stranger.

Blake folded his arms, his jaw firm, his eyes narrow. "I had my suspicions. I've always had my suspicions."

Cally left Jim's bedside, moved close to Cody, and confronted Blake. "He's innocent. You know he's innocent. You can't talk to my client. You have no jurisdiction here."

Blake ignored her. He walked over to Jim's bed and peered down at him. "You crazy fool. You should've let me help you."

Jim stared back. Color crept back into his face and confusion gave way to a recognizing chuckle. He raised his shaking hand and gave Blake the finger. "What kept you, Blake? The last time I saw you, you were unconscious, sucking air out on the highway."

"I almost lost my job over that. I should've shackled you to a tree."

"Would've ripped it out and taken it with me." Jim was about to say more, but started coughing. He reached for the plastic water bottle on the TV tray close to his bed. He took a long drink. Water dribbled down his chin.

"Take it easy." Blake waited until Jim caught his breath. "Mo helped you, right? And, you stole things from the Lake Store and the cabins? That has to be it. That has to be how you survived and eluded us."

Jim didn't answer. He continued to sip water. He set the bottle back on the tray and wiped his chin with the bedsheet. "You're like a bad case of the runs, Blake. There's no stopping you." He had an amused smirk on his face.

"You killed Len Roster, didn't you? And you saved that other little boy, Jason Atwater, right? It was you I saw that day, running from that car on the highway?"

Jim's lips curled up into a sly smile. "You'll never know," he managed to say in a wheezing voice. He gasped for some air. "I'm frigging dying here, Blake, and all you want to do is play twenty questions."

Nola bit her lip and shook her finger at Blake. "You better leave."

Jim waved her off. "It's okay, Nola." He took off his glasses and set them on the TV tray. "You're too late, Blake. You came all this way for nothing."

"You half-assed hero." Blake grabbed Jim's right hand.

Cody thought he was going to shackle him. "Don't!" he cried.

Instead, Blake entwined the fingers of their hands, extended his index finger and clenched it against Jim's.

Cody looked at his own finger. He instantly understood. Those were the fingers with the faded scars. The fingers they'd cut years ago, now with swollen knuckles, vowing to be blood brothers, friends forever.

"Remember?" Blake asked. "When we were kids?"

"Yeah, we snuck off into the woods and smoked cigarettes. Mo was mad as hell."

Blake released their hands. "He didn't like us smoking out there."

"Yeah, and we ran off with his favorite knife. Good ol' Mo. Hell, I had to steal those cigarettes."

Blake's voice caught. "I could've helped you, buddy. You should've let me—"

Jim gave another weak laugh. "You couldn't of helped. Not with the way things were back then. They were after my ass. Wanted to hang it from a tree."

"I would've tried."

"Take your head out of your ass, Blake. You couldn't of done nothing."

"You haven't changed." Blake laughed. "You're still full of piss and vinegar."

"And you're still two quarts low." Jim paused. "I . . . I always thought I did it. All these years, I thought . . . Until the kid there—" He looked at Cody.

Nola's lips twitched. She turned to Cody and said in an accusing voice, "Why did you bring the police?"

Cody raised his hands in front of his chest as if to fend her off. "I didn't mean for this to happen. I didn't know he was following us."

"Now, we're all in trouble." Nola flittered toward the bedroom door. The hospice nurse, a chunky Modoc woman carrying a tote, hurried into the room.

The nurse looked down at Jim and then at them. "I have to ask you all to leave," she said with the authority of a general. She pulled out a blood pressure cuff. "You can stay," she said to Nola. The nurse ushered the others into the small living room. "Shoo."

In the living room, the three stood silent, uncomfortable, not knowing what to say. Blake picked up Jim's eagle carving from the shelf and fingered it.

Finally, Cally approached him. "I suppose you're going to go back to Oregon and file a damn report," she said in her lawyer voice. She crossed her arms. "You know, you could get a whole bunch of good people in trouble. He's dying, why can't you—"

Blake gave her a level look. "Yes ma'am. You're right. I'm going back to Oregon." He set the carving back on the shelf. "And then I'm going to turn in my badge and take Lydia on that cruise she's been nagging me to do." He headed out, stopped, and turned. His voice cracked. "I got what I wanted . . . you know, to see him." He shook his head. "We grew up together. Since grade school. He was my best friend." He paused and cleared his throat. "One sideways decision, and his whole life went to hell. It's just a damn shame. All of it." He swallowed several times, his eyes rheumy. "All of it," he said again. He turned the doorknob. "You folks have a good day."

When the door closed behind him, they slumped into each other's arms. "Whew," said Cody.

Nola came into the room. "Where did that cop go?" she asked.

Cally stepped forward and took her hands. "He left. Don't worry. He just came to say goodbye like the rest of us."

"He's not going to arrest me?"

"No one is going to arrest you. Trust me."

"The nurse gave Jim some medication," Nola said. "He needs to sleep now. This was too much for him. You'll have to come back tomorrow." She went to the door and opened it. "Don't bring the cop."

* * *

The next morning, after checking in with Britt on the phone for the umpteenth time, Cody and his mother caught a late breakfast at a small café in downtown Miami before heading out to see Jim again.

"Britt's doing well. She sends her love," Cody said. He pulled the Banjo charm bracelet from his pocket and held it out in his palm. "I gave this to her for her birthday. She wants me to give it to Jim. It's special. It's our totem."

269

"Ah, that's so sweet." Cally said. "I'm sure he'll love hearing that."

"And speaking of love, I'm glad Jim found Nola and that he had a reasonably good life." He poured ketchup over his scrambled eggs."

"If he hadn't escaped and run, he probably would've gone to prison or worse," Cally said. "Everyone was convinced he killed that girl. He's Indian. Oregon has the death penalty. This oatmeal is not so hot."

"You should have ordered the eggs. Did you catch what Blake said about Roster?"

"I believe he accused Jim of killing him. Small loss. Roster abused and murdered a child and was about to harm another one." She raised her cup. "Here's to Jim," she said loudly.

The server, a young girl in jeans, refilled their coffee cups. "Is everything okay?" she asked, looking at Cally.

"Yes, fine," Cally said, avoiding her eyes.

"I think that's true," Cody said, once the waitress left. "It's possibly one of those other issues Bobby was concerned about. Jim would still have to account for that, wouldn't he?"

"Considering what Roster did, I doubt that any jury would convict him. Jim rescued an endangered child. Plus, he's and old, sick man. He did assault Christie Jenkins and put her in harm's way. It doesn't matter, though. Blake's not going to pursue it. Jim will die a free man."

Cody paid the bill at the register. "I never will adjust to this humidity," Cally said as they climbed into the car for their trip to visit with Jim again.

Cody's thoughts shot back to the time Jim told him he was taking him home. He said he'd gone "shopping" and brought Cody a new set of clothes. Cody knew now that he'd stolen them. But he arrived at the cave out of breath, and it looked like he'd been in a scuffle. He had blood on his jacket sleeve. He said he tripped on a deer trail and slid down a ravine. Jim must have encountered Roster, overpowered him. *No, say it. Killed him. Then made it look like a suicide and ripped buttons from Roster's clothing. It all fit together. That's why I had those buttons in my pants pocket when I was found, and why everyone was so certain Roster had kidnapped me.*

"There's our road coming up," Cally said, breaking into his thoughts. "We need to turn there."

"Yeah, I see it." Should he ask Jim about Roster? The buttons? Would Jim tell him? Probably not.

"That's the driveway up there. Just past that little tree," Cally said. "See the mailbox?"

It was around 10 a.m. when they pulled in and parked next to the green Chevy.

A somber, puffy-eyed Nola greeted them. Her shoulders slumped. Her voice sounded like she had a cold. "Last night," she said. "H-He passed."

"He's gone?" Cody asked. Those words hit hard.

"An ambulance came." Her voice cracked. "They tried. There was nothing they could do. This is all too much, too much."

Cody wondered if she were telling the truth or if, still fearful, she had Jim spirited away. He rushed past her toward the bedroom. The door was open, the unmade bed empty. There was a large wet spot in the middle, the oxygen concentrator silent and the tubing lay on the floor. Jim's glasses were still on the TV tray. The room smelled of urine. Cody turned to face Nola. "What happened?"

"Around midnight," Nola said. "I was sleeping on the couch, and I heard him moaning. He couldn't breathe. I went in to help. He looked at me and said, "What's that noise?" At first, I thought something was wrong with his oxygen machine. Then he started gasping, making odd sounds, so I called the ambulance, but they couldn't do nothing." She started to cry. "They asked me to wait in the living room while they worked on him. The man came back in and said, 'He's gone. I'm so sorry.' I didn't get to say goodbye. Not really."

Cally put her arm around her and led her to the easy chair. "Why don't you sit down here for a while? Can I get you a drink of water? Is there anyone I can call for you?"

She shook her head. "I called Bobby. He's coming. I didn't know how to get hold of you or what else to do, so I just sat up all night, rocking. Hugging my pillow."

"I'm so sorry," Cody said. He sat down next to her. "I hoped to spend more time with him. I—" He wiped his eyes on his sleeve. He couldn't finish.

"It's okay, son," Cally said. "It's absolutely okay to cry." She handed him a tissue. "At least, you got to see him in time. That's the important thing."

"Please stay for a while," Nola said. "I have some coffee. Would you like coffee?"

"Don't go to any trouble," Cody said.

"It's no trouble." Nola went into the kitchen and returned with coffee in three different kinds of mugs.

"Do you use cream and sugar?" she asked.

"No," Cody said. "Black is fine for both of us." Actually, he didn't want coffee at all. They'd had plenty at the restaurant, but it seemed like Nola needed to take care of them.

Nola sat in the easy chair while Cally joined Cody on the couch.

"Jim had a good life here," Nola said. "Showed up one day with his dog. Needed a place to stay. My uncle, Frank Blaze, helped him get here. Picked him up some place near Tule Lake and drove all the way here in that old blue Ford of his." She sipped coffee. "Frank and Mo were friends back in Oregon. We couldn't say anything to anybody about Jim." She paused, swallowed, and looked up. "The plan was for him to move in with another fella we know, but Jim and I sort of hit it off. I was alone. My husband died of the jaundice. Jim was a hard man to love, like an untamed coyote, living off by himself. But we did okay."

"Of course you did," Cally said, trying to comfort her.

"The first few months he couldn't even sleep on the couch or the bed. He slept on the floor. When the weather got warm, he'd take a sleeping bag out in the backyard."

They both laughed when she said that. Jim had been isolated for so long. Cody remembered his blank look when he told Jim he had a computer at home.

"He did woodcarvings, and I sold them at various fairs," Nola said. "I went alone. We had to be careful. One of his favorite things was to plant tomatoes. He loved digging in the dirt." She set down her cup. "Would you like to see his garden?"

"Sure," said Cody, glad to take leave of his coffee, which tasted like it had been in the pot for a while. "I'd love to see it." As they stepped out onto a small back porch, Cody saw Jim's well-worn boots with bits of mud clinging to the soles. They looked empty. Lonely even. He wished he'd come sooner. At the bottom of the porch steps near a shrub, Cody spotted a coffee can half full of cigarette butts.

Nola noticed Cody staring at it. "Those are mine," she said. "Jim couldn't smoke no more, so I'd come out here for my smokes, but not in the house." She didn't wait for a response. "These are his tomatoes." She gestured toward the garden. "His pride and joy. He must have a dozen plants."

A wooden fence enclosed the backyard. The tomatoes were starting to wither, their leaves and vines yellow-tinged. A few plants still had fruit. There was some struggling squash, a few cucumbers, and cornstalks. The soil was hard, in need of water.

"In May, I helped him put the garden in. He liked the little things in life," Nola said. "This was the last thing we did together. Then he got real sick. Jim had lung problems. He was a heavy smoker. He said he lived in a dark, damp place for a long time, and the air was bad."

"A cave," Cody said. "It was a cave."

"He had a good seventeen years here, I think. He never left the house. Just stayed inside and worked out back in the yard. Never let me or anyone take pictures of him." Nola was rambling. "I did the best I could."

"I'm sure you did," Cally said.

Cody walked around the garden. Weeds were everywhere, most likely due to Jim's illness and Nola's need to care for him. In one corner, a clump of black-eyed Susans grew. Nestled beside them was a small, stone carving. It simply said *Wolf.* He stood there looking.

Nola came up beside him. "That was his dog."

"I know," said Cody. He often wondered what happened to Wolf, the first dog he knew. It made him happy to know Jim hadn't abandoned Wolf, but then that was the kind of guy Jim Fallingwater was.

"He loved that dog," Nola said. "When the dog died, he never wanted another one." She peered up at Cody through swollen eyes. "I have something for you."

She led them back inside and went to a cupboard in the small kitchen. Cody could see clutter on the counters and wooden table. The sink was full of dishes. Nola retrieved a crumpled manila envelope and handed it to Cody. "Jim wanted you to have this."

Cody undid the clasp and unfolded a piece of yellowed notebook paper. "This note is dated some years back."

"Jim told me to give this to a young man if he ever showed up."

Cody read the note:

> *Kid,*
> *I knew one day you'd come. Don't know why, just did.*
> *Thanks for letting me have some life left.*
> *Ben (Guess you now know who I really am.)*

He handed it to his mother. There was something else inside the envelope. He reached in and pulled out a heart-shaped necklace and a dried yellow rose.

"Let me see that." Cally reached for the necklace. "That's mine. The one I left on the stump in the woods that day. I never expected to actually find you. I left it as a memorial for you along with a bouquet of yellow roses. It was my way of saying goodbye. He must have been there, watching me." She looked at Nola, her eyes teary. "He kept these all this time?"

"Yeah," said Nola.

Cody reached into his pocket for the tissue. He dabbed at his eyes and blew his nose. "That's the hell of it. I came to thank him, and he ends up thanking me."

"I think he thought of you as his boy," Nola said.

Jim's funeral, Nola said, would be in two days. "We're gonna have graveside services. It'll be just me and Bobby . . . a couple of others. We always kept to ourselves. You know, because of his past. You'll come, won't you?"

"We definitely want to be there," Cody said. He looked at his mother.

Cally nodded. "Yes. Absolutely. And, when the time is right, I hope you'll come to Oregon and visit."

That made Nola smile. "Yes," she said, "We'll stay in touch."

Cody ran his fingers over the writing on Jim's note as a way to connect with him. There wasn't anything more he could do. His anxiety-plagued soul had sprung free. His whole body gave into a sense of peace. He had found Jim who'd led a free, although humble, life with someone who loved him. All of that was a gift from the innocent child he'd been. He folded the note and placed it, the necklace, and dried flower back into the envelope. *I need to get back to Britt and focus on our life together. Jim would want that.*

CHAPTER 42

Bunches of yellow and brown oak leaves pirouetted in the light breeze on a warm Sunday afternoon in late October. Bobby carefully escorted Brittany, bareheaded, down the steps of Eaton Hall out to the green grassy quad of Willamette University. As the two approached the back of a small tent awning set up on the lawn, a fresh-faced young woman with shoulder-length blond hair began playing Pachelbel's Canon on a large harp.

Inside, a four-foot stone statue of a meditating Buddha, eyes half-closed sat at the front of the tent. A single yellow rose and Cally's heart-shaped necklace lay across his hands. A lighted lotus flower lamp floated in a shallow glass bowl of water next to his crossed legs. On the right side of the Buddha was a large, flaming white candle. There were no other decorations.

Seated on folding chairs, were Cally Benson and her companion, Wyatt; Pete Benson, arms crossed and frowning, with his wife; Cody's half-sister, Lacy; department head Luci Maxwell; Anne Ferguson, Cody's landlady; Dr. Aanandi and his wife, Leila, and a few of Cody and Brittany's friends and colleagues.

Cody, standing in a dark suit and beaming, waited. His eye caught Dr. Aanandi's, who winked, causing both to grin. Omar, his black hair slicked back, looking like a budding rock star, stood next to Cody as best man. Dulcy, the proud matron of honor, in a flowered, empress-style dress, stationed herself directly across from them. In the center was a tall middle-aged man in suit and tie.

Everyone rose as Bobby and Brittany entered the tent and walked down the aisle between the rows of chairs. Cody gave Brittany an adoring look, proud to see her walking with such ease. She was stunning in an ankle-length silver and ivory vintage Titanic dress with empire waist and soutache embroidery.

Bobby escorted her to Cody, who took both of her hands. When the smiling couple faced each other, Bobby stepped away and seated himself by Nola. Next to her sat Sue Bolin and Dottie Johnson, both fighting back tears.

When the music stopped, the tall man stepped forward. "Good afternoon. I'm Mark Melroy, an ordained Buddhist Dharma teacher and a professor of English at Portland State University." He smiled. "I met Brittany several years ago at a retreat. I'm honored that she asked me to preside at her wedding today. Before we begin, I'd like to acknowledge Betsy Carson, who played the beautiful harp solo and Jake Kerry, who will honor us later with his trumpet. Both are students here in Willamette University's music program. Thank you so much for joining us today.

"In Buddhism, marriage is not a religious sacrament, but a personal decision, a partnership between two people who have deep, mutual respect for one another," he continued.

Cody glanced at his father, who tugged at his collar and stared at the Buddha statue, bewildered. Lacy, a petite slip of a girl, was teary-eyed. Cally, in a cool, mint green dress, seemed serene. She dabbed at her eyes with a white hanky.

"Since Buddhism practices acceptance of all cultures and spiritual paths," Melroy said, "the ceremony today does not follow any prescribed traditions, but is what Cody and Brittany wanted." He took a breath and gave Brittany a sympathetic look. "It will also be short, so that our dear Brittany does not have to stand too long on her still healing leg."

He turned his gaze to the audience. "Please, be present and put your heart's full attention to this ceremony. Look and listen with your whole being."

He opened the large folder he held and read, "'Nothing happens without reason. Even the chance brushing of one's sleeve against a stranger's may be the cause of their future encounters.' The union of Brittany and Cody is not accidental. Indeed, due to the law of karma, it is the inevitable consequence of all the actions of their lives. They, from their very beginning, have been coming together to this sacred moment. Therefore, this union must never be broken or dissolved."

He turned toward the couple, who were staring into each other's eyes.

"You look beautiful," Cody whispered.

Brittany beamed. "You're pretty hot yourself," she replied softly.

"Will you take the Threefold Refuge?" Melroy asked.

"Yes, we will," they said in unison and pledged to take refuge in the Buddha, the Dharma, and the Sangha.

"Dear Brittany and Cody, marriage is a journey of your deepest expression of intimacy. It is your lifelong commitment and true spiritual practice.

"Do you pledge to help each other to develop your hearts and minds, cultivating compassion, generosity, ethics, and wisdom as you undergo the various ups and downs of life?"

"We do," they said together.

"Recognizing that the external conditions of life will not always be smooth and that internally your own minds and emotions will sometimes get stuck in negativity, do you pledge to see all these circumstances as a challenge to help you grow, to open your hearts, to accept yourselves and each other, and to generate compassion for all beings who are suffering?"

"We do."

One by one, they pledged in unison to share, preserve, and enrich their affection for each other and to be aware of Buddha nature in themselves and all living beings.

Melroy turned to the audience. "Let us pause for meditation." Dulcy handed him a small brass bowl. He held it in the palm of his hand and struck it three times with a padded mallet, producing a lovely bell sound. Moments later, he rang the bell two more times. He faced the couple. "Do you, Brittany, take Cody to be your husband?"

"I do," she said.

"Do you Cody take Brittany to be your wife?"

"I do."

Melroy handed the bowl back to Dulcy. "The wedding ring is the outward sign of an inward and spiritual bond which unites two loyal hearts in partnership." He nodded at Omar, who stepped forward, fumbled in his pocket, and gave a ring to Cody and then Brittany.

Once the rings were on the couple's fingers, Cody produced the Banjo charm bracelet and slipped on Brittany's left wrist. "Totem," he whispered.

Brittany's eyes glistened. She fingered the dog charm. "Totem."

"According to the wisdom of Buddha and by the authentic rights vested in me," Melroy said, "I joyously pronounce you husband and wife." He nodded at Cody. "You may kiss the bride."

"I love you," Cody said.

"I love you, too," she replied.

Cody pulled Brittany close. She wrapped her arms around him and they kissed. A hum of laughter came from the audience.

Melroy said, "Ladies and gentlemen, may I present Mr. and Mrs. Cody Benson."

Everyone applauded.

Jake, the young man holding the trumpet, stood. He waited for Betsy to take her place behind the harp. In those few minutes, Cody caught sight of his mother, who was softly crying. His heart ached for her, but he understood. Earlier, while straightening his tie, she'd said, "When you went missing, I thought I'd lost my son forever. I never thought I'd ever witness this day. I'm so very happy."

Betsy began playing the introductory flourishes to Tomaso Albinoni's Adagio. Jake placed the instrument to his lips. Clear, soothing sounds of the trumpet filled the air.

Holding hands, Cody and Brittany slowly walked out together, followed by Dulcy and a jubilant Omar who shouted, "Woohoo!" Anne gave him a thumbs-up sign, but as he passed by his parents and little squirming sisters, his mother shot him her no-nonsense-now look.

Once out of the tent, a group of Cody's students released a cluster of white balloons applauding, as they drifted into the blue sky. "Way to go, Professor," they called.

Cody waved them closer. "Follow us. I know where there's food."

The story of the attractive young couple who brought down a prominent timber barren politician, solved an age-old murder case, and saved sawmill jobs in a small Southern Oregon town continued to get play in the press. A KGW News 8 cameraman captured footage of the two for the nightly news, while a *Statesman Journal* photographer shot stills for the newspaper. "How do you feel?" shouted a reporter. "Do you have anything to say?"

"Great. We feel just great," Cody replied. "And we wish everyone peace and happiness."

Brittany bowed to them, her hands in prayer pose. "Shanti."

Inside the tent, the music stopped. Melroy faced the audience. "Please, you are all invited to the reception in Goudy Commons. I'll lead the way, so you won't get lost." He hurriedly departed, waiting outside for the guests to line up behind him.

"This is a beautiful campus," Sue said to Dottie as they sauntered down the sidewalk, admiring the green, the trees, late blooming shrubs, and the flowing millrace filled with quacking ducks. She looked around to see who was in earshot before lowering her voice. "Are they really married? I mean, that guy's not a minister."

"I'm sure they are *very* married," said Dottie, her cane clacking on the concrete. Bobby looked at Nola and chuckled.

Sue frowned. "But that statue, that idol . . . her father is probably turning over in his grave."

"If he's leapin' around down there," Dottie said. "He's probably jumpin' for joy."

CHAPTER 43

Cody and Brittany honeymooned in a small rented cabin at Cannon Beach on the Oregon coast in perfect fall weather. During the day, they took reflective strolls or sat outside on the deck planning their future, tasting the fresh ocean air, and enjoying the spectacular views. In the evenings, they snuggled next to a warm fire, listening to the rolling sound of the waves.

One afternoon, after a long solo walk, Cody showered, threw on a white terry cloth robe, and relaxed on the couch to study flyers about Colombia, South America, where they would go in January, so he could begin his research.

Brittany brought two glasses of champagne and joined him. She handed one to Cody. "Here's to us." She curled her legs under her body and sat beside him. Their glasses clinked.

"And here's to Jim Fallingwater," Cody said. "Thank you, Jim for bringing us together." He leaned forward and kissed Brittany.

"I'm going to tell Jim's story," Cody said, his eyes determined, "in a memoir about this whole experience. I want the world to know this man. He deserves credit for saving the lives of two children. He was a hero."

"I think that would be excellent therapy for you, too. Writing about it, I mean. I'll help with the research."

"When we get back from Colombia, I'm going to track down Jason Atwater, so he knows the truth about who really saved him."

"He's probably a young man by now," Brittany said. "Just starting out in life."

"Yeah and—what the . . ." Cody felt something cold and wet on his neck. He turned to look over the couch. "My God! It's Banjo. Where'd he come from?"

Brittany doubled over with laugher. "Bobby dropped him off while you were out walking. Banjo didn't like Oklahoma, so he's going to live with us, and when we're in South America, he'll stay with Bobby in Forest Lake."

Cody rubbed Banjo's ears. "You're a wanted dog. We better get you some shades and a hat before someone recognizes you." Banjo planted a sloppy kiss on Cody's cheek.

Brittany had a mischievous look in her eyes. "His accusers have moved out of state. Everyone thinks Banjo disappeared, so there's no culprit. Lupe got another dog from the shelter, a small one. I told her the whole story. She thinks Banjo will be safer with us. So she's happy. I got Banjo a license and a chip, only I said his name was Bingo."

"You never quit, do you?"

"Nope."

He raised his champagne glass to her again. "We've cleared the reputations of two fugitives."

He leaned over to kiss Brittany, but Banjo nuzzled between them, panting, his tongue hanging out. Laughing, they both planted a warm kiss on each of Banjo's furry cheeks.

* * *

Memorial Day, Three years later ...

Cody swung open the door of the Flower Peddler. A dark-haired little boy with big brown eyes ran ahead of him.

"Well, hello, Professor Benson," said Pamela, the proprietor. "Do you want the usual?"

"Yel-yole," said the little boy. "We want yel-yole."

Cody grinned. "That's right. One dozen yellow roses."

Pamela reached for her order pad. "Which we will have delivered to the cemetery in Oklahoma."

"Yes."

"Daddy. Daddy." The little boy fidgeted.

"I think your son wants your attention."

"Look. Look." His little finger pointed at a display in the center of the shop, which featured a cute golden ceramic puppy with a shiny black nose and pink tongue. He rushed toward it.

Pam laughed. "He likes that little ceramic dog planter. It's a popular item for baby showers, or you can use it on your desk to hold pencils."

"I see it, buddy." Cody said. "Don't touch."

"I've been meaning to tell you," Pam said, writing up his order. "I just loved your memoir, *Finding Jim*. Your illustrations are exquisite. Our book group is reading it. When we finish, will you come and talk to us?"

"Thank you. I'd be happy to."

"Would you mind signing my copy?" She retrieved the book from behind the counter.

"Not at all. Do you happen to have a pen?"

"I sure do." She pulled a pen from a drawer. "I see you'll be doing a reading at the library."

"Yeah, I'm really pleased with how well the book has been doing. It's overshadowing my dry treatise on tribes of Colombia."

"*Finding Jim* is a great story . . . and all you went through. Goodness."

"Daddy, doggy," called the small boy. Frustrated, he stamped his feet. His little mouth formed a pout.

"Okay, okay, why don't I get that, too." Cody went over to the display, got the dog planter, and brought it to the counter. The boy clapped his hands.

Pam happily rang it up. "You want me to wrap it?"

"No, that's okay." He handed the planter to the child, who squealed with delight.

"For Mommy," he said, his eyes big. He hugged the dog to his chest and rocked it back and forth.

"You be careful with that," Pam said. "Hang on tight. Make your mommy proud."

Cody smiled. "Thanks, Pam." He patted his son's head. "Come on, Jimmy, let's go home."

ACKNOWLEGMENTS

Special thanks to Jane Fernandez who never faltered in her belief that Jim Fallingwater was innocent, and to Lois Rosen, my first and always fan, for her helpful suggestions. Thanks also to Dawn Eisler Smith, Margo Hampton, Sandy McDow, and the Thursday Night Group for being patient readers and top-notch editors, and to Marge French, my favorite heroine and grand member of the Trillium Writers group, for her willingness to read the entire manuscript.

To the late Cathy Ingalls, a stellar journalist and fellow animal lover, who told me the story of Blue, a special dog in trouble. Blue was the inspiration for sweet Banjo.

Thank you to Marcia Vargas and Angie Bartel for your enthusiasm and encouragement as well as a good laugh at all those breakfast get-togethers, and to all my dear friends along the way—so important to the solitary writing life.

I can't forget sweet little Tara, my most ardent follower, who gets up with me each morning, follows me to my writing room, and patiently waits for treats, a tummy rub, and that special romp in the yard. And to Forester who snuck into our backyard and wrapped his paws around both of our hearts.

We've gone through a lot while this book was in the making—a pandemic, wildfire threat, terrific ice storm, a war overseas, numerous mass shootings, and a setback in women's rights. May our future days be blessed with justice, kindness, and love.

Finally, if you enjoyed reading this story, please consider posting a review. A few sentences will do, and it will make Banjo and Crackers especially happy.

ABOUT THE AUTHOR

Jean Rover is the author of *Touch the Sky*, a heart-rending novel, filled with intrigue, about a missing child in Oregon's backcountry. Her writing has received awards or recognition from *Writer's Digest, Short Story America,* Willamette Writers, Oregon Writers Colony, and the International Association of Business Communicators (IABC). Her work has appeared in various literary magazines and anthologies, including the Saturday Evening Post's Great American Fiction Contest Anthology. Other stories were performed at Liars' League events in London, England and Portland, Oregon. She has also authored a chapbook, *Beneath the Boughs Unseen,* featuring holiday stories about society's invisible people. She lives and writes in Oregon's lush Willamette Valley.